I0678175

The Road Back Isn't Straight

A novel

by

James E. Gottesman

Do not copy, reproduce, forward, or transfer in any format without the permission of James Gottesman
This is a work of fiction and all characters and events appearing in this work are fictitious. Any resemblances to real persons, living or dead, or events are purely coincidental.
2.19.

©copyright, 2012
Do not copy, reproduce, forward, or transfer in any format without the permission of James E. Gottesman

ISBN-10:0615711243
ISBN-13:978-0615711249 (JayEddy Publisher)

This is a work of fiction and all characters appearing in this work are fictitious. Any resemblance to real persons, living or dead, is purely coincidental.

ACKNOWLEDGMENTS

Thanks go to many. Gloria Brown Gottesman, my longtime co-conspirator, read it first and, like always, was brutally honest, but said that the story was rock solid.

My muses, Grace, Ellie and Sophie Gottesman, have pleaded with me for years to tell them stories, and I tried. Afterward, if the story was worthwhile, Grace would always suggest that I write it down. I finally did.

I need to thank the initial readers of the book, particularly Tony Wartnik, the first one to read the book and tell me I was on the right track and make some valid comments. Chuck Caplan, a good friend and ENT surgeon, educated me on the fine art of punctuation, plus lots more. Laurie Cohen, Helene Fleisher, Linda Current, Carol Leibowitz, Jerry Hahn, Jason Black, Mike Backes, Ruth Bunin, and Greg Gottesman, to name a few, gave valuable insights.

Also to Diane Mackay Richie, the first person to really teach me how to write. She may not remember, but I do.

Although I listened to everything, I didn't always follow their suggestions.

The medical portions, despite my forty-two years in the business, needed some tuning. For that I am thankful to Drs. Michael Hart and Steven Wald.

I am sure more will need to be thanked, but for now...jeg

DEDICATED

To no one else but Mrs. Brown's Lovely Daughter

Mrs. Brown, You've Got a Lovely Daughter, sung by Herman's Hermits, #1 on the U.S. Billboard Hot 100, May 1965

Prologue - Fear and Fate.

Mid-October, UW Med School, Seattle

Emma Braza loved Dr. Agotini's class. Few things made her forget her demons, but this did.

Emma, the only undergrad in the class, looked out the window of the small second floor lecture hall and quickly looked back again. Worry lines furrowed her brow as she thought, *It's very dark outside. Too dark. This doesn't make sense. What time is it?* She knew her cell phone was dead and the hands on the classroom clock hadn't moved for three weeks. She leaned over to the grad student next to her and quietly asked, "Excuse me, what time is it?"

"4:45."

"Why is it so dark?" Emma asked.

The student, annoyed, whispered, "Daylight savings ended yesterday," and turned back to the lecture. Agotini had completed only two-thirds of the day's class outline.

A seed of doubt crept into Emma's mind. She had forgotten the lost hour of daylight. The darkness drew the first bead of sweat on her brow. Her aloneness drew the second. Both triggers that might call back terrors that she couldn't handle. The muscles around her right eye and cheek started twitching.

Can I wait until class is over and plead for someone to drive me home or borrow someone's cell phone to call the sorority to see if someone could pick me up?

Maybe, but that would be defeat and I must try to be strong.

But doubt was now firmly rooted and the battle had

begun. A battle Emma had little chance of winning. But she would try. She always tried her hardest, but winning, no, not in the past year. Her breathing quickened into shallow hiccup-like breaths. The doubt became fear. Emma could see Dr. Agotini's mouth moving, but the words made no sense. Emma looked to the window again.

I can't concentrate. I need to get back to the sorority, now, while there is still a wisp of daylight remaining.

Emma hastily gathered her notebooks, eyed Dr. Agotini and mouthed, "Mi dispiace." She ran through the empty hallway to the elevator and hammered the down button until being rewarded. Exiting the elevator, she walked quickly through and out the main lobby of the medical center onto Pacific Avenue. Her tongue had stuck to the roof of her dry mouth. With some difficulty she wiggled it free.

Two taxis stood at the curb. Emma looked inside both, hoping to see if either had a woman driver, but she had no luck. She hurried to the crosswalk and waited at the stop light with a small group of people. Emma kept pushing the crossing button, knowing full well that the light would turn of its own accord. Nonetheless, she kept pushing.

In the crowd waiting to cross, Emma noticed an unshaven man in a faded parka wearing a threadbare ski cap, pulled down to his eyebrows. His glasses were fogged, so she couldn't make out his eyes.

He's staring at me.

Emma focused on him for a second then turned away. Though he was six or seven feet away, and one of ten people at the curb, she could hear only him breathing. She wouldn't look back again. She thought only of those two men of a year earlier, those terrible two men with ropes and plastic bags, taking turns.

Please don't follow me. Please don't follow me.

When the light turned green, she crossed swiftly and headed north into the campus.

I hope everyone at the stoplight turned east to catch the bus. I can make it to the sorority in 25 minutes. I know I can, she thought, *30 minutes tops.*

Emma kept her head down, trying to think good thoughts and breathe normally, as her counselors had recommended when her fears started taking control. Try as she might, sensations of cigarette burns on her chest and breasts quickly overrode conjured calm sunsets and lush vineyards. Emma's jaw clenched.

Away from the clang and clatter of traffic, the almost-windless night was quiet, other than the whispering of the few leaves remaining in the trees. As Emma focused on listening, she thought she could hear quiet footsteps behind her. She looked quickly over her shoulder, praying that her senses were playing tricks, only to find the unshaven man ten steps behind.

Emma started to run. Within a few paces, books and papers flew out of her backpack, which in haste she had forgotten to close completely. She turned quickly and removed her backpack at the same time, intending to snatch up her fallen objects. The unshaven man moving out of the darkness at what seemed a very quick pace, walked directly at her.

Emma could feel her heart slam against her chest and she barked, "Leave me alone."

The man continued to close the distance between them.

Oh, please God. He's going to hurt me.

Emma could feel her hands and feet being bound

again, the sheer darkness, and the pain. She panicked and abandoned her backpack, books and papers and started to run. Run anywhere. Hoping to find help, she headed toward the nearest building. She didn't notice the yellow caution tape and the scaffolding as she entered Anderson Hall. Semi-darkness enveloped the building and the construction debris covered the floors. Luckily, with little ambient light left, she found an unlocked door and entered a small room, a men's bathroom. A semi-opaque window gave little light. She bolted the old door then backed up slowly, hitting her leg softly on the edge of the toilet and then pressed herself against the back wall. She hoped that she hadn't been followed. Between quiet sobs, she prayed, "Leave me alone. Leave me alone."

A minute of deathly quiet passed, other than Emma's rapid breathing. Trying to hold her breath to listen, she could hear soft and slow footsteps, then saw tiny bits of intermittent searching light coming under and around the doorframe. "No, please, no. No, please, no. No, please no," she whispered to herself.

Emma could not help seeing and feeling her worst memories. The footsteps ceased and a bright light circled the doorframe and all was quiet.

I think I smell smoke. Is this man smoking a cigarette? The burning sensations on her chest and breasts intensified.

Emma continued her mantra, "No, please, no. No, please, no. No, please no."

A voice shattered the silence and slammed her head and back against the wall of the darkening bathroom. "I know you are in there. I am not going to hurt you. I did not mean to scare you."

Despite the semi-darkness, she closed her eyes and covered her face with her arms. She peeked and closed her eyes again. Emma could not talk. She tried to inhale but couldn't.

The voice, feeling like thunder, repeated itself, "I know you're there. I am not going to hurt you."

Finding just a bit of courage, Emma pleaded, "Please go away."

Chapter 1

Three years earlier. September, UW campus

Francine Frost, Gamma Gamma's square-jawed, mid-fortyish housemother, shut the door to her study and took a seat. Opposite her sat sorority president, Melissa Cornelius. With the completion of rush, Francine and Melissa started reviewing individual requests and assigning rooms for the new pledges.

"Why are the forms on Emma Brazza and Sophia Picone empty?" Melissa asked. "I don't remember talking to either of them during rush."

"Emma was here briefly and both are legacies. We have to deal with it, like it or not."

Melissa nodded.

"Emma lives outside of Walla Walla," Francine continued, "and is plain as wheat. I expect she'll last a quarter, then bail to some Moo U with the rest of the farmers. Sophia couldn't make it to rush because of 'family commitments', whatever the hell that means. Her mom's national connections apparently put her above our rules. Sophia Picone is going to be a GiGi, end of story."

"At least this part is easy," said Melissa. "Ten groups of three each and the two misfits, Emma and Sophia together in the last room. No downside there."

Frost typed the room assignments onto a spreadsheet and printed it. Melissa posted the list in the sorority entryway. The pledges would be moving in the next morning.

* * *

Emma Braza, wearing Wrangler jeans, ankle high work boots, and a 4H T-shirt, moved into her room, alone. Tallish and thin with light auburn hair, Emma's

T-shirt revealed a muscular physique, toned from years of outdoor work. Her deep summer tan highlighted brilliant aquamarine blue eyes, but hid the saddle shaped peppering of freckles across the bridge of her nose. Her slightly square jaw had a small chin cleft giving her just an air of authority. Emma was country-girl pretty.

Emma's mysterious roommate, Sophia Picone, had yet to arrive. Emma could hear a constant chatter from rooms filled with new girls. She made it a point to introduce herself to each of her pledge sisters, but little was said after "hello" and "where ya from?" Each pledge was busy trying to make a portion of their assigned room a piece of home. Emma smiled, thinking that the quiet would not likely last and she might as well enjoy it while she could. None of the other pledges or sisters knew anything of Sophia Picone and strangely, to all of them, none had seen her during rush.

In the early afternoon, while lounging on her newly made bed, Emma heard a loud "Oh my God" from the hallway, followed by a stampede of feet and then a symphony of "Oh my God"s."

Scrambling out her room door toward the noise, Emma entered a room packed with pledges, stretching, straining, bobbing and weaving, trying to peer out the sole front-facing window in the pledge wing. The pledges parted to let Emma get a front seat to the silent show. Exiting a taxi was a multi-pierced, rainbow hair-colored girl in classic Goth dress with black stockings and lace from head to toe. Francine Frost was there to meet her. Wild gestures and apparent screaming left little doubt that their first meeting was going poorly, or worse. Sophia Picone had arrived.

Chapter 2

Pledges crowded the doorways with disbelieving stares as Sophia Picone lugged her suitcase and large box up the stairs. Francine Frost, frown glued in place and offering no help, followed.

Between labored breaths, the sweating young girl asked, "So which room in this nuthouse is mine?"

Francine offered coldly, "Last room on the left. Your roommate is a girl named Emma. Be nice."

Sophia, clenched her jaw at the comment, continued down the hall, not bothering to acknowledge the mouth-ajar pledges in each doorway. She arrived at her appointed room, pushed the door open with her foot and backed into the room. After dropping the box noisily to the floor, she confronted Emma.

Sophia, with an oval expressive face and a smooth, dark olive complexion, stood half a head shorter than Emma. Penetrating large brown eyes diverted Emma's attention from a nose that was just a little too large. Sophia was thin-waisted, even petite, but amply endowed. Piercings and rings dotted her nose, ears, brows, and lips. At least, those were the places Emma could see.

"So who'd you piss off to end up rooming with me?" Sophia asked.

Emma gave the statement a bit of thought. *I guess she means to be the alpha.* Emma paused and said in a clear, calm, monotone voice, "Actually, no one was pissed. I chose you specifically. Frost said that the last girl in was apparently a flaming asshole and did anyone want to room with her? I figured after castrating two hundred head of cattle a week before rush, that a flaming asshole would be welcome relief."

Sophia laughed. "Cool. Finally someone with a sense of humor."

Emma smiled. "Hi, I'm Emma."

"I'm Sophia Elena Vittoria Maria Picone, but Sophie or Soph works for me."

Within the first two weeks the other pledges started socially segregating Sophie and Emma and made it painfully obvious. Sophie was clearly the cause. But Emma made no attempt to rid herself of her unusual and malapropos roommate, as most of the others might have. In front of Sophie and Emma's door, in a hallway full of other pledges, one girl asked Emma if Sophie was as weird as she looked.

"She's amazing. Smart and so interesting. Totally fabulous. I'm so lucky to have her as a roommate," retorted Emma.

The other pledges rolled their eyes. The pledge that asked the question turned to her friends and snickered loud enough for Emma and Sophie to hear, "Emma is either dumber than wood or as whacko as the roommate."

When Emma entered the room Sophie was grinning like a Cheshire cat. "Well, it's you and me against the rest."

"There's a lot of them," Emma deadpanned.

Sophia offered a suggestion to Emma "Yeah. But let's make a promise that we watch each other's backs. We can ask or tell each other anything without judgment or getting mad. Okay?"

"Fine with me." Emma agreed. A few minutes passed.

Emma, testing the new rules, asked, "What's with the Goth? I think you'd be really pretty if you dressed a little more, I hate to use the word, *'normal.'* Just a simple observation, but at the mixers the guys seemed to ignore you, not to mention the rest of the sorority."

"In tenth grade," Sophie said, "my parents were driving me up the wall, not trusting me, angry about everything. Goth was the only way I could show them that I was in charge of my life. Parental hysteria followed, so I became Gothier and Gothier. Is Gothier a word?"

"Doubt it."

Sophie continued, "Whatever. Everyone at school thought I had gone all bonkers, was drugged, or something. I didn't deny it but I did squat except smoke a little grass and have a beer or two.

"Anyway, I had to get as far away from my parents as I could. The UW looked the farthest from Jersey. My mom was ticked; Dad didn't care. Once Mom realized I was going, she bargained that if I joined GiGis here, she'd go along with it. The reason I didn't show up for rush was that my mom assumed that no matter how important she was nationally in GiGis, they'd never take me. From Frost's comments at the taxi that first day, I have to give points to Mom. Anyway, after a while, I got used to the look and people left me alone. I'm not changing just to fit the GiGi image. Don't even ask. Got it?"

Emma listened.

Sophie continued, "Okay my turn. Why no make-up and hair and clothes that you look like my four-year-old cousin, who's a boy?" Sophie laughed at her own humor.

Emma responded quickly, as if she had been thinking about the question herself. "It's socially competitive as hell. I grew up in a farming community and most kids don't go to college. Most here are going to typecast me as 'farm-girl-hick' no matter how I act, look, dress or speak. So why waste the time trying to be cool so they can say, 'look she's trying to be a big city girl.' I don't have to prove myself to anyone. I thought I'd play the unsophisticated farm girl to start with."

"Oooooh, bitchy and sensitive Emma, I like it," said Sophie.

* * *

Francine Frost mumbled something of a cautionary warning to Emma about the blatant segregation from the rest of the pledge class.

"Emma, you seem reasonable. Picone is going to drive a wedge between her and the rest of the house. You're going to have to make a decision what side of that wedge you want to be on. Do you really want to be a GiGi?"

"Thanks, Francine. I'll give it some thought." *NOT!*

The more Emma got to know Sophie, the more she liked her, despite Sophie's dress and facial accoutrements, a hindrance in an uber-conservative sorority.

A small contingent of senior sisters had already confronted Sophie. "Have you even considered trying to look and dress like the rest of us. I mean 'normal'"

"Fuck off," Sophie said, immediately ending the conversation.

Emma knew that Sophie wasn't going to change just by asking but also realized that her roommate needed to drop the attitude a large notch. Something would need to happen.

Emma hatched Plan A. "Wanna have some fun. I'll be like you for a week and then you have to dress like me."

Sophie thought a second, "Nah."

"What do you have to lose? I think it'd be a hoot. A week of this, a week of that. We'll have them thinking...What are they going to look like on Monday?"

Emma had no Plan B but her cajoling went on for two days until Sophie caved.

"Jesus, Emma, you're a pain in the ass. Aw, what the hell, why not, but you're going Goth first."

"Cool, but I'm not piercing anything permanently."

Sophie nodded assent and spent the next two hours splitting and coloring Emma's hair into light pink and blue. A quick trip to University Avenue got Emma the straps and faux-piercings she needed.

At dinner that night, Francine was so upset she left the dining hall early after asking to see Emma and Sophie in her office. The meeting went badly. Francine ranted for forty-five minutes with a three-sentence summation. "I had hoped you two would have tried to fit in. The whole image of the GiGis is in the toilet. Sophie, if you try to change anyone else to crazy, I promise I'll find a way to get you booted from GiGis, no matter who your mom is."

Sophie smiled, "It's a free country, last I looked. Do what you want. Can we go now?"

Emma returned to Francine's room later in the evening, alone.

"Francine, I know you and Sophie don't see eye to eye on just about anything. But under her crazy looks is a really neat person," Emma said, "who's funny, smart, caring and loyal, at least to me. Her dress is merely a statement that she is in charge of her life. Anyway, I'd like you to give me a little time and a bunch of slack. You are just going to have to trust me a little."

“Why should I trust either of you? Sophie is so disruptive to the house. And now you. There are a lot of very unhappy sisters right now,” said Francine.

“Driving Sophie, and possibly me, out of the house isn’t going to happen, and you have to realize that it won’t make our parents happy if you do. Just give me a little time. That’s all I’m asking.”

Francine nodded, “Okay, a little slack and a little time, but very little trust.”

The next night, a local fraternity, Lambda Chi, arrived at the Gamma Gamma house for formal introductions of the new pledges to the Greek system. The ceremony would repeat itself to many fraternities over the next three weeks.

The Lambda Chis thought Emma and Sophie might be in costume after the first thirty pledges descended from the second floor dressed to kill. The two misfits were largely ignored when the boys found out the look was real.

The following morning Emma received an email from her mother.

"Surprise. Just left Walla Walla. Dad and I driving in to see GiGis & meet pledges and roommate. Be there about noon"

To this point, Emma had told her mother close to nothing about Sophie.

Emma, close to hysterical, found Sophie doing her wash and explained the situation.

Sophie smiled. "I'm cool. Remember, I had to introduce my new self to my parents too."

"Yeah, but you don't know my dad."

"You don't know mine either."

An upbeat Sophie straightened up their room, while Emma, lying on her bed, awaited Armageddon. Emma went to the front door at eleven thirty and paced around the foyer trying to imagine what she would say.

Clara Braza walked into the sorority at ten past noon while Joe searched for a parking space

"Hi, Mom," Emma said.

Clara's jaw dropped while a grocery bag full of treats fell to the floor. "Oh my God. Emma is that you?" Clara gasped.

Emma spoke rapidly. "Mom, you've got to listen. I'm going to need you to control dad."

"Is this some kind of joke? I don't know that I want your father controlled after seeing you," Clara said. "Have you lost your mind."

"Please just listen. It's complicated. My new roommate, Sophie, is nice, but different. She came from New Jersey and dresses and looks unlike anything you or Dad have ever seen. Ever! The rest of the sorority is not very happy about Sophie. That includes the housemother. It'll be okay in the end but I have made Sophie a deal that I would dress like her for a week, if she'll dress like me for the week afterward. We're only two days into her week and I can't change back now."

Fifteen minutes later Emma and her parents found themselves in Francine's office with the door closed. Closing the door made little difference. The conversation was audible throughout Sorority Row.

Joe Braza sat grinding his teeth, with his arms folded tightly against his chest. Emma and her mother sat to the side.

"Mrs. Frost, we trusted you, your sorority, and this

university with my daughter, our daughter," Joe Braza said, "against my best wishes I might add. In less than a month you have her looking like a drugged out Berkeley hippy. God knows what else she's doing or already done. I want her transferred into a new room, now. No, better yet, yesterday. Am I making myself clear? If not, I will pull my daughter out of this sorority and this school."

Francine hesitated. *I have no other rooms. No one would room with Sophie. If Emma left, then Sophie would likely follow.* "Mr. and Mrs. Braza, I understand your concern and I hope you know that I have been as upset as you but..."

Emma jumped in. "Mom, Dad, you know me. You have always said you trust me. Well, I am asking you to trust me now. I am fine, and I have not changed, and I know what I am doing. I am not swapping rooms, or roommates, or schools."

Turning to Francine with a glare that would melt steel, Emma continued, "Don't even think about moving either of us."

Looking back to her parents, Emma said, "Mom, Dad, say goodbye to Mrs. Frost. I'd like you to see my room and meet Sophie."

A minute later, the Joe and Clara Braza entered Emma's room. Sophie was reading on her bed. "Mom and Dad, this is Sophia Elena Vittoria Maria Picone from the great State of New Jersey. Sophie, my mom and dad, Clara and Joe Braza."

As Joe and Clara's eyes widened, Sophie quickly stood, put on her best smile and approached the Brazas quickly and held out her hand. Her shake was confident and firm. She kept eye contact between both Brazas. "It's my pleasure to meet you both. I've heard so many wonderful and remarkable things about you two from

Emma already. My parents were so worried about the people I would meet and be living with. From what I've told them about Emma, they couldn't be happier. They'll be here in a couple of weeks for the Open House and I'd love to have them meet you."

Clara was not prepared for Sophie's appearance, but equally not prepared for the sincerity, tone and confidence of her introduction. Clara Braza relaxed, smiled and gave Sophie a hug. "It's nice to meet you too, Sophie."

Mr. Braza stared, his jaw clenched so tightly that his head had a slight tremor. He said nothing.

"Dad, this is my bed and my side of the room. We're lucky to have only the two of us in a three-person room, so we have a bit more space. Nice, eh?"

Mr. Braza looked around. "Very nice. We'd like to take you out to dinner." He did not look at Sophie and did not invite her.

About to ask if Sophie could come, Emma thought better of it and said nothing..

As Joe Braza exited he turned back to Emma, who was getting her purse, and announced to the room, the door and the hallway, "If my daughter puts one hole in her body that God didn't give her or one tattoo anywhere, this experiment is over."

Two hours later Emma returned to the room.

Sophie squinted and grimaced, "So?"

Emma plopped on Sophie's bed. "We're cool."

"C'mon, Emma, it can't be that simple. What did you say?" Sophie asked. "I thought your dad was going to explode."

"I told them I've never done anything crazy. I wanted

to have some fun and do a little experimenting and where better to do it than at college. I promised them I'd be back to myself next weekend. I asked my dad how many things he did in college that weren't straight arrow. My mom backed me up and Dad relented."

Chapter 3

For the rest of her week as a Goth, Emma ignored the looks and snotty comments from the rest of the sorority. The week of many-colors ended on Sunday, the day before a multi-fraternity and sorority party.

"My turn to dress you and if we're going to do it, let's do it right," Emma said. "I've got the name of a salon downtown to get made over, I pick the style, and it won't be farm girl either."

Sophie frowned and said, "Emma, this is total bullshit. I'm happy the way I am."

"No way, Jose. This is not up for discussion. We made a deal and I'm making you go through with it."

"One week, Emma. That's it. You are such a shit."

Monday afternoon led to four hours of reconstruction, coloring, highlighting, waxing, eyebrow arching, exfoliation, facials, and styling. Next came Nordstrom's to buy Sophie a dress.

Early that evening, Emma and Sophie made it back to their room through the pledge wing's back door, encountering no one.

By seven p.m., the fraternities and the other sorority had entered Gamma Gamma. The active members were already downstairs. The pledges from the other sorority had been herded into the upstairs hallway outside the pledge's rooms. All the doors, save Emma and Sophie's, were open and pledges from both sororities mingled comfortably. The pledges would be introduced, alternating between the two sororities as the girls descended the stairs to the main foyer. Assuming the 'Goth Girls' would disrupt the introductions, Francine had demanded that Emma and Sophie be last down the stairs. As the announcements proceeded, the hallway emptied. When Emma and Sophie exited their room, the effect on the few pledges remaining was one of absolute astonishment.

Clara Hartley, a pledge from Tacoma, who had not been particularly nice to either, shook her head in questioning disbelief. "Emma, Sophie? What did you two do? You guys look great."

Emma and Sophie descended the stairs hand in hand, doing a pose at the middle landing. The loudest gasps came from the GiGis, but their response only added to the oohs and aahs and stares from the fraternity boys.

Somewhere in the evening, Mrs. Frost approached Emma and Sophie with a look of sly satisfaction. "Well, it's about time you two came around and started looking like GiGis," Francine said.

Emma had feared solicitous sarcasm. Before Sophie could run upstairs and re-pierce herself, Emma responded. "Tomorrow we're going back to Goth. We just wanted to show you we can do whatever we like." Sophie looked at Emma and nodded 'thanks' for the support.

Frost retreated with a grumble.

A couple of the older sorority sisters had similar unwanted and unwarranted comments.

Sometime during the evening Emma cornered Francine and unloaded a litany of complaints.

"How dare you and some of the older girls tell Sophie that she needed to change to fit their profile," Emma said. "Her whole Goth thing is a control issue and now I can promise you that she'll go back to Goth tomorrow. If everyone had just kept their mouths shut, this might have been so easy."

Francine had just been taken down a notch by a freshman pledge. "Emma, I'm sorry, you're right. I underestimated you."

Sophie's hair was dyed pink and blue at two a.m. and the piercings returned. Emma went back to understated and plain. Francine Frost, forewarned by Emma, kept her comments to herself.

Two nights later, a group of pledges filed into Sophie and Emma's room just after dinner. The leader of the group was the 'bitch in the hallway' who had declared Emma and Sophie to be wackos two weeks earlier.

Emma and Sophie looked at each other, rolled their eyes and said in unison, "What now?"

"We came to say we're sorry. Talking it over with ourselves, we think it's pretty cool that you two have total control over what you do and how you look. You've not bowed to pressure from any of us or from Francine. Anyway, we'd like to start over. We are sisters after all."

Chapter 4

Emma invited Sophie home to Walla Walla for the first Thanksgiving weekend. Emma's father had a meeting in Seattle a week earlier and left Emma a car to drive home.

As the two girls headed east on I-90, Sophie asked a simple question that demanded a very long answer. "So tell me about your family and the deLorraine winery?"

"My family's winery was started by my mom's grandparents, like a hundred years ago..."

The four and one-half hour ride east over the Cascade Mountains into the Palouse gave Emma a chance to tell Sophie the entire saga of the Braza family as seen through her biased eyes. Emma drove and spoke almost without hesitation from North Bend, at the eastern foot of the Cascade Mountains, all the way to Columbia River, in eastern Washington, about two and one-half hours.

At the end of her epic tale of the deLorraines, Emma went off on a tangent and talked about her personal interest in wine. Sophie hadn't seen this coming.

"Sophie, I feel the winery is as much my legacy as it is my lazy-ass brother's. Plus that, I love the winery and I'm really, really, really good at it. From as long as I can remember, I've worked around the winery. I have tried to learn everything from putting the plantings into the ground, crushing the grapes to bottling and distribution. I didn't play sports and didn't have many close friends. Just came home and worked because I wanted to. I learned from everyone, especially my grandfather. He and my brother, Alan, didn't get along well because Alan didn't care. But I cared, and Gramps knew it. Gramps would walk me around the winery, and as early as I can remember, he'd tell me everything he could about growing grapes and making wine. Our relationship was so special.

"He died when I was 16. I was devastated for the longest time. Gramps would tell me I was gifted with a natural nose for wine and an accurate sense of taste. My brother received few of these gifts, a fact not lost on anyone, except my brother and dad."

After talking for most of two hours, Emma quieted. Sophie was quite taken aback by "*The History of the Brazas, as told by Emma Braza.*"

From her two months as roommates, Sophie had firmly thought Emma was understated, almost self-deprecating about herself. Her description of her obsession and expertise with wine caught Sophie completely off guard. Biting her usually loose tongue, Sophie mused to herself, *Okay, wine is wine, but if she needs to believe she's a wine expert, so be it. I'm not the one who's going to burst her bubble, if it makes her feel good.*

Heading east and south on US 82, just past Yakima, Sophie's story was easier.

Sophie summed it up in a simple paragraph, "My family comes from pretty much nothing. Low end Newark, third generation Italian family. My dad, Rocky, has driven a truck from the time he was 19. Joined the Teamsters and worked hard enough to buy his own rig at 25. He got lucky with some contracts, paid the right people, and then bought another truck. *Badda Bing Badda Boom*, one thing led to another and he's got his own trucking company with 15 trucks. Met Mom at a church wedding. Mom's family wasn't happy because Dad hadn't gone to college, but Dad's got a ton of street smarts. Mom was doing low level editorial work at Vogue, being paid nothing, after graduating from Vanderbilt. She quit after getting married. No need to work, and I appeared 7 months later. We now live in upscale Morristown, New Jersey. Mom, totally, and Dad, a little, are trying to wedge into local society. Actually Mom fits, Dad doesn't really. My conversion to Goth didn't help their image. Two brothers, Tony and Rocky Jr., are already anxious to be truckers, and neither will likely go to college. Mom's is ticked about that too. Dad's elated. Not much else. I had to get as far away from them as I could. The UW looked the farthest from Jersey."

As they neared Emma's home, and without being asked, Sophie removed most of her piercings and had only wisps of blue and pink remaining in her hair.

Clara Braza greeted both at the front door with generous hugs..

"Thank you so much for having me this weekend, Mrs. Braza," said Sophie.

"It's Clara. Mrs. Braza was my mother-in-law."

A large Thanksgiving dinner with friends in the wine trade went off without a hitch. Joe Braza treated Sophie with indifference and without teeth grinding or looks of disgust. The dinner party moved to the veranda for coffee and dessert.

Emma's brother, Alan, seven years older, remained charming to a point, until he had too much to drink and started hitting on Sophie.

"So Sophie," Alan said, "my dad tells me you're weird. I think you're pretty hot actually. How about I show you the highlights of metropolitan Walla Walla tomorrow night? My dead-ass sister will probably stay home the rest of the weekend and sniff grape leaves. That's about all she's good for. Boring."

Clara, hearing the end of the conversation, pounced on Alan, "Alan, back off. You've had way too much to drink and Sophie is spending the entire weekend here at the winery with Emma and me. And your father never said that Sophie was weird, he said she was 'unique', so apologize.

"Bullshit, Mom. I talk to Dad every day at the office. I know what he said," Alan said.

"Alan, get your coat and I will have Ramon drive you home. We'll get you your car in the morning. Now, go."

Alan had enough sense to back off before a simmering Emma picked up a candlestick to convince her brother to stay away.

Clara turned to Sophie, "I'm sorry for my son's actions."

"It's okay. Emma gave me a heads-up in the car."

Later that evening, Joe and the other men started discussing some of the union worker issues coming up that spring.

"Joe, did you see that memo about what the fucking *'spics'* want in terms of health care. We might as well build a Wetback Mayo Clinic right here in Walla Walla."

"Yeah, that Jew lawyer from Seattle, what's his name, Daugherty, is apparently telling them that we'll cave if they strike," Joe responded. "Fuck'em, I say."

Another friend piped in, "The fucking Teamsters are going to screw us too. We can never give those assholes enough."

The conversation deteriorated further, getting uglier and uglier for another forty-five minutes. Even with the Hispanic help well within earshot of the group, the comments continued, louder and angrier, *'fucking Jew lawyers'*, *'fucking wetbacks'*, and *'spics.'* Sophie asked to be excused and Emma followed her out.

"I'm sorry," Sophie said. "I had to get out of there. My dad's business works with the Teamsters and other unions and they get along great. Dad was a Teamster first and many of his best friends are Teamsters It's one of the reasons he's done so well. Not all the lawyers they talked about had Jewish names but everyone was a 'fucking Jew' lawyer. What's with that?"

"I warned you," Emma said. "This rhetoric has been going on as long as I can remember. My grandparents, as much as I loved them, weren't too different, but Dad and Alan are worse."

"How'd they get that way?" asked Sophie.

"I don't know. They distrust anyone, or anything, that isn't white, conservative and Christian. I'm not sure why Dad's like that, but it's pretty deep seated. I'm pretty sure it started with growing up with the wrong friends in Toppenish and then Dad passed it onto Alan. At least Dad is fair with the Mexican workers and he has their respect for that. My brother spends his days pissing off everyone at the winery, causing Dad one headache after another trying to fix up his messes.

Emma continued, "My uncle Arnie, Mom's brother, died in Viet Nam. You didn't get to hear about fucking Asians, which are all lumped into one."

"Gee, what's your dad think about me?" asked Sophie.

"Not to worry, Dad loves Italians, French, Spaniards and Germans," Emma said. "After all, they're white, Christian, grow grapes and make wine."

"Thank God for little things."

"My mom will go out there in a few minutes and tone things down and then throw them all out," Emma said. "She's way more accepting. If not for her, I suspect the men would go out with hoods and shotguns looking for some *fucking* group to shoot at. It's my family, good and bad, warts and all."

Sophie deadpanned, "And here I thought my family was strange."

"Sorry about my brother, but I warned you. He's a piece of work. My dad, a guy's guy, of course, expects Alan, a worse guy's guy, to someday take over the business. I suppose that's going to happen. He's athletic, good looking, and smart enough. But he's a lazy shit and totally irresponsible. He likes the money, cars, women and the entitlement that comes from my dad's success. Alan could care less how or where money comes to him, as long as he doesn't have to work for it."

* * *

A large travelling group from the UK arrived the morning after Thanksgiving for a scheduled tour of the deLorraine Winery. Alan, still hung over at his apartment, begged off doing the tour and Joe asked Emma to lead it. Sophie tagged along not knowing what to expect. Emma had been leading winery tours since she was fifteen. She enjoyed interacting with touring groups, and knew more about the minutiae of the winery than Alan.

Initially, the English amateur oenophiles appeared upset at the apparent youth of their guide, but after fifteen minutes the mumbling ceased. Emma knew considerably more about wine than anyone in the group. The group toured the vineyards, mostly barren in late November, where Emma explained new plantings to harvesting and destemming. Moving from the fields, they learned reds versus whites, crushing techniques and fermentation, pressing, cold and heat stabilization, laboratory testing to check the status of each wine, blending to achieve desired taste, filtration, bottling, and storage. From the storage areas, Emma let the guests taste young wines that hadn't aged enough and then let them try older wines from the same grapes that had reached maturity. Emma knew every intricacy of the process. Additionally, Emma knew all of the staff, gave them important titles, and used them to add snippets at each station. The staff loved the recognition and, just as clearly, they respected Emma. Not uncommonly, and today was no different, a feeding frenzy ensued at the order desk for cases of wine to be shipped to the UK.

As Emma and Sophie left the touring group and walked back to the house through an edge of the vineyards, Sophie put her arm around her friend's waist and said emphatically, "You told me you knew wine, but, heck, I had no idea that you *really* know wine. You are amazing. My dad's in the trucking business and I don't know a goddamn thing about a truck except that the wheels go 'round and round.'"

"It's my life's passion, honestly," Emma said. "I told you on the ride here how, as early as I can remember, my grandfather would hold my hand and we'd walk through the vineyards and he'd talk and we'd feel and smell the grapes and the stems and the earth. I really loved him.

"I'll tell you a story I've never shared with anyone. One night, I must have been about thirteen or so, Gramps and I walked up to a work shed that had a side door and was always locked. We went in and he put on a lantern. Pictures of my grandfather and great-grandfather and pictures of my uncle Arnie, before he went off to Viet Nam, adorned the walls. Kind of a shrine to select members of our family.

Gramps told me that I had been given a gift by the 'wine' gods and then showed me a little scar on the inside of his right wrist that his father had created with a penknife and some cuttings from the vineyard. He told me that his grandfather had the same one, as did Arnie before he shipped off. I asked if my dad had one, he said no, he wasn't a blood deLorraine and Mom and Alan weren't given the gift. He made this little cut on my wrist and told me to keep the cut in the sun for a few days so it would be permanent. He then tacked a picture of me on the wall next to him. Anyway, this little scar on my wrist was from Gramps. He swore me to secrecy and, like I said, I've never told anyone about it, except you. He did show me where he kept the key. After he died, I cleared out the shed and stored the pictures in a box that I keep. It's my Grandpa box and I open it once in a while to talk to him."

"That's kinda of creepy, no?" asked Sophie.

"Yeah, probably, but my grandfather was old school, as they say. You'd have loved him. Anyway, it bound us together and I miss him. I have a thousand questions I'd like to ask him. He really loved this land and the grapes. Hard not to admire someone with that much passion and not want to emulate him."

The weekend ended peacefully and on Sunday morning, While Sophie packed, Emma went to say good-bye to her mother.

"Thanks for being so nice to Sophie," Emma said. "It's not been so easy all the time for her at the sorority."

"Emma, you were right," Clara said. "Sophie is nice and smart. She'll find her way. She's welcome anytime you want to bring her. Even your father admitted to me that she's 'not so bad', which for him is a huge concession."

Emma and Sophie returned to school, dove into their studies and took their finals before Christmas break. Emma and Sophie, carrying full academic loads, had the two highest grade point averages in the pledge class.

When Sophie returned from New Jersey after Christmas break, she no longer wore lip piercings and after the spring break the brow piercings disappeared. Emma said nothing and the rest of the house, now smarter, followed suit.

The entire pledge class, with Sophie's help, surprised the rest of the house by having pink and blue hair and faux piercings for a party after initiation. For most, the dyed manes vanished within a few days, but some kept them for a while.

Chapter 5

Before returning home from school after freshman year, Emma called her father.

"Dad. I just want to let you know that I'm going to work in the business office this summer. I've already talked to Henry Watson and he says it's okay with him. I know you were upset and surprised that I picked the business program at the UW rather than the agricultural program at State. But I've learned so much this year already. I think working in the business office makes sense."

"I dunno, Emma," said Joe Braza. "They're busy and I don't want you getting in the way."

"Dad, hopefully, one of these days, you and Alan will realize that I have a little bit of talent. Besides, when have I ever gotten ***in the way***?"

"Okay, Emma, whatever you want to do. But I thought you and Mom were going to go to Europe earlier this year."

"Nope. I plan to work."

Within two weeks of Emma returning home, Alan entered his dad's office and took a seat.

"Dad, Emma is being a pain in the ass. She's trying to tell me how to run some of the invoices. I don't like being lectured to by my kid sister, who should be in the kitchen with Mom."

"Alan, cool it. The accountants have called me a couple of times to tell me that some of the changes she's made in the bookkeeping department are effective and are saving us money. She has the bookkeepers using spreadsheets that she's created. Now when I need specific information, it's there quicker."

Alan rolled his eyes and slid down in the chair. “I know. I know. But I don’t like it. All everybody does around here is swoon over Emma, telling me how much they adore her. I’m sick of it.”

“Alan, give it time. You’re so goddamned impatient. I don’t know what she’s going to do in the end, but you’re going to run deLorraine. That much I’m sure of. She’ll find some guy, settle down, raise kids, and make your mom happy with grandchildren.”

“Fine, but I can’t wait for her to go back to school.”

Emma and Sophie talked, emailed or texted every day.

“Sophie, I have never had anyone I could be so honest with,” Emma said one night. “Well, maybe my mom, but there’s just some things you really can’t talk about with your mom.”

“I feel the same way,” Sophie said. “I can’t wait until September when we get back to school.”

Their bond had been forged by the social exclusion experienced together at the onset of their relationship. They knew that their relationship was gut deep.

Starting as toddlers, Alan and Emma, at the very end of each summer, headed to Europe with their mother to visit wineries, friends and family. Joe would come for a week sometime during the trip. By age sixteen, Alan saw no reason for the trips and stopped coming. By the time Emma reached college, she spoke French and Italian fluently and German nearly so. Emma's Spanish was natural, influenced by the Mexican workers at the winery.

In early August before Emma’s sophomore year, Clara and Emma left for Europe. Emma diverted her return to spend time with Sophie and her family in New Jersey. The girls then flew into Walla Walla until they had to leave for school

Returning to school for sophomore year, Emma and Sophie, again roomed together.

A hip, small diamond stud now replaced Sophie's nose ring and her hair had only subtle streaks of pink and blue.

Both girls assumed *de facto* leadership positions in the sorority. They established themselves academically and offered assistance to any one in need. Francine Frost did a complete one-eighty on the two girls and often, in confidence, would ask them advice about one situation or another.

The summer following sophomore year, Emma worked in the bottling and distribution part of the winery. The employees loved having her around. And again, Alan resented her presence.

That summer, during her free time at lunch or before dinner, Emma would walk the vineyards, sift the soil between her fingers, smell the grapes, and talk to the staff. When asked what she was doing, she would likely say with a huge smile, "Looking for Gramps. He's here somewhere."

Back at school for junior year, after Europe and a trip to New Jersey, Emma continued her business studies with the unwavering intent of going to work for her family's winery.

Meanwhile Sophie had not the slightest interest in her family's trucking company. She decided early her junior year that she would attend law school. Unfortunately she wasn't going to graduate in four years but she was having enough fun at the UW that the extra quarter or two wouldn't be a big deal. So happy about Sophie's new personality, her parents would have agreed to just about anything.

Sophie Picone returned for junior year and rush with natural, beautiful jet-black hair and diamond studs in both ears.

Sophie had her own thoughts. "I am my own person, I make my own rules and I'm not angry at my parents right now. I reserve the right to go back and be a pain in the ass whenever I want."

Emma thought better of saying anything and didn't even nod assent.

Emma's transformation from country girl to city girl took place slowly and with purpose. By junior year she subtly became one of the most stylish and copied dressers in the sorority.

The summer after junior year, Emma worked in distribution again before heading to Europe. Sophie was working full time in New York at a law office, so Emma came directly home with Clara. Sophie planned to come to eastern Washington a week early to drive to Seattle with Emma.

Back home awaiting Sophie, Emma looked forward to her last year at the UW.

A few days before Sophie arrived, Emma told her mom that she was going to Richland, Washington, to do some light pre-school shopping.

As Emma wrapped up her mini-expedition in Richland her cell phone screen flashed a near-dead battery warning. Using the last of her charge, she texted her mom at 8 p.m.

'on the road. phone almost dead. home b4 9:10.'

Just past the small city of Touchet, Washington, on

Highway 12, Emma's left rear tire blew and she pulled to the side of the road. A trucker, following her, stopped, but took an hour to change the tire. She thanked the trucker who would accept no money. He left before she could ask him to use his cell phone to call home.

Now past 9:15 p.m., Emma resumed her drive home a mere twenty-five minutes away. A small roadside eatery, Jolene's Joint, near Touchet seemed like a good place to stop, get a bottle of water, and let her mom know she'd be a few minutes late.

Chapter 6

Tom Carter had just been released on parole from the Washington State Penitentiary in Walla Walla. An armed robbery three years earlier in Everett had gone badly, and the judge, showing little mercy, gave Tom ten years. Tom's priors included two different airtight sexual assault rape charges, but when the brutalized victims chose not to appear, he walked. He had also done ninety days for pistol-whipping an ex-girlfriend and her new boyfriend.

Once released, Tom moved in with his mother, who had relocated to Walla Walla, but not to be near her son, whom she regarded as a 'bad apple.' Once Tom located her secret cash stash in the apartment, he took the money and left. He picked up two new friends, also recently released from the state penitentiary. 'Friends' would be the loosest of definitions to Tom.

Manny and Paco, long-time compadres, had worked as itinerant farm laborers before turning to petty crimes and assaults. Uneducated and lacking street smarts, Tom felt he could control both. Buoyed by Tom's mother's money, the three headed west from Walla Walla toward the Tri-Cities to cause mischief as the sun started to set. Intending only to get beers and sandwiches at a dive on Highway 12, Tom realized after fifteen minutes that no one else had entered the eatery. The older woman/cook/cashier with a big name tag that read *Jolene* was clearly alone. As Tom watched, Jolene had already turned off some of the interior lighting preparing to close for the night. Tom quickly cased the restaurant to be sure no surveillance cameras existed.

Tom thought to himself, '*So what the hell, easy as pie.*'

The three approached Jolene, without weapons drawn. Jolene, smiling, stood at the register assuming the three men would pay their bill and leave.

"I'll make this easy on you, lady," said Tom. "We want all the money in the till. I don't want nobody to get hurt."

"Sure, sure," Jolene said, surprised. "Please don't hurt me."

"Just give us the money and no one gets hurt."

Jolene didn't seem overly excitable and calmly opened the register and pulled the money drawer out of the register. She appeared to accidently drop the drawer on the counter with coins and bills falling both ways over the edge at the feet of the three men and Jolene.

"Oh, I'm sorry," Jolene said, a bit too calmly for Tom.

Manny and Paco immediately scrambled to the floor for the fallen money.

Jolene bent down behind her side of the counter, appearing to look for money, and came up with a twenty-gauge, sawed-off shotgun, leaned over the counter and calmly shot Paco in the back, killing him instantly.

Off to the side, Tom watched the ordeal play out. He spit out, "Aw Shit," and quickly shot Jolene before she could shoot again.

Manny started screaming, "Tom, we need to vamos."

Tom pointed the gun at Manny's head, "Shut the fuck up, Manny. I needs to think."

"Manny, take about half the money and leave the rest," Tom said. "We need to make this look like Paco was alone."

Tom wiped his gun, the one he had just used to

shoot the Jolene, and then put it in Paco's lifeless hand. He rescanned the register area and confirmed the absence of video cameras. He then used a mop from behind the counter to erase the different sets of footprints in the blood.

"Okay Manny, let's get the fuck outta here," Tom said. "I'll get the lights so no one shows up until tomorrow."

As Tom searched for the light switch, Emma Braza entered the restaurant.

Chapter 7

Emma knew within a second that she did not want to be there. Tom Carter knew in half a second.

She spun to exit when Tom grabbed her by the hair and pulled her to the floor.

"Leave me alone, you fucking asshole. Leave me alone. Help. Help," Emma screamed.

Emma, continuing to scream, fought as hard as she could, flailing at her assailant's face, biting his arm, and trying to kick him in the groin. Tom banged her head hard against the linoleum floor, once, then twice and a third time, until she stopped moving. He then looked out the door to make sure no one else occupied Emma's car.

"What we gonna do?" Manny asked. "What we gonna do, Tom? We gotta kill her too? Tom, she awful pretty and I ain't had a piece of ass in long time that looks this good."

As Tommy looked at the unconscious girl, he nodded agreement. "I know we can't leave the bitch here," he said, "that's for fuckin' sure. I'll turn off the lights; you tie her up and put her in the trunk. But look careful before you step out the door that nobody else is around. I gotta think hard."

Manny removed Emma's shoelaces and bound her feet and hands. He then tore a swatch of Emma's blouse to wipe the blood from the floor around her head. Next, he peaked out to the front of the restaurant, now dark. He saw no visible traffic and no other cars in the almost dark lot other than their old Sentra and a newish Honda. He easily lifted Emma's limp body from the floor and dumped her in the trunk of their Sentra. Dripping blood from the back of Emma's head left a trail to the car.

Tom quickly found the keys to Emma's car in her pocketbook. "Follow me up 12 goin' west," he shouted to

Manny. “There's a ravine a couple of miles before the river. We'll dump her car there and take her plates." He didn't want to give Manny too many instructions at once.

“Then what, Tom, then what?” Manny asked.

“I’ll tell you when we get to the ravine.”

“No, Tom, then what? I gotta know.”

"Okay, asshole. We'll follow the river south into Oregon. I know a motel near Hermiston that's a shit hole, but the guy asks no questions as long as you pay cash up front."

They arrived at the ravine after the sun had set but the early evening summer glow gave just a bit of light. Tom had been in the ravine before. He drove Emma's Honda, lights off, downward. Manny stayed up top after turning the Sentra around, shut off the lights and engine, and waited. Tom, now halfway down the steep road into the ravine, exited the car and set the parking brake. He hid Emma’s pocketbook between two large rocks. With a screwdriver on his multipurpose knife, he removed the license plates from her Honda. He then put her car in neutral, released the parking brake and watched as the car descended off the road into the ravine. The crashing sound echoed around the ravine for a few seconds, but unless one counted jackrabbits and coyotes, no one heard a thing.

Tom walked back up the road. As he approached Manny, Tom could hear Emma screaming in the trunk. He threw Emma's plates in the back seat of the Sentra.

"Manny, get the roll of duct tape off the back seat. We gotta make sure the bitch don’t make no noise for the rest of the trip."

They popped the trunk. Emma, at first disoriented, lay face up then started kicking and screaming.

"Help. Help. Help," Emma screamed.

Tom grabbed Emma's mouth and she bit him on the left thumb as hard as she could.

"Ow. You fuckin' bitch," Tom screamed. He slapped Emma hard with his right hand but she wouldn't let go of the thumb.

"Fuck, fuck, fuck." Tom pinched Emma's jaw with his good right hand forcing her mouth open until she lost her bite grip on the thumb.

"Let me go. Let me go. Help," Emma screamed.

For good measure, Tom banged her head against the floor of the trunk, which did little to quiet her.

"Help. Help."

Tom grabbed Emma's hair, pulling her head backwards and placed a chokehold around her neck with the opposite hand to keep her quiet while Manny put duct tape over her mouth. Manny slammed the trunk shut while Tom sucked on his bleeding thumb.

Tom took the wheel of his car and reentered the highway. He shook his aching thumb repeatedly. Emma had drawn blood over the knuckle and he sucked it clean. He'd worry about it later and said nothing to Manny.

Tom and Manny headed west on WA-12 to the Columbia River and turned south on Route 730 crossing into Oregon. Before entering Hermiston, Tom pulled off the road and swapped the license plates from Emma's Honda.

They pulled into the sleazy motel in Hermiston, Oregon about 12:30 a.m., parking well away and out of earshot from the manager's office. Tom had correctly guessed that the motel would be void of cars. Emma, now fully conscious, started kicking the trunk, but too far from the manager's office to be heard. Tom rang the night bell and moments later the manager opened the door.

Tom asked, "You guys not too busy, don't see no cars?"

"Nuttin' goin' on here for a few days," the manager responded, looking over Tom's shoulder at the car parked at the far end of the lot.

"I need a room with two beds for me and my buddy. Something quiet, maybe at the end of the motel."

"That'll be $75 bucks and I prefer cash," the manager said. "What's your license number, I can't see it from here?"

Tom had memorized Emma's plates. "Washington, MPA 343."

The manager wrote the number down.

Tom then gave the man seventy-five dollars and said, "We'll likely be here a few days, maybe more. I have business in Hermiston. I'll give you seventy-five dollars cash every morning." Tom didn't want the manager calling the cops and knew he wouldn't call if he thought that he'd be getting seventy-five dollars cash every day.

Tom returned to his car and backed up to the door of a motel room at the end of the strip.

Manny, shaking, had his hand on his gun. "Tom, I need whiskey, bad."

Tom looked over his shoulder saw the manager peering out from behind his desk. Tom put his hand on

Manny's shoulder and said, "Cool it, amigo. The asshole's watching us. You can get a drink as soon as you get into the room, not until then. Get out of the car and walk real slow into the room. Here's the key. I'll follow. We'll get the bitch out when it's clear."

"Okay, Tom," Manny said, continuing to sway back and forth.

Tom grabbed a small duffel bag from the back seat and followed Manny into the room and closed the curtains. He peeked out the window every few minutes.

Manny had already opened the duffel bag and had his first few shots of whiskey. He knocked the no-smoking sign off the desk into the small garbage can at the side of the dresser as he lit up a cigarette.

Tom waited until the manager had turned off the lights and left his desk. Tom rechecked every few minutes and until he was certain that the manager had gone to sleep. Tom walked out first, and stood off to the side of the car, shielding the trunk as he watched the manager's office.

On Tom's signal, Manny followed, opened the trunk and grabbed a kicking Emma and hustled into the motel room with Emma over his shoulder. Never taking his eyes off the office, Tom slammed the trunk shut, casually lit up a cigarette and took five or six huge drags. Seeing no activity from the manager's office, Tom smiled, chucked the cigarette butt, re-entered the motel room, bolted the door and wedged a chair under the doorknob.

Manny had put Emma on the double bed farthest from the door. Emma's clothes were in tatters from her attempts at self-defense. Her head turned violently side-to-side. Her mouth was still covered with duct tape and the bed sheets under her head were already blood soaked. Tom could hear the deep throated muffled sounds coming through Emma's nose and vibrating the tape over her mouth like the tight skin on a snare drum. He thought she was saying "No, No, No." but didn't give it any thought. Tom held her arms above her head as Manny duct taped her wrists to the headboard. Together, the two men taped her ankles to the bed frame rollers on each side at the foot of the bed spreading her legs apart.

Tom, smiling, flipped a coin. "Heads I go first with the girl. Tails you get the whiskey first."

Manny thought for a second and even he got the joke. But Manny, still a bit shaky, needed to get real drunk anyway. "You go, I needs more booze."

Emma would lose consciousness repeatedly, only to be awakened by cigarette burns to her chest and breasts. Literally, the evening would only last until 4:30 a.m. when both men were spent and too drunk to do any more to Emma. Figuratively, the evening would last the rest of her life. She remained strapped to the bed with her wrists together, although they had re-taped her prone at three a.m. for the last ninety minutes and moved her down to the foot of the bed. The bed covers at the bottom of the bed were covered in blood and small amounts of blood oozed down Emma's legs. Tom slept on top of the unused bed and Manny was sound asleep on the floor.

At seven a.m. the next morning, Tom arose and checked to see that Emma's tapes remained secure. He kicked Manny to tell him he'd be back in twenty-five minutes. Tom drove to a Safeway he had seen on the way into town and purchased more duct tape, a box of large plastic lawn and leaf bags and seventy-five dollars worth of Cokes, Pacificos, snack food, and three cartons of unfiltered Camels.

Tom needed a plan, quickly, but not easily conceived hung over. The throbbing thumb annoyed him; his aching dick did not. As he drove back to the motel he thought.

'Shit, can't talk to Manny, he's one dumb asshole. I gotta figure this out myself. The cops will figure out sooner or later, probably sooner, that the stick-up and murder wasn't a solo job. They're too stupid to put the girl in the middle of all this, but someone could see the car in the ravine in the next day or two. By then, I'll be in Mexico. I'm 'sposed to personally check in with my parole officer in Richland tomorrow. Fuck. No way I coming back to Washington, ever. They'll be looking for me in a day or so, but not hard looking.'

Back at the motel, Tom re-taped Emma's mouth. The fight had gone out of her early in the morning and all she could mount in defense was a slow shaking of her head and a low groaning, "No more, no more." Her clothes were largely gone, cut to shreds the night before with Tom's utility knife after the first few minutes in the room. They cut the tape from the headboard, keeping her wrists bound and then rebound her ankles together. Tom poked breathing holes in one large plastic bag and used it for Emma's upper body and head. Another bag was used to cover her abdomen and legs. The two bags were duct taped together so that no skin showed. Tom watched the manager's office for a few minutes. Seeing no one, Manny dumped Emma back into the trunk.

Off they went, heading west on US 84 toward I-5 and then, with luck, south to California and Mexico. Tom had given the motel manager another seventy-five dollars that morning with a promise of another seventy-five the following day. Tom told the manager not to clean the room.

Tom told Manny as he re-entered the car, "We're heading to Mexico, Manny. No stopping for nothing but gas and food. Just keep driving. We'll have to dump the girl after one more night."

Manny nodded in agreement. Even more hung over

than Tom, Manny's head ached, made worse by the bright light of the morning sun.

Tom finally had a plan. He, of course, hadn't told Manny that travelling with three people was two too many. Tonight, somewhere in southern Oregon or northern California, Tom would be the only one travelling, or alive.

Emma, in the trunk, fell in and out of consciousness. *It hurts so bad. I'm so thirsty. Where am I? I'm in the trunk of a car, but where? It hurts so bad. That must be oil or gasoline that I smell? It's sickening. It hurts so bad. What can I do? It hurts so bad. I've got to do something. We're moving. Oh, we just turned. We're slowing down. We've stopped.*

"Help. Help. Help." But the tape on her mouth made her pleas sound like dull and soft 'uhs.'

I've got to move and kick. Move and kick. Move and kick. It hurts so bad.

Oh, we're moving again.

Chapter 8

Charlie and Ruth Munro maneuvered their 43' Winnebago, pulling a Toyota Corolla, into a Mobil station just outside Tualatin, Oregon, on US I-5, heading south. Charlie found it always a little tricky to find a station that could handle his twenty yards of rig and tow. Charlie had been with the RCMP in British Columbia for forty years and had been retired for four years. Charlie and Ruth bought the RV to live in after selling their home. They would head south, slowly, starting sometime in the fall and make it to Mexico by early November. As Ruth headed into the station mini-mart to buy Diet Cokes, Charlie started refueling the Winnebago. His rig held more than one hundred fifty gallons, so filling would take a while.

A beat up Nissan Sentra with two unsavory characters pulled up into the station's adjoining bay. Charlie had seen hundreds like these idlers but not in a while. Charlie thought to himself, *once a cop always a cop.* To Charlie, these two not only looked like trouble, they acted like they were '*in* trouble.' Charlie watched closely, he couldn't help it. An air of tension, darting eyes, trying to act like they're not in a hurry, but were, only added to Charlie's level of suspicion.

Tom kept the pump handle compressed to the max after sliding forty dollars in tens into the pump's cash slot.

Charlie smiled when Tom glared at him. *Bad guys. They're running from something.*

"I gotta take a piss and a crap," Manny said.

"Make it quick. Me too, I don't want to stay here any longer than we have to." Tom added.

Manny took off for the bathroom, getting the key from the cashier. Tom, holding his aching thumb, walked a few steps away from the car to get a little sun in his face.

Charlie shrugged and checked his pump. He'd only gotten to fifty gallons. He then noticed the back of the Sentra. The tail end was moving up and down ever so slightly, but moving nonetheless. He saw no occupants or animals in the back seat. The Sentra's engine was turned off and he saw the car keys twirling in the hands of the guy in the sun. Then the tail end moving stopped. Strange he thought. He kept watching the car. A moment later, the tail end moved once again. Charlie's hunch was that there was something alive in the trunk. The moving stopped again. The guy in the sun turned and gave Charlie a look that spelled *'stay out of my way, asshole.'* Charlie tried his best to appear to be watching only his pump. The back end of the Sentra was moving again.

Manny returned and he and Tom exchanged car and bathroom keys. Tom headed for the bathroom.

Charlie needed a ruse to get closer to the back of the Sentra. As Manny looked away, Charlie rolled a coin toward the Sentra. It stopped just under the left rear tire.

"Oh darn", Charlie said loud enough that Manny turned around. Charlie walked to the back wheel of the Sentra.

Manny shouted, "Back off, asshole."

"Excuse me but I just lost some money and it rolled under your car," Charlie said loudly.

Charlie bent down to his knees to pick up the quarter, shouting, "I found it, it's right here."

"Back off," Manny repeated, even louder.

"Ooh, hard to get up. Sorry." Charlie stopped

moving and listened. The car was moving and a soft thumping sound came from the trunk.

Manny came behind him and gave Charlie an unsubtle nudge in the left hip with his foot. "Hey, asshole, get out of there."

"Okay, okay, I'm getting up. I've got a bum back so I'm not bouncing anymore. Here's my quarter." Charlie stood slowly, showed Manny the coin, and arched his back to feign stiffness. He moved back to his pump and carefully checked the reading. "Thirsty son of a gun, eh."

A few moments later, Tom returned and Manny told him about the rolling quarter. They both looked at Charlie who was seven-eighths through his fill. Tom mumbled loud enough, but the only word Charlie clearly understood was "asshole."

The men jumped into the Sentra and took off. Charlie noted the Washington plates and the number. The car sped onto the ramp leading to I-5 South.

Charlie got into his rig and waited for Ruth. Once in the RV, they headed south onto I-5 as well.

“Ruthie, I just saw something.”

“You're always seein' things. What did you see this time?” Ruth asked.

“There were two guys in that red Sentra parked next to us and they looked like they were on the run.”

Rolling her eyes, Ruthie said, “Really, Sherlock.”

Charlie disregarded the sarcasm. “Anyway, there was nobody in the car and yet the back end kept bouncing up and down. I think there was something alive in the trunk. I swear.”

“So now what?”

"While we're driving maybe we can see if anyone knows something."

He flipped on his CB radio and starting asking if anyone knew of any serious crimes or kidnappings that had occurred in the area within the last couple of days. He picked up a trucker outside of Troutdale who had heard about a murder robbery in southern Washington near Walla Walla the night before. The guy had not heard of any kidnappings.

"See, Ruthie. Maybe these are the perps. Just do me a favor and see if you can get a number for the Walla Walla PD, eh."

While Charlie drove, Ruth *Googled* the contact number of the police in Walla Walla on her iPhone and dialed. Ruth, who'd done this before, told the operator that she was calling for Inspector Charles Munro of the RCMP in Vancouver, BC, and he needed to talk to a detective. She folded her arms, shook her head, put the phone on Bluetooth and waited.

"Detective Erik Rawlins here, whom I talkin' to?"

Charlie spoke up quickly. "Detective Rawlins, I am Charles Munro, formerly of the RCMP in Vancouver. Can you hear me okay?"

"I hear you fine."

I was a detective for 20 plus years, mostly Narcs and was Drug Enforcement Commander for the Greater Vancouver area. I am in an RV heading south of Tualatin, on I-5 below Portland and the US-205 interchange."

"So why the Walla Walla PD?" asked Rawlins.

Charlie explained the entire scene from the gas station and the information from the trucker to Rawlins.

"Just on a hunch, I wonder whether there had been a kidnapping or missing person report as well."

"Actually there is a missing person report on a young college girl from Walla Walla who didn't get home last night, but no one has suspected that the two events were related."

"Rawlins, I'm telling you that these guys were running hard," Charlie persisted. "And no question, something was moving in the back of their Sentra. The license plates were from Washington, MPA 343."

"Humph, that does sound familiar, hold on." After a moment of silence Rawlins came back on.

"Those plates belong to the girl that is missing but she was driving a white 2009 Honda Accord."

"These guys were driving a beat up late 80s red Nissan Sentra and those were the plates on the car."

"Holy smokes, buddy. I think you just hit the jackpot."

"Detective, these guys are heading south on I-5. I expect they'll be outside Salem in forty minutes. I'm in a RV, towing a car, and I can't keep up with them."

"Charlie, you've done plenty. I'll take it from here. I've got to call the Oregon Highway Patrol and the Salem PD. I've got your number on my screen. Thanks. I'll get back to you." Rawlins never did get back to Charlie.

Chapter 9

An Oregon Highway Patrol helicopter was already in the sky just south of Salem and, within seconds, turned and headed north at full throttle. Assuming the Sentra was travelling at no more than 70 miles per hour, the car would be at least 25-30 minutes north of Salem. If the perps wanted to stay under the radar, speeding would be the last thing they'd do.

OHP officers up and down the I-5 corridor were alerted and units from north and south converged toward Salem. A SWAT team from the Salem PD that kept its offices at the state capitol helped the OHP set up a roadblock just before I-5 split at OR 22.

Twenty-three miles north of Salem the OHP helicopter spotted the red Sentra going a steady 60 miles per hour in the right lane.

The roadblock was set up away from exits to prevent the fugitives from turning off the highway. The site was just south and below a subtle rise in the highway to prevent the oncoming drivers from seeing the extent of the preparations. Four OHP cruisers were in place, ready to straddle all three lanes and the sides of I-5, awaiting a signal from the observation helicopter. Temporary large orange construction signs were deployed along both sides of the highway.

The helicopter laid back, three quarters of a mile behind the Sentra, and remained undetected. When the cars were within ninety seconds of the roadblock, the helicopter radioed, a 'go' signal and traffic was halted at the top of the rise. The cruisers formed a solid line across the highway out of sight, south of the rise. The visible officers, while armed, had no guns drawn to give the appearance of a routine traffic slowdown. The Sentra was nine cars back at the stop point in the middle lane. Within another ninety seconds, all lanes of I-5 South were filled with cars and trucks behind Tom and Manny's Sentra. Concealed sharpshooters were placed out of sight on the east and west side of the elevated highway. OHP patrol cars were now three abreast 250 yards behind the Sentra.

Tom realized quickly that he and Manny had fallen into the police snare. Tom tried to turn the Sentra around but there was no room to wiggle. The roadblock's lead officer, Captain Reggie Phillips of the OHP, bull-horned the drivers to stay in their vehicles, keep their doors locked and windows closed.

"Fuck, fuck," Tom screamed as he pounded the steering wheel. "What the fuck are we gonna do? Fuck. Fuck."

"Tom, we're fucked," Manny shouted. "Now what? I don't see no way outta here."

Tom pointed his gun at Manny and spoke firmly, "Calm down, amigo. Getting fucking crazy now is not going to help. We gotta use the bitch as a shield and make some kind of deal. They won't dare shoot if they think the bitch might get popped."

Tom waited for a second so Manny could agree. Manny nodded, and mumbled, "Si."

Tom jumped into the back of the Sentra and ripped the back seat off its frame, which opened into the trunk. He grabbed the black plastic bag covering Emma's head and torso.

"Manny, help me here. Pull."

With Manny's help leaning over the front seat, they pulled the plastic bag and Emma through the opening. She offered no resistance. The car seat frame edges ripped the lower bag during the pull. Other than shreds of the black plastic, Emma was now naked below the waist while her ankles remained bound with duct tape. Fresh bleeding oozed from leg scrapes also caused by the car's sharp frame edges.

Tom opened the back door, keeping low, and dragged Emma onto the pavement.

He yelled at Manny, "Asshole, get out your side, keep low. Don't fucking point your gun at anyone. If you point it, you're dead meat. And don't open your fucking trap. I'll do all the talking."

Manny, visibly shaking, exited the passenger side and kept low as instructed. Tom tore open the top of the upper bag to reveal Emma's face, bruised and bloody with duct tape over her mouth. Her head fell to the side and moved little, as if she were shaking it to say 'no.' The plastic bag remained bunched around her neck. Tom stood, grabbing Emma by her chest with his left arm to brace her, and pulled the gun out of his belt with his right hand and pointed it at Emma's left temple.

"Manny, walk together," Tom shouted. "Walk real slow and let me do the talking. Don't do nothing stupid."

Tom started walking toward the roadblock holding Emma by the neck, the gun now pointed below her right ear. Emma was conscious enough to hold up most of her weight. Manny, agitated, walked in parallel on the opposite side of the car, gun drawn but kept against his chest.

Tom, holding Emma, and Manny cleared the front of the first stopped car together. On seeing Tom and Manny's guns, every officer on the roadblock drew weapons.

Manny, without cover, saw the drawn weapons and panicked. He ran to the west edge of the freeway, jumped the rail and started down the embankment, running straight at the sharpshooter sitting behind a large boulder.

The sharpshooter in full Kevlar stood up and yelled, "Stop now! Put down your weapon."

Manny immediately turned and ran back to the north along the embankment. The sharpshooter repeated, "Stop, now. Put down your weapon."

Manny looked back, raised his gun and fired two haphazard rounds toward the sharpshooter, missing badly. The OHP sharpshooter had dropped to the ground as soon as Manny raised his gun. Before the sharpshooter could return fire, Manny was killed with a head shot from the sharpshooter's partner from the east side of the road who had crossed over the freeway behind Manny after seeing him run to the west. Both marksmen immediately repositioned themselves to cover Tom and his hostage.

Tom turned to see the effects of the shot, then quickly looked back to the main roadblock and screamed, "Put down your guns or this bitch dies."

The roadblock officers did not move, looking only to Captain Phillips for instructions. Phillips shouted back, "We're not going anywhere. Your only chance of living is to let the girl go and drop the gun."

Tom screamed again, "Put down your guns, you assholes, or she dies, I'm not bluffing. We've gotta talk. I don't care if I die, but you care if she does. Put down your guns. I need a car."

Distracted, Tom had allowed Emma to slip down in his grasp. Tom now held Emma's neck so tightly that she lost consciousness. Her head drooped and her arms dangled limply to the side. Her dead weight and profuse sweating inside the plastic bags made supporting her almost impossible. Emma began to slip down through the plastic bag and her head disappeared downward. Tom went to regrab Emma's head but she continued to slide downward toward the pavement. Tom had let go of the emptying bag intending to re-grab Emma. As he did his gun pointed upwards, away from Emma. Both repositioned sharpshooters saw the brief opening when Emma, now on the ground, was not in danger. Shots rang out simultaneously from both sides of the road, and Tom Carter's head split in two.

Chapter 10

The SWAT team, forewarned that only two men were known to be in the car, nonetheless, carefully approached the Sentra to ensure that no other shooters remained hidden. EMTs from the Salem Fire department, on the scene from the beginning, sprinted to the fallen girl once given the all-clear from the SWAT team.

Within seconds, the EMT team radioed for a Med-Evac helicopter.

The lead EMT, Samantha Croft, and her team made a quick evaluation of Emma. Over the surrounding noise, she screamed her report in the radio microphone to the incoming Med Evac helicopter, "We've got a young woman, semiconscious, in deep shock, responding to only deep stimuli. Pulse one-forty, thready, BP seventy over forty. Respirations thirty, labored and shallow, oxygen saturation initially eighty-nine, up to ninety-two with eight liters of O-two by mask. Severe dehydration with sunken eyes and no skin turgor. She's got a three inch ragged laceration on back of her head with large hematoma, oozing blood. Fresh skin loss on thighs and calves, oozing, probably from being dragged out of the car. Innumerable punctate cigarette type burns over her breasts and chest, front and back. Abdomen distended. Blood stains, old and fresh, in the perineum. Can't evaluate further here in field. We've found a vein in left arm and have RL running wide open. Needs transfer to OHSU stat."

Emma remained semi-conscious despite oxygen and elevating her blood pressure ten points with IV fluids by the time the Oregon State Med-Evac helicopter arrived seven minutes later. The flight, north, to the University of Oregon Health Sciences Level I trauma center in Portland lasted twenty-five minutes.

OHSU had a complete surgical and medical team waiting for her arrival. The Med Evac EMTs had called ahead and by the time the copter landed General Surgery, Neurosurgery, Gynecology and Urology were in the ER to evaluate rectal, head, vaginal, and urethral trauma.

At OHSU, Emma's pressure was up to ninety with a heart rate of ninety-five. She remained semi-conscious responding only to deep stimuli. A quick exam by the neurosurgical chief resident did not reveal any specific findings other than her semi-conscious state, which, according to the EMT reports, had not changed. Emma was sedated by the surgical team and then intubated to control her breathing. Another large IV line was inserted in her neck veins. The perineal bleeding came from the vagina and rectum. The gynecologist, Dr. MaryJo Gaspar, found multiple significant, but non-penetrating, lacerations within the vagina along with copious amounts of semen. The urologist, finding no injury to the urethra, easily catheterized her bladder to monitor urine output. Finding very little urine confirmed her state of shock. Telescopic examination of the anus and rectum showed two lacerations of the anus with bruising of the lower rectum but no apparent perforations. The surgeons ordered intravenous, broad-spectrum antibiotics to cover vaginal and rectal injuries and STDs.

Emma's blood work revealed anemia consistent with the loss of at least two units of blood. As her blood pressure, pulse and peripheral perfusion improved, the ER team determined that she would need no blood replacement. Her kidney function improved dramatically as the IV hydration kicked in and Emma started to make urine. Now apparently stable enough, the surgical team moved her to the ER X-ray department for CT scans of head and abdomen. The scans showed no free air within the abdomen confirming the telescopic findings that the rectum and vagina had not been perforated.

The good news was soundly trumped by the head CT scan which showed a large, left subdural hematoma, a threatening collection of clotted blood pressing on her left brain, likely from blunt head trauma.

After another quick evaluation, the neurosurgical chief resident started barking orders to the ER staff. Emma was started on intravenous mannitol, a concentrated sugar-type solution to reduce brain swelling.

The neurosurgical resident called the OR to secure a room for a cranial exploration and then he called the Chairman of Neurosurgery, Dr. Steve Walle, to give a report. The resident had noted that Emma's pupils, previously normal, were now slightly dilated and barely reactive to light, an ominous sign, suggesting increasing pressure within the brain cavity from the expanding subdural hematoma. Emma's life was in danger.

Dr. Walle took command of Emma's head injury as soon as the gurney wheeled into the operating room.

Asleep and positioned, Emma's entire head was shaved. Dr. Walle made an large incision over the left side of her skull. Guided by the CT scan, Walle removed a four-inch oval of Emma's left skull over the apparent blood clot. The dura mater, the normally pearly white covering layer over the brain, was dark and bulging as the clotted blood pushed hard against it. Opening the dura revealed a large formed blood clot, which was carefully extracted, relieving the pressure on Emma's brain. Bleeding points were then cauterized. Comfortable that the bleeding had been controlled, Walle placed a small suction drain over the brain to ensure that blood did not re-accumulate post-operatively and closed the dura. He then replaced the oval flap of left skull, and closed the scalp incision. Walle next explored, cleaned, and sutured the head laceration on the back of Emma's head.

An intra-cranial pressure monitor, or ICP monitor, was then inserted through a separate drill hole through the right side of Emma's skull and dura to observe the pressures within the brain in the post-operative period.

Dr. Walle commented to the OR nurses and residents, "This young lady is lucky to have been found when she was. Doubtful she would have survived another two to three hours untreated. Probably less."

Once in the ICU, Emma had a nurse placed at the bedside to watch her neurological signs.

Notified fifteen minutes after Emma's rescue, Joe and Clara Braza, accompanied by the Washington State Highway Patrol, drove to the Oregon border. The Oregon State Highway Patrol escorted the Brazas to Portland and OHSU.

Dr. Walle gave Joe and Clara a complete report of the neurosurgical condition and procedures just performed. He deferred the rest of the injuries to the other specialties. When informed by Dr. Gaspar, the gynecologist, of Emma's vaginal and rectal injuries, Clara vomited, and then fainted.

By morning, her anesthetic had worn off and Emma fought her endotracheal breathing tube. She passed a trial of breathing on her own. The anesthesiologist removed the breathing tube.

An hour later, Emma opened her eyes staring blankly at the ceiling, moving her head slightly side to side and kept softly repeating "Please, no more, please no more, please no more." She would then fall back to sleep, awaking intermittently to continue her pleading of "Please, no more."

Medically Emma continued to improve. However,

she remained uncommunicative making her mental status difficult to assess. Her intracranial pressures stayed normal by postoperative day three and Dr. Walle removed the pressure monitor and drain.

Sophie, after talking with Clara Braza, had flown from Newark into Portland two days after Emma's rescue.

Emma remained at OHSU for six days until Dr. Walle agreed that she was medically fit for travel. A private med-evac helicopter transferred Emma to Walla Walla General Hospital to finish her recovery.

Psychological and sexual trauma specialists were culled from the region. The Rape, Abuse, Incest National Network or RAINN provided names of people in the northwest who could assist in Emma's recovery. Emma remained largely incoherent for two more days after the transfer to Walla Walla.

When semi-awake, Emma would alternate between repeating, "Please, no more," "Help me," and "Mom." On the eighth evening post rescue, Emma slept quietly in her room. The Brazas had gone home to get some sleep, while Sophie read on a second bed brought into the room. Sophie noted Emma fidgeting with her IVs.

Sophie got out of bed and approached her friend, expecting no lucid response.

"Emma, Hi, it's me Sophie."

Emma looked into Sophie's eyes, "Sophie," Emma said clearly, "you're here. I am so scared. Where's my mom." Clara and Joe raced back to the hospital after Sophie had called to say that Emma was awake.

Chapter 11

Newspapers, blogs, Facebook, news channels covered Emma's kidnapping, assault and rescue from A to Z. Grisly details appeared in every format, obtained from the police, EMTs, nurses, IV techs, helicopter pilots, and drivers observing the shootout from the roadblock. Friends from Emma's high school and sorority were interviewed.

Rape victims pleading to have their stories told again, and with no knowledge of Emma's plight, added to the media circus.

Without any other major national or international news for two weeks, Emma's story sold copy and attracted viewers. Police footage and private cell phone cameras documented the gunfight between the SWAT team and Tom and Manny.

Emma Braza was famous, and her plight infamous. In any event, most Americans knew the name of Emma Braza.

Chapter 12

Emma's superficial bruises transformed from deep blues and purples to yellows and browns, then faded away.

The multitude of burn marks on Emma's chest and breasts healed to pinpoint scars that would remain the rest of her life, like mythical constellations of warriors and doomed gods.

Emma's hair grew back covering the deep purple scalp laceration and craniotomy incision.

Emma would talk only in short sentences and then have long quiet times, as if she resided somewhere else. Her mom or dad alternated spending evenings and nights in the hospital with her except for times when Sophie would drive in from Seattle to relieve Joe and Clara.

Even though Emma said little to nothing, she became unsettled when left alone or in the dark. Emma also let it be known that she could not be alone in the room with any male other than her father. The male nurses knew to stay away. Her brother, Alan, came infrequently and his presence always unsettled Emma. He stopped coming altogether.

The Walla Walla doctors discharged Emma seventeen days after the transfer from OHSU. During her hospital stay and for the first few weeks at home, Clara prevented any well-wishers from visiting other than Sophie.

By month four, trauma and sexual abuse experts in Seattle and Spokane had seen and evaluated Emma. All concurred that she had a severe case of Post Traumatic Stress Disorder or PTSD. Most felt that she would likely require prolonged and intensive psychotherapy for months or years or, possibly, forever, along with trials of various drugs. The family even had discussions with the psychiatrists from Madigan Army Hospital at Ft. Lewis, in nearby Tacoma, who had special interest in PTSD found in returning veterans of the Middle Eastern and Asian wars. The Army doctors had nothing more to add.

The most helpful consultation came from Dr. Sarah Cohen-Finer, a psychiatrist at the University of Washington. Clara, Joe and Emma sat in her office after Emma had been examined. Dr. Cohen-Finer addressed her comments to Emma.

"Emma," Dr. Cohen-Finer said, "I believe you to be extremely intelligent, so I'm going to tell you, flat out, my feelings. I'll hold nothing back. You have Post Traumatic Stress Disorder. I would say a fairly severe case at this point. As you must know already, PTSD, as we like to call it, is a potentially debilitating anxiety disorder initiated by exposure to a traumatic experience such as physical or sexual assault. You've had both. PTSD patients are often plagued with clusters of symptoms.

"First is the sense of reliving or re-experiencing the original event in flashbacks or nightmares. These can be brought on by the slightest of incidences or triggers."

"I see them every day," Emma said, nodding yes. "Will they ever go away?"

"Maybe. Usually they get better. But not always. But let me finish talking about PTSD and then I can answer all your questions."

Emma, Joe and Clara nodded assent.

"Next are the clusters of symptoms such as increased arousal, sleeplessness, anger and hypervigilance, brought on by trying to avoid events that might bring on triggers."

"I'm not angry. I am just so scared all the time."

"Yes, I know Emma. And we're going to work on that. What you are seeing is the distress and functional impairment caused by both your memory of what happened and the attempt to avoid things that remind you. Does that make sense?"

"Yes," Emma said, "I understand."

Dr. Cohen-Finer continued, "Your doctors and therapists in Walla Walla have been doing a good job trying both psychological therapy and drugs. The combination of these treatments is usually more effective than either alone, but not always, and not in you. I see that trials of sertraline, amitriptyline, and carbamazepine to help with panic attacks and nightmares had little effect and all medications were stopped. I don't see that adding any more drugs makes sense at this point."

"Will Emma ever get better?" asked Clara.

Dr. Finer-Cohen responded, flatly and without conviction, "Yes, she should. She will need to continue to see her psychologist, Dr. Krehmen, in Walla Walla twice a week. I know Marilyn and will keep in touch with her. We will make follow up appointments to see me when needed."

On no one's specific advice, other than Clara's innate judgment, the Brazas moved a twin bed into Emma's room, and Clara would sleep with her daughter almost every night for the next four months. Darkness triggered anxiety attacks, so Emma's bedroom was kept dimly lit at all times. Clara's few nights of reprieve would be when Sophie would come to visit for the weekend.

The Brazas let Sophie have a car to allow her more freedom to visit. Early on, Emma had no desire to leave the confines of her parents' house. If the Brazas went out for the evening and Sophie was not visiting, Emma would wait up with the maid in the den until her parents returned. Clara told the maids, explicitly, not to go to sleep or leave Emma alone until they returned.

Sophie's visits remained Emma's few bright spots. Sophie lifted her spirits with half-empty promises of a return to normalcy. Sophie, back at school for her senior year, had left the sorority and moved into an apartment with some other friends.

At every visit, Sophie made the same pledge. "Emma, you will return to the UW and finish. I will move back into the sorority with you, I promise. You've just got to come back and graduate."

Sophie understood that Emma would not be able to be alone in an apartment and the sorority gave her the best chance of security, physically and psychologically.

Nighttime represented the biggest hurdle for Emma. For the first five months, about every third night, she would awaken with deep and fearful nightmares. Clara, or Sophie, would get into bed with Emma and hold her tight until sleep refound its way. Rarely, when Emma could not be calmed, Clara would give her a sedative and then held her tight for thirty minutes until the drugs allowed Emma to find sleep.

In three months, all physical signs of Emma's ordeal had resolved other than shorter hair. Emma started taking long walks with Clara or Joe about the winery. The workers would nod hello. Emma, on seeing a group of men, many she had known her whole life, would alter directions, as would the men, to avoid even eye contact.

By month six, Emma started making progress. Serious nightmares would occur only once every two or three weeks. She would walk the grounds during the day on her own, started engaging the workers, even men, in conversation, and reassumed some of the jobs around the winery that gave her comfort.

Emma had not lost any of her love for the winery, and had not lost her senses of taste and smell. The hard physical work around the winery became the best therapy Emma could receive. The entire staff of the winery did everything in their power to help Emma's recovery.

Emma, with her mom, saw Dr. Cohen-Finer in June to ask if coming back to school made sense.

"Emma, you have done so well. I am very proud of you." Turning to Clara, she said, "Emma should come back to finish her education. The return will be difficult and may not work, but your daughter's best chance of regaining some semblance of a normal existence rests on handling her fears."

Clara said, "My husband is dead set against her leaving home."

"I really want to try to come back," Emma said.

"Emma, your dad may be right, but we won't know until we try. Emma, you need to do this. I will be available to help you on a regular basis. I do suggest that moving back into the sheltered environment of the sorority makes sense. If you can get your friend, Sophie, I think that's her name, to move back in with you, the chances of success would rise immeasurably."

Arriving home, Clara and Emma discussed Dr. Finer-Cohen's suggestions with Joe.

"No. No. Emma's not ready," Joe said emphatically. "She needs to be here. She doesn't need college and she certainly doesn't need to be so far away. I don't want her to go."

"Dad," Emma pleaded, "I need to try this. If Sophie will move back into the sorority with me, I want to try. Please. If it doesn't work, I'll come home."

When Sophie agreed to move back to the sorority house to live with Emma, and with Sophie's solemn promise to Joe to get Emma through the year, Joe relented.

The following September, Clara drove Emma to Seattle to restart school. Sophie and Francine Frost posted themselves at the front of the sorority awaiting Emma's arrival. Francine could not stop crying, which didn't help settle nerves.

Emma and her mom went to the UW Medical School the next day to see Dr. Cohen-Finer. Dr. Cohen-Finer scheduled a weekly, two p.m., Tuesday afternoon session. Emma and Clara felt better after the visit, hoping that another pillar of support might be in place. The only minor glitch recognized by Dr. Cohen-Finer was that her backups were both male psychiatrists. Dr Cohen-Finer gave Emma the name of a local woman clinical psychologist, Bev Green, who was in private practice off campus, but usually available. Emma, Clara and Dr. Cohen-Finer agreed that seeing Ms. Green, a time or two, in the next few weeks would give Emma comfort that she would always have help, if needed.

After the meeting with Dr. Cohen-Finer, Emma and Clara had lunch in the UW Med School cafeteria. On the bulletin board at the entrance to the cafeteria Clara saw a flyer announcing a class posting entitled, *Medicinal Value of Wine Over the Ages,* to be given by Visiting

Professor Agnello Agotini from the Department of Medicine, Milan, Italy.

"Emma, look at this. I think you'd really like this class," said Clara.

Emma looked over the flyer. "You're right, it does sound like fun. I don't know that I'd get credit for it, but I can check with the Business Department tomorrow."

Emma took one of the tabs off the bottom of the flyer that listed a website locale to enroll. The class convened every Monday, Wednesday and Friday from three thirty p.m. to five p.m.

When Emma went to see her class advisor, Professor John Miller in the School of Business, Clara came and sat outside knowing that Emma still had issues about being in a room alone with men, even ones that she knew.

Professor Miller adored Emma. She had been one of his star students and never disappointed him.

"Emma, it's so nice to see you again and looking so good. I am so sorry for your incident and hopefully you'll be able to put it behind you."

Emma merely nodded and said nothing.

After waiting a moment, Professor Miller started up again, business only. "Emma here's a list of the requirements for the School of Business to graduate and here's another printout of the classes you've already taken. I don't think you'll have any trouble finishing by the end of spring quarter, even if we go slow this quarter until you get your feet on the ground."

Emma looked at the lists, and, again, merely nodded.

"You still have four hours of Fine Art requirements to get your Degree," Miller said. "There are a multitude of classes that will fill this requirement. It shouldn't be a problem."

Emma finally responded, "I found this flyer for a class held in the Med School yesterday."

She showed Dr. Miller the printout from the website describing the class.

"Any chance I could take this class and count it toward my Fine Art hours?"

Dr. Miller, trying to be as accommodating as possible, "I'll make some calls and find out more about the course and then email you, maybe tonight or tomorrow morning. In any event, I think you need to keep your workload light this quarter. No more than 10 hours, I'd guess. You have to take a minimum of eight hours to stay in school. But you'll have plenty of time Winter and Spring quarters to finish."

Emma, smiling for the first time, said, "Thanks, Dr. Miller. You've always been so nice to me."

Dr. Miller grinned back, "Emma, I will say this now and say it again every time we meet. You are an extraordinary young woman, and one of the best students I've ever counseled. I will help you any way I can."

The next morning Emma received an email from Dr. Miller saying that the class had been approved by the Department of Business and they would give her 4 hours of credit. Emma immediately returned to the class's website and tried to enroll. There were no boxes to check for undergraduate students. She emailed the Department of Medicine to let them know that she was an undergraduate, but with specific interests in wine, and would like to take Agotini's class for credit, and that the School of Business had approved her request.

An email came back that late afternoon from the Department of Medicine saying "Sorry, no undergraduate students allowed and no credit can be given, only students in the Health Sciences." No name was given on the email.

It was getting dark outside and Sophie wasn't around, so Emma put off going to the Med School until the next morning.

Emma called the Med School at eight a.m. and asked for Dr. Agotini's office. He was not on any phone roster. Emma, looking at the flyer, then asked for the Department of Medicine. The secretary said that Dr. Agotini had been there only two weeks and didn't have a phone number or secretary, yet. Emma asked for his office room number.

Thirty minutes later Emma knocked on the door of Health Science West, Room 434.

"Comma in, thanka you," a man said in a heavy Italian accent.

Emma opened the door, smiled and said, "Buon Giorno. Professore Agotini?"

"Si."

"Io sono Emma Braza. Ho un piccolo problema."

Agotini enrolled Emma in his class, for credit, fifteen minutes later.

Emma signed up for two more classes, Accounting Principles 202c and Business Management 214b which were 4 and 3 hours each giving her a total of 11 hours of classes for the first quarter. Dr. Miller happily signed off on her schedule.

Chapter 13

Emma became involved in that year's sorority rush as much as she could. Emma remained quiet and subdued, but clearly knew the routines, and she needed routines to feel comfortable. The sisters, who had known Emma from prior years, tried to engage her whenever they could. At this point, Emma didn't let many people in.

Even with Sophie, she often acted detached.

"Emma. You okay?"

"Sure, Sophie, why?"

"You seem to be in another world sometimes."

"Yeah, sorry."

Sophie thought. *What would I have done had I been there? Killing Tom Carter would have been so easy.*

Emma had more difficulty with the usual and expected sorority social exchanges after selection of the new pledges. A good number of the frat boys knew Emma from prior years, but other than the perfunctory greetings, she had no desire to talk to any of them.

Emma confided to Sophie, "I know I may be overreacting but I don't want to continuously hear about how sorry they were. It's even worse when someone asks me to tell them about it. I freak."

"Everyone cares," Sophie said, repeatedly, "and they were trying to be nice. They just don't get it."

"I know. But those types of questions just represent vicarious thrill seeking, nothing less."

"I don't think so. I think they do care. They just

don't know what to say,." Sophie said.

"Then, they're just insensitive."

"You're frustrating me," Sophie pleaded. "You know you used to like to dance, not that you were any good at it. Actually you're a crappy dancer. But why won't you dance with some of these guys that know you. You used to be the last one off the floor in the old days. Now you seem to leave whenever the music starts."

"I can't Sophie. The thought of any guy touching me is…."

The sentence remained unfinished.

Classes started and Emma seemed to get into an acceptable routine. She never missed her meetings with Dr. Cohen-Finer and the occasional visit to Ms. Green, the backup psychologist. Emma, with her doctor's help, wanted to get better, to change, to be more accepting, to be more trustful around men.

As Emma put it to Dr. Cohen-Finer one afternoon, "I'd like a normal life, neat, with just a touch of chaos, but no fear."

Dr. Cohen-Finer smiled at the comment. "Your recovery will come at its own time but I can't say when. I admit that you will never forget your ordeal and that certain events or situations are likely to cause flashbacks. Your nightmares will become less frequent, but may, possibly, never go away completely."

Dr. Cohen-Finer let her comments set for a moment, then continued.

"PTSD is different for each individual. I feel, in time, you will need to learn to deal with men. Avoidance merely perpetuates the problem. At some point, trust will need to creep back into your life."

Emma nodding her understanding, but little

changed.

Sophie couldn't help notice Emma's restlessness attempting to sleep. A small lamp was always left on and Sophie, being as tolerant as she could be, said nothing.

Every night, as Sophie went to bed, whether Emma was up or not, she'd say, "I'll be there for you, Emma. Wake me if you need to talk."

Emma denied nightmares to Sophie but Sophie knew Emma lied. She did confide in Drs. Cohen-Finer and Green.

Emma had no difficulty managing her accounting and business classes. Though she had forgotten some of the basics of her first three years, the facts and figures came back quickly enough that Emma had little to no stress. With ample free time, she often read alone in her room. Anything she read that contained sex, she bypassed.

Dr. Agotini's class became her one true enjoyment. Only thirteen students enrolled in the class and once Dr. Agotini realized that Emma had a complete knowledge of wine, the relationship flourished. On occasion, Dr. Agotini's lack of command of the English language would arise and he'd ask Emma to translate. A couple of the male grad students tried to start conversations with Emma but she dismissed their advances quickly.

In June, in Washington State, with daylight savings in place, the sun sets around ten p.m. and rises around 4 a.m. But by late October, daylight is at a premium and daylight savings stops on a Sunday in late October.

That October Sunday, the day that daylight savings changed, found Emma swamped with work. She had papers due on Monday morning for both business classes. She remained up much of Sunday night writing and editing until early on Monday afternoon. The business professors cancelled classes, wanting only to receive the papers by 4:00 p.m. Emma joined a few sorority sisters to walk to campus that afternoon. She would turn in her papers and then head to the medical school for Agotini's class. She had forgotten, as she often did, to charge her cell phone but expected no calls. She kept the dead phone in her backpack anyway.

After the two-day writing marathon, Emma looked forward to relaxing, taking a few notes, and enjoying Agotini's always-animated lectures.

Near the end of Agotini's lecture, Emma looked out the window of the small second floor lecture hall and quickly looked back again. She thought to herself, *"It's very dark outside. Too dark. What time is it?"* She leaned over to the grad student to her right and quietly asked, "Excuse me, what time is it?"

"Four forty-five"

"Why is it so dark?" Emma asked.

The student, now a bit annoyed, whispered, "Daylight savings ended yesterday," and turned back to the lecture.

A tiny seed of doubt crept into Emma's mind. She had reset her watch that morning but had forgotten the lost hour of daylight. The darkness drew the first bead of sweat on her brow. Her aloneness drew the second. Both triggers that might call back terrors that she couldn't handle. Dr. Agotini was only two-thirds through his outline. The muscles around her right eye and cheek started twitching...

Chapter 14

Being dumped so unceremoniously by Sally Feldman put Dr. David Milton in the foulest of moods. A glib text message, thirty-six hours old, said only, “It’s over. Don’t need to call.” The unbelieving David reread the message ten times over the next day.

Somehow he'd have to explain to his parents that all their plans, and his, had been derailed. He had now been around the medical center for two straight days, and in the ER for twelve hours. After signing out with the next shift, David, a third year surgical resident, wallowed in self-pity in the Emergency Room Doctor's lounge, too tired, too depressed, and too angry to get up and walk home. *My life is shit.*

The ER head nurse, Delores Bryant, entered the lounge and saw the morose resident, and friend, motionless, like an inert blob of unhardened Play-Doh. David had already confided in her about the cryptic text dump.

"You are done now,” Bryant said. “Get your butt off the seat and get home. You look like a total pile of dog poop, I might add."

"Okay, okay,” David said, “I'll move. My life is so in the toilet right now. My glass is half empty, and the stuff remaining is poison."

"You'll be fine. Get some rest, take a shower, shave and change clothes, and we'll see you in thirty-six hours. Now git, you big sloth!"

David stood slowly and opened his locker in the lounge. Without bothering to change out of his surgical scrubs, he grabbed his backpack filled with clean clothes he hadn't had time to use, threw on his faded, weather beaten parka and ratty ski cap. He headed for the door and Pacific Avenue. Only a wisp of light remained in the sky. The early night air was refreshingly cool and wet but did nothing to change his foul mood and the mist fogged his glasses. He would head north through campus to the HUB, as the Husky Union Building was called, and grab a sandwich to take to his apartment.

At the stoplight heading across Pacific, a small group of people stood with him waiting for the light. He couldn't help staring at the pretty coed with a half-open backpack punching and re-punching the stoplight button on the post.

"Like that's going to help", he mumbled, to no one in particular. However, the unknown coed was pretty enough to keep his attention. The girl looked at him, her eyes widened and then she turned away. Curiously, though gloved and dressed warmly, her teeth chattered, her hands shook and she seemed to have some kind of nervous twitch around her right eye.

The light turned and the group started across Pacific, led by the attractive, fast-walking button pusher. Across the avenue, everyone turned right to the bus stop except the girl, who headed north into campus. David followed the same path on the way to the HUB. He loved walking at a brisk rate and with his ano-reflexive, competitive, Type A, surgical personality, he kept pace with the girl, staying twenty or so yards behind.

After a bit she looked back. He smiled. She appeared frightened, turned, and started to run. Within a few steps, a book and some papers fell out of her backpack. She swung around, pulled the pack off, and bent to grab the fallen objects. Approaching to help her, she looked at David and yelled something unintelligible. David continued to walk toward the girl to help.

Abruptly, the girl stood and ran northward toward the center of campus, abandoning her backpack and the fallen objects. David, confused, stopped to pick up the book, papers and pack and followed her. She ran without stopping or looking back and entered Anderson Hall. The building, under renovation, was surrounded by yellow caution tape and scaffolding. She didn't belong there and he couldn't tell why she had reacted so crazily. He also had her backpack, as well as his own.

David entered the building and found it dark, damp, cold and eerily quiet. The electricity and heat had been turned off. He took out his iPhone and opened the flashlight app. *This was not a place to be.* Debris and construction detritus was strewn everywhere. Even with the flashlight, little could be seen. Dust hung in the air like swarming black flies.

The girl had to be near - no place else to go. He stopped, put down both backpacks and listened. He could hear faint noises coming from a door twenty feet ahead. He approached, stepping carefully. The weak light illuminated hazy footprints in the dust. The ancient door had a "GENTLEMEN" sign on the front. He listened closely and heard muffled sobbing. The door had been bolted.

Not knowing how thick the door might be, David stood back a few feet and announced loudly, almost yelling, to the old door, as if challenging it to open, "I know you are in there. I am not going to hurt you. I did not mean to scare you."

David listened but heard nothing.

"I know you're there. I am not going to hurt you."

David paused again to listen.

A soft voice came through the door, "Please, go away."

"I have your backpack and..."

"Leave them and go," she interrupted.

"Listen, I am sorry if I scared you," David said. "You can't spend the night in a building that has no electricity or heat. It's not safe or healthy. I am a surgical resident at the med center and was walking home. I did not mean to scare you."

"Are you smoking? I don't want to be burned."

David, at first confused, responded angrily, "What? No, I'm not smoking. Why would you even ask?"

She's got to be completely insane.

But David knew that getting angry would be of little help. "I am not going to leave until you come out. Isn't there anyone you can call? You must have a cell phone?"

"My cell is dead," said the girl.

David thought. The door was at least an inch above the floor. "I am going to gently slide my cell phone under the door. Call whomever you like."

David turned on his phone and sank down to his knees, realizing only then that the floor was filthy. He put the phone onto a bed of dust. The phone slid easily, like a shuffleboard disk, under the door. David listening through the door heard the plaintive girl's conversation.

"Soph, it's me Emma. Where are you? I'm stuck in a building on campus across from the med school. I need you to come pick me up, now. Please call me back at, oh shit, my phone was dead so I borrowed a phone... at whatever number shows up on the screen. Please call."

David now at least knew the girl's name, Emma, but would not use it.

Emma, now sobbing, yelled at the door. "My friend didn't answer. I left a message. Please go away. Please."

"I heard." David hesitated. "Listen, I'm not comfortable leaving with you here. I have an idea, call 206-543-2000, that's campus police, and ask for Sgt. Gomez or better yet slide the phone back and I'll call him."

The phone was kicked back under the door. David made a hockey goalie save with his foot or the phone would have slid under a pile of cut up wood, sawdust, and two by fours.

"Sgt. Gomez, please, tell him it's Dr. Milton from UW Med." Seconds later, "Rafe, it's me David."

David told Gomez the events of past ten minutes and asked if Gomez could please come to the east side of the Anderson Hall. Gomez said he'd be there in fifteen minutes.

Talking to the door again, "The campus police officer said he'll be here in fifteen minutes. Knowing him, it won't be more. Are you okay with that?" David heard no answer, just muffled sobbing.

David continued talking to the locked door, "Again, I am sorry that I scared you. I am going to slide my phone back under the door. Keep it for a bit. You might try your friend again. When you send it back, tell me it's coming and don't kick it."

David slid down against the wall outside the bathroom and put his head against the wall. A swirl of dust flew up and forced David to close his eyes and pull the collar of his parka over his mouth like a surgical mask. Two days of no rest was catching up with him and he fought sleep. The girl left two more voice mails, each one more frantic, to Sophie from Emma.

The crying inside the men's room continued intermittently.

Raphael Gomez, sergeant on the UW police, showed up on time. His powerful flashlight, scanning the hallway, blinded the sitting David when the light found him. "Hey Doc, what the hell is going on?" David got to his feet.

"I dunno, Rafe, but I do know her name is Emma. She tried to call a friend and I overheard the conversation. Friend never picked up."

Gomez turned to the door. "Emma, this is Sgt. Gomez of the UW police. You are safe now. Can you open the door?"

"How did you know my name? How do I know who you really are?"

"My friend here heard you leaving a message and you used your name. Look out the bathroom window to the east if you can, you can see the flashing lights on the patrol car."

"Okay, I see them. I will come out but make that man go away and then I'll come out."

David shook his head. "Rafe, that plaid backpack by the entrance is hers. I am going to walk to the HUB, pick up a sandwich, and then back to my place. Call me when sanity resumes." David thought for a second. "Actually sanity is unlikely to resume, so call me anyway."

David grabbed his own pack and walked out of the building heading, as he had intended from the start, north to the HUB and then to his apartment.

Chapter 15

Emma unbolted the door and came out slowly. Even with the indirect light from Gomez's flashlight, he could see that she had been crying. Her gait was unsteady.

Gomez held out his arm saying, "Hello Emma, I'm Sgt. Rafael Gomez of the UW Police. Hold onto my arm and we'll walk out slowly and I'll drive you home."

She tentatively held his arm and Rafe escorted her to his patrol car. She continued to sob silently. He helped her into the back seat behind a wire grill and Gomez sat in front and picked up a clipboard.

"Emma, I need your full name."

"Emma Braza."

Gomez appeared startled at her name and hesitated for a moment. "Emma, what is your address and phone number?"

"4711 18th Ave NE. The Gamma Gamma sorority. 503-746-8207."

Gomez wrote the information down on the top of a police report form, but asked no more questions and wrote nothing else on the form. He started the patrol car and proceeded, slowly, through the campus toward the north exit.

Gomez kept looking at Emma in the rear view mirror but said nothing for the first minute. Finally, he spoke in a soft and gentle voice. Gentler than she would have expected for a policeman.

"Emma, I am just going to take you home, nothing more. I have enough information from Dr. Milton to fill out the report. As an aside, Dr. Milton is a very nice man. He would have never hurt you and he's sorry that he might have scared you. Also, I know who you are and what happened last year. I am sorry for your trouble."

"Thank you. Can I make a call?"

"Sure. Do you need a phone?"

"I have that man's phone. I'll just use it."

Emma dialed the phone and spoke haltingly between soft sobs, "Sophie, it's me... No, I'm okay now. I am in a UW police car and he's bringing me back to the house. We just crossed the 45th Street booth so we'll be there in a minute."

Emma listened to her friend and then held the phone to her chest.

"Do you think you can drop me off at the corner of 47th and 18th rather than take me to the front door? The police car will create a ton of questions which I don't want or need to answer."

"I don't mind as long as there's someone to hand you off to. Can your friend meet us at the corner?"

"Soph, can you come to the corner of 47th and 18th and meet us. He won't let me out alone.... Thanks."

Emma pressed the 'off' button and leaned toward the front of the patrol car, "She'll be there."

Moments later Gomez parked his cruiser at 47th and 18th and waited 30 seconds until a young woman in a black pea coat arrived.

"I have to open the door for you," Gomez explained to Emma, "because it won't open from the inside." He then exited the patrol car and stood in front the back door, but did not open it. He turned to meet the girl's escort first.

The girl spoke first, "Officer, I am Sophia Picone, Emma's roommate. I'd like to get her inside as quickly as possible."

"I'm Sgt. Gomez. I happen to be from Walla Walla, so I know a little about your friend."

"Well, she's fragile and this episode didn't help. Still getting therapy."

"I completely understand. I'll likely call you later to get some more information."

Gomez wrote Sophie's name and number and had her sign the release at the bottom of the form. He opened the door and Emma exited. He watched the girls hug and heard Emma's muffled sobbing and saw the tearing in her friend's eyes. Sophia kept murmuring to her friend, "Everything is going to be all right."

Not letting go of Emma, Sophia turned her head to the officer, "Can we go?"

"Sure. We're done here," Gomez said. "Emma, good luck. Here's my card if I can be of any assistance."

Emma and Sophie said, "Thanks", in unison.

Sgt. Gomez returned to his car and drove away.

Sophia gently grabbed her friend by the shoulders and pushed her to arm's length. "What the hell happened?"

"This man was following me. It was dark. I was alone. I was so scared."

"Let's finish the story later. Dinner is in fifteen minutes. Time to get you in a hot shower. Looks like you've sweat enough for a marathon."

The two walked a few steps and Emma stopped.

"Sophie, I wasn't ready to come back to school. I think I need to go home."

Sophie wheeled around to face Emma and grabbed her again by the shoulders, but not gently this time, forcing her beleaguered friend against a retaining wall at the sidewalk's edge.

"Ouch. That hurts," Emma cried.

"God damn it, Emma," Sophie said, "I don't care if it hurts. You are not bailing on me. Your doctors told you this might not be easy, there'd be ups and downs, but you'd have to fight. I don't see the fight in you. I'm fighting for you every day and in every way I can. I need to see you fight too. I promised your parents I'd get you through to graduation and I am not going to fail. *We* are not going to fail. Do you understand me?"

Emma nodded softly. "I'll try or I'll try to try."

"Not good enough. I don't want you to try. I want you to fight, okay?"

"Okay, I'll fight. You can let go of me now."

Now let's get you back to the house. Forget this creep, we'll never see him again."

The two started walking again.

Emma hesitated, "I think we'll probably see him tonight."

"What, why?"

"I've got his cell phone. Forgot to give it back to him or the officer."

"You mean the crazy, lunatic, madman stranger out to kill you, loaned you his phone and you kept it?"

"Well, yeah," Emma said.

"I've heard enough. I will get you showered and warmed up and calmed down. Then I am going to strangle you."

Chapter 16

Halfway home David came to an abrupt stop and swore under his breath. He realized that he had left his cell phone with the crazy one.

David walked straight home without getting a bite to eat, which only made him angrier. The hospital operator only had David's cell phone number, and as second backup for the hospital's surgical services, they needed to be able to reach him. He needed the phone.

He lived in a house on the north side of campus. A three story 1900's mansion on 16th Avenue NE turned into a three-level triplex that his parents owned as a rental property. For some unknown reason, the building was called the Alamo. The Mexican army, Davy Crocket and Jim Bowie were nowhere to be found. Mike and Laurie Milton gave David the middle floor, called Alamo B, until he finished his residency.

Two days of mail had piled up in the box. The upstairs, unit #C, and downstairs, unit #A, were lit up and voices could be heard coming from above and below. Four guys lived in Alamo #A, the basement or the so-called 'garden apartment.' *It's still a basement*, David mused.

Six girls from the UW women's crew team lived above David in Alamo #C. The girls had become friends and had invited David upstairs on two occasions for a meal. Two of the girls, very tall, rowed. The other four girls served as coxswains, two from the women's team and two from the men's team. The four coxswains appeared half the size of their rowing roommates. The Mutt and Jeff dichotomy between the rowers and coxes was not lost on David.

David borrowed a phone from one of the rowers and called the UW police, told the operator who he was, and asked to speak to Sgt. Gomez.

“Gomez is out. Can someone else help you.”

“No, I need to speak to him and him alone. I think he’s got my phone and I’m on call for the ER and hospital.”

“Calm down, doc. I’ll radio him and he’ll call you back on the number you’re calling from.”

Raphael Gomez called the rower’s cell phone ten minutes later.

"David, Rafe here. You know who that girl was? Emma Braza."

"Nope, don't care either. A total whacko as far as I'm concerned. I did nothing to cause her to bolt. The whole thing was surreal. You have my phone?"

Not answering David's question, Rafe continued on his own thread of thought, "Well, do you remember that murder-robbery-kidnapping outside of Walla Walla about a year ago? Three ex-cons robbed and killed a truck stop owner during a holdup. The owner had a sawed off shotgun under the register and blew a hole through one guy's back and then got shot by one of the other bad guys. As they were about to leave, in walks a UW coed. Talk about bad timing. She had the works done to her over the next 24 hours. The Oregon Highway patrol gunned down the kidnappers outside Salem. Was in all the papers and TV for at least a week. You had to be brain dead to have not heard."

"Maybe rings a little bell but remember I was doing a trauma rotation at San Francisco General Hospital last year from July to September. Must not have gotten the same attention down there. So? Anyway, you got my phone?"

“Well, this is the girl that was kidnapped and

screwed up. I called her roommate after getting back to the station. Getting shrink treatment for a year and tried to come back this quarter. Screwiest thing is that I know her family. Well, actually don't know them, but know who they are. I grew up in Walla Walla and played football with this girl's brother. Total asshole, if I remember. The Brazas are big shot wine makers and would have never talked to the likes of me. One of my uncles used to pick grapes for them. Anyway, I'd cut her a little slack. From what I gathered from her roommate, she's still pretty fragile."

"I'm fragile too. I haven't slept in a couple of days and my life is shit right now. You couldn't know that Sally and I just broke up. She left two voice mails, and then a text, dumping me. Screw it. So, where's my cell phone?"

"Shit, David, the girl's got it. I forgot to take it back. I meant to, but she was so upset that asking her anything seemed loco. They only live a block and a half from you on 18th in the Gamma Gamma sorority, middle of the block on the west side. Big white house. Can't miss it. Ask for her roommate Sophie Pecan, or something like that."

"Got it, Rafe. Thanks again for coming over so quickly. I've got to get over to that sorority, pronto. I'm backup for the ER, so I'm in deep shit if they call and I don't answer. The only number they have is my cell. "

"David, watch out. These girls think you are the perp. I told them you're a really nice guy and wouldn't scare anyone. That said, you might wear a cup and helmet," Rafe laughed. "Anyway, good luck, amigo."

David returned the phone to the girl upstairs and walked the block and a half east to 18th and knocked on the door of the Gamma Gamma house. He assumed he'd grab his phone and be gone in a minute or two, get back to his apartment and get some sleep. Bad guess on the doctor's part.

An attractive young girl answered the door and showed David into the foyer.

“Hello. I am David Milton. I need to see Sophie Pecan, or something like that. She has my cell phone.”

Eying David, she did not like the way he looked and he could care less. Girls were milling around talking, getting ready for dinner. They all ignored David. The girl that had let David in got on an intercom and asked Sophie to come down.

She then turned back to David and said, "She'll be down in a minute. Are you the whack job that scared Emma? You ought to be ashamed of yourself." She left for the dining hall before he could formulate a response.

David, speechless, shook his head trying to figure out how many kooks could live in this house.

A few moments later, down the stairs, steps a pretty dark haired girl with a very sour look on her face.

"Are you Dr. Milton?" she asked.

"Yes," David said.

"I'm Sophie Picone, Emma's roommate." An accent from Jersey that you could stop with a tennis racket, but cute.

David started, taking the defensive, "I don't know what you've gotten from your friend, but I did nothing wrong. I was getting off work from the ER at UW Med Center and was walking home. I live on 16th and 50th and the way to my place would be the same as your sorority. Your friend just looked at me and freaked. It was so totally weird. After that I couldn't leave her alone in the building under construction. That's it. I'd like my phone back and I'll get out of your life."

Sophie looking very concerned, countered, "That's not it. I've got a hysterical friend upstairs. Her parents entrusted me with her safety and I'm blowing it."

Sophie hesitated. David could see that she was crying.

Sophie continued, not embarrassed by her emotions, "She thinks it's all her fault and she's ready to pack it in and go home. She's afraid to go back to the med center to take a class that she needs to take to continue to be a student. I don't know what the hell to do."

A moment of silence passed between the two of them. David asked, "So you're really not pissed at me?"

"No, I'm just scared for Emma and trying to keep her sane and in school."

David responded, "Okay, okay. How about I apologize to her, personally, as best I can, and take full responsibility for the whole deal, as long as you know that I didn't do squat to cause this."

Sophie thought for a second.

"Well it's a start. Can you come back after dinner, maybe ninety minutes. Another thing, you look like shit. I would have been scared looking at you. Hair, unshaven, dirty parka. I'd like you to come back cleaned up."

David, stunned at the sorority girl's hubris, decided against commenting, as she wasn't totally wrong either. Delores Bryant had said the same in the ER before he left. "Can I at least have my phone back?" David asked.

"No, I'll wait for you to come back. If I give it to you now, I figure you'll never show."

David was about to explode, but took a deep breath. "I am a surgical resident at the medical school and I'm on call for emergencies. I need the phone now. I will return in ninety minutes, you have my word."

Sophie hesitated for a moment, then reached into her pocket and brought out David's phone and handed it to him. "You better be back", said in a tone that wasn't threatening, but pleading.

Chapter 17

As promised, David returned to the Gamma Gamma house an hour and a half later. He had showered, shaved, eaten and put on a clean shirt and jeans with a sweater tied around his neck. He had time to get on the web and researched Emma Braza. Two million hits told him that Rafe Gomez's description of the events were not exaggerated.

David knocked again at the front door. A different girl answered and the routine repeated itself. This time, at least, he didn't get any lip.

Sophie called down and asked the girl to put David in the small library and kick out anyone else in the room. She escorted David into a paneled room filled with books and comfortable chairs with a few small desks.

A minute later Sophie and Emma walked into the room. David rose quickly and started to approach the girls with his hand out. Sophie stopped him with a quick but subtle hand sign that meant 'stop.' David stopped.

Sophie spoke first. "Emma, this is Dr. David Milton. He's a resident in surgery at the medical center and was the one that followed you after crossing Pacific. He lives around the corner and was merely on his way home."

Emma, eyes mostly down, responded with a simple, "Hello."

Sophie spoke next, "Let's all sit down." Then she spoke words with her eyes pleading for Dr. Milton to say something.

David, picking up the clue, began, "Emma, first of all, let me say, in the sincerest way that I can, that I am sorry for scaring you."

Realizing that there was a kernel of truth in what he was to say, he continued.

"It was totally my fault and I hope that you will forgive me. You couldn't have realized that our paths home were the same. I had been in the hospital for two days and hadn't shaved or cleaned up and was wearing an old parka. I can see why you became frightened. In hindsight, I can clearly see that my actions were intimidating and thoughtless. Once I realized my mistake, I did feel responsible to see that you were taken care of. I wasn't going to leave you in that building, but I am certainly responsible for you being in there. Again, I hope that you can forgive me."

Sophie smiled and thought, *He's doing better than I could have ever imagined. Something to work with.*

No one knew what to say next. Emma, looking down, had not verbally accepted the apology, her hands clenched to whiteness in her lap.

But then, David continued, "I am curious, what were you doing at the med school? I didn't think that any undergrad classes were given there."

Emma relaxed her grip and looked up, but not directly at either Sophie or David. "Oh, I was taking this class on the medicinal uses of wine from a visiting professor of medicine from Milan. Dr. Agotini."

"I don't know him, but he's in a different department," said David. "The class sounds interesting."

As Emma described the class her persona changed. She smiled and started gesturing with her hands. For a moment, she looked at David, then averted her gaze, only to return.

Emma continued, "It's really a cool class and I've enjoyed it, so far. My family's in the wine business. I am going to work at the winery when I'm done with school."

"I hope you'll stay with the class," David said.

"I don't think so," Emma, looking away, quickly responded. "It ends after dark and I don't want to walk back to the north side that late. I can't have people picking me up just because of my fears. That would make it worse."

"This was all a weird mistake," Sophie said. "There's nothing to worry about and you need the class to stay in school. You know the rules. If you're not taking more than eight hours, you'll be dropped. Besides, you need the class to graduate. You don't want to be here any longer than you need to. Please."

Emma shook her head, "I don't think so."

David watched the two of them. Their relationship appeared far deeper than just sorority sisters or roommates.

"Emma, what time does the class end?" David asked.

"Monday, Wednesday and Friday at 5:00 but sometimes he's not done until 5:15. Why?"

"I'm rotating in the emergency room until January 1st. My schedule gets me off at four thirty every weekday and I'm usually ready to leave around five o'clock after some paper work and rounding with the incoming docs. I'd be glad to escort you home."

Another pause.

David continued, "I'll try and look better too."

Sophie was speechless.

Emma thought for a second and said, "No, I can't have you do that."

Sophie was about to plead to Emma when David

continued.

"You don't have a choice here," David said. "I created this situation and if I ended up causing you to drop out, I'd feel terrible. The least you can do is give it a shot, and if it doesn't work out, at least, we tried. It's not out of my way. You have to help me out here. What'ya say?"

"Well, hmmmm", Emma stammered, seemingly paralyzed.

David knew instantly that he couldn't take a chance on Emma making the decision. "Okay it's done. If you don't have a class before 'whateverhisItaliannamewas' on Wednesday then come by the ER thirty minutes early. The ER is on the very east side of the med center. You can have Sophie come with you. Ask for Delores Bryant. She's the head nurse."

David wrote down the information on a piece of paper.

"I'll tell her you're coming and I'll come out to see you, unless I'm dealing with an emergency. There's a nurse and doctor's lounge in the ER and you can have a seat there. If for any reason I am ever late or held up you need only to come to the ER and have Delores or one of the nurses park you in the lounge until I'm ready. My cell phone number is on there too. 206 290 0553. It should be on Sophie's phone already. If she can't reach you on the walk back, she can call me."

Emma hesitated, and then said, "Well. Okay, I'll try."

Sophie's eyes were glassy and she had a bit of a smile. A load had been lifted.

David rose up and said. "Emma, thanks for being so understanding. Anyway, I have to go. I haven't been to sleep for a couple of days. I'll see you Wednesday, okay? Don't stand me up."

David did not attempt to shake either girl's hand. He left the sorority and started his walk back to the apartment when the cell phone rang. The screen showed Sophie Picone.

"Hi, did I forget something?" asked David.

"Forget something, are you kidding, Dr. Milton, you were incredible. I can't thank you enough."

"Fine, but stop with the Dr. Milton, it's David. Got it. Tell Emma too that Dr. Milton's not going to work for me. Just David. Okay?"

"Okay, thanks again. Oh, one thing. Emma's not real touchy feely right now."

"Sophie, duh, I get it."

David ended the call and thought to himself. *What the hell did I get myself into?*

Chapter 18

The next forty-eight hours went quickly. Emma had second, third, fourth and fifth misgivings about the escort-bodyguard plan. For the next two nights, she slept little.

"I am so frightened," Emma admitted to Sophie on Tuesday night.

Sophie, of course, anticipated Emma's reluctance.

"We need a mantra," Sophie suggested, "words that you and I will use to get through this year."

"Like what?"

"Remember that paper that you wrote sophomore year on Eleanor Roosevelt. You finished it with a quote that you thought remarkable. What was it?"

Emma remembered the quote, *"You gain strength, courage, and confidence by every experience in which you really stop to look fear in the face. You must do the thing which you think you cannot do."*

"Great, we're going to say that every time we have doubts."

Sophie then changed her tone to a bit more forceful.

"Your doctors have told you more than once that your fears around men, when alone, needs to be dealt with," Sophie said. "Shit, this opportunity with some guy that's actually a doc is like too good to be true. You've had so much bad luck in the past year, why not take advantage of some good luck when it comes your way. Please try."

"Okay," Emma said, without conviction.

"I'll meet you at the HUB and then walk with you to the med school."

Emma, acquiescing, said, "Okay, okay, okay. I'll meet you at the HUB."

Sophie also made sure that Emma had connected her cell phone to its charger remembering clearly that an uncharged cell phone had played a part in both of Emma's catastrophes.

Emma, as she turned off the room lights, save her desk light, said, "Sophie, I'm scared. I don't think I'm going to sleep very well."

"I know, me neither. But try," Sophie said. "I'll be there for you. Wake me if you need to talk."

The next afternoon the two girls, holding hands, entered the ER at the UW Medical School. They walked immediately to the front desk.

Sophie approached the desk with Emma trailing. "Is Delores Bryant here, she's expecting us. Emma Braza and a friend."

The receptionist, a thin Asian woman with glasses three sizes too big, asked, "What do you want with Nurse Bryant?"

"We need to meet with Nurse Bryant and Dr. Milton," Sophie answered, "and were told to ask the receptionist to find Nurse Bryant first."

"Please have a seat. You might be waiting here a while. I don't know how busy Nurse Bryant is at the moment."

Emma and Sophie sat in plastic chairs near the desk. Emma leaned over to Sophie and whispered, "I have only thirty minutes before Agotini's class starts. Now what if we have to wait and..."

But before she could finish the thought, a middle-aged African American woman stood in front of them.

"Hi, I'm Delores Bryant," the nurse said, directly to Emma. "Welcome to my Emergency Room." Emphasis on the '*my*.' "Let me show you to the lounge. Dr. Milton is just finishing up with a scalp *lac* and will be there shortly."

From the looks on the coeds' faces, Bryant realized that neither knew '*scalp lac*' from a blue Oldsmobile. Emma and Sophie both stood but Bryant grabbed Emma's arm as she walked into the ER after swiping her ID card at the electronic double door.

Another card swipe and into the lounge they went. Two nurses and a female doctor sat talking. A full kitchen with appliances lined one side of the room. Stacks of peanut butter and jelly jars and loaves of bread and graham crackers lined the counter along with a coffee machine, and microwave. Computers filled the opposite wall and a large table with surrounding chairs in disarray occupied the center of the room.

"Carol, Joan, Dr. Billings, this is Emma," Bryant said. "She's a friend of Dr. Milton and may be here on some weekdays waiting for him. Be nice."

The three nodded.

Looking back to Emma, Bryant said," Emma, anything you want to eat, eat. You don't need permission. Take a seat anywhere."

They sat at the large table in the middle of the room.

She then handed Emma a blank ID card with a strap neckband.

"This will open that big door we went through first and will also open the door to this lounge. You're smart enough to realize you shouldn't have this card, so you'll take care of it...right?"

"Yes, thank you," Emma said.

Delores left the girls at the table.

David came in a few minutes later wearing surgical scrubs. He nodded at the other occupants and stepped up to Emma and Sophie. "Hi, glad you two could come early. I know Delores was nice, she always is. Don't want to cross her though. She thinks she owns the place. Been here long enough. Anyway, Emma you should be able to find your way back here after class. Yes, no?"

"Sure, no problem. Mrs. Bryant gave me an ID card to get through the doors."

"Cool. She said she might," David said. "Don't tell anyone. Well, OK, gotta get back to work. See you at five or so. I'll be here."

David exited the lounge door back into the ER.

"This was easy," chirped Sophie. "I'm going back to the house. So I don't worry, call or text me when you're on your way. Okay?"

Emma puffed and noted the comment with, "Yes, mother."

"Let's do a quick Eleanor to keep us focused, just like last night."

Together they repeated the mantra.

Sophie laughed and gave Emma a hug. They both left together. On the way out Sophie ran into Delores Bryant and said to Emma, "You go ahead to your class, I want to thank the nurse."

Sophie and Delores watched Emma walk into the

medical school, then they faced each other.

"Ms. Bryant, just wanted to thank you for being so nice to us."

"It's nothing," Bryant said.

"Curiously, how did you know which one of us was Emma?" asked Sophie.

"I've been doin' this stuff for thirty years. I can spot wounded a mile away. Not sure what her relationship with Dr. Milton is yet. I'll get it out of him. I will tell you that he's a special doctor and a good friend."

Sophie noted the comment and said, "Thanks again." Sophie headed back to the sorority.

Agotini's class went well. After class he asked Emma to stay a minute.

“Emma, how come you leave so fast on Monday? I had some notes I needed translated.”

"Nothing really." Emma didn't lie well, usually, and this lie was no exception. "I realized I had forgotten something important and had to leave. Of course I'll translate the notes for you."

Agotini didn't look convinced, but let her excuse stand. "Bene, a venerdi." He gave her the small pile of papers to translate.

Emma took the papers with a faint smile. “All right. Until Friday.”

Emma walked back to the ER, swiped the entry card at the main door and swiped it again at the lounge. There sat David Milton eating a PB&J sandwich and reading a journal.

"Great, let's go," he said, grabbing his backpack along with a newer parka and knit cap.

Off they went, out to Pacific Avenue, across the light and past Anderson Hall, still being renovated. So far, nothing had been said.

David, smiling, spoke first, assuming that Emma wasn't going to. "I had a dream about you last night...well maybe a nightmare."

Emma wrinkled her brow, clearly uncomfortable with David's opening remark.

"I dreamt that we did this walk three times a week for the next two months and despite my pleading and cajoling, you never said a word, not a single word. We'd just walk for forty-five minutes, you'd get to your house, enter, and never look back."

Emma paused, took in the offhand comment, smiled or smirked, David couldn't tell.

"Oh my God," David said, "there is somebody in there."

"Funny, amazing, I had the same dream," Emma said.

David, now caught off guard, "You mean I never said anything to you either?"

"No, that I never said anything, just as you dreamt."

Silence...and then they both smiled.

"Where you from?" Emma asked.

The forty-minute walk went quickly and the banter remained light. Without mentioning Emma's missing year, each learned where the other came from, education, and siblings. Sophie called Emma on her cell about halfway through the walk. Emma refused the call and texted Sophie back…'OK.'

"So what's your relationship to Sophie? I can tell she's from New York. Is she related in some way?" David asked.

"No, just a really close friend," Emma said "She's from New Jersey. Met her after rush four years ago and have roomed with her ever since. Neither of us have a sister, I mean a real sister, so we just got close. I really don't know what I'd do without her."

"She seems pretty protective of you."

"Mother Hen to the max but she's been there for me in so many ways." And then they were in front of the sorority. "Thanks again for doing this, I know it must be a burden."

David shrugged, "No, no big deal really. I like to walk whenever I can and now I have an excuse. See ya Friday, OK?"

"Yep. Really, thanks again." Emma was up the sorority steps and disappeared into the house. David headed to his apartment.

Sitting at her desk, Sophie waited for Emma to return. "So, how'd it go?"

"Great." Emma dumped her pack on her bed.

"What did you talk about?"

"Nothing much, really. Got a ninety-four on my accounting paper. Only two people higher in three sections. It's been a good day, a really good day."

Sophie knew Emma. The paper meant nothing, but walking back from the class with a relative stranger, who happened to be a male, was huge.

Friday's walk back was just as uneventful.

"What you doing this weekend?" halfway through the walk," David asked.

"Nothing much, a party at the house with a fraternity from Wazzu."

David said nothing expecting Emma to ask what his plans might be.

After a brief interlude of silence, Emma picked up the clue, "And you...I mean what are you doing?"

"Family stuff, our holidays come thick and heavy this time of year."

Emma didn't understand exactly. She knew of no holidays of any import until Thanksgiving. She let it slide.

The weekend came and went. Emma knew some of the Washington State University boys from her high school days, which helped a little. She stayed longer than usual, but left when the music started.

She slept peacefully both nights.

On Monday, light rain began as they left the ER. Emma and David departed the ER fifteen minutes late while David tended a head trauma case that needed to be dealt to the neurosurgeons. David didn't want to leave the ER until the head-crackers arrived. Within a few minutes the rain started to pick up along with a brisk southerly wind that made them feel as if the rain was falling horizontally at their backs. They talked little and kept their heads down. As they neared the HUB, and though both Emma and David wore raingear, David suggested that maybe they should stop for a few minutes to see if the rain might subside a bit.

"Sure, why not. I better text Sophie that we'll be late and have them hold me a dinner."

"You hungry?" David asked as they entered the HUB cafeteria.

"No, I'll wait for dinner," Emma said.

"I'm famished and no one cooks for me. Only so much PB and J one can eat. Do you mind if I get a burger?"

"No, of course not."

David ordered a burger with a fruit side and a large coffee.

"Want something to drink," David asked.

"Maybe a latte, why not." The HUB's baristas were actually pretty good at making lattes. "Single, skinny with extra foam."

David couldn't help notice that Emma was edgy. He could feel the tap tap of her thigh against the table leg and could see the slightly tense look to the muscles in her neck and jaw. Her menu didn't include a stop at the HUB and he surmised that any deviation from the planned walk home would create anxiety.

The HUB was packed with people, most coming in from the downpour. Seattle rains were notoriously variable and the true Seattleite knows that the deluge would lighten. Regardless, most eyed their cell phone apps that showed the weather sonar. The rain would largely pass in 30 minutes.

As David ate, Emma quietly watched, sipping on her latte.

"That burger would go well with a 2007 Merlot from our winery. Don't know why, but at home and Dad's barbequing, we all seem to go for that vintage."

"I never really put burgers with wine much. I'd guess that most would have had a beer. Maybe a 2005 Miller Lite or maybe a 2006 Corona."

Emma didn't respond and pouted a bit, looking down at her latte.

"I'm sorry, didn't mean to have it come out sarcastically," David said. "Just a crappy sense of humor. I know your family is in the wine business. I like wine but really have never met anyone who actually makes it. On the TV ads, it's always some swarthy looking Italian or French guy yapping in front of a zillion acres of grapes. You'll have to get me one of your Merlots for the next time I have a hamburger. I'll test it out."

"Sure."

That evening Emma related David's comments to Sophie.

"I was being serious and he just flipped me off," Emma said.

"Don't you think," Sophie asked, "that you're being a bit over-sensitive here? Matter of fact, if I didn't know you and was sitting in a dumpy university cafeteria eating a dumpy burger with plastic trays and plastic knives and someone dropped an '07 Merlot into the conversation, I'd probably have laughed."

"Well maybe so."

"Not maybe so, SO! You might tell him you were being an erudite, uppity wino bitch."

On Wednesday, Emma started the conversation. "You remember the conversation we had on Monday at the HUB."

"No, not really, remind me."

“I resented your comments about beer and burgers.”

“Oh yeah, I put years on Millers and Coronas. I thought I was being funny.”

“Sorry if I acted upset. I thought you might be making fun of me.”

“Nah, just my sense of humor, David said. “I don’t do well with doctor jokes, so there. You don’t bash docs and I won’t bash winemakers. Come to think of it, I don’t think I’ve ever heard a winemaker joke. Are there some out there?”

Emma deadpanned, “No, not too many. We just tell doctor jokes.”

David started laughing and Emma followed.

"Touché," David said. “That was funny.”

Sophie beamed later that evening as Emma related the conversation.

“He really thought I was funny,” Emma said. “It was cool. I like him.”

Sophie grinned from ear to ear. Sophie also realized that Emma had not been complaining about sleeplessness.

Another week went by and David sensed her fragility lessening with each walk. Emma talked freely and admittedly she started looking forward to these forty-minute mini-hikes. David steered clear of any personal topics for obvious reasons. He didn't know what might trip a switch like the night in Anderson Hall. Her business classes sounded like total bores, so he tried to show some interest in Agotini's lectures, hoping she'd open up. She loved talking about the lectures, but it was also obvious that her knowledge of wine in general far exceeded what she had heard that day. David even started doing a little Googling of wine so he wouldn't sound quite so unknowledgeable.

On the first Wednesday of November, Emma was in a great mood. She looked forward to the walk home. They talked about Agotini's lecture and she related a funny anecdote imitating Agotini's Italian accent perfectly. David started laughing and Emma followed.

As they approached the HUB, on a beautiful November evening, David suggested they stop for a coffee.

"David, how did you decide on being a surgeon?" asked Emma, sitting at a table, sipping on her latte.

"In the middle of my third year of med school at UCSF, I rotated onto surgery. It was the best quarter of my four years. Two of the residents in general surgery were uncommonly nice to me and I loved working with my hands. That was it. I was hooked. I loved UC, but after four years at Cal and four in med school at UCSF, I decided I'd been away from home long enough. So I applied to the UW for general surgery residency."

Emma looked at David closely for the first time. She figured he had to be at least 6 foot 2, sandy hair and blue eyes covered by glasses. His hair was thinning a bit and clearly he wasn't the smoothest dresser. He had a killer smile and exuded confidence and warmth.

"How come you're living on the north side of campus away from the hospital?"

"My parents own the triplex as a rental. They call it the 'Alamo' for some reason. Anyway when I told them I was coming back to Seattle for surgical training, they offered me the middle unit. It's way bigger than I need but I really like living there."

Emma looked at her watch. "Uh oh, time just flew by. I was supposed to be back a while ago. We're having a big homecoming dance on Saturday night and I'm supposed to help Sophie with the decorations. She's going to kill me."

Emma looked down sheepishly at her empty latte cup and said slowly, "What are you doing Saturday night? I don't have a date."

"I'd love to come but ..."

Emma didn't like the '*but.*'

"...but what time does it start?"

"It's supposed to be at 6:30," Emma said. "Most don't show up 'til 7ish."

"I'm pulling a later shift on Saturday this weekend," David said, "and don't get off until 7:30 but I should be able to make it by 8:00."

"That'd be okay with me. I have some setting up to do at the beginning anyway. It's kind of formal. You are supposed to wear a suit. Okay?"

"No problema. I'll drive to work take a suit with me. One thing though that you have to understand. I'm on an ER rotation so things happen. I could get stuck, not likely, but possible I'll never make it. My last girlfriend couldn't handle my no-shows, among other things. So you're warned. But if it's between someone bleeding to death and coming to the party, he dies. Just kidding. Anyway we better get going. Don't want Sophie on my bad side."

They both got up and headed for the door. David couldn't help noting that Emma had a huge grin.

As they exited the HUB, David stopped walking for a second.

"Oh shoot. I forgot something. I had a manuscript to review. I'm writing a paper on post op pancreatitis, that's an inflammation of the pancreas after surgery. One of the attendings had handwritten comments on my paper and I left it in the lounge. Now I've got to schlep back to the ER."

"What's 'schlep' mean. I've heard it but never really knew exactly what it meant."

"It's a Yiddish word that can be a verb or noun," David said. "Usually it means a journey or trip that is essentially a pain in the ass, either because it's far or because you're lugging something. Walking home with you is not a schlep. Going back to the ER because I forgot something is a schlep."'

"David, are you a Jew?" Emma asked, changing the tone of her voice.

"Yeah. That a problem?"

"No, no, not at all."

But it was.

After his comment about being a Jew, Emma seemed to shut down. David thought it a bit strange, as they, particularly Emma, had been talking pretty much nonstop. Also the tone of the query differed from Emma's usual questions. She hadn't asked whether he was Jewish as a query but asked *was he a Jew* as a statement. The subtle difference of Jew versus the softer Jewish was not lost on him. David tried not to make too much out of it after he dropped Emma at her house. He walked back to his apartment and got in his car to drive back to the ER to pick up the manuscript. He decided he'd find out more on their next walk. He didn't have to wait that long.

Emma entered her bedroom finding Sophie on her bed reading her LSAT prep book.

"Soph, I've got a problem."

"So."

"David is a Jew."

"So."

"I've never been out or been friends with anyone who's a Jew, male or female."

"One, you're not going out with him. Two, he's been a gentleman in every way. Three, he's saved your ass by allowing you to get through the class at the med school. Four, you've met tons of Jewish people here at the UW, but just didn't know it.

"Now that you mention it, your advisor Dr. Miller is Jewish. I'm pretty sure, or at least I read in the Daily that the Jewish studies program honored Miller for something. Meant to tell you but never did. It wasn't a big deal. I'm pretty sure that both your shrinks are Jewish. Half my school in Morristown were Jewish and most were friends. To be honest, I've never challenged your dad or brother when they say something so bigoted that I cringe. It's the only thing about your dad that makes him seem small but I've let it slide and never thought it would come up. I don't give a shit about Alan. He's not worth my time or yours."

"Okay but I've just complicated things by inviting him to the homecoming dance."

"You what?" Sophie blurted.

"You heard. I asked him to come to the dance on Saturday. But that was before he told me he was a Jew. Honestly, Sophie, I really like him. He's easy to talk to and I feel comfortable with him. I've found myself actually thinking about him when I'm alone. You know I wasn't sure I was ever going to feel safe again with any guy. Sophie I feel more than safe with him."

"Did you ask him to marry you?"

"Don't make fun of me. You know how crazy my dad and brother are about Jews in general. I know they're not right but I'm not going to change them. I know my mom doesn't feel the same but she's not going to buck up against dad on this. I'm thinking of calling and canceling. Maybe tell him I'm not feeling well or have too much to do or some crap."

"I love you more than anyone in the world," Sophie said. "You're over thinking this one. Shit. Go out Saturday and have a good time. He's a nice guy and your dad and Alan aren't here. Girl, this is an easy call."

"Well I may have screwed things up already. I really stopped talking after he told me. He asked if it was a problem but I said 'no.' I don't think I was very subtle. I really didn't talk after that."

"Do you think he got it? I mean that it's a problem for you."

"I don't know. I sensed that he knew it surprised and probably upset me. That it might be a big deal."

"Well you might let it slide and see what happens."

"Maybe better if I bring it up before Saturday night. I don't want to feel funny and it's not going to be easy to talk when the party's going. He's been so nice that I just think I need to talk to him before."

"Your call. I don't disagree. You know this may blow up in your face and then you're not going to have him bringing you home after class."

"Not lost on me. But I just feel that talking to him..." Emma stopped talking for a moment. "Oh Soph, I really like him."

Tears started flowing from Emma. Sophie moved to her side and gave her a hug until the crying stopped.

"Emma, call him now."

Chapter 19

"It's me Emma."

"What's up?" David asked.

"Where are you?"

"I'm coming back from the ER. I had to go back to pick up the paper."

"I'd like to talk to you. Can you come back to the sorority?"

"Emma, are we still on for Saturday?"

Emma, hesitated, and said, "Sure."

David said, "Emma, that wasn't a very convincing 'sure.'"

"No, I really want you to come to the party. Really."

David now knew exactly what was on her mind. It was on his mind as well.

"Emma, I can't come over right now. I've got a plumber coming to my apartment in ten minutes to fix my garbage disposal. I'm pretty sure the motor's burned out. Anyway, I have to be there for the next hour or two. He's doing some work for the unit above me as well, and I need to be around. Can you come to my place?" David thought, *No way she's coming here.*

"Sure. I'll come."

"5015 16th, third house from corner north of 50th, on west side. Unit #B. I'm pulling in now."

"I'll be there in a few minutes." Emma turned to Sophie and said, "Sophie, will you walk with me to his place. Take just a minute. I don't want to walk alone."

They grabbed coats and left immediately for the five-minute walk.

"Sophie, what am I going to say? How do I even start?"

"Be honest and truthful. That way there would be no need for second explanations. Seems like a plan."

As Emma and Sophie came up to David's house, two girls, one very tall and another very short, were at a three-posted mailbox sorting through mail.

The two girls eyed Emma and Sophie coming up the stairs past the front garden.

Emma smiled and asked "Excuse me, where does David Milton live?"

"He's in Unit B. That's the one that opens in the front, just behind us, up the stairs," said the taller one.

The shorter one said. "I assume you two are not the plumbers."

All four laughed.

"No, just a friend," said Emma.

"And another friend," Sophie said to the group, and then faced Emma. "I'm going back, Emma, you're solo from here. Call me if you need me to walk back with you." She waved at the three and turned back to the sorority.

"Are you the one he walks home some nights?" the taller one continued.

"Yeah that's me, name's Emma."

"I'm Kasey and this is Sandra. Well, he's certainly been in a better mood for the past couple of weeks."

Emma smiled and walked up the short set of stairs to the house's main entrance and knocked.

David answered quickly and smiled, "You Joe the plumber?"

"What's with this house and plumbers? You need a toilet fixation to live here?" Emma jokingly asked.

"Come on in."

David looked out the door to the two girls from unit #C watching David and Emma.

"Hi guys. Plumber's not here yet. I'll send him up after he fixes my disposal," David said.

Emma turned around as both girls gave David a thumbs-up. Emma walked into David's apartment. The main floor of the old mansion had been converted into a four-bedroom unit.

One small bedroom seemed to be just storage, one a study, one a guest bedroom, and the largest bedroom was David's. Nice dining area and kitchen but no real living room or den.

"Have a seat. Want me to take your coat?"

"No. I'm fine like this."

Emma unzipped her parka, but didn't remove it. A sign to both that she might not stay very long. Emma sat at a dining table just off the kitchen.

"Want something to drink, Diet Coke, coffee?"

David hadn't seen Emma this nervous since the first evening after he had gone back to the sorority to apologize. The splotchiness around her eyes made it abundantly clear that she had been crying.

"Well, maybe a glass of water."

"Sure, ice?"

"No thanks, just some of Seattle's finest." Emma tried to smile.

David took a clean glass from the cupboard and filled it from the kitchen sink, placed it in front of Emma and sat opposite her.

"Your dime," David mumbled.

"Do you know why I'm here?" Emma asked.

"Pretty good idea. When I told you I was Jewish you switched persona."

"Was it really that obvious?"

"Yep."

"I'm sorry."

"So am I."

"I guess we need to talk a bit about me." Emma hesitated. She thought to herself, *"Where do I start this? No, first I want to talk about you and me. I want whatever I say to come out right.* "David, I like you. I don't know if you know all my story but ..."

"I know enough," David interrupted.

"Well, asking you to the party was a really big deal for me," Emma said. "I did it because for the first time in over fourteen months I feel safe when alone around a guy – you did that for me. You saw me that first night. How utterly out of control I can be."

"So how did that change, me being Jewish?"

Emma's eyes saddened quickly as her face sagged, her gaze lowered and her lower lip pouted, "My family, well, my dad and my brother are bigoted. They are extremely and utterly and without reason, bigoted. I've never had a Jewish friend, never been out with someone Jewish and if my dad finds out, I might, well, get pulled from the UW. My parents weren't all that excited about me coming back to school and this is the kind of thing that might show them that they were right. That, in their eyes, I wasn't ready."

Emma's shoulders sagged even lower and she placed both hands on the table for support. Tears started flowing and her breathing became labored. David got up and brought a box of tissues from the bathroom and placed it in front of Emma.

"Thanks. I don't know what to do. I want to know, but I don't," Emma said.

They sat for a while saying nothing. David couldn't stop looking at Emma's face. She looked so vulnerable, so desperate. Wishing he could walk around the table and hug her, he knew that was out of the question.

David finally spoke. "Well, it must have taken a bit of courage even to come here now. What were you thinking? Do you want me to go to the party with you? Do you even want me to be walking home with you?"

"Yes and yes. I don't want to change anything."

Tears were coming without letup and Emma was too distraught to even wipe them before they spilled onto her unzipped parka and blouse.

"I told Sophie. She thought I might just let it slide. But I knew that wasn't right. I needed to talk to you."

Emma's face reddened, the tears continued and she started breathing deeply through her nose trying to keep her composure.

"So your biggest fear is that your dad will find out, right?"

"Yes."

"So here's the deal, or at least the way I see it. You don't tell him, you're a wreck, worried 24/7 that he'll find out and go ballistic and yank you from school. You don't need that stress. So why not 'man up', bad word choice, and just tell your parents. Maybe tell your mom and let her deal with it." David hesitated then restarted, "No, just face the firing squad and tell your dad. Then he can't get mad at you for not knowing or finding out last."

"I'm scared."

"Better scared, but in control. If he asks who already knows, you can say no one but Sophie and him. Besides, you've only known for an hour."

"Sophie knows my dad, and she'll try to talk me out of calling. David, I feel so bad about this. So conflicted."

"Why's he so bigoted?"

"I'm not sure when I knew first." Emma then gave David the same summary of her father and brother's issues that she had given Sophie after Thanksgiving dinner on the veranda.

David spoke forcefully, "Emma make the call. Call your father."

"I'll give it some thought."

"Make the call," David said.

"Boy, am I going to have a bunch to talk about with my shrink on Tuesday."

"Who's your shrink?"

"Dr. Sarah Cohen-Finer at UW, she's so nice."

"Another Jew."

"I don't think so."

"Wanna bet?"

"Okay, her backup is Dr. Bev Green."

"Likely batting a thousand."

"Jesus Christ!"

"Him too."

David walked Emma back to the sorority and wished her good luck. Emma ran up to her room and found Sophie sitting at her desk.

“I'm going to call my dad,” Emma said.

"Ooh. Did you think this out? Maybe not a good idea," Sophie said.

"David's suggestion. Then I don't have to sit around worrying dad will find out on his own and he'll be upset that he didn't know."

"Want me to leave the room?"

"No. I might need moral support. He may even want to speak to you."

"Go for it," Sophie said.

Emma, too nervous to sit, paced the room to make the call. Clara Braza answered the call.

"Hi Mom. Yeah, things are okay. I'm really happy and doing well in my classes. Say, is Dad there? I've got to tell him something."

Emma looked at Sophie and crossed her fingers.

"Hi Dad. Things are great. Sophie's here and says hi."

"Tell her hello from me," said Joe Braza.

Looking at Sophie, Emma said, "My dad says hi to you. I want to tell you about something, do you have a second?"

"Sure."

"Great. Anyway you know I've been taking that class on wine and medicine, right. Well the class gets out at 5 or 5:15 in the evening, so it's dark when I walk back to the sorority. Anyway, I met this guy on the walk about two weeks ago. He's a surgical resident at the hospital. He lives a block from the GiGi house. So I've been going down to the emergency room after class and when he's done, he walks me back. Okay, here's the deal. I asked him to a party that we're having tomorrow. Homecoming. It's a big deal and he said he'd go with me."

"Good for you, honey but where's this going?" asked Joe. "You've never told me about a date before. Is he a serial killer or something?"

"Dad you're worse than Sophie, let me finish. Well after I asked and he accepted, I found out that he's Jewish. I know that you have some issues with that and I didn't want you to be upset."

Silence.

"Dad, you there?" Emma asked.

"I'm thinking. Mom know?" asked Joe.

"No, Mom doesn't know. Other than Sophie, nobody knows. I thought I needed to talk to you first."

"No chance you can cancel?"

"I could," Emma said, "but then I won't have a date,

and I'd like to go. I'm not going to go solo. This is actually the first time I will have gone out since you know what, and I was looking forward to it. Plus, if I biff on this, I don't know that he'll still want to walk back with me for the rest of the quarter. I really don't like coming back alone when it's dark."

"You could take a cab."

"Dad, please. Then I'll be getting into a cab with a different driver each time. That's worse. He's been a gentleman."

"Sophie met him?"

"Yep."

"Let me talk to her."

Emma handed the phone to Sophie.

"Hi, Mr. Braza."

"Sophie, you've met this guy?"

"Yes I have," Sophie said. "He came by the first night and said hello. He lives on 16th, we're on 18th. He seems nice and can't be too dense to get into the surgical program. Emma's been home, on time, every night."

"Okay. Thanks, Sophie, and say hello to your mom and dad for us. Tell them we're looking forward to Mexico. Put Emma back on."

"Me, again," said Emma.

"First, thanks for calling," said Joe. "You know we worry about you. Your call here, Emma. Go if you want and have a good time. We'll talk more."

"Thanks, Dad. Luv ya. I'm going down for dinner now. Bye." Emma disconnected and declared, "Yes," with a fist and a smile. She dialed David.

Chapter 20

Joe slammed the receiver hard enough that the entire phone bounced and then fell to the floor.

"Clara, what the hell is going on with your daughter?" Joe yelled. "God damn it. I knew she wasn't ready to go back to school. If she were here and not so fucking fragile, I would have thrown her in her bedroom."

"Joe, stop swearing. Cool down and tell me what she told you. I'm clueless."

"She's going out with some Jew doctor on Saturday, who's also walking her home every night. I'm not happy. You're going to have to talk to her. I don't want her hanging around with the wrong people. You understand me?"

"I hear you," Clara said, "but I'm not sure I agree. She needs to find her own way right now. She knows how you feel and she did call us."

"God damn it, Clara. She's my daughter and I don't want her seeing any fucking Jews or Muslims or blacks or Asians. Why can't she find a date from our kind of people? If we don't nip this now we may be sorry. I don't trust Sophie's judgment on this either. You need to call that Frost lady and get her on board."

"Joe, Calm down. I'll call, but you've got to stop swearing and get hold of yourself. You're getting too worked up over something that's probably nothing. Please calm down."

Chapter 21

"Emma, you look so lovely," Francine said. Francine's eyes were a bit misty. Emma wore a black dress, heels, and pearls. Her hair was up. Francine gave Emma a long hug and added, "More than a few of the girls have come up to me to say how glad they are to see you going out again. I certainly hope tonight works out for you. I've never met this young man. It certainly didn't start off very well, I guess."

"Thanks, Francine," said Emma.

"I have a message to call your mom. She called every other day when you first came back, but not for a while."

Emma, trying not to worry about the upcoming evening, furrowed her brow and said, "Don't know about anything. Let me know if you talk to her."

"Sophie told me your date isn't coming until 8 or so."

"Yeah." Emma looked at her phone. It was 7:55. She had missed a called from David stamped at 7:35, twenty minutes earlier and the voicemail icon showed a waiting message. "Oh, oh. He left me a message," Emma said, walking away.

Emma walked into the pantry in the kitchen, closed the door, slid to the floor against the back wall and punched her voice mail button.

I hope he's coming. I wish I could think more positively. I miss being positive.

"Emma, it's just after 7:30 and I am leaving the hospital now. Going to park at my place and walk over. Should be there by 8."

Emma smiled. "See," she said out loud to herself.

Sitting there quietly, Emma realized that David had never touched her. Not a handshake, helping hand, pat on the back. No physical contact of any kind that she could remember. *Strange.*

Sophie walked into the pantry to find her friend sitting against the back wall. "Emma, you okay? Francine said you'd came in here."

Emma got up. "Yep, David's on his way. Soph, just curious, did you ever tell David not to touch me?"

Sophie paused and thought for a second how to respond, "Well, I might have said something that first day about how not touchy-feely you might be."

"How could you say that?"

"Emma, I had to talk you into going through with the walk home every thirty minutes for two days. I was..."

Before Sophie could finish the sentence Emma's phone made a short jingle... *'text coming.'*

"Outside front door help dm."

"He's here," said Emma.

Sophie gave Emma a hug and said, "Good luck. Maybe you can get a dance out of him. That's touchy."

Emma thought for a second and said, "Surgeon. Dancing. Doubt it."

Emma pushed through the crowd to the front door and exited. Sophie decided against following Emma.

The noise from the DJs music and the throngs of young people dancing and mingling was palpable. David waited, facing away from the stairway, toward the street.

"David," Emma shouted.

David, wearing a pin-striped blue suit, light blue dress shirt with a hand painted multicolored tie showing a boy sitting on his father's shoulders, turned to Emma's voice. David had a box with a corsage. She hadn't mentioned that he needed to bring one. Emma stopped at the top of the stairs.

"You are stunning," David smiled.

"Thanks. You clean up pretty well too. I had hoped you'd be wearing your old parka and knit hat," Emma said.

Emma walked down the five brick steps to the bottom of the landing.

"Would have, but both are at the dry cleaner. I threatened to sue them for not having them back in time. So I asked the girls in unit #C what to wear. They also told me that corsages were not mandatory but nice. I didn't know the color of your dress, so they said white always works."

"The flower is lovely."

"I walked into the ICU until I found a comatose patient who had flowers parked outside the door and voilá. I stole a white one."

"Really?"

"Nah, florist on 43rd and Roosevelt." David put the corsage on Emma's wrist. "There you go."

Emma laughed and without thinking or hesitating she grabbed David's left hand in her right. His hand was warm and strong. It felt good. *No-touchy-feely* was now off the table.

"Come on. Let's go in," Emma said.

For the first time in more than a year, Emma Braza felt no fear.

People packed the dance floor while undanceable rap boomed through the room.

"I want to find Sophie, so you can say hello," said Emma.

Sophie, in a corner with her date and two other couples, saw Emma coming and waved her over. After the intros, Sophie pulled David aside.

"Thanks for everything. You have been a godsend beyond belief. The change in Emma, how happy, how carefree, has been nothing short of miraculous. Anyway, thanks."

David nodded.

The DJ had switched to some rock and roll, John Lennon's 1975 rendition of *"Do You Want To Dance."*

Emma grabbed David's hand again. "Want to dance? I'm not so very good at it, but I love trying." *He's gonna to say no.*

"Sure, love to," David said, as he pulled Emma onto the dance floor.

Almost without exception the guys she had dated her first three years were, at best, terrible dancers. A few would go through the motions for a song or two and then beg off. Some wouldn't even try. Emma, ready to accept anything from David, had not been prepared. He was good. Really good. The DJ continued with a 60s swing dance, the Beatles' version of Chuck Berry's, *'Rock and Roll Music'*, one of Emma's favorite dance songs. Many of the nearby crowd stopped dancing to watch Emma and David. Most just to be happy that Emma was on the floor, all knowing what a huge step she had taken. The rest watching the two dance. After the song ended, the group around them gave a brief round of applause.

As they headed to the beverage area Emma beamed. “My goodness, David, where did you learn to dance?"

"My parents are good dancers. Mom would make me dance with her whenever Dad got tired or wasn't around. Remember, she grew up in the fifties and sixties, so swing was huge, and she showed me all the moves. By the way, you're good. Most girls these days can't follow. Where'd you learn?"

""Now you're lying,” Emma said. “I know that I am not a great dancer, not even good, but I love being out there.” Not much to do fifteen miles outside of Walla Walla. So our family would dance."

"Maybe our families aren't so different?" declared David.

"I wish it was that simple."

Back to the dance floor they went. The DJ played a Ricky Martin Latin swing, some hip-hop and finally another Latin song.

David asked, “Do you know the tango?” David asked.

"Not really."

"I know a little more." David grabbed her forcibly and pulled her close.

"Okay here's the deal. My mom says for the tango to work you have to be an actress, I only have to be aloof. They have to believe you hate me at first and love me at the end. She said that dancing the tango with me never worked. I mean how can you hate your son? She said she could hate Dad more easily.”

They both laughed.

"Anyway, ready?"

"Yep."

“Nose to nose, eye to eye. Remember, you hate my stinking guts. I'm a scum sucker and you're being forced to dance with me or I kill your sister.”

“I don’t have a sister.”

“Then your brother.”

“Most of the time I wouldn’t mind.”

“Your dog?”

“I’d kill you in a New Jersey second.”

“Something like that."

Emma found it hard to hate David when she wanted only to laugh. They started and Emma tried to act aloof and uninterested.

Halfway through David said, "Okay, you've changed your mind, you can't live another second without me, you need me, you have to have me right here on the dance floor."

Emma burst out laughing. As the tango ended, David swirled Emma, dipped her to the ground, raised her up to his face and kissed her. Emma looked stunned, but happy stunned. Sophie and Francine Frost watching from the side were both tearing up.

As they walked back to get some water, Emma wouldn't let go of David's hand. "I am really happy you came."

"So am I," David said.

After a glass of water, Emma excused herself to go to the bathroom.

"David, don't leave."

Not able to wipe the grin off his face, he said, "I'm out the window as soon as you're gone."

As soon as Emma left, two sophomore girls near the punch bowl approached David.

The taller one said, "You're the doctor that walks Emma home?”

"Yep."

"You can really dance."

"Thanks."

The better looking of the two spoke up, "While Emma's gone would you mind dancing with me?"

The other chimed in, "and me next."

"Well it's up to Emma. Whatever she wants."

"I'm sure it's fine with Emma, she doesn’t socialize much and we're sisters, right?"

"Just the same, let's wait."

The three made idle chit chat.

Emma returned and greeted the two sorority sisters. She didn't know them well. They had joined the house during her year in recovery.

David grabbed Emma’s hand, then said, "These girls wanted to know if you'd let me dance with them?"

Emma, taken aback, said, "David, do whatever you want."

"I don't know protocol at these functions. You mean

it's my decision?" asked David.

"Yes," Emma said, as the two intruders nodded yes.

"Okay, easy." Turning to the two girls, "I choose to dance only with Emma," he said bluntly.

A moment of silence ensued until the two girls understood David's message and left in a huff.

"I guess I'll need to talk to them in the morning," Emma mused.

"Don't waste your time. Not worth it. Let's dance."

He grabbed Emma and back to the dance floor they went.

By 10:30 p.m., many of the couples had left. Sophie and her date had joined Emma and David. Sophie suggested they might go out for a quick bite.

"Why not?" Emma said.

David said, "Great, I'll drive. My car's a block away."

On the way out, Emma introduced David to Francine. She was oddly detached during the conversation. Emma did not know that Francine had talked to Clara Braza during the party.

The two couples went to an Indian restaurant on University Avenue. Animated, engaged, talkative and smiling, Emma cornered the conversation. Sophie mostly sat, listened, and watched her best friend, back from the dead. Sophie thought, *'How lucky were we both tonight?'* They finished eating after midnight and headed back to the sorority.

David double-parked in front of the house. Sophie and her date exited David's car and headed up the stairs.

"I've had the best time," Emma said.

"Well, we're at that moment, Emma Braza," David said.

"What moment is that?"

"When I wonder if I can give you a kiss good night? Always tense and full of suspense."

"I don't do well with tension you know."

She leaned over and gave David a kiss on the lips. "Now ask me."

He didn't ask. He kissed her again.

He walked her to the door and she hugged him at the doorsteps.

"See you on Monday afternoon."

"Sure, unless you want to go out for breakfast tomorrow. I'm on at noon until 11 p.m."

"I'll be at your place at 8:30, okay?" Emma asked.

"Great."

Emma plopped on Sophie's bed, spread out her arms and smiled.

"Emma, we need to talk."

"Sophie, he's amazing."

"Francine was up here five minutes ago. Your mom called at 11 and 11:30. Francine told her you were so happy, and that David appeared to be a gentleman. Not what your mom wanted to hear, apparently. Francine is supposed to tell you tomorrow to break it off, and then she's got to call your mom back. Guess you misread your dad. I'm sorry."

"Don't spoil my night."

"Emma, he's Jewish. The shit is going to hit the fan."

"Screw them. I had a great time and I'm going out for breakfast with David tomorrow morning."

She did, and did not bring up her parents with David.

Chapter 22

Emma returned to the house after breakfast with David. Emma drove David's car and dropped him at the ER. David planned to sleep at the med school, conduct some early morning library research for a scientific paper, take his Monday rotation at 9 a.m. and finally walk home with Emma after work. Emma took his car back to David's apartment, parked it, threw the keys in the unit and walked back to the sorority.

Francine had posted a note on Emma's door, "Come to my office, ASAP, Francine." Emma went immediately downstairs to Francine's office.

Once Emma sat, Francine said, "You had a great time last night, eh?"

Emma nodded and smiled. "I had a great time. I had no idea that David could dance. He was amazing. We went out for breakfast at Carillon Point this morning."

Francine looked distraught and remained silent.

"Okay, let's have it," Emma said. "What did my mother want?"

"I'll come to the point," Francine said. "Your parents are upset over your seeing Dr. Milton. I did what I could to smooth the waters, but I don't think I registered."

"I assumed as much. How can they be so judgmental without meeting him?"

"I told them that from what I saw last night, and from what I've heard from Sophie, that he's been a gentleman. I'm not sure what the repercussions might be if you continue to see him, but from your mom's tone, there's going to be some fallout."

Emma closed her eyes and nodded a soft no, no.

"You are an amazing young woman and a role model

for the house," Francine said. "I'll do whatever I can to help but...but I'm not sure what that might be.

"Nor do I."

"Your mother did say that you had talked to your father about Dr. Milton. Anyway you might keep the lines of communication open. If they don't hear from you, they will surely assume you're doing something they don't like. My suggestion to you is to try going out with other guys. Whether you continue to see Dr. Milton is up to you. Dating others may buy some time."

Emma, thinking, folded her arms and said nothing.

"I got the feeling this is not your mother's doing," Francine added, "yet she's trying to fix it, as the middleman."

"This is my dad's issue, but he's dumped it on my mother. I'm not sure what to do either, or whom to talk to. My appointment with Dr. Cohen-Finer is Tuesday. I might see what she says."

The rest of Sunday was unbearable. Emma wanted to call David but discretion for lack of a game plan made the call impossible.

Sophie agreed with Francine's appraisal of the situation.

Emma had her first really bad night in three weeks.

When Emma showed up at the emergency room on Monday she ran into Delores Bryant. She came into the doctor's lounge and sat next to Emma.

"Hi, nice to see you again Emma. I just wanted to remind you that when your class is over, I'll need you to return the passkeys for the ER. I wasn't worried, but I have to keep track of them."

"No problem. You've been great. Thanks for everything."

"I'd say you've been great as far as Dr. Milton is concerned. Don't know what's in the coffee you're serving him, but it's got him out of the doldrums."

Emma smiled and reiterated her appreciation, "Thanks, thanks so much."

On the way across campus with David, Emma suggested a stop at the HUB. After ordering two lattes they sat in a corner.

"Well I guess my dad's not as liberated as we thought," Emma said. "He was so nice on the phone to me, but he must have unloaded on my mom, who then unloaded on my house mother. Like either control my life. I'm twenty-two and they have no confidence that I can make decisions."

"What's all this mean?" David asked. "I don't know your family enough to formulate an opinion or plan. I can say that this sucks. Growing up on Mercer Island and then Cal and UCSF, I never ran into any serious anti-Semitism. I know it's out there; it's just not gotten to me before. I'd really like to keep seeing you, but if it's out of the question, you have to let me know. If your parents, or at least your dad, really have the power to control your life by pulling you from school, I'd say their love is pretty conditional."

"I agree," Emma said. "Growing up, my dad wasn't a control freak at all. Actually quite permissive as far as I was concerned. He's changed. I can see it and so can my mom. If you hit the right buttons, he lights up. He's *Las Vegas lit* right now. Anyway, the only decent suggestion I've gotten is from Francine. She thought that I should try to date other guys and she'll keep my parents in the loop."

"Whose side is she on?"

"She's on my side and, from what she's seen and heard, she likes you. She told my mother that, but it didn't go over very well. My dad wants to hear that you had horns, ate Christian livers, and were dripping blood from your fangs or something."

"Actually, in my job, I do sometimes drip blood, it's just not mine. Not funny, sorry. Is Francine to be trusted?"

"I think so. Double agent-like. The downside of all this is my dad pulls me out of school, which I guess he could do. I don't have the money to finish school without him. Once I graduate in June, I've got more options. I want to still see you. But I have to keep the animals in their cages as long as I can."

"I'm sorry for all this," David said.

"I don't know what's going to happen, but I do know that you've helped me more than anyone outside of my parents and Sophie. Please try to be understanding. I'm going home for Thanksgiving and maybe I'll be able to get a better handle on things."

David, subdued, said, "Why can't life be simple once in a while? Am I still going to walk you home?"

"I hope you will. I don't really want anything to change right now. Will you bear with me?"

"Sure."

Emma returned to the sorority and sat down with Sophie.

"I need to start dating again. Maybe my parents are right that I'm over the top with the first guy, when I truly believed there would never be any guys."

"Maybe, but I don't believe it. I think if you had met

David two years ago you'd be engaged...and probably disinherited. But, let's see who we can find."

Emma's nightmares returned.

Chapter 23

On Friday, the week before Thanksgiving, David called Emma early in the day before she left for school.

"I was hoping that you hadn't found anyone to go out with yet."

"Not here, but I am going out when I get back home. He's a high school friend who's going to Gonzaga Law School."

"Can we do something tonight?"

"I'd love to. What do you have in mind?"

"Surprise. You need to wear a black skirt and white blouse and flat shoes but you have to bring a change of clothes and heels for something nice. We'll leave about 6:15. You might eat a little something before."

"David, that's not fair, I need to know."

"Nope. Tough."

David started doing the two-note low background music from the Jaws soundtrack. "Da-Dum, Da-Dum, Da-Dum. Suck it up and live on the edge."

"I'm not going then."

"Okay, I'll ask someone else. Maybe Francine Frost."

"I hate you, David Milton. Okay, I'll go, but you'll pay for this."

David dropped Emma at the sorority at 5:45 p.m. They had walked back quickly, but David, despite pleas for mercy, would not relent. The evening was to be mystery to Emma.

She had the skirt, blouse and flats to match David's

dark slacks, white shirt and tie. He had a sports coat in a travel bag and she brought a black jacket to go over her blouse, her lucky pearls and four inch black heels."

Emma demanded, "Okay, so now what are we doing?"

"I assume you know who Samantha Stone is?"

"Yes, of course. She's in town for a week doing a Marilyn Monroe biopic, a one-woman show. A bunch of us tried to get tickets, but they've been sold out for months. Please tell me you bought tickets."

"Nope. Didn't buy tickets. Too expensive."

"Shoot. You had me there. So what is it?"

"You'll now have to wait. Sorry, Charlie."

David drove to downtown Seattle and parked a block from the 5th Avenue Theater. David took Emma's hand and grabbed the clothes bags in the other and they entered the theater at a side door an hour before show time.

"David, what's going on here?"

"Okay, here's the deal. My uncle, Bob, manages the theater. For fifteen years, on and off, I've worked as an usher in exchange for a seat, if there are any seats. Tonight, we ush.'"

"Wow, I didn't see this coming," said Emma.

They entered the theater manager's office and placed their extra clothes on the couch. As they were about to exit, Uncle Bob appeared. David gave him a big hug.

"Uncle Bob, this is the magical Emma I told you about."

"Nice to meet you young lady." Bob shook Emma's hand. "David's been babbling about you for a couple of weeks."

"Nice to meet you too," said Emma.

"Anyway, get your butts out there and earn your keep. David will show you the ropes. Believe it or not, he actually knows Ms. Stone. She's played Seattle a few times over the years and David always gets to congratulate her on her performance."

David and Emma went to a nearby room marked "Ushers only" and grabbed two flashlights. The room had a steady stream of ushers entering, hanging up coats, grabbing a flashlight and looking on the wall for their assignments.

David seemed to know half of them. Most were pleasant enough but there was no time for introductions. They walked up three flights to the balcony.

David, speaking rapidly, said, "We can't work the same section. I am going to take Balcony Center Left, Aisle B and you're going to take Balcony Left, Aisle A. It's the easiest, usually, but tonight every seat is sold. You'll be working with a guy named Harry Kraft. He will hit on you, but disregard him. He'll get the picture. I am going to retrieve you at 7:15, fifteen minutes before curtain. Don't ask questions, when I grab you, you come."

Emma's head was spinning as David walked her to Balcony Left, Aisle A.

"Emma, this is Harry. He'll show you how the seating goes. Harry, you know I'll be back fifteen minutes before curtain."

Harry was a double seventy. Seventy years old and seventy pounds overweight. His breathing was still labored from walking up three flights of stairs.

"Yes, David. Hi, Emma. Will you marry me? Don't answer that just yet. I have a hard time with instant rejection."

Emma smiled.

Harry showed Emma the seating arrangements and gave a few suggestions.

"Harry, where will you watch the show?"

"Honey, this ticket's harder to get than the Inauguration Ball. I'll be standing behind the last row up here in the nosebleed section with the rest of the ushers."

Emma nodded. The stage was a long way off. She thought, *'What the heck, a new experience.'*

Seating people wasn't rocket science, so Emma got the hang of it immediately. Some of the theatergoers were a bit put off by the distance to the stage. Emma assured them that the sound system was top notch and that they would hear just fine. She had no idea really, but the ruse got people into their seats.

At 7:15, David grabbed Emma's hand and they barreled down three flights back to Uncle Bob's office. David put on his suit coat and quickly combed his hair. Emma didn't have to be asked. She put on her jacket and pearls and her high heels. Out the door they went and up one flight to the main level. David pulled tickets from the jacket and they entered the theater, center right on the main level. The usher, another older woman knew David and nodded. David gave her a quick peck on the cheek, grabbed two programs.

"I know where to go."

At 7:24 p.m., David escorted Emma to the 4th row, center. Seats that love or money or both couldn't buy.

"It's never who you are, it's who you know," David quipped.

The evening was magical and up to all the hype. Ms. Stone received a standing ovation for fifteen minutes and three curtain calls. During the second curtain call, Emma saw Samantha Stone wink and point at David.

As the crowd started to exit, David lingered with Emma.

Emma, still dazzled, said, "I could stay here forever. Best thing I've ever seen. Samantha Stone is my new idol. David, was she winking at you?"

David not responding to the question said, "Hmmph. And you almost didn't go."

"I am so mad at you. You could have told me."

"Nah, better this way. Follow me."

They went back to Bob's office and grabbed Emma's flats and coat. Around the corner and up a half-flight of stairs were a group of doors. Two guards stood in front of the stairs.

"Hey, Freddy. Hey, John. How things going?"

John, the larger of the two, said, "Great, David, or is it Dr. David?"

Freddy quickly responded, "It's Dr. Milton, asshole." Freddy then saw Emma standing behind David. "Oops sorry ma'am, that was meant for my Neanderthal friend."

"Is Ms. Stone accepting guests?" David asked.

"I think so? Your uncle is in there now. Just knock," Freddy said.

David knocked and a muffled, "Come in," returned.

David found Uncle Bob sitting on a couch sipping a gin and tonic. Ms. Stone, wearing a Chinese silk robe, worked busily at her mirror removing makeup. She spun after seeing David in the mirror.

"David, how are you?" She stood and gave David a big hug.

"Great, Sam," David said. "So good to see you. You were beyond spectacular. I'd like you to meet Emma Braza."

"David", Stone said, frowning, in lowered voice, "how dare you bring someone into my dressing room who looks better than I."

Emma eyes widened then relaxed as Samantha smiled and gave Emma a European faux cheek-cheek kiss. "If you're a friend of David or Ben, then you're a friend of mine."

"It's a great honor to meet you, Miss Stone," Emma said. "You were simply magical, and I enjoyed every second."

Samantha looked at Emma, "It's Sam to everyone in this room." Samantha then turned to David and said, "A keeper."

Ben stood up. "I've got work to do. Sam, you okay? Need anything?"

"I'll let you know. I am famished. David, Emma, would you like to have a bite with me? I despise eating alone and your uncle always begs out. Your aunt must really be the suspicious type."

David looked at Emma, "Well, can we get a bite?"

"I'd love to," said the totally bewildered Emma.

Samantha Stone's limo was parked out front.

Freddy, the guard from the stairs, was driving. "Where to, Ms. Stone?"

"How about Canlis? David, Emma?"

David responded instantaneously, "That sounds fine with me."

Emma spoke up for the first time. "I've promised my parents and Sophie that I would call if I'm going to be back after 12:30."

Samantha snorted, "Curfew, gee whiz, forgot about those things. Where do you live?

"We don't really have curfews any more at the GiGi house or any of the other sororities, just a promise I made this year. It's a long story."

Samantha thought the need-to-check-in comment sounded odd, but didn't give it more thought when she heard that Emma lived in the Gamma Gamma sorority.

"Really, no kidding. I'm a GiGi, Southern Cal," Sam said. "I was in the film school. Didn't graduate though. I really did enjoy the sorority. They're pretty much my only friends outside the industry. Who's your roommate? Hopefully she's got a sense of humor."

"Sophie is her name," Emma said. "She's cool, but will be jealous as hell."

"What's her number?" asked Sam.

"You're not really going to call her, are you?"

"Why not, can't have you getting into any trouble."

"I'll dial it on my phone, she'll answer it. Otherwise

she might not."

Sophie answered, "Hey, Emma, what's up. You okay?"

"Sophie, this is Samantha Stone."

"Who?"

"Samantha Stone, like in Hollywood, Samantha Stone."

"No, really who is this and what are you doing with Emma's phone? Is she okay?"

"Emma, you tell her who I am." Samantha put the phone on speaker.

"Soph, this is Emma."

"Hi Emma, who was that on your phone? Some kind of joke?"

"Actually not. David Milton took me to see the Marilyn Monroe play at the Fifth Avenue tonight. Turns out he knows Samantha Stone. Anyway, we're going out for dinner and I don't think I can get back to the house before one."

"Unbelievable, Emma."

"Give me the phone back," demanded Samantha.

"Sophie, Samantha again. Here's the deal. I am keeping Emma until 1, 1:30. I will send David packing and then I'll put Emma in my suite at the Four Seasons. There's actually three bedrooms. We're off to Canlis for a bite, but I'm going to have my limo driver, named Freddy, come by the GiGi house in thirty minutes. If you, or someone, can get a change of clothes for Emma for tomorrow morning, that'd be nice. We'll both be by the house at 10:45 tomorrow morning. I am a GiGi, you know, so I expect some sisterly cooperation here."

"Okay, I guess. Uh, can I speak to Emma again?"

"Hi, I'm listening," Emma said.

"Emma, is this on the level?" asked Sophie.

"Trust me, it's on the level."

"Well, I'll be..."

"Bye, Soph. You'd better tell Francine what's up. I guess we'll be there before 11:00."

"I've already started walking toward her room with my phone. See ya tomorrow. You're going to be okay, right?"

“Yep. So much to talk about tomorrow.”

The three ate lightly at Canlis, ordering exclusively from the starters menu. Emma ordered a bottle of wine from her family's winery. The sommelier carded her, which she was used to. Samantha berated the sommelier for not carding her too, again with a smile.

David, needing to drive home afterward, had only one glass of wine. Samantha and Emma finished the bottle. Samantha talked about her four husbands for much of the evening. Emma told a funny Agotini story in her best Italian accent that had Samantha and David roaring.

The limo headed back to the Four Seasons at 1:15 am. Emma's change of clothes and toiletries were in the back seat of the limo.

The limo dropped David at the parking lot near the theater. Samantha exited the limo to give David a hug.

"David, is she okay? Something about her, I can't put my finger on it. That business about checking in with her parents was a bit odd."

"Google the name Emma Braza, B-R-A-Z-A, when she's not looking," David whispered, "but, please, say nothing."

After checking her clothing and toiletries, Emma exited the car. David gave Emma a quick hug and smooch on the lips, and said, "Talk to you tomorrow, sometime, okay?"

Emma, almost singing, "Okay. What an evening."

"Pretty cool for me too," David said. "We need to write a note to my uncle thanking him for the seats."

"Absolutely."

"Okay you two," Samantha said, "Come on Emma, I'm beat." When Emma joined her, arm in arm, Samantha continued, "How long have you known David?"

"Couple of months."

"You like him?"

"Yes. Yes, I do, a lot. But we've got some issues."

"Like?"

"My parents aren't very happy that he's Jewish."

"My grandparents on both sides weren't happy either, and that was thirty years ago."

"Really."

"Yep, my dad is Jewish and my mom is Episcopalian. Mom was an actress and my dad did some directing. They are still in love, but both sets of parents were really upset. But they got over it in time. Not all the way over, but pretty good."

"How were you raised?" asked Emma.

"Both ways. I played it however worked best for me."

"When I rushed GiGis, I was pure Episcopalian, as far as they were concerned. I also went to the AEPhi house and told them I was Jewish. Both houses wanted me. Hey, if you ever need to talk, call me." She gave her a card that said simply SS with a phone number as they entered the suite.

"I'm beat, Emma. Last performance is tomorrow night at 7:30. Thank God. Anyway, my stylist will be here at 9 am and get us both ready. The hotel will bring up breakfast for both of us. Freddy will pick us up at 10:30, and then back to the GiGi house."

"Samantha, I've had a night I'll never forget. Thank you."

"Good night, Emma."

Samantha, silk pajamas and all, slid into bed and grabbed her laptop and Googled, *Emma Braza*. She started crying within minutes.

When Emma and Samantha arrived the next morning, Francine was at the front door. When they walked in, every member of the house was present, surrounding the foyer and filling the stairway. The GiGis sang their traditional welcome song and Samantha sang with them. She shook or hugged every sister and signed a few autographs. They took a group picture, subsequently published in the Seattle Times, as well as the GiGi national magazine. A blow up photo, framed, soon hung on the wall in the dining room.

Ready to return to her hotel suite, Samantha asked Emma into the limo. She told Emma that they were now friends, no matter how things worked out with David.

Samantha held herself together until Emma left the limo and then cried softly until she reached downtown.

After Samantha left, Emma retold the entire evening to the sorority from David's invitation until the arrival that morning. A handful of girls came up to Emma afterward to say they would marry David tomorrow. Emma couldn't tell if they were joking, most were not.

Emma called David at the ER later that morning.

"Just needed to say that I'll never forget the last twenty-four hours. I'm even happy you didn't tell me what we were going to do. It did make it even more special."

"Actually, I knew about the seats, but I didn't think we'd get to go out to dinner afterward. That was pretty cool for me too. If you didn't notice I couldn't take my eyes off of you. When you are happy and engaged, you just light up. Pretty special."

"Two things, before I let you go," Emma said. "First, I'm still scared about my family. I just don't know where they stand. Second, if you don't stop acting like you've been acting, I could actually really like you."

"Emma. Uh oh," David said. "A nurse is waving at me frantically, I gotta go. Call you later or see you tomorrow night after class. I'm not acting."

Samantha Stone called David the next day from the airport. "David, sweetie, I really enjoyed Emma. She is so courageous. I can't stop thinking about what she's been through. If I can be of any help to either of you let me know. You can always reach me through your uncle. I'm off to New York tomorrow morning and I have no immediate plans to come back to Seattle. So you take care of yourself and Emma. She's special."

Emma floated home with David on Monday's walk as she talked about Samantha's visit to the sorority.

As many in the class hoped, Agotini cancelled his Wednesday class so people could get out of town before the afternoon pre-Thanksgiving holiday traffic.

Chapter 24

Sophie flew to Newark on Tuesday. Emma left for Walla Walla, the Wednesday before Thanksgiving, at 1:30 p.m. She had not talked to David since the walk home on Monday. Anxious about what to expect at home, she slept poorly the night before.

Emma arrived home at 6:00 p.m. Her parents seemed happy, but Emma knew that some sort of reckoning would happen before she returned to Seattle.

Emma had the one planned date on the Friday night after Thanksgiving with Hank Ward, a classmate from Walla Walla High School. Hank had started law school at Gonzaga University in Spokane. He entered the house and reintroduced himself to the Brazas. They had remembered Hank vaguely and knew his family from various local events. Hank's father was a prominent local attorney, although the deLorraine Winery used different counsel. Hank and Emma departed, ate a quick dinner, movie and then a nearby Starbucks.

Conversation was light and both were a bit guarded, even tense.

"I am still trying to find myself. Most days are really good lately," Emma finally said, bluntly, "but I have some dark days too."

"I understand. That sounds good." Hank responded.

While not discussed specifically, Hank knew every detail of her kidnapping and recovery. Everyone in Walla Walla did.

Emma thought to herself, *'Of course, he knows everything, every gory detail. How could he possibly be comfortable, knowing what he knows, sitting across from me? He probably had a thousand questions he'd like to ask, but never will. Who would or could be cruel enough to ever ask?'*

Emma snapped out of her thoughts to see the anguish in Hank's expression. She was trying to think of anything to say.

"So have you seen Phil McCloskey, you and he were best buds, right?" Emma asked.

"Funny, I just talked to him yesterday. He's at Central getting a teaching credential."

"That's cool."

They caught up on more people in common from Walla Walla. Emma had largely been out of the loop for a year.

Driving up to the Braza's house, Hank said what he'd wanted to say all night, "I am so sorry about your troubles from last year. I hope you'll be able to put it behind you some day."

Emma looked away, but in the end, couldn't even say 'thank you.' Hank's comments were heartfelt, but to Emma, tragic, nonetheless.

At the Braza's front door Hank gave Emma a hug. All in all, a nice first date, and last. Emma knew that he wouldn't call her again. Just a second sense that he didn't need her problems. That said, she knew they might be friends if she returned to Walla Walla. Nothing more.

Emma entered her house to find her mom reading in the den. She gave Emma her *"so, tell me look."*

"Hank's really nice," Emma said, "but I sense, pretty strongly, that he doesn't want baggage and I'm carrying steamer trunks full of it."

Clara understood and said nothing for a while.

"Thanks for giving it a try. We'll need to keep looking."

"Mom, I love you. I'm going to bed."

"Honey, we, I mean you, me and your dad still need to have a talk before you go back, okay?"

"Yeah, Mom, I know."

Emma called Sophie who said to call at any time. It was 2 a.m. in New Jersey but Sophie expected the call and kept her cell under her pillow.

After relating the evening, Sophie suggested, somewhat sleepily, the witness protection program.

"All you have to do is rat on a mafia capo and let Uncle Sam do the rest. I think my family can help. Nobody will know you. Fresh start. I'd pick a name like Mary Smith and live in Duluth."

They both laughed.

"Sophie, I love you. I can't imagine life without you, ever. Thanks."

They hung up. Emma texted David, "miss u."

He responded, "miss u 2."

On Sunday morning, Emma sat down with her mom and dad in their study.

"Honey, we're so proud of how you've done at school this year," Clara said. "We were concerned that you weren't ready to return but you've shown how tough and resilient you can be. On the other hand, we're not so excited about some of the friends you've chosen to associate with."

"Mom, Dad," Emma said, "I appreciate everything you both have done for me. I mean that for my whole life, not just since you know what. You two mean everything to me. Plus, you have both trusted my judgment when I've had to make big decisions. I remember four years ago you were ready to kill me about Sophie, and that's turned out better than any of us could have imagined. Sophie, other than you guys, is the best thing that has ever happened to me. She's a rock."

"We agree," Joe chimed in.

"Dad, it's not in Mom's makeup to have deep seated dislike for other people, I mean other types of people. I've seen her with the laborers, the Asians in town, and the few blacks that live around here, like Mr. Adams at high school."

Joe grumbled and folded his arms. Clara sat quietly.

"At the moment, I have had a couple of dates with a guy named David Milton," Emma continued. "David is a surgical resident at the U and he is Jewish. He's been a godsend because without him I don't know how I would have been able to finish the class that gets out late. Bad choice of class times, I guess, but I really enjoy the class and I needed the credits in Fine Arts to graduate.

"I did ask him out and then found out afterward that he is Jewish. I had a great time that night, my first night at a social gathering with a guy. And I felt comfortable. That was huge for my confidence, which hadn't been so good before that. Dr. Cohen-Finer, you know the shrink, also agreed that getting my confidence back is so important."

"I understand all that, dammit. But I'm not going to change," Joe said, fidgeting in his chair. "Sorry, it's the way I feel. Lots of people feel that way too around here."

"Let me finish," Emma said. "I plan to date other guys when I return and see how things go. My date with

Hank on Friday showed me pretty much that people around here are always going to judge me. For good or bad, judge my character on the events of last year. They can't help it, and you would probably do the same, maybe me too."

"So, it's over with this Jew asshole," Joe said.

"No, I didn't say that I wouldn't see him. He's been nice and we're friends, maybe even good friends. At this point, I don't care who his parents or his grandparents are. He's kind, he's super intelligent and he doesn't care that I am Christian. We're not getting married, we're not having sex."

Clara eyes opened wide. Joe clenched his jaw.

“And I think you know that I'm not having sex with anyone, so put that out of your mind. Please. And..."

“Okay, okay,” Joe interrupted. “I get a little of the picture. We'll give you a little discretion here but I have concerns you are not making really wise decisions. And I'm not sure when you might be trusted completely. These Jews are all sneaky and I don't know what his motives might be but his kind always has some agenda."

"Please stop that. David Milton does not have an agenda. He's working his butt off to become a surgeon. That's more than my lazy brother ever did or will do. Do you want me to tell you what Alan's agenda is? Numbers one to ten are to mooch off you while doing as little work as possible."

"Watch it Emma," Joe, now angry, said. “You're skating on very thin ice right now. This isn't about Alan. This is about you and your choices. This is about your choices and how they affect my family. Our support for you staying in Seattle is conditional on me feeling comfortable that you are thinking about the family. Right now I'm not so sure. I want you to think good and hard about these things when you return to Seattle."

"I called you first, remember," Emma said to her father. "I was thinking about you. I didn't try to do this behind your back, right?"

"Right. But calling me just before you're about to rob a bank doesn't make it any less of a crime." Joe laughed at his own lame humor.

"Not funny...well maybe a little funny," Emma said.

All three smiled a bit.

"Well, I want to start getting packed. Don't want to be on the road too late."

"Go," both Clara and Joe said together.

Chapter 25

Back at school, Emma had only a few classes left in the quarter.

She met with her advisor, Dr. Miller, who reminded her that a senior project was a requirement to graduate and gave her some suggestions. Dr. Miller hadn't pressured Emma with the needed project when she first returned to school, knowing that she didn't need any additional stress.

"Dr. Miller, you've been so kind to me. I can't thank you enough."

"Emma, you have thanked me. You are one of the best students I have now, or ever have had, for that matter. Given your trauma, to come back like you've done, is close to Herculean."

Emma nodded and paused, then spoke, "Dr. Miller, you're Jewish aren't you?"

"Why yes, why do you ask?"

"If you have time I'd like to talk to you?"

Emma and Dr. Miller talked for three hours. Dr. Miller cancelled two scheduled meetings. His brother's wife had not been Jewish and when she converted, her family cut all ties. Their marriage had not been easy but they persevered and, in time, her family acquiesced to a degree.

"You know that I will be there for you whatever happens," Miller said.

"Professor Miller, thanks again. Could I come back and talk about issues if they come up."

"Of course, Emma. Planned or unplanned, I'll try to make time. I would suggest that your life would be simpler if you could find someone of the same background. You must know that dating other men now seems like a reasonable plan, but you might lose this David by so doing. Life isn't easy and the choices we make are sometimes impossible. Often the choices are not between good and bad, but bad and even worse."

As she was about to leave, Dr. Miller reiterated that he'd do what he could if she needed anything.

Agotini cancelled Monday's class, but Emma went to the ER anyway at 3:30 to talk with David. She wanted to explain the Thanksgiving weekend in person.

Unfortunately, David came into the lounge to explain that one of the residents was ill and he'd have to pull an extra half shift.

As he retreated back into the ER, David said, "I'll give you a call tomorrow after work."

Emma had her regular appointment with Dr. Cohen-Finer on Tuesday. David and Sophie had been correct that Cohen-Finer was also Jewish. Dr. Cohen-Finer worked on the clock and Emma couldn't nearly get everything out that she wanted to say.

David didn't call Tuesday night.

Wednesday evening was crisp and clear for the walk home with David. Emma wanted to tell him the varied conversations she'd had over the past five days: mother, father, brother, Sophie, Dr. Miller and Dr. Cohen-Finer.

Her brother's one liner of 'I'll kill the Jew prick before he marries into my family' stung more than her dad's lecture. Her mom just wanted Emma to be happy and put the events of last summer behind her. Clara, however, did think that life would be easier if she met someone her dad and brother might like. Drs. Miller and Cohen-Finer had also the same comment that Emma should see other men.

“If I were you, I'd marry David tomorrow, no questions asked.” Sophie said, balancing the equations.

Onto their second latte huddled in a corner of the HUB's cafeteria, Emma said to David, "I don't know that I'm strong enough to fight my family right now. I need as many people in my corner as I can muster. I don't think I can handle my parents pulling the plug on supporting me. My dad said as much."

"I'm not giving you up so easily,” David said. “But, if you need to date a little bit, I'll try to understand. Shit, no! Actually I won't understand. We'll still be able to go out some, right?"

"Of course. Maybe a little more on the QT, though."

"Whatever," said David.

"Yeah, whatever,” Emma said. “God, I hate the word, whatever. Anyway, I am going to Cabo over Christmas with my parents and Alan and my new ditz sister-in-law. Sophie's family is flying in from Jersey and we've rented a large house, 8 bedrooms with servants and all. Should be pretty cool and I could use some sun. Maybe the trip away will give us a little reflection time."

"Yeah, but that's not for three weeks. That's nine walks home. You're going to be miserable in Mexico, so there."

"David, don't make it harder, please. I’m only so tough."

"You're tougher than you look and I'm the weak one here because I don't want to stop seeing you."

Chapter 26

David and Emma walked home every time Agotini had his class but they saw each other no more than that. He acted no differently, nor did Emma, but a little of the chemistry had been eroded with Emma's declaration of the need for variety.

The following week, both Emma and David went out on set-up dates.

David's Aunt Alice found him a 'nice Jewish girl', although two years older and already divorced. They had little in common other than David's aunt. He called his aunt to thank her. He didn't tell Alice that he'd have divorced the girl faster than her first husband.

Emma's date with an engineering graduate student bored her to tears. She couldn't tell if he knew anything about her past and, in fact, couldn't tell anything about him at all.

Finals week came and Emma and Sophie spent most of the time studying. Emma did not call David. Agotini had already given Emma an A+ with recommendations to match. Emma's Business Management final was inconveniently scheduled on the very last day of finals week.

Sophie's last final ended three days before Emma. As soon as Sophie finished, she left for the east coast. "See you in Mexico, be good...but not too good" was her standard goodbye phrase.

By Thursday night, three-quarters of the house had already left for home or vacation. Emma went to bed at 11:00 p.m. The final was not until 1:00 p.m. the next afternoon.

At 3:00 a.m., Friday morning, two intoxicated

fraternity boys, on a dare and a bet, put a twenty-two foot ladder against the GiGi house, broke a window, and entered a room in Emma's mostly vacated wing. Emma, dead to the world, heard nothing.

As a disguise, the boys covered themselves from head to toe in foamy shaving cream once inside the sorority. Their mission was to steal, undetected, at least five different size bras on a one hundred fifty dollar bet.

After getting lucky in the first room with three different bras, they entered the hallway. The first two rooms were locked tight. Emma's room, the third, was also locked, a new, but understandable, habit for Emma. The boys, now frustrated, were cranking hard on the doorknob. Hearing the ruckus, Emma, alone and without Sophie for the first time in three months, was awake but disoriented.

Unfortunately, the two crazies now assumed that all the rooms would be locked. The bigger, and likely drunker, of the two stood back and kicked in Emma's door. They both rushed in, flashlights scanning the room frantically searching for dressers, needing only two bras for one hundred fifty dollars of glory and fame.

Emma cracked. The screams she emitted were so intense and loud that the boys, now frightened, starting yelling back obscenities trying to quiet Emma. No luck. The two left, only to find the door to the original room which held the open window and ladder locked behind them. They kicked in the door, shattering the frame, then rushed to the ladder. The first boy fell ten feet from a missed rung and broke his leg. The second, sliding down the ladder too quickly, lacerated both hands down to the tendons. The Seattle and University police were there within minutes and both boys were arrested. By 4:20 a.m. all the commotion had died down, the remaining girls had gone back to their rooms to try and get some sleep. Most were leaving early in the morning to go home or out of town.

Francine never left Emma's side. An uncontrollable anxiety attack hit Emma. Emma began hyperventilating until her lips and fingers became numb. Francine Frost gave Emma two doses of Xanax as prescribed by Dr. Cohen-Finer for such an event. Dr. Cohen-Finer's answering service got them to an on-call psychiatrist at the UW who calmly suggested taking Emma to the ER where she could be evaluated.

Using Emma's cell phone, Francine called Clara Braza for permission to take Emma to the ER. The phone kicked over to voice mail. Francine, identifying herself, left a frantic message to call immediately that a crisis had developed. She did the same for Joe Braza, who also didn't answer. Their house phone forwarded to Clara's cell and Francine left a third message.

Francine was frantic. She then called Sophie in New Jersey realizing that it was already 7:30 am on the east coast.

Francine updated Sophie on the evening's catastrophe and that she couldn't reach the Brazas. Sophie thought for a second. "Call David Milton. His number is on Emma's speed dial. He'll come. First, let me speak to Emma."

Francine walked back into Emma's room and handed her the telephone.

"Emma, it's me Soph. Doing okay now?"

"I wish you were here," Emma said. "I got so scared. It was crazy. We're trying to reach my parents. I am so tired. Francine gave me some pills to relax, but I am so wired I can't relax."

"Emma, you're going to be fine. Just another bump in the road. See you in Mexico. Call me when you get home, okay?"

"Sure, Soph. God, I'm so tired. I wish I could sleep." Emma dropped the phone on the bed but remained wide-awake and severely agitated.

Francine took the phone and walked into the hallway and called David Milton. He had been sleeping, but as only surgeons can do, he was awake, alert and competent within seconds.

"Dr. Milton, this is Francine Frost over at the GiGi house. We had an incident tonight. Two drunken boys broke into Emma's room on a prank. She is rattled and I can't reach her parents. Sophie Picone, who's back east already, suggested that I call you."

David said, "I'll get dressed and run over. I'll be there in less than 10 minutes."

Within seconds of hanging up, Clara Braza called. Francine filled her in on everything, except talking to Dr. Milton. Clara asked if she could talk to Emma.

"Emma, Emma, this is Mom."

"Mom, I am so scared right now. I know that the break-in is over and I wasn't hurt, but I can't stop seeing things. I feel like I'm being burned alive, my chest, my breasts are on fire, the cigarettes are burning me. I'm afraid to close my eyes."

"Honey, everything is going to be all right."

"Mom, Sophie's gone home. I'm all alone. I don't trust being alone. Can you or Dad come here?"

"Dad's in New York City and I'm in Ellensburg visiting Marv and Sarah."

"Mom, can you come here. I don't want to go to the emergency room and have strange people asking me hundreds of questions. Dr. Cohen-Finer is signed out. I need someone that I can trust. I don't feel safe."

"Emma calm down. I will leave in the next twenty minutes. I will be there in two hours or so. I'll have Marv or Sarah come with me."

"Mom, don't speed, be safe. If I know you are coming, I'll try to be okay. Keep your cell phone on so I can call."

"I'll be there as quickly as I can. Goodbye, honey. You hang in there. Let me speak to Mrs. Frost."

"Mrs. Braza, it's me, Francine."

I will be leaving Ellensburg in twenty minutes or less. I will be there in under two hours. Keep Emma in the house unless you feel something is terribly wrong."

"Okay, Mrs. Braza. I'm scared. Emma's not been like this since coming back to school. Before you called back I talked to Sophie in New Jersey. She thought I should call Dr. Milton, that boy that walks her home. He's very calming to her although I haven't seen him since before Thanksgiving. He said he'd come over."

"That's okay, Mrs. Frost. Sounds like it can't get worse. If he's no help, send him away. We saw these attacks a fair amount in the first few months. She may only need someone she trusts. I'll be there. I am giving you permission to use your best judgment. Goodbye. I'll be there as soon as I can."

Francine held Emma's hand and said, "Emma, your mom is on her way. She's only a couple of hours away. We're going to be just fine."

Seven minutes later, David called on Emma's phone and Francine answered. "I'm here outside the house. Knocking isn't working and I don't know where Emma's room is anyway."

"I'll be down in 20 seconds," said Francine.

Francine let David in and he followed her up the stairs. A few heads popped out of the doors. Francine had broken at least five house rules already letting David in and up.

Francine entered first and alone and sat at Emma's beside.

"Where did you go, Francine? You said you wouldn't leave me until my mother came."

"Emma, your mom is on her way. I have someone to see you."

David stood in the doorway but Emma didn't recognize him at first. Emma sat in the corner of the bed against the wall, wearing a T-shirt, and a pair of long pajama bottoms. Soaked wet with sweat, Emma's T-shirt outlined her breasts and her neck and face glistened from moisture. Her left hand clutched a blanket.

Emma's teeth chattered despite the heat in the room. Initially, Emma could only make out the outline of a man in a doorway. Her eyes widened and her teeth clenched and her arms started to rise together in a protective maneuver.

"No, please go. Please go."

"Emma, it's me, David."

"David?" Emma asked.

"Hi Emma. What's doing? I heard there was a break in by some crazy drunk frats. All okay now?"

"I'm so scared."

"Nothing will ever happen to you while I'm here."

David moved to Emma's bedside as Francine moved away.

David asked sweetly, “May I hold your hand.”

She nodded yes.

Her free right hand shook visibly as she brought it up to her chest, not to David. With both his hands, he reached over and surrounded Emma's hand with a firm grip and slowly pulled it toward him. Within seconds the shaking lessened dramatically.

"I'm here. You are safe. I am not going to leave you until you feel safe, okay?" David said.

"Yes, yes. Please stay. My mom is coming too. I didn't think you'd come if we called. Thank you, so much."

Francine showed David the bottle of Xanax. "She's taken two of these, one two hours ago and one forty-five minutes ago."

"Thanks, that helps." Turning back to Emma. "It's been a long night and you must be exhausted. Why don't you try to shut your eyes and get some sleep."

"I can't shut my eyes. I see things and I feel things."

"Okay, then, just put your head on the pillow. Don't close your eyes but get comfortable. The wall is cold and it doesn't help your shaking."

Emma moved away from the wall and turned parallel to the bed to lie down. David released one hand and tried to straighten out her blanket.

"Emma, let go of my hand for a second and I'll straighten out your blanket."

"No, no, Don't let go of me. Don't let go."

David returned both hands to Emma.

"Okay, Emma. I'm here and I'm not leaving and I'm not letting go." David eyed Francine to help.

First, Francine brought one of Sophie's pillows over to prop up Emma's head. She then straightened out Emma's blanket and said, "There you go. That should make you comfortable."

Emma looked at David with soft eyes that said 'thank you' and 'help' at the same time.

David spoke in a low smooth melodic tone, "Emma, I'd like to keep your desk light on, but turn off the overheads and Sophie's lights. Sound okay? I'm not leaving." He gripped Emma's hands a little firmer.

Emma nodded.

David motioned for Francine to turn off the lights. "Okay, let's see how it feels."

Francine turned off the overhead light at the door and then turned off Sophie's desk light. The room was considerably darker but light enough that everything could be seen.

"Emma, I am not going to leave you until you say go, or your mom comes. I promise. If you fall asleep, and I think you will, given the medications you've taken, I will not leave. You don't have to close your eyes, but I want you to relax. I am not going to stop holding your hand, so you'll know I'm here. Now try to rest."

The room was too hot to be comfortable, so David told Francine to lower the heat a few degrees.

Over the next fifteen minutes, Emma's pulse slowed, her breathing returned to normal, her skin color improved and her clamminess disappeared. She finally closed her eyes and fell asleep.

"Francine, she probably won't wake up for three or four hours. She's not likely to have any nightmares with that amount of drug in her, or at least until it starts to wear off. Does she take Xanax often, that might change things a bit? I'm not going to leave anyway. Promised I wouldn't."

"This is the first time I've given her these," Francine said. "Her parents gave them to me, through Dr. Cohen-Finer when she first came, to be used only in emergencies. I didn't know what they meant until now."

"You did good. Wanna be an ER nurse?" David smiled.

David had Francine bring a small ottoman next to Sophie's bed over to his chair.

"Don't turn off the light, I'll be okay," said David.

He put his legs up, never letting go of Emma's hand. He was asleep in ten minutes, another trait of surgeons, knowing how to catch winks of sleep on demand.

At 6:55 a.m., Clara Braza arrived. A sorority girl, on her way out, met Clara at the door. She introduced herself to the girl.

The girl, upset enough to forget introducing herself, started in, "Emma had a really, really bad night, Mrs. Braza. She scared me more than the crazy guys that broke in. She's better now. I think she's sleeping. Her doctor friend is still in the room alone with her, I'm pretty sure." She paused, thinking about what she said, "I mean he's in the room sitting near her."

Francine was paged and appeared, worse for wear.

"Hello, Mrs. Braza. Let me fill you in on everything, especially after you called."

"Sure. But let's go up," Clara said.

"Actually, Mrs. Braza, let me tell you how this all played out first. Once you go in there, I don't think it will come out as easily."

"Okay."

She related David's arrival and the events that transpired.

"Mrs. Braza, I don't think I could have gotten Emma calmed down. I gave her two sedatives, which did nothing as far as I could see. The on-call doctor told me not to give more. I don't know how much more harm could have been done by letting her go another two or three hours. I didn't know what to do but Sophie did when she thought you or Mr. Braza weren't reachable. Anyway, Dr. Milton was incredible. He was here in ten minutes. Calming, soothing, understanding. I don't know how much of his actions were just professional, being a doctor and all. But I think he clearly cares for Emma and that helped. Mrs. Braza, honestly, she clearly feels safe around him. Anyway, let's go up."

When they walked into the room, the small desk lamp remained on and Emma and David had not changed positions. Emma had kicked off the blanket as it took a while for the room to cool. Her T-shirt, still clinging wet, was rolled a bit above her belly button. Her left arm was across her chest. David's right hand held Emma's right and his left sat over his chest, mirroring Emma's position. Both asleep and both breathing easily.

Francine shook David's shoulder and he awoke quietly and was alert quickly. He didn't let go of Emma's hand until he saw Clara Braza. He slowly peeled his hand away from Emma who subconsciously searched for the missing grip, then fell back to sleep.

"David, I mean Dr. Milton, this is Emma's mother, Clara Braza."

"Hello, Mrs. Braza. It's nice to meet you. I've heard a

lot about you from Emma."

Clara didn't know what to say or how to say it. This man had just helped her daughter immensely. The thoughts of past and future horror never left Clara on her drive to Seattle, of going back into the hospital, more and more months of intense therapy, new drugs to try, new doctors to help, and then to find her daughter safe and calm.

"I can't thank you enough for being here. I was so worried that I didn't know if I could drive. My friend Sara drove and is downstairs, too afraid to come up and see Emma like she was just after the kidnapping. I know you've got to be exhausted. I think I can take it from here."

Francine chimed in. "Emma has her last final at 1 p.m. We post all the finals on the wall so no one ever sleeps through. I don't think she'll be able to take it though. I know she was ready because she went to sleep early."

David responded. "The sedatives will be out of her system by 8 or 9 a.m. If she's up to it, I'd let her take the final. Not doing so might just reinforce her fright. Can't tell what the prof might do. He'd have to create a whole new final just for her. He might balk at that. If she knows the material, well...well Emma's call I guess. Might just ask her."

Clara thought for a second, "We'll see. You may be right about not reminding her that she didn't finish out. Anyway, I can't thank you enough."

"I'm off today, or at least until 10:30 p.m. when I pull a week of evening duty. Call me if you need anything. Nice meeting you, finally." When Clara Braza said nothing, David left.

Emma woke up at 7:30 a.m.

"Where's David?" Emma asked.

"Emma, it's me, Mom. I'm here. I sent David home to bed. He'd been up all night with you."

"Oh, David promised he wouldn't leave."

"David told me he said he wouldn't leave until I got here, so I made him go home."

"Mom, he was so nice. He came right away. I hope you were nice to him."

"I was honey. He helped you, that's huge to me. I was very nice and very appreciative. You can ask Mrs. Frost."

Emma's grogginess lasted another hour. Francine, Emma and Clara had breakfast with the rest of the diminished house. Scrambled eggs, toast and coffee. Barely edible to Clara, who lied. Emma knew and said nothing. Clara and Francine couldn't help notice Emma's clipped speech, a sign that the effects of the prior night and the drugs lingered.

Clara, not sure what to do next, asked Emma, "You think we should just leave for home?"

"Well, I have a final at 1:00 p.m., " Emma said. "I'd like to take it."

"I don't know if you are up to it," Clara said. "You might not perform well or not be able to finish. I think maybe we can see if you can take it later?"

"You might be right. I am nervous," Emma said, "but taking it later, I don't think so. The professor is really tough and I don't think he'll make a new final for me. I'd like to try. I know the material pretty well."

"Okay. I'm exhausted and so was Sara. She checked

into the Deca Hotel on 45th. I'm going to join her and try to sleep, if I can."

"Mom, did David say he was going to work?"

"Actually, he said he was off today. He was going to work late tonight."

"Thanks. I'm going to see if he can take me to the final and then come back and walk me home."

Francine cringed a bit. Not what she wanted to hear from Emma in front of her mother.

Clara said nothing, just nodded and thought, *At this point all I can hope for is that Emma is safe, nothing more. I'll deal with Joe later, he's not here and doesn't understand.*

"If he can't, I think I'll be okay," Emma said.

Clara feeling very second fiddle, "Can you call him now and find out?"

"I should let him sleep and I'll call around 11:30."

Francine then stepped in, "Listen, if Dr. Milton isn't available, I'll walk you over. Your mom really should get some sleep until you are ready to drive back. She's got to be tired."

Emma and Clara nodded acceptance.

Clara left for the hotel and Emma went back to her room to study. She was still a little woozy from the drugs and thought she'd study lying on the bed. With a little forethought, she suspected she might just fall asleep, so she set her alarm for 11:15 and then opened her Business Management notes. She fell asleep within five minutes. At 11:15 she was awakened by the alarm. After a second or two of fear that she might have missed her final, she realized that she had more than ninety minutes to go. She immediately dialed David.

"Hi, Emma. Doin' OK?" asked David.

"Yes, ...yes. Thanks to you. My mom is here but I guess you knew that? Did you talk to her?"

"Well, pretty much to say 'Hello, you're welcome for helping Emma, let her take her final, good-bye."

"I'm sorry she acted that way."

"Your mom was fine. Francine introduced me as Dr.-Milton-the-Jew, and the one personally responsible for killing Christ. That probably kept the conversation shorter than it might have been."

"David, not funny."

"Actually it was that short but she acted appreciative and nice. She was so concerned about you and was obviously stressed to the max by the situation and the late night drive. She knew I had been there for a while and thought it wise to let me get home and sleep. She was okay, don't be too harsh."

"My final is at 1:00 p.m. at the Business School. After last night, any chance you could walk me there? I'll be leaving for home right after the test and...

"Emma, stop, of course, I'll walk you there. I have to finish my article so I'll take my laptop and work in the Business School library. Then we'll walk back."

"Really, that's great."

"I've got to get a few things together. Is there WiFi in the library?"

"Yes, but you might need a business school login. Not sure the Med Center login will work there. Keeps the riffraff out of the library. My ID is easy...emmab123. My password is 321Bamme, which is the ID backwards with only the B capitalized."

"Cool, I can remember that. See you at 12:20, okay?

"Perfect, bye and thanks again."

Francine came into the room a few minutes later knowing Emma might fall asleep.

"Doing okay."

"Yep, David will be here at 12:20 to walk with me. Thanks anyway. You've been great. Hopefully when we've all left, you can get some rest."

It was a blustery mid December day in Seattle, but no rain. The outdoor wind and chill felt good and helped Emma get rid of the drug effects from the night before. The two didn't say much during the walk as Emma's mind focused on the upcoming final. As they neared the Business School, David crossed to Emma's opposite site and took her left hand in his right.

"I held on to the other for so long, I didn't want lefty to get upset at being unnoticed," he laughed.

He let go of her hand and she immediately regrabbed it.

"You are such a cornball. Thanks so much again for coming. I don't think I would have ever gotten to sleep."

"I'll be in the library, so when you're done come and get me. I've got your ID and password."

"The final is over by 3:30 so I shouldn't be later than 3:45, okay? Wish me luck."

"Knowing you Emma Braza, luck will have nothing to do with it, but good luck and break a leg. Just in case you forgot, here's an energy bar for the break, if there's one."

Emma smiled and produced the same energy bar in a different flavor. "I'll keep yours for luck and you keep mine for the library."

The final format had been published: sixty minutes of multiple choice questions, then a fifteen minute break and then sixty minutes of short essay questions. Emma breezed through the exam.

As they exited the library, David asked, "So how'd you do?"

"Really good, I think. I am so glad you suggested to my mom and Francine that I take the final. They may have talked me out of it. That would have been a huge mistake."

"Not all my advice works out."

"This one did. My mom will probably be at the sorority waiting to go. She has her friend, Sara, from Ellensburg with her so we'll need to stop to drop her off. I am sure she's talked to my dad by now and I'm not sure how that might have gone. Knowing him, he'll not want me to come back for winter quarter.

"I expect a little fight in Mexico but I'll have Sophie to help. I hope that my nightmares don't come back. That won't help my argument. Maybe better if you don't say hello again. She'll just tell my dad that you came back to the house and that'll make him even more leery of my mental status."

"Emma, you'll be fine. You have to believe that."

"I just couldn't stop being scared. I haven't felt out of control like that for months. I mean the nightmares come and go, but I just felt like I was being burned again. I was really scared. I'm not going to tell them. I will tell Sophie, though."

"You might have Mrs. Frost put a few Xanax, those sedatives she has, in an envelope for you to take to Mexico. Tell Sophie you have them and if you, or she, feel that you're getting out of control, take one. Okay?"

"Why do doctors always think the worst can happen?"

"Actually, the best happens mostly, but when the worst arrives, a little preparation can't hurt."

As they neared the sorority, Emma stopped.

"Close enough. I wish you could come to Mexico with us. I wish my family could see how nice you are and how much you've helped me. I wish we could go dancing at Señor Salsas in San Jose del Cabo and take a day trip to Hotel California in Todos Santos and lie on the beach, talking and soaking up the rays."

"Me too. But, I gotta work. I traded call around so I'm covering for most of Christmas. Not so bad, usually really slow."

Emma gave David a big hug and a kiss on the cheek and a soft kiss on the lips. "I am really going to miss you."

Emma walked the half block to the house alone. Clara was waiting in the dining hall having a cup of coffee with her friend, Sara, and Francine Frost.

"Hi Mom. Hi Sara. Ready to go?"

She gave Sara a big hug and kiss and an even bigger one to her mom.

Emma's bags were mostly packed and she threw them into Clara's car. Emma, in the back, fell asleep for most of the ride to Sara's house in Ellensburg. They stayed for dinner and then mom and daughter drove back to Walla Walla. Emma had so many thoughts racing through her head on the drive. David, Jewish, Joe, Alan, Cabo, finish school whatever it takes. The sun and warmth of Mexico, two days away, didn't even make it onto the radar.

Chapter 27

Joe Braza started in minutes after Emma walked through their front door, "No way you're going back to Seattle. I've had enough sleepless nights for a lifetime since you left. Getting that call in New York City, twelve hours afterward, scared me half to death. You are so lucky Mom was close to you at Sara's place and that she was willing to drive with Mom. You know you risked Mom's life, and Sara's, trying to get to you at breakneck speed."

"Dad, I'm fine. Honestly, I am. Any girl in that sorority, or anywhere, would have freaked out if two drunk crazies entered their room at four in the morning, covered with shaving cream and yelling. I was disoriented, alone in the wing, and I'm okay now."

"Clara, help me out here. You were there. You said she was a mess."

"Joe, we've just had her back for 12 hours. The whole incident was absurd. I remember a couple of your friends at WAZZU did the same thing to a group of new pledges at one of the sororities. One girl ended up in the infirmary. Duh. Let's see how Emma does over the next couple of weeks, here, and in Mexico. If she's okay, I'd like to see her finish school. We both know how important that is for her."

Joe, upset at the lack of Clara’s parenting cooperation, eyed his wife and spoke harshly, "I wish you'd support me on this."

Clara, hoping to end the discussion, said, "Joe, we'll see."

Before Joe could say more, Emma gave her dad a big hug and kiss. "Thanks, you guys are the greatest."

Emma headed for the door.

Joe, not done with his directives, said, “Whoa, there. Where ya goin?”

“Dad, I've really got to get packed for Mexico.”

“Emma, you are trying to dodge me. I don't think you're listening.”

“I hear you Dad but I'm okay. Mom was there. She heard how crazy everything was from Francine Frost. I'll be okay. Sophie and I made a pact to get through this year so we could both graduate. I've just got to go back.”

Clara immediately ended the conversation, “Go, finish packing so we're not up all night.”

Emma knew that her mom rarely stood up to her dad. By doing so Emma felt her mother had made a statement. *The winery is yours, Alan may be yours, but Emma is mine. I would like to have the final word on some decisions regarding my daughter.* Sometime in the next day or two, Emma knew that she and her mom were going to have a talk with some laws laid down.

Clara came into Emma's bedroom minutes later, “Need any help?”

“No, I think I've got it. Thanks so much for being in my corner. I needed that. I needed to know that someone trusts me and will let me make my way. Mom, I am going to finish school on time. I've got to. I promised Sophie that I'd finish the year with her. She would have stayed in an apartment but chose to return to the sorority to be with me. I can't abandon her. Be my champion. I won't let you down.”

“Let's get through this vacation with no melt downs. Then, I'll get you back to school.”

Without saying a word, Emma circled her bed and gave Clara a long overdue "*i luv u*" hug.

* * *

Baja California Sud was glorious.

The villa sat in a semi-contained beach front development between Cabo del Sol and San Jose del Cabo.

Alan came with his current wife, number two, Monica, a hair dresser/private masseuse. Monica was the same age as Emma and Sophie but any comparisons ended after the year of birth. The 'lights were on but nobody was home' described Monica perfectly. Alan didn't see it or didn't care.

Next door, sharing the beach in a similar villa, was a family from Columbus, Ohio, the Bairds. They came with two sons, a daughter-in-law and two delightful granddaughters, 2 and 4. One son, Brad, single, was a second year law student at the University of Michigan.

Sophie, Emma and Brad found each other on the first day. Together they explored all the nearby towns. Emma's fluency in Spanish made for some delightful stories. Emma and Sophie loved to bargain. The girls would place Brad at the store entrance while they shopped. During the bargaining, the girls would keep looking back at Brad who had been instructed to keep shaking his head 'no' until the best deal was reached. Worked like a charm.

The three drove up the west coast to Todos Santos, and had drinks at the landmark Hotel California, made famous by the 1977 Eagles song of the same name.

When the men chartered a boat to go fishing, Emma, Sophie and the Bairds' daughter-in-law, Carol, with the two babies, decided to go snorkeling at Playa Santa Maria, just a few miles from their rented villa. Monica came but had no interest in getting in the water.

"Shit. Too cold and too salty for me. Don't know how you tolerate it." Monica declared. Monica hadn't realized that the Gulf of Mexico had salt water.

When two large snorkeling boats from Cabo San Lucas dropped anchor in the bay and discharged fifty snorkelers, Monica decided she needed to be the show rather than the fish. She took off her flimsy bikini top and walked the beach. Her store-bought forty-six D cups kept the men on top of the water until the police showed up and explained to her that topless was a no-no in Mexico. Only Emma's knowledge of Spanish kept her from getting arrested. Emma explained to the Federales that her sister-in-law had been injured in an auto accident and wasn't right in the head. Emma promised to watch her more closely and that the topless exposure wouldn't happen again. Monica had no idea what Emma was saying. Alan thought the incident was hilarious when told that evening. Clara prayed silently that night that this daughter-in-law would have no children. Emma, if she had been asked, would have thought they deserved each other.

Brad liked Emma and Sophie equally in the beginning and gave both the same attention. On the fourth or fifth day of the two week trip, he started directing attention almost solely to Sophie. On the way to breakfast in the morning, Emma asked Sophie what was going on.

"Sophie, is Brad ignoring me on purpose. What'd I do?"

"I don't know Emma. You didn't do anything but I agree he's ignoring you. I'll ask him when we're alone."

"Sophie, I'm not jealous, if fact, I'm happy for you. Just thought it a bit strange."

Later that morning, Sophie pulled Brad aside.

"Brad, pretty obvious that you're not talking to

Emma. What's up?"

"Is it that obvious," Brad said. "Alan got me alone yesterday morning after breakfast. He told me about Emma's kidnapping and rape and that she'd developed a unpredictable and volatile personality. He suggested not to try to get close to Emma, that she was damaged goods and could become violent. He suggested I Google her if I didn't believe what he was saying. He also told me that she had a thing for Jews. Alan then went off on how he'd never allow a Jew into his family. I admit I didn't see any of this in Emma, but I did Google her. I had no idea."

"Emma's fine," Sophie, spitting mad, responded. "Emma is my best friend and if I had a real sister, I would want her to be Emma. When the three of us are together, your attention needs to be shared. Alan Braza is a low-life-piece-of-shit and a liar. If you can't see that you're blind. Emma is the least volatile person I know. The business about Jews is absurd. She went out with one Jewish guy and her father and brother went ballistic."

"Sophie, Sophie. Hold on. I didn't put much stock in Alan's advice but the Web stuff is pretty out there. As for the Jewish business, I didn't believe a word. Half my class at Michigan Law is Jewish and a good percentage of my friends from high school in Columbus and undergraduate years at Ohio State were too."

"Then why are you being so mean to her."

"I'm sorry. I should have talked to you first. I won't let it happen again. Shit, I feel sorry for Emma having to deal with a jerk for a brother."

Sophie recounted the conversation with Brad to Emma, which in hindsight was a mistake.

"Sophie, I swear I am going to kill him some day. I hate him. I hate him with all my soul. He's a rat bastard..." Emma went on for another minute.

"Stop. Stop!" Sophie pleaded. "If you get too emotional with Alan or your parents, you could jeopardize your return to the UW. Just calm down and let's take a long walk on the beach to gather our thoughts."

Emma confronted Alan alone in the house the next day.

"You are a fucking asshole," Emma said. "Who gave you the right to talk to Brad about me? Why would you say all those vicious lies. I am doing the best I can and you don't have enough decency or sense to stay out of my way."

"Fuck you," Alan said. "I can say what I want, when I want, to who I want. Plus, to me, you are one crazy bitch. You treat my wife like shit. So, fuck you."

Emma, doing everything she could to keep her composure, said, "You stay out of my life and I'll stay out of yours."

Emma didn't have leverage. Alan didn't care and, worse, didn't need to care.

Against Sophie's better judgment, Emma complained to her parents.

"Mom, Dad, Alan has been undermining my relationship with Brad. He's been telling Brad terrible lies about me. I tried talking to Alan and he just doesn't care."

"I'll talk to him." Clara said. "He feels you and Sophie aren't being nice to Monica. She is his wife and your sister-in-law, like it or not."

Looking only at her mom, Emma added, "You know

that any relationships I might have in the future will be made difficult because of my past. You saw that with Hank Ward. Having Alan lie to any potential boyfriend that I'm crazy doesn't help."

Clara repeated, "I'll talk to him."

Joe Braza showed little or no understanding at all, arms folded and lips pursed, perhaps as a test to see how she'd handle stress, or that he agreed with Alan.

Sophie and Brad continued to be attracted to each other and for the last four days of the trip, Emma covered for Sophie who would sneak out at night to meet Brad. Emma thought that the two of them matched perfectly.

As the vacation wound down, and with Emma as a witness, Brad promised Sophie that he'd call her when he got back to Ann Arbor.

"Spring break is only three months away," Brad said. "Maybe we can meet somewhere."

Later that evening, Emma, alone in the bedroom and waiting for Sophie to return, closed her eyes and thought. *I am damaged goods and will be damaged goods my whole life, regardless of what I do or don't do. I feel like I'm navigating in the dark, without lights, on a winding road with potholes. I guess that the road back isn't straight.*

Emma, keeping her thoughts to herself, even from Sophie, made a monumental decision as the families said "Adiós" to Mexico.

Sophie came back to Walla Walla with Emma and, with no visible objections from Joe, they both headed back to Seattle for the start of winter quarter.

Chapter 28

The girls returned to school on the second of January. School started on the fourth.

Immediately after throwing her suitcase on her bed, Emma called David. She got his voice mail and left a message that she had returned and wanted to see him.

David called back fifteen minutes later.

"Emma, hey, you're alive," David said.

"And tan. I missed you," Emma said.

"You didn't call."

"It's too expensive to use my cell from Mexico unless you're on some special plan. The house we stayed in had no Internet. My dad got one for his cell phone for business and we were supposed to make all our calls back to the states on it. I didn't think calling you from his phone was a good idea. I'm sorry. Still, I did miss you."

"Okay, I admit, I missed you too."

"School starts on the fourth. What's your schedule like?" asked Emma.

"ER is done. I'm in Dr. Henderson's lab doing some research this month. Then I have a two month elective at UC San Francisco, February and March. Starting in April, I am back on general surgery until July 1. Next year, as senior resident, I will be at the UW most of the year running one of the surgical services. I don't need to walk you anywhere this month, do I?" asked David, knowing the answer.

"No, no. All my classes will be during the day, I made sure of that. I'll be fine. I am going to take a full load this quarter and then I only need to do a senior Business School project in the spring and I'll graduate in June. I've got to get my proposal in to Dr. Miller by the end of the month. Still don't know for sure what I'm going to do."

"Did you meet any interesting guys in Mexico?"

"Actually, I did. Brad Baird, second year law student at Michigan. Tall, handsome, athletic, intelligent, total hunk and eligible. I think he fell in love."

Silence until David said, "And?"

Emma, laughingly continued, "And what? Oh, that. He fell in love with Sophie, not me. He thought I was dog meat."

"You are so mean," David said.

"When can I see you?"

"Lab animals and test tubes don't care when or whether I come or not. How about dinner at a Turkish restaurant I found in Madrona. There's a special ice cream place a few doors down and we can get a scoop of salted caramel. To die for."

"Sounds good after two weeks of burritos and enchiladas."

"Sophie wanna come? Okay with me."

"I'll ask, but I think she'll bow out."

"By the way, what's your schedule on Fridays this year?"

"11:00 to noon and 2:00 to 3:00. Why?" asked Emma.

As I'll be gone February and March, I do have a request for one evening this month. Friday after next.

Starts at 4:30 p.m. Wear grubby clothes and bring a change for something nice. Not a play or ushering. I have to make sure that this will work, but I should know by tonight. I couldn't have set these plans for sure since I didn't know if you'd even call."

"Of course I was going to call you. No confidence. This party, that's all you'll tell me?"

"Yep, you need to have a bit of mystery. See you at say 6:30 tonight for dinner, okay?"

"Come on, David. Tell me what it's about."

"Nope, bye."

Turning to her roommate, "Sophie, I missed him."

"I could tell from your voice. Another mystery evening, eh."

"Yeah. Every guy I go out with takes me to a movie or a cheap restaurant or a frat party. David always seems to find something really different and interesting."

"Shut up and enjoy the moment. Brad hasn't called me since we left Mexico. I bet he's got a girl in Ann Arbor he didn't tell me about."

"He'll call. Want to bet?"

Brad never called. For the first time in more than a year, Emma got to placate a distraught Sophie for a few days.

At dinner that night, Emma told David all about Mexico. Her mom sticking up for her, her brother being a shit, her brother's wife shedding her top, and Brad and Sophie." After a bottle of Cabernet, Emma and David were very relaxed.

"David, I have to ask you a serious question, okay?"

"Shoot."

“We’ve never broached this subject, but how much do you know about what happened to me last year?”

“Fair amount, I guess.”

“From where?”

“A bit from Sophie and my friend at the UW police, Rafe Gomez. I did a web search after talking to Sophie that first night before coming back later to meet you. Since then nothing.”

“Every guy I meet wants nothing to do with me once they've heard the story of my kidnapping. Happened even in Cabo with this guy, Brad. At the start, I’m pretty sure he was interested in both Sophie and me. Then he just stopped talking to me. Turns out my brother had told him to stay away from me, that I was damaged goods and unstable. But other guys too. I don’t even know how many guys won’t even go out with me just because I was news fodder for a week, 18 months ago. Anyway, why aren’t you put off by it?”

“Fair question. Admittedly, if I had been set up with you on a blind date, and had been forewarned, I might have said no," said David.

“Yeah, but you did accept the job of escorting me, knowing what had happened.”

“My agreement to escort you had totally to do with your kidnapping in a way, but those were not social dates. I was actually helping out Sophie more than you. She wanted you to feel safe. After two or three walks, I didn’t care what had happened to you. I liked what I saw and heard and felt."

Emma smiled.

David thought for a moment before continuing, "Maybe a fault of mine, being a rescuer and all. That’s what my mother has told me and my last girlfriend, Sally, said as much. When I first met Sally, just before she started law school, she was unsure of herself on a few levels. She needed the security of a boyfriend with a future, I guess. As she was finishing law school, she realized she didn't need anyone to watch over her. She, also, was intolerant of my work schedule, which interfered with her social goings on."

"Do you miss her?"

"Not a bit. Not even a little bit. And actually, I don't believe I'm a rescuer at all. I like you because you are smart, beautiful, funny, and make me laugh and I missed you. I wanted to call you in Mexico so bad it hurt. If you need rescuing once in a while, so be it. Most of the time, I think you'd be rescuing me from myself."

"Thanks, I guess."

"Actually, it's a good thing for me that men are turned off by your bad fortune. That leaves me as the only one who'll tolerate you." David smiled and held his hands up to protect himself.

Despite his protective posture, Emma threw a small piece of pita bread at him.

"So what's this thing we're going to Friday after next?"

"It's not a done deal yet. News at 11:00. I'll have to get back to you. All I can tell you is that we work, then eat, then listen."

Emma smiled. *I like him. I missed him. I am pretty sure that I need him.* The decision she made to herself at the end of the Cabo trip stood, unchanged. She, again, did not tell Sophie.

The next morning, on the way to class, she detoured to the Walgreens on 50th and the University Avenue. Two nights later David texted to say that "Friday is a go.

Grubby clothes and nice clothes to change into. I'll let you know what's up two hours before and not sooner."

Emma re-texted. "I hate u, I shouldn't even go out."

"u luv me and u will go out and have a great time."

Emma dove into her studies and finally came up with an idea for her senior project, '*Marketing of Wine using Social Networking.*' Dr. Miller signed off on the project so her last quarter at the UW was set.

The following Friday, David called her at noon.

"Okay, here's the deal. Tonight at 7:30 is the annual Juvenile Diabetes Foundation meeting at the Westin Hotel. My uncle, Bob, bought cooking lessons for ten at a charity auction to help prepare the dinner in the Westin kitchen, and then a place of honor at the banquet. So at 4:30 we start to prepare dinner for four hundred fifty people and at 7:30 we eat. The after dinner speaker is Ralph Potro who is talking...."

"I know Ralph Potro. He's sort of a friend of my dad. Actually a competitor."

"I knew you would know him. But I thought it would be fun to do all this anyway."

"I've heard his talk, if it's the one I think it is. *History of Winemaking in Washington State* or something like that."

"I guess that sounds right. I still want you to come."

"Who are the other people besides your uncle?"

"My mom, dad, sister, grandmother, Ben, of course, Aunt Alice and two of Alice's bridge buddies."

"David, how could you do this to me without notice?

Now, I am not coming."

"You are coming and there'll be no pressure. We're preparing a meal and then we eat and then we listen to a talk you've heard, and then you go home."

A nor'wester storm clobbered western Washington with blowing, cold rain and even a touch of non-sticking snow. David picked up Emma at 4:00 p.m. and fought traffic to be at the Westin by 4:30.

"I could hate you on so many levels," said Emma, arms tightly folded against her chest for the ride downtown.

"Oh, by the way, everyone else has been there since 4:00, so we'll be the last ones in." David said, handing his keys to the valet at the Westin.

"Wonderful, I'm late, great first impression," Emma said.

"They knew you had a class, no biggy."

As they entered the kitchen, everything and everyone stopped.

"High everyone, this is Emma, Emma Braza," announced David.

Emma remembered Uncle Bob from the theater. Everyone shook Emma's hand, if they had a free, clean hand or else waved. David's parents, Mike and Laurie Milton seemed nice but not effusive. David's sister, Rachel, a senior in high school, acted the most distant. Totally a 'whatever' look. Off in the back, chopping vegetables stood an older woman, smiling and waving a large knife, 'hello.' She had stacks of carrots and celery and peppers next to her on a chopping block.

"That's my grandmother, Esther Milton," David said. "She's a terror with a knife in her hand, even at eighty-one."

The head chef, Emile Vitresse, spoke up in a strong voice with a heavy French accent. “Everyone back to work. Vite, vite!”

“I can chop vegetables,” Emma said.

Aunt Alice quickly said, “Not a good idea. Grandma is a wizard with a knife and if you slow her down she’s likely to stab you.”

Grandma smiled. “Send her over. We’ll see what she can do. If she’s no good, I’ll send her back to David in pieces and he can put her back together.”

The entire entourage laughed, including Emma.

David let everyone know, “Emma’s tough.”

Emma settled to Esther Milton’s left with a prep sink in between, and without asking for any direction, grabbed a large knife and a cutting board and attacked the carrots. Stroke for stroke, slice for slice, carrot for carrot, celery stalk for celery stalk, pepper for pepper, Emma kept up with Esther Milton. Comically, Emma and Esther had identical strands of hair in their face and with each finished piece of chopping, Emma or Esther would blow the strand out of their way and go to the next vegetable. The rest of the amateur cooking staff could only watch with amazement as the two vegetable henchwomen finished off the stack in no time at all.

Emile Vitresse, also watching, remarked, “Trés bon, trés bon. Would both of you like to work for me full time. I can fire five of my staff, they are so slow.”

David, working with his sister, said, “Pretty amazing, eh?”

Rachel Milton responded, “One point for the blondie, I'm impressed. She’s obviously been in a kitchen.”

"Sis, technically she's not really blonde, more light brownish."

"Bro, technically she's auburn. But her hair is lighter than mine and she's not a member of our tribe. Therefore, she's a blondie. Live with it."

After chopping, Emma stood off in the corner, her arms folded like she was cold or protecting herself. Grandma Esther watched her and wondered what Emma was thinking.

Vitresse then gathered everyone around and taught them the correct way to pound veal and gave everyone a chance.

As they were pounding, a server came around with glasses of white wine on a tray.

"I thought a little 'vin blanc' with work would go well," said Vitresse. "Don't get so drunk that you pound a finger, eh." Vitresse then laughed at his own joke.

Everyone took a glass. Rachel, seventeen, looked at her mother, who shook her head, NO.

"Cheers and thank you for coming," Vitresse declared.

The whole group sipped the wine. David thought the wine tasted bitter, but he thought, *what do I know.*

Emma, not looking at all happy, looked at the chef, "Ce vin est mauvais." She turned to the group and said, "Don't anyone drink this."

Emille Vitresse responded, "Pas possible. Not possible."

The Milton crew stood dumbstruck at the audacity of this young and impertinent guest.

The hotel's sommelier came into the room and asked

what had just happened.

"I'm sorry. The wine has turned. It's no good," Emma said.

The steward carefully took the remaining glass meant for Rachel, still on the tray, smelled and then tasted the wine. He ran to the sink and spit it out.

"I am so deeply sorry to everyone here," the steward said. "I've never had a bad bottle of this wine before. It's pure vinegar."

He turned to Emma, "Thank you for calling it to our attention."

"No problem. What was it?" asked Emma.

"It was a Chardonnay from Potro's Vineyard."

"Those are usually pretty good wines."

"You know wine? You're young."

"I know wine," Emma said.

"Any suggestions then?"

"Potro's 03 Sauvignon Blanc is really good if you have it. Better than the Chardonnays."

"That is a great wine. I think we have a few bottles left."

Rachel Milton, and the rest of the Milton brood, stood in awe of this strange girl. David smiled.

David looked at Rachel. "Two more points for blondie, eh?"

Rachel just nodded.

Emma then worked between David's mother and aunt as they seasoned halibut. The three carried on light banter with a laugh or giggle every moment or so. All three enjoyed each other's company.

Aunt Alice came by David on the way to the sink and merely said, "Wow."

David's mom trailing a few minutes later gave David a peck on the cheek, "Emma's a doll. Why haven't we heard about her? She says you've been friends since mid-October."

"Sorry, Mom."

The 03 Sauvignon Blanc was perfect.

Once the guest pounders and cutters and seasoners had completed their tasks, they retired to reserved hotel rooms to change.

The table of ten sat in the front of the packed dining hall. Forty-four tables with ten guests each. Emma went to look for Ralph Potro to say hello, but did not see him, so she returned to the Milton table as dinner started. The emcee, a local TV newsman, greeted everyone and thanked them for coming. He made special note of the Milton table that had helped prepare the meal. He next welcomed the French, Italian and Spanish consuls and their staffs, in English. They had been invited because of the topic of the after dinner speaker. Each consulate had made a generous donation to the Juvenile Diabetes Foundation as well. The food was excellent and the wines, all from Potro's vineyards, reds and whites, were well chosen.

Emma sat between David and Rachel. Rachel, by this time, realized that Emma was the real deal and decided she needed to make friends. David could hardly get a word in to Emma as Rachel pried her with question after question about the UW and college life in general. Rachel had applied to the UW as a backup. She was hoping to get into an Ivy League school or the University of Michigan as first choices. On a large screen behind the dais, appeared the first slide of a Powerpoint presentation, entitled, *History of Winemaking in Washington State by Ralph Potro*

"Having a good time?" David asked Emma.

"Yes, your family is so nice. I hope they like me."

"You fishing for a compliment?" David asked. "Of course, they like you. I guess the talk is coming up pretty soon. If you want to leave early, let me know."

"I'll stay, but I haven't seen Ralph Potro."

An older man approached the dais, and pinged the mike.

"Can you hear me? Ladies and gentlemen, apparently a snow storm on Snoqualmie Pass had blocked I-90. Mr. Potro, our after dinner speaker is stuck and will not be able to give his talk tonight. I am so sorry for this big disappointment. You are all welcome to stay and talk for as long as you wish. Again I am sorry."

The man returned to his seat at the head table. Emma leaned over to David. "I've heard this talk twice before. I think I could give it if I had to. I've given wine tours at our winery since I was sixteen. Maybe not as well as Mr. Potro, but I know the material."

David hand wrote out Emma's credentials and approached the head table.

The president of the JDF read David's notes and scurried over to Emma. "Young lady, do you really think you can do this talk using Mr. Potro's slides?"

"Yes, I think I can." Emma said. "If I'm lousy, it's

still better than no talk."

"Oh God help me, I hope this works out," the JDF president mumbled.

David gave her some advice, "Emma, you know the subject, but you don't know his slides. Don't read from the slides, walk around and just talk like you talk to me. Throw in some of the good Agotini stories. They'll love them. Break a leg."

The president of the society ascended the dais and received everyone's curious attention.

"Excuse me, excuse me. Ladies and Gentlemen, as you know our featured speaker, Mr. Ralph Potro, is stuck on I-90. We are, however, fortunate indeed, to have a back-up speaker. Miss Emma Braza, currently living in Seattle, is a fourth generation wine maker, a friend of Mr. Potro and has heard him speak. Miss Braza's great-grandfather started the deLorraine Winery in Walla Walla almost a century ago. DeLorraine is one of the great Washington treasures."

The president had run out of information on Emma.

"Without further ado, I'd like a big welcome for Miss Braza."

Emma didn't even know the society president's name to thank him. As she mounted the dais, everyone could feel the tension. They were to be lectured by a pretty girl who was no older that most of their granddaughters. The audiovisual technician pinned a lapel microphone on Emma's dress.

"Thank you, everybody. I am sorry Mr. Potro could not make it, but I hope I can keep you entertained for the next hour."

She then welcomed the French, Italian and Spanish consuls.

"Bienvenue au consul français."

"Benvenuto al console italiano."

"Bienvenido al cónsul español."

Emma's apparent command of three languages calmed most people.

Emma understood that she couldn't talk exclusively from the slides. She asked for the first slide, a picture of Mr. Potro.

"Well, clearly I'm not Ralph Potro, sorry about that."

Microphone in hand, Emma started walking the stage, visually engaging people at the tables, turning only to quickly look at the slides as they came up. If she knew the subject or remembered Potro's talk, she would talk to the slide. The slides that specifically dealt with Potro's holdings she skipped.

Anything that reminded her of an Agotini story prompted a, *"Ya know there's an old tale about this."*

The gathered couldn't take their eyes off Emma. She was radiant, articulate, knowledgeable and told some of the most outrageous stories that Dr. Agotini had spun.

Emma talked for seventy-five minutes. Nobody stirred, nobody left.

"Anyway, I'd like to thank the JDF for allowing me to talk tonight," Emma said, ending the talk. "It was an honor. Merci beaucoup, molto grazie, y muchas gracias a todos," directing her final remarks to the consular tables. She then stood at the lectern, not sure of exactly what to do. A moment of eerie silence preceded eruptive applause. Emma just stood there smiling. The JDF president came up the stairs and helped her get unhooked from the microphone. He then thanked

Emma and had parting words for the audience.

David met Emma at the bottom of the stairs and gave her a hug and whispered, "You big show-off. You planned this. You brought on the storm just so Potros wouldn't show. You are too much."

Emma took a seat between Esther and Rachel. Rachel Milton couldn't speak. She was in total awe of Emma.

Grandma Esther couldn't stop smiling. She had only known Emma for four hours and for some reason they seemed to have a special kindred.

Emma then had to stand as a line of well wishers formed. Each consul came by to say hello and Emma spoke to each in their own language. A local reporter came by when much of the crowd had gone.

"Emma, I see you have recovered from your kidnapping and assault," the reporter said loudly. "It was sure big news. Do you think about it often? Do you think I might be able to set up a time for a private interview?"

Completely caught off guard by the question, Emma started looking around for David. A trigger had just been pulled. Joe and Clara Braza had cloistered Emma for months after her kidnapping to ensure that she was never interviewed. Emma walked around the table to grab David's arm for support as the reported followed. Her head turned right and left, looking for an escape and she said nothing.

Esther bounded out of her seat and insinuated herself between the trailing reporter and Emma.

"Young man, I don't know who the hell you are or what you represent, but this girl has just single handedly saved the JDF thousands and thousands of dollars in donations. How rude can one be to change the subject when we are all glowing in her aura. Kindly remove yourself and do not, and I mean do *not*, speak to Miss Braza again. I know the editors of every Northwest paper, personally, and I'll make sure you are summarily dismissed if you don't clear out."

Esther, hands on hips, didn't move until the reporter backed off a step. The reporter let out a mini snarl, turned and departed. Esther and Emma sat back down. Emma was now the one with the mouth agape.

Rachel added, "Atta way, grandma. You tell'em."

Esther asked Rachel and David to let her and Emma have a few moments together.

"Thank you, Mrs. Milton. I didn't know what to do," said Emma.

"Emma dear, I am not sure why, but I had suspected there are things about you that are guarded," Esther said. "Secrets for only the closest of the close."

"Thanks, I do, I guess. David knows and I don't really like to speak about it."

Esther rolled up her left sleeve revealing a series of numbers tattooed on her forearm. "We all have secrets that we can't really share comfortably."

"I've never seen concentration camp tattoos in the flesh. Where were you?"

"Auschwitz."

"I am so sorry," Emma said.

"Well, we're here talking, so we've both made some tough journeys. Maybe before I head back to Palm Desert for the rest of the winter, you'll come over to my place for tea and we'll talk."

"I'd like that. I'd like that a lot," said Emma.

"I am not going to ask David about you. I'll hear it from the horse's mouth, better."

The president of the JDF offered Emma the speaker's stipend intended for Mr. Potro. She declined and noted that since she used his slides it wouldn't be fair to pay her.

Emma and David arrived back in front of the sorority at 11:00 p.m. and David parked. Emma wasn't tired at all.

"I am on such an adrenaline rush right now. That was so fabulous. Your family is so nice. I really liked your grandma."

"She liked you and she's pretty picky."

"David, can we go to your place and talk."

"Sure, do you need to call Sophie?"

"Maybe, but we have an hour."

Off to David's apartment they drove.

Chapter 29

The weather outside remained Pacific Northwest miserable, cold, wet and windy. Even the short run from the alley parking, through the tricky locked security gate to the front of the house, chilled Emma and David to partial numbness. David opened the door to let Emma in first. The apartment was dark and cold. David switched on the light to the main hallway and then cranked the handle on the old water-heated radiators. To get the unit even modestly toasty would take ten to fifteen minutes.

David took off Emma's coat and had her put on his heavy sweater conveniently left in the foyer for his first fifteen minutes home. The sweater smelled of David. He ran into the bedroom and brought out a similar sweater for himself.

"Emma, want something to drink?"

"Bottle of water. Well, it's cold, maybe you could put on a pot of tea."

David started the water to boil and grabbed a small bottle of water from the fridge. He was tired from a rather full day. Emma, looking at photos on the wall, seemed to be full of energy, or was she just nervous? David couldn't tell for sure. David sat on the couch and slumped down.

"I'm beat," he said.

Emma approached the couch. She took her cell phone out of her pocket and silenced it. She put her left knee on the couch to David's right and then face to face quickly straddled him with the other knee. David was a little stunned with the seemingly aggressive move from the always guarded Emma.

"I had the most wonderful evening," Emma said sweetly.

"Me, too."

She stared for a moment at David's tired eyes, removed his glasses, then circled David's neck with her arms and kissed him deeply on the mouth. Then snuggled with David, putting her head in the crook of his neck.

"Emma, you okay?"

"Yes. I'm fine... David,... Will you make love to me now. I don't know when else I'll have enough courage."

She leaned back and pulled a small pill disk out of her pocket and popped it open, revealing oral contraceptives with five pill slots empty. David didn't need to be told twice.

David sat up with Emma still on his lap facing him. He put his arms under her, leaned forward and stood up. He carried Emma into the kitchen to turn off the boiling water and then carried her into his bedroom. The radiators now had the room warm enough to shed their sweaters. He laid Emma down on his bed and sat next to her.

He bent and kissed Emma on the lips softly and then repeated, "Emma, you okay?"

"Go slow. I'm scared."

"I will go very slow. Tell me if anything I do brings up bad memories. I don't want you to feel like you have no control. Okay?"

"Okay." Emma's eyes were glassy. "It was all so violent, so fast, please don't be in a rush."

David nodded and said, "Emma, will you help undress me?"

Emma nodded yes.

David unbuttoned the top button on his shirt to give Emma a lead as to what to do. Emma undid the rest. They took off his shirt together. He took off his undershirt halfway and let Emma pull it over his head. Emma had never seen him with his top off. He had a beautifully toned chest. She slowly massaged the front of his chest with both palms.

"Emma, can I undress you, slowly?" Emma nodded yes with just the smallest movement of her head.

David started with the top button, never taking his eyes off of her eyes. Certain that during the kidnapping and assault her clothes would have been ripped from her violently and painfully, David would move ever so carefully. After unbuttoning her blouse, he gave her a hug and then sat her up. He dropped the blouse behind her shoulders and let it fall gently onto the bed. He slowly undid her bra and allowed it to fall slowly forward as he gently and slowly moved the straps off her arms and let the bra drop to the side. Emma shivered even though the room was warm enough now.

She looked down at her chest and breasts and said, "The burn marks will never go away. I see them every time I look into the mirror to remind me who I am now." She slowly rubbed a punctate scar just above her right breast and then took David's hand to feel the same disfigurement. "They don't hurt to touch but I feel them when I'm scared." She then looked back into David's eyes, keeping his hand on her chest.

"I have never lied to you," David said, "nor will I. I know that the burns are there, but I don't see them. You know our lives are stories. I don't know how mine will turn out, nor yours. I know that your story will be full of wonders and awe. I'd bet the ranch that your story will have nothing to do with your kidnapping. It will be a small footnote at the bottom of an insignificant page. At least, it will be to me when I read it."

He moved his hands to her shoulders and held her at half arm's length.

"I will be strong for you and protect you for as long as it takes for you to be strong for yourself. I will try to never let anyone or anything hurt you again. You have to believe me."

"I know you will. I need to know that," said Emma.

"Emma, I am going to turn down the lights a little, okay?"

She silently nodded yes.

Remembering Emma's sorority room from the night of the break-in, he turned off the lights in the room, save a small desk lamp. David stood and undid his belt and the buttons on his slacks and slid them down with his underwear. Emma undid her skirt and slid it off. David put them on a bedside chair. Under the covers, she removed her underwear and left them at the bottom of the bed as David slipped in beside her.

He enveloped her in his arms and held her tight.

"Emma, I want you to relax and close your eyes. I don't want you to have any thoughts in your mind but you and me. I am going to kiss and explore every part of your body. I want to know everything."

"As tears flowed freely down her cheeks, Emma spoke, "David, I want you to know that I never stopped fighting. I never stopped trying to stop them. They would beat my head against the floor or the headboard to get me to stop, but I never stopped trying to stop them. You have to believe me that I did everything I could. They were too big and too strong for me to win or set myself free, but I never stopped trying. I never stopped."

"Emma, I know."

"David, let me finish. People said to me in the beginning, why didn't you try to fight them. I did. But then, someone else would ask me if I tried to stop them, so I thought that no one believed me. I fought, I never stopped trying."

"Emma, I know you did. You didn't have to tell me because I know you well enough that you would have never stopped fighting unless you were unconscious or they had killed you. You have to believe that I know how hard you tried to stop them. Never doubt that I think otherwise. But if it makes you feel better to remind me, that I need to know you tried, then tell me. Tell me whenever you think someone is doubting you and I'll confirm that you never stopped trying, not for a second."

David made love to Emma all night. He moved slowly and passionately bringing her to places she'd not been before, nor him. Twice during the night, while both were spent, she told him again "I never stopped fighting, I never stopped trying to stop them." She would tear up and so would he. Wounds that were so deep and in so many places, they both understood that they would have to visit them again and again.

Finally, Emma curled up in a ball and David surrounded her. They slept soundly until 10:00 a.m. when Sophie called David's apartment. Sophie had called or texted Emma's cell every thirty minutes since 7:00 am to no avail. She finally, out of desperation, tried David.

David looked at his phone and told Emma it was Sophie. She took the phone and spoke, "Hi, it's me."

Sophie, clearly perturbed, spoke quickly, "You okay? I was worried. I've called your cell every thirty minutes for the past three hours. You're supposed to call me if you're not coming back."

"I'm okay. Maybe better than okay. I'll be back to the house in an hour or two. Thanks. Yeah, I'm okay." Emma disconnected and turned to David who was just watching her talk. "David, what am I gonna do? I wish I knew."

"You'll figure it...no, we'll figure it out, somehow. I love you, Emma Braza."

"I love you, Dr. Milton." Emma smiled.

Emma returned home at noon in time for lunch. She had already eaten at David's. Francine Frost did not ask where she had been, she knew. Sophie had said something at 8:00 a.m. to Francine about not hearing from Emma. Both knew that Emma had gone out with David. Emma looked radiant which answered any questions that Sophie and Francine might have had.

After lunch in their room, Emma lay on the top of her bed just staring at the ceiling.

Sophie entered the room and watched her friend for a moment and said, "A penny for your thoughts."

"I've gone out with guys from the U, from Walla Walla and even Ohio slash Mexico. My past is always going to be there and, so far, no one wants to deal with my struggles, except David. I can look for ten years and never find anyone who will not have their doubts. David not only doesn't doubt me, he makes me feel strong, he makes me feel whole."

"Emma, I agree with everything you said. David is the best thing that could have ever happened to you."

"Sophie, I didn't tell you but I started the pill the day after we returned to Seattle. I didn't realize how much I had missed him. I had the most amazing time last night. Every time I go somewhere with him it seems to be amazing.

“I needed to find out for myself, and for David, whether I could ever truly make love without being afraid, of putting all my fears somewhere else and just enjoying the moment. Sophie, it was so wonderful. Maybe better than wonderful because I didn't know if I had the strength. He was so gentle and so understanding.

“I don't want to keep looking for other men. I may have to keep my dad at bay, but unless something crazy happens, I am going to live with David the rest of my life. I haven't told him that but I know it to be true."

Sophie had tears as she sat on Emma’s bed and hugged her, "Emma, you may have gone from the unluckiest girl in the world to the luckiest. I am so happy for you."

Chapter 30

The next three weeks, before David left for San Francisco, went quickly. Timing is everything. David had more free time as a lab rat than he'd had in five years. He and Emma spent as much time together as they could, without drawing attention from Francine Frost. Sophie made excuse after excuse for Emma's absences.

David and Emma made love as often as they could in the secure confines of David's apartment. Emma, so joyful about a step toward normalcy and a giant leap from her demons, looked at herself differently. Sophie jokingly told Emma that her constant smile was wearing on her. Emma felt completely at ease and started to take an active role in their love making. She felt whole, and free, for the first time in eighteen months. Her nightmares disappeared.

For appearances, Emma had two dates with graduate students. She made sure that both came into the sorority to wait for her, so that Francine would see them and then report back to Clara Braza. Emma made sure neither would ask her out again.

Emma enjoyed her classes and remained actively involved in sorority functions. She continued to leave the social events early to be with David, but her departures were consistent with her activities of the past year and raised no eyebrows.

Emma called home at least every other day, at times that she knew her father would be around. Joe Braza wasn't used to Emma's attention, but never complained when she talked about her classes and her social activities without mentioning David.

Near the end of January, Joe called Emma.

"Hey there, honey. How things going?"

"Great, Dad. Why the call?"

"I ran into Ralph Potro the other day and he told me about you speaking at some function in Seattle that he couldn't make. He said he had tapes of the talk and you were very impressive."

"Oh, didn't I tell you guys about that? Sorry. It was the Juvenile Diabetes Foundation Annual Dinner."

"How'd you get invited?"

Emma needed to lie to her father, hoping she wouldn't get caught. "I was invited by friends from the wine class at the last minute. One of their parents couldn't go and had paid for the seat. When Ralph Potro didn't show up, I told the officers that I had seen the talk before and could try to give it. Having no plan B, they let me go on. I thought I did pretty well. Not too different from giving a tour of deLorraine and then I added some stories from the wine class."

"Emma, I'm really proud of you. Ralph told me that he had gotten some great new material for his talk listening to you. I'd like to hear more."

"Dad, I've got notebooks full of good stuff from Agotini's lectures. I'll bring them home at spring break. Is Mom around?"

"No, she's out doing something. I just wanted to call."

"Thanks. I love you both."

The call ended and Emma was relieved that David hadn't been discovered.

Emma asked David to set up a meeting with his grandmother, Esther. Emma, using David's car, went over to Mercer Island on a Tuesday afternoon after classes. Esther, delighted to see Emma, had prepared some light sandwiches and had opened a bottle of deLorraine Pinot Grigio. Esther sipped her wine gingerly saying that she didn't handle alcohol like she used to. Emma laughed.

Esther told Emma again how mesmerizing she was at the JDF function.

"My grand-daughter Rachel has not stopped talking about you. Emma this, Emma that. She has raised you to 'goddess' status and wanted to come over today for the meeting. I told her no, that we had stuff to talk about, girl to girl."

"I'll get to the point, Emma dear. I felt that two different Emmas were present that night. The Emma, most seen, was the powerful, smart, hip girl in total control. The other Emma was scared and tentative, and holding something back. I may be wrong, but as one who has spent most of my life holding things back, I should know. I have not spoken to David, so I don't know any of your story, but that miserable son of a bitch reporter suggested that I am right. There is something you are hiding, no?"

Emma nodded.

Esther continued, "I've got things to share with you as well. You'd like to go first, or me? Either way is fine. If you can't talk about it now, then maybe sometime in the future."

Emma started and told everything she could remember about the kidnapping and assault and rape and torture, and what she'd learned afterward about the times she was unconscious.

"I really thought I was going to die. I really did. But I didn't want to die. I never stopped fighting or trying to escape."

Esther wept with Emma listening to her saga. Emma talked of her rehab, of her return to school, of her meltdowns, her nightmares, of Sophie Picone, of failed dates, of being tainted, of the eyes of people who knew, looking differently at her.

She told Esther how David had scared her, and then how he had rescued her on more than one level. She talked of her parents.

"My mom is somewhat weak, now, although I remember her as being pretty strong when I was young. She does what she can to protect me. My father and brother are both dominating and bigoted beyond reason."

She talked of the support she was given by Professor Miller and Dr. Cohen-Finer. Emma talked for much of two hours.

When done, Esther could only say, "Thank you for sharing. You are one of the most remarkable people I have ever had the pleasure of meeting. Even if you don't continue to be friends with David, I hope that we can remain close. I will always try to be a source of strength for you.

"I am planning to tell you things, some that I've never told anyone, not my children, not my friends, and not any psychologists that I've seen in the past. For sixty-five years I have been looking for someone to share these terrible, deepest thoughts. Our stories are so different in many ways, but so similar in others. We will never forget, we will never be completely free of the shame. My torture lasted for almost two years, although, unlike you, I was never physically harmed. Nonetheless, I continue to suffer and have nightmares to this day.

"My maiden name was Esther Wilensky. I was born in 1931 and I grew up in Lodz, Poland. I was the middle child of Chaim and Leah Wilensky. I had a brother, Saul, two years younger and a sister, Rene, who was seven years older. Rene was a talented ballet dancer with hopes of dancing at the major ballet houses around Europe. Rene was smart, tall, and athletic but, most of all, breathtaking to behold. I loved my sister with all my heart, as she loved me. But I admit to being jealous because of the attention paid to her wherever we went. My father was a chemist and my mother a concert pianist and piano teacher. Our family was well to do and respected throughout the Lodz community. Our family friends were both Jewish and non-Jewish.

"World War II and the Nazis changed everything abruptly. Some of the local non-Jewish authorities protected us as much as possible. We didn't have to wear Jewish armbands, when most did, and we didn't enter the Lodz ghetto. We moved house to house, wore disguises, and hid in attics. In the end, like most Jews, we were betrayed.

"Our family was rounded up in late 1943 and sent to the concentration camp at Auschwitz. Some of the families that helped us were shot by the Nazis. My brother and father were separated from us upon arrival at Auschwitz, and I never saw them again.

"Saul was gassed twenty-four hours after arriving. To the Nazis, he was too young to be of use. My father died in early 1944 from starvation and pneumonia. My mother's and Rene's arms were tattooed immediately. I was too young and would have likely been gassed, so I wasn't tattooed in the beginning.

"At the camp intake area one of the prison officers, in fact, the commandant, a Major Bermann, had been a dancer in his youth. On seeing Rene, the way she held herself, the way she walked, he knew she was a dancer. He asked if she would dance for him. Rene, seeing the reality around her, sensed that this might be our only chance of survival. Anyway, she danced for Major Bermann, and he spared her life. He wanted her to be his personal housekeeper, but we all knew what that meant. He was a mean and sadistic tyrant who asked everything of Rene, and she did her best to comply.

Quickly, she lost any sense of dignity and self respect, but she kept at it.

"My sister's only demand, from the start, was that my mother and I be spared. Then, I was tattooed, as the other workers, and they found a place for me on the assembly line at a nearby machine shop, even at age twelve. My mother died of typhoid fever within the first few months of being in the camp. She had completely disowned Rene for her actions. As long as I was alive and fed, Rene whored herself with this pig, Bermann. He beat her, tortured her, and disfigured her. She came to see me every day or two to make sure I was alright, and brought food from the officer's mess.

"As time went on, she was no longer the beautiful Rene that had entered the camp. She was still a teenager but looked so tired, so defeated and so beaten. Her face in those last months is etched in my mind. Major Bermann was growing tired of Rene and, as he did, he became meaner and more vindictive. Berman didn't hide the fact that he was culling the new arrivals to find a replacement. Later Rene told me she was certain that she would be gassed, as would I. But Major Bermann was summarily summoned away and we never knew what happened to him. Before the Germans could kill all the remaining Jews, the Russians arrived and freed the camp.

"Instead of being joyful by gaining our freedom, my sister was viewed as a pariah by the other surviving inmates. They taunted her day and night. I can certainly see why they thought that. Rene refused to use me as an excuse, for fear of getting me in trouble too. Seventy-two hours after being freed by the Russians, my sister hanged herself or was hanged by the remaining Jews. I never really knew for sure and it probably doesn't matter. If they hadn't hanged her, she would have done it herself. She told me she wanted to die. Regardless, I am alive today because of what she did.

"I have never stopped feeling the guilt and shame that I lived, when so many died. So many times I wished I were dead, and seriously considered suicide in the first year. But then everything Rene did would have been in vain. I finally decided that her sacrifice demanded that I pick myself up and make something of my life. But never have I stopped feeling remorse for being alive at the expense of my sister and the other Jews. I am regarded by many as a hero for surviving the camps. I don't feel anything like a hero, I only hope God will forgive me."

As they parted, Esther told Emma, "I am leaving for Palm Desert in a few days. I own a home there at an enclosed golf community called Indian Ridge. I haven't played golf or tennis for years but I enjoy the social aspects, friends, and the nice weather. Here's my address down there. Come whenever you want or call whenever you want. I'll be back in late May, but I want to see you again. If you ever need anything, I will be there for you, like your friend Sophie, or your professor, Dr. Miller."

Emma and Esther hugged and Emma drove back to the UW.

David left January 31st, for the Bay Area and a trauma rotation at San Francisco General. They would talk every day by video phone or on the web. Emma breezed through her courses and finished the quarter in late March. She still wasn't sure what would happen to her after graduation, but she knew that David had to be in the equation. Sophie was accepted to law school at the UW, but also at Columbia and Duke, both closer to home.

Emma came home after finals for Spring Break, and started to work on her senior project. Most of the work could be done away from school, but she didn't let on to that tiny tidbit of information to her mom and dad. Her parents had paid her tuition for her last quarter as an undergraduate and she returned to Seattle.

Emma made a decision that her family would need to know about David, and she tried to imagine of all the possible retributions that could happen.

Emma went to the registrar's office at the UW and asked to speak to one of the senior people on a personal note.

Mrs. Gladys Rogers, a veteran of thirty-two years in the Registrar's Office, said she had five minutes to spare to talk to Emma.

Emma laid her story out quickly. “I have one quarter to go, I am over 21 and my parents have already paid my tuition for the quarter. I need to know if they could demand the tuition back, if they are not happy with something I am doing?”

"Why would they possibly do that?" asked a curious Mrs. Rogers.

"I am going to tell them I have a boyfriend. A boyfriend that they are not going to be happy about. I was warned three months ago that seeing him might cause them to withdraw their support. Now that I am only a quarter from being done, I feel I can take that chance, depending on what you say."

"Not that it makes any difference, or is any of my business, but can I ask who or what your boyfriend might be? Just out of curiosity.”

"He's a surgical resident at the med school."

"Am I missing something?"

"He is Jewish."

"Oh, hmmph. I see. That's too bad, I'm sorry. Well Emma, there is little your parents can do against you for this quarter. You are no longer a minor and you've already started classes, right?"

"Right."

"Your tuition is not refundable. Trust me, I know," Rogers said.

"Thanks. Thanks for your time."

"Good luck. You may need it."

David returned from San Francisco on the evening of April Fool's Day. Emma picked him up in his car at SeaTac airport. David's return to work was not until the next morning. David drove to his apartment. As they exited I-5 at 50th Ave NE, he suggested they turn off their phones. He left his suitcases in the trunk and they walked quickly into the unit. Emma had been there earlier to straighten up and turn on the heat. David threw his carry-on bags and laptop on the couch. Pulling each other's clothes off, they dove into bed in seconds, laughing when they realized that both had forgotten to remove one sock. They didn't leave for the next three hours.

That evening, in the glow of each other's warmth, Emma told David, "I want to tell my parents about us. I am done with the facade."

"Do you think that's a good idea, at least until you finish with school?"

"I'll be done at the end of the quarter and I've checked, they've already paid my tuition for the quarter."

"Well, maybe you should wait until you've graduated and gotten a job before pulling the possible plug."

"David, I am tired of hiding. It just creates more

stress in my life. They are likely to find out anyway and, if I haven't told them, they'll think that I knew I was doing something wrong or bad. Well, I am not doing anything wrong or bad, I am doing what my heart tells me is the right thing to do. If I can't tell my parents, well that sucks."

"Okay, okay. Let's say they pull your support. Where are you going to live and eat?"

"I'll get a part-time job, move out of the sorority, eat less well."

"Well, I could let you stay in the storage room. I'd have to move some boxes."

"David!"

"Well, I guess you'll just have to stay in the master. Sorry."

"David, you are such a shit sometimes."

"Yeah, but one that loves you. So when are you going to do this?"

"When I get enough nerve. But I need to do it before they ask. I'll talk it over with Sophie. She knows my situation better than anyone else. I am going to ask my parents for a period of grace and then ask them to not make any decisions until they've met you. How can they summarily dismiss someone whom they've not met? Be prepared to go to Walla Walla around Memorial Day when school's over."

Sophie was no help but brutally honest.

"Emma, I know your family," Sophie said. "This is not going to go well, no matter when you do it. I don't care how you spin it, your life may come unglued."

"You'd wait?"

"No, I didn't say that. You'd have to live with the stress of them finding out, which they will. In the end, I don't see things being good or bad, just really, really bad or worse. You might want to get a good leg up on your senior project though. If the shit hits the fan, and it will, you might not feel like working for a while."

"Good thought. I've already got a good start. David starts a new rotation tomorrow and will be really busy for the next week. I am going to bust my ass until he's off next."

David didn't come home for a week.

With more than 80 percent of the project done by May 1st, Emma decided to call. She had already run into a friend from high school on campus had heard Emma was seriously seeing a resident from the med school. Emma needed to act.

She called after dinner on May Day.

"Hi Emma, what's up?" Clara asked.

"Got most of my senior project done. It's due by May 21st but I should be okay. Is Dad home?"

"Yes, why?"

"I want to talk to both of you."

"Joe, Joe...pick up the phone. Emma's on the line."

"Hi Emma."

"Hi Dad."

"I want to tell you something together. It may not be easy, but I need to do it."

Joe and Clara simultaneously said, "Okay..." Joe, having no idea that Emma was still seeing the 'Jew', had no clue. Clara knew right away.

"I am tired of looking for a guy that might like me and I like him. I have one. I am really fond of David Milton. He likes me and makes me feel safe. He doesn't care about my kidnapping, in fact, it may have drawn him closer. I need to let you know that I am not going out with anyone else for now. We are not married and I've not even spoken to David about that remote possibility."

Angrily, Joe interrupted, "This is the Jew guy, right?"

"Yes Dad, he is Jewish. Mom met him for a second when she came into town after the sorority break-in, but doesn't know him. I'd like to wait until the quarter is over and then bring him to Walla Walla to meet you. You can do that for me, can't you?"

"Emma, we discussed this," Joe yelled. "I am not happy, not happy at all."

"Please don't yell, Joe," Clara pleaded.

"Dad, I know how you feel," Emma said. "You are wrong, though, trust me. David is a good person who you would like, if you could see past your whatever, you know what I mean."

"Clara, aren't you going to say something here to straighten out our daughter?" Joe said, a decibel lower but dripping with anger.

"Joe, I don't know what to say. Emma is twenty-three years old and she's about to graduate college. I don't think she'd be making this call if she hasn't already made up her mind, regardless of what we say. Is that true?"

"Pretty much," Emma said.

"God damn it, Emma. I am going to talk to your mom and we're going to call you back," Joe said. "I may even talk to our lawyer, I'm so *effing* pissed. You knew how I felt, yet you proceeded to be manipulated by this Jew, prick, weasel. You've not heard the end of this by a long shot."

"Dad, that's enough. You don't know him, at all, yet you've judged him guilty. All I am asking you to do is meet him. If you don't think him worthy, then you can tell me. Talk to Mom, talk to whomever you want, but let me bring him home..."

Joe slammed the phone down.

...after school ends," Emma said, finishing the sentence.

"Emma, you are not making my life easy," Clara said. "I don't think you've thought about the repercussions for the family. I'll talk to Dad and see if I can have him wait until you come home with David. Have you met his family?"

"Yes, they are wonderful. David's grandmother is a survivor of a concentration camp."

"I've got to go. Your dad is breaking things in the kitchen. Bye."

"Mom, I love you."

Sophie came into the room a little while later. "How'd it go?"

"Not well."

"How not well, I mean there's not well and deeply and profoundly not well."

"DAPNW."

"Eh?"

"Deeply and profoundly not well."

"What now?"

"I've asked them to not do anything rash until I can bring David home after the quarter ends."

"And..."

"My mom is going to see if that'll fly. Dad was breaking dishes in the kitchen when I hung up."

"Ouch...DAPNW. Do you think it's even safe for David to go to Walla Walla?

"Please. That's ridiculous. It may not go well, but no one's going to get hurt."

Joe or Emma did not call back that night.

Emma received a call the next afternoon from Mrs. Rogers in the Registrar's Office.

"Emma, this is Gladys Rogers from the Registrar's Office."

"Hi, Mrs. Rogers."

"After our little private discussion, I had your account flagged to notify me in case a call came in. Your father called this morning, so I ended up with the call. He tried to get your admission pulled and he didn't even care about getting back the tuition. I told him that you were an adult and that the tuition was not refundable. I told him that only you could withdraw yourself. I think he knew the answer before he called. He screamed a word that started with an 'F' and slammed the phone down. Anyway, I assume you told your parents what you told me you were going to tell them."

"Yeah, last night."

"Well, as I said when we last talked, good luck."

"Thanks Mrs. Rogers. At least it tells me where they are."

Emma wondered whether the sorority, cell phone, and credit cards would be stopped. She called her mom.

"Mom, I thought you and Dad were going to talk and call me back."

"Dad was beside himself for three hours," Clara said. "He now blames himself for letting you go back to school, in fact, even letting you go to Seattle in the first place. He feels betrayed after all he's done for you. Your brother is even madder, but I'm not going to tell you what he said."

"I don't care what Alan says. You know that, so I don't need to hear it. He's worse than Dad and half as smart. All he cares about is his car and the current idiot he's dating or married to."

"Okay, okay, enough about your brother. I know his failings, although I don't always know that Dad sees them. "

"Did you know Dad called the registrar to have my admission revoked."

"Actually I did catch the end of that conversation. I was furious because he did it without talking to me. He's changed, Emma, really changed. He never would had done this in the past without talking to me. I deserve to know. Anyway, he was going to call the sorority next. I stopped him. I told him that you deserve the chance to bring David here. This whole thing with David may blow over, I mean relationships do. You might realize he's not for you, or he, or his family, feel the same about you."

"Maybe." Emma said.

“You've been forthright with us,” Clara continued. “You know my parents were furious with me when I brought your father here the first time. They felt he was beneath us. I reminded him today of all that. He seems to have conveniently forgotten. He says he won't do anything until you come home, but I can't promise what will happen then. Your brother is crazed and although you may not care what he thinks, he is your brother, and he is my son, and he and dad talk all the time. For now, keep in touch and we'll see you at Memorial Day. Not likely that we'll come to Seattle before that. Be strong Emma, I need you to be strong."

"Thanks, I'll try. When I'm around David, I feel so strong and so safe. Can't explain it better than that, but he keeps me from being afraid. Nice feeling after so many months of feeling afraid all the time."

Chapter 31

Joe Braza entered Alan's small office at the winery. *Alan Braza, Executive Vice President* was on the door. Alan was sitting back with his feet on the desk, reading 'Hot Rod' magazine, while ESPN blared from a flat screen TV on the wall to the side of the desk.

"Hey Dad, how's it hanging?"

"Alan, can't you say hello like a normal person," said an already angry Joe Braza.

In a monotone, Alan came back, "Hello Father, how are you today?

"To be honest, I've been having headaches lately. Probably because your sister is driving me crazy."

"Why don't you call Doc Franklin."

"Nah. He doesn't need to know what's goin' on with Emma. It'll just get around. By the way, did you call Richmark, the label guys in Seattle, about another run for the Chardonnays? We need fifteen hundred more labels."

"I'll do it today. What's the guy's name, Donny Williams? Got the number, somewhere around here."

"Alan, damn it, You promised you'd do it before last Wednesday. Please take some responsibility. I give you a task, you have to do it and do it well."

"Sure, Dad. What's bugging you?"

"I'm not good. Your sister called last night and confirmed what you had thought all along. She's been hoodwinked by the Jew doctor and now she wants to bring him home to introduce him to the family. She's seriously making the wrong decision. I know I shouldn't have let her go to the UW in the first place and, for sure, not to go back after her head got fucked up. I don't know what to do and your mother is less than helpful. She only cares that Emma is happy and can't see the big picture. I feel betrayed, screwed, blued and tattooed."

"Want me to do something, if I can?"

"Your sister is not going to listen to you. She's not even talking to me."

"You talked to her uppity bitch friend, Sophie Pecan Nut?"

"Sophie is on her side. Says the guy is great."

"Dad, I'll make you a deal."

"What?"

"You handle the labels and I'll deal with the Hebe. You can't do it, you're too close to Emma. I give a shit, and I am certainly not letting this turd into our family."

"Whatta you thinking?"

"Don't know just yet. I'll give it some thought. Better you not ask, then you can't be held responsible by mom or Emma. You know what I mean? When is he supposed to come?"

"Looks like he'll be here the Friday night before Memorial Day. I said I wanted him put in the maid's room. Mom wanted to put him in your bedroom, which is now supposedly a guest room. I said no. Don't really care where he stays, as long as it's not permanent."

"Dad, I'll do what I can. Remember, don't ask me about it."

Chapter 32

The month of May sped along. Emma's senior project was very strong and Dr. Miller, a confidant on more than one level, was incredible help and inspiration. David's hours at the hospital were horrific but every squeezed-in meeting with Emma confirmed how they felt about each other.

One night in early May, David ran into Rafe Gomez, his buddy on the UW police force, in the ER. Rafe had been in the ER following another UW officer who had been injured chasing a thief. David had seen the officer for a possible ruptured spleen.

The two unlikely friends, David and Rafe, sat down for a cup of coffee in the ER lounge to catch up.

David had met Rafe three years earlier as a second year resident rotating the county hospital. Entering the hospital through the ER at 5:00 a.m. to start his morning rounds before the rest of the team met at 6:30, David spotted a young Hispanic couple exiting. The man looked familiar, but he couldn't place the face. The young lady, his wife or girl friend, was holding a child of about three or four years of age in her arms. The mother was crying, the child was moving very little. David moved to the couple to see what was going on.

Looking at the man, David stopped them from exiting, "Hi, do I know you?"

"Dunno, I'm Rafael Gomez, out of the US army, was in ten years, last four as an MP. Got a job at the UW in security two months ago."

"Oh, I've seen you around the ER at the UW. I just got off a surgical rotation there. Nice to see you. What's wrong with the baby?"

"This is my wife Nadia, she speaks only a little English. Bito, our only child, is 3. He's been in good health his whole life. Super kid. He's been complaining about his tummy hurting for the last day, but the docs in the ER didn't feel it was a big deal. Gave us some baby Tylenol and said come back tomorrow if he's not better. Nadia thinks he's sick, really sick, just a mother's intuition. Would have taken him to Children's, but our UW insurance doesn't kick in for another 30 days."

"I'm sorry for you troubles. I'm a bit late for rounds but come with me, let me examine Bito in the outpatient clinic. I don't want to take him back to the ER. Looks bad to the ER staff and it will only take a second. I'll get his labs from the computer."

David escorted the Gomez' to the nearby surgical clinic and Nadia took the listless Bito into the exam room and undressed him. David downloaded Bito's blood work and was not surprised to find a relatively normal white blood count of seven thousand which would be low for a serious infection. What was not normal was a so-called '*left shift.*' Almost all the white cells were granulocytes. Normally the percentage would be about seventy percent or lower, Bito's granulocytes measured ninety percent. The left-shift made the total count less important, suggesting a possible serious infection or inflammation.

David's examination of the young child took only a minute. Bito had pain in the lower abdomen, particularly on the right side. David would have bet the moon that the youngster presented a classic case of appendicitis. David did not want to get into an embarrassing shouting match with the current ER doctors about a missed diagnosis, so he called his chief resident, Mary Ward, whom he was to meet at 6:30.

"Mary, David here. Long story, but I intercepted one of the UW police officers leaving the ER with his three year old son. Kid didn't look good and the ER thought he had nothing. Anyway I examined him in the clinic and I'm pretty certain that he's got a hot *appy.*"

"Did they get a white count?"

"Yes, it's only seven thou, but with a huge left shift. Any chance you can come to the clinic first?"

"Sure, I'm walking into the hospital now. Be there in a second."

Mary Ward agreed totally with David's assessment and called the OR to bump the least important case for an emergency appendectomy.

She said to David, "I've got a couple of things to do on the ward first. You stay here with the Gomezes and get them consented for the appendectomy. It's your case to do. I'll handle the idiots in the ER later today. I'll see you in the OR in thirty minutes. Okay?"

"Got it chief." David responded.

David explained everything to the Gomezes, who consented quickly. Nadia Gomez told her husband, who then told David that God had not been fooled by Bito's illness and had put David in their path. The case started forty-five minutes later. David and Dr. Ward found Bito's appendix severely inflamed and likely to have ruptured at any time. Had it ruptured, Bito could have died without ever making it back to the hospital. The ER doc, who missed the diagnosis, was a rotating resident from another surgical program. The resident was sent back to his own program to learn about appendicitis after Mary Ward went ballistic. David hovered with Bito and his parents on and off all day. The next afternoon, David discharged Bito to home. Certain that David had saved Bito's life, Rafe and Nadia would be eternally grateful to David.

As they left the hospital, Nadia Gomez, in her broken English and tears in her eyes, said to David, "Djyou come our house to eat, please."

"That's not necessary, but thanks anyway," David said.

Rafe Gomez, interjecting, "Doc. She's not going to take no for an answer. She knows you probably saved Bito's life and she's got to repay you in some way. Just say 'yes' so we can leave."

"Okay, okay. Sure, I'd love to come for a meal."

David did come a few days later, and they showered him with homemade presents and cakes.

After dinner, Rafe told David about his life. "I grew up in Walla Walla and most of my family still lives there. Growing up, I wasn't such a good guy. I was in a gang from the time I was twelve and in and out of minor scrapes with the police. I went into the army right after high school, mostly on the advice of my juvenile parole officer, to stay out of trouble. The army turned me around and I qualified for the MPs. Ended up as a Master Sergeant and had the job skills to be hired by the UW police department as soon as I got out."

David and Rafe became friends and would call each other for advice. David gave medical advice to Rafe and his family and Rafe fixed things for David around the apartment.

Twelve months later, Nadia, whose English had improved, left a message on David's phone to call her, which he did.

"Hello Nadia, this is David Milton."

"Doctor David, hola. I need talk to djyou."

"What can I do for you?"

"Doctor David, I have cousin in Walla Walla, Selma Rodriguez. Selma has bump in her breast. She just have her baby, number six, a few week ago."

"Okay, how can I help your cousin?" asked David.

"You need to know that Selma mother die from breast cancer when she very young. Selma has papers, and has insurance, but her English is not so good. Maybe worse than mine. She try get into doctor's office in Walla Walla, but no doctor will see her for three weeks. She is scared and call me because I tell her about djyou."

David, understanding completely, said, "Nadia, I am sorry that your cousin can't be seen in Walla Walla. I don't know any of the doctors there. Can your cousin find a way to Seattle?"

"Si, si. She can get here," Nadia said, "even if Rafael need go there and get her."

"Okay Nadia. I am in clinic tomorrow morning until noon. The same place that I saw Bito. I will see your cousin. Okay?"

Nadia, sounding relieved, said, "Thank djyou, thank djyou, Doctor David. We will be there."

The painless right breast lump was distinct, measuring about an inch in diameter. David pulled some strings and got Selma in for a mammogram that afternoon and broke away from the afternoon clinic to review the films with the radiologists. The mammogram suggested a benign fibroadenoma, a non-malignant tumor, but they could not be one-hunded percent sure.

Given her family history, Selma Rodriguez wanted no part of watching and waiting. David gave her two options, a needle biopsy or removal of the entire lump. She thought about her options for three seconds. David presented the case to the chief resident. David, aided by the chief, removed the lump the next day. The pathology report confirmed the benign diagnosis. David shared the good news with both families. He told them that had it been his sister or mother, he, too, would have had the lump removed.

Selma and her family were back home within three days and made David promise that if he ever got close to Walla Walla, he would have to come to their house for a meal and to meet the rest of the Rodriguez and Gomez families. David, a native Seattleite, had never been to Walla Walla and would have guessed that he'd never take the Rodriguez' up on their offer. Nonetheless, David's star had risen immensely in a faraway place.

As the two friends were finishing their chat in the ER lounge, David told Rafe about his likely trip to Walla Walla around Memorial Day.

"I'm not so concerned about myself but Emma is worried to death," David said. "Her father is totally pissed and she can't even describe how bad her brother is acting."

Rafe reminded David that he knew Emma's brother from football days in Walla Walla.

"Alan Braza is an asshole and his reputation amongst the Hispanic community is shit," Rafe said. "He can't get any lower. I'm not so sure you should be going there from what you've told me. Alan Braza is crazy."

David, knowing this from conversations with Emma, said, "I've heard this from Emma as well. Alan Braza is not nice to the Hispanic workers at the winery, even to some of the senior men with more experience. Joe Braza spends a good deal of time smoothing ruffled feathers. As for me, I'm not worried. I can take care of myself. I'm just worried about Emma."

They both shook their heads.

Rafe said, "Don't forget, if you do get to Walla Walla,

you promised Nadia's cousin, Selma, that you'd have a meal at the Rodriguez's house."

David responded, "I don't know what the actual plan of events will be, but 'getting out of Dodge' in one piece, with or without Emma, seems like a distinct possibility. I'll call Selma, no matter what, but I can't promise I'll be free for a meal."

Rafe made the call the next day to Selma. Selma understood that David might not come for dinner but couldn't figure why anyone as nice as David Milton would consider even talking to, least enough dating, anyone in the Braza family. Selma promised Rafe she would say extra prayers for David at Mass, and light a few candles.

Chapter 33

Emma told her mom that she would be home late on the Thursday before Memorial Day. Emma added that David was leaving for San Francisco on the Tuesday before Memorial Day for the Pacific Coast Surgical Society meeting. He had a paper to deliver on Friday at 8:00 a.m. His flight north was at 11:00 a.m., and with a stop in Seattle, was scheduled to arrive at 4:00 p.m. into Spokane. He'd rent a car for the three hour drive to Walla Walla and be at Braza's house at 7:30 p.m., in time for dinner and to meet the family.

On the Monday before Memorial Day, Emma presented her senior project to a panel of business school professors and MBAs from the private sector. For luck and support, David went with her and waited outside the presentation. She would receive her final grades on a special website along with a critique. She thought it went well. Dr. Miller recused himself as a judge but he glowed and smiled during the entire delivery and question period. Both of the private sector judges asked if her contact information would be the same after graduation if they wanted to call her. She said it would be. Dr. Miller had given her a *'two thumbs up.'* David returned to the hospital and she returned to the sorority to start packing.

As she and Sophie packed, Emma could only think about what might happen in Walla Walla.

Emma, pontificating, said, "I hope, at the least, my mom and dad will return to Seattle for graduation ceremonies in June. Dr. Miller told me that I would easily be cum laude, but possibly magna cum laude, and would be awarded some special honors at the graduation rites. It would be nice for them to see that."

Sophie, always the comic, replied, "I'm just hoping that you and David are alive after Memorial Day."

"That's not funny," Emma said.

"Wasn't meant to be."

Chapter 34

On the Wednesday morning before Memorial Day, Rafael Gomez was sitting at his desk at UW Security making up the rotation schedule for the next four weeks.

The security operator paged into Rafe's office, "You've got a call from eastern Washington. Some guy named Rico Rodriguez. Says it's personal, but important, and refused to leave a message. Says he knows you."

Rico Rodriguez belonged to Rafe's old gang in Walla Walla. Rico had made little of his life and included jail time for petty crimes. Rico mooched off his family for money and odd jobs when his cons or minor drug dealings weren't going well or it was 'too' hot to deal. He was the younger brother to Selma Rodriguez and cousin to Nadia Gomez, Rafe's wife. Rafe had to take the call. Rafe and Rico no longer called each other friends, but Rico wouldn't call unless something bad was going down in the family.

"Hey, Rico, what's happenin' cabrone?" Rafe said lovingly.

"Hey Rafe. This line, is it safe?"

"No. Call me on my cell, 206-789-2646."

"Si."

Rico and Rafe hung up simultaneously. Rafe grabbed his cell and walked out of the back door of the police station into the parking lot.

Rafe's cell phone went off as he walked down three stairs to the pavement.

"What's up that's so secret?" Rafe asked.

Rico, clearly nervous, said, "I'm gonna tell you something that I didn't tell you, got it?"

"Okay, okay. I never heard it."

"I try to be quick," Rico said. "This story is a bit loco. One of the gang members, whose name you don't need to know, was called two, three weeks ago by some dude, your age, that we both know for years and is a pinche cabrone. His family makes vino."

"Okay, I gotcha." Rafe knew exactly who Rico was talking about – Alan Braza. Pince cabrone loosely translated meant fucking bastard.

"He want to buy fifteen thousand dollars of coke, one-time deal," Rico said. "But that's not the loco part. He do not want it to use or sell. Even more loco. Second part of the deal, for another five thousand dollars he want us to plant it in the car at his house of some guy he try to set up for the cops. The deal is supposed to go down this Friday after midnight. My buddy says he get back to him in thirty minutes. This deal had *somebody's gonna get fucked all over it* and my buddy wasn't sure that we wasn't gonna get fucked too. He call back Señor Cabrone and tell him that the heats been on him, and he no want to handle the risk. He suggest some guys in Spokane, but Señor Cabrone said he had other guys if we don't do it."

"Rico, why does this interest me?" Rafe asked.

"I'm getting to there. So I'm ready to forget the whole deal. I be at Selma's house last night for her birthday. Whole family there. Selma tells the family that the doctor from Seattle that help her out, and is an amigo with you and Nadia, is coming to Walla Walla. He going to meet the Braza family, cuz' apparently he's poking the daughter, whatever her name is. Word is that she as nice as the brother is an asshole. We were laughing about why anyone would want to get mixed up with those locos if they don't have to. I knows doc, he a good guy, and has help you, and I know my sister think he close to God. So I put this all together, and you didn't hear this from me, but I think your doc amigo is about to get fucked, big time. I don't know, and don't want to know, who doing the plant. Remember, we never talked. Got it. Adiós and let's see you back here once in a while."

"Gracias, amigo," Rafe said, ending the call.

Rafe first thought was to call David but Rafe hesitated, thinking he needed to have the counsel of somebody who knew drugs. Rafe called a friend at the Drug Enforcement Agency or DEA in downtown Seattle.

Dick Hawkins had been in the army with Rafe and had joined the DEA after discharge. They met by chance at Seattle Center during the Cinqo de Mayo festival a few years earlier and would socialize on occasion.

Rafe explained to Dick the *unknown conversation* with his cousin and also the fact that David Milton was one of his best friends and a guardian of his family.

Dick thought for a second, "Where is Dr. Milton now and how and when is he was getting to Walla Walla? Until I know that I can't make plans or even know if we can do anything. Don't tell Dr. Milton anything, yet."

Rafe said, "I'll find out if I can and get back to you ASAP."

Rafe hung up, collected his thoughts, and dialed David Milton's cell phone.

David answered immediately. "Hey Rafe, why the call? I'm in San Fran at a meeting."

"I was kind of thinking I'd go to Walla Walla this weekend," Rafe said. "Nadia reminded me that you might be there too. Maybe going to take Selma

Rodriguez up on a meal?"

"Yes I am going to be there. Sorry, don't know what the schedule might be, so I couldn't make Selma any promises."

"You coming home first?"

"No, flying Alaska Air to Spokane on Friday morning from here. Get into Spokane about 4ish and then rent a car and drive to Walla Walla. Get there around 7:30 or so. From there, it's a wing and prayer, with mostly prayer."

"You're renting a car?" asked Rafe.

David responded, "Yeah, why, wanna pick me up?"

"No, not enough time. Cost much, who ya renting from?"

"Got a deal from National, one hundred fifty bucks. Planning to drive back to Spokane and fly back to Seattle. Cheaper and quicker than taking the car one way back to Seattle and paying a drop-off charge. Emma's not coming back with me. That's the plan."

"Hey, not sure what we're doing, but I've got your cell and I'll call you if we go, okay, buddy?"

"Sure," David said. "Thanks for the call."

Rafe called Dick Hawkins back and told him David's plans.

Dick Hawkins, thought for a moment, then said, "This may be a go. Let me run this by my boss."

Dick called back ninety minutes later.

"Rafe, probably a good idea that you not come to Walla Walla. If it's merely a drug drop, I don't see your friend being in danger. If we let it run its course, we might be able to get the supplier and the local dirty cops in on the setup. I'll call and get the DEA office in Spokane up to date, then fly to Spokane to make sure we don't put your buddy in jeopardy. We'll make sure his car is clean and then tail him to his destination. Airport security will check his bags in San Francisco. We want to certify that he's not carrying."

"Dick, I'd stake my life, and my family's life, on the fact that he doesn't use or carry or sell drugs."

"Regardless, we'll make sure he's as sterile as the emperor's eunuch," said Hawkins.

"Then what?"

Hawkins continued, "We'll try to get cameras on the car once he's there. Let the arrest go down and when he gets to the jail, we'll take the case over. Then we get him out of town and take care of the bad guys."

"He'll be safe, my friend?"

"Rafe, I promise. If I think anything puts him in harm's way, I'll blow the cover, promise. You got pictures of your friend?"

"Yeah. I have one of him and me on my phone. I'll send it over. I assume you'll be smart enough to figure out which one is him."

"Rafe, you're such a asshole."

"Dick, don't you think we need to tip off the Walla Walla PD or Sheriff's office. I just don't want Dr. Milton to get in the middle of something."

"No, Rafe. If they're dirty, then we've tipped them off. Don't worry, your buddy is going to be safe."

Rafe Gomez hung up the phone. He sensed a tightness in his chest that he hadn't felt since Bito had appendicitis and before that Afghanistan six years earlier. He would not tell Nadia, and now he couldn't warn David.

Dick Hawkins immediately set into motion the big wheels and long arms of the DEA. Any luggage carried or checked by David would be searched by SFO security. The Spokane office of the DEA would screen, check and clean his rental car and he'd be tailed all the way through to Walla Walla and the Braza residency. A federal judge gave them permission to tap Alan Braza's phones. The Spokane DEA dispatched agents to scrutinize the sight lines to parking at the Braza house and try to position cameras on Friday night for surveillance.

Chapter 35

Emma had said her good-byes to the sisters and Francine, and spent as much time with Sophie as she could. They had been inseparable for most of five years and, at this point, she felt as close to Sophie as she did to anyone, save her mom and David. Sophie had decided to go to Columbia Law School to be closer to home. She'd get a small apartment in Manhattan with some friends and see how Sophia Picone, Doctor of Jurisprudence, sounded in three years.

"I may want to come back to Washington State after law school but I'd have to live in Seattle. Walla Walla is *so not me,*" Sophie told Emma.

Emma agreed.

Emma arrived at home at 1:00 p.m. on Thursday to be greeted by her mom who seemed warm, friendly and happy to have her daughter home.

"Where's dad?" Emma asked.

"He's at work, so is Alan. So, how are you doing, honey? I mean okay and all?" Clara asked while helping Emma lug suitcases and boxes into her bedroom.

"I'm scared, but not scared of the boogie man."

"I don't follow you?" Clara asked.

"I only want Dad and Alan to give David a chance. David is so kind and doesn't understand the bigotry that sometimes dwells around this house. I don't either now. I've lived with it for years and it didn't affect me, but now it does, and I am scared. I don't want to lose David. I don't want to have you mad at me or be disappointed in me for no reason. Hating David because he happens to be Jewish is no reason."

"I've talked to your dad at length. He has been quite subdued for the past week, as if he's finally realized that it's your life. I think Dad will give David a chance. Can't promise but, well...," Clara hesitated, "I just can't promise..."

"I love you, mom. You've been so understanding," Emma said.

"Your brother is another story," Clara continued. "Alan is a big baby in a man's body. He doesn't reason like you or me and, sometimes, doesn't reason at all. I can give him ten reasons to give David a chance. All make sense but he'll respond by saying something like, 'Fine Mom, but no fucking Jew is going to be in this family. This Hebe's got an agenda. Don't know what it is, maybe he thinks he can steal the business from us. He's not going to last. I just know it.' Then, he'll repeat the whole thing. I don't know where the hate comes from."

"Why is Alan like that. Anyway, all I care is that Dad gives him a chance."

"I think he will. Let's get you unpacked."

That evening, the welcome Joe gave Emma appeared subdued compared to Clara, but not out of character. Alan chose not to eat with the family, which in itself was not unusual. He had his own house in town and didn't come to dinner during the week unless a special occasion called for his presence. Emma coming home was, to him, not a special occasion. Joe did ask about Agotini's class and the stories told at the JDF banquet and he seemed genuinely interested. Emma went to bed with a ray of hope.

Chapter 36

Dick Hawkins, otherwise known as "Hawk" flew into Spokane on Thursday afternoon. Local agents, William Baker and Harry Connors, met Hawkins at the airport. Together they drove to the Spokane field office and picked up what gear they thought they may need including automatic weapons, cameras, night gear, focused microphones and armor. They downloaded maps and information about Walla Walla into their laptops. They drove in separate cars to Walla Walla that night arriving at 10:00 p.m.

After checking into a motel, Hawk divided the terrain into thirds with each officer getting lines of sight and entrance and exit strategies for bad guys. Hawkin's plan had weaknesses because they didn't want to be spotted before the drop and they didn't know when, where or how the drugs would be carted in. But no one had any better suggestions. In addition, many small homes for the employees had been situated on or near the many service roads that surrounded the thirty-five acre Braza home site.

Most likely the bad guys, one or two at the most, would walk in, plant the drugs and walk out. Hawkins estimated the walk in would take no less than ten minutes, two minutes for the drop and ten minutes to walk out.

The agents selected two excellent high ground spots with good lines of sight but not near any roads or walkable terrain. Spotters, with night vision cameras would be placed at each location. The rest of the DEA crew, twelve in all, arriving the following afternoon from offices around Washington State and Idaho, would be sequestered two miles away. The agents would wait for instructions from Hawkins.

Hawkins, Baker and Collins discussed every

possibility they could imagine and the probabilities of each. Hawkins summed up their conclusions, "The person doing the drop would not be the same as the one supplying the drugs. Too risky to put that person *on the ground*. The dropper or droppers might not know the source of the drugs or even what was in the package to be planted. The seller might not know the droppers, if middle men were used. Only Alan Braza would know the seller."

The other two agents nodded agreement.

If they didn't have enough to nail Alan Braza after the drop, their plan was to work with the prosecutor's and sheriff's offices to trap Braza and get him to lead them to the source of the drugs. They would have David released out of jail the next morning, declaring publically that the parcel contained only sugar and no drugs. A very pissed off Braza would then lead the DEA back to the dealer. At least, that was the plan.

Chapter 37

On Friday, the day of David's arrival, Emma tried to be hopeful. She texted David to call her in between meetings. David waited until after his presentation and called Emma from the taxi on the way to the airport.

"David, there's hope," Emma said. "My mom thinks everything would be okay with my dad. My brother is being a shit. You can't get baited into any arguments. He'll try, but don't fall for it. I am so excited to see you. Call me when you've left Spokane."

David drove up the driveway to the Braza house in his rental, a plain green Kia Rio, at 7:25 p.m. Emma had been waiting on the porch for twenty minutes and scurried down the quarter-mile driveway to meet him. She jumped in the passenger side after moving the empty cola cans off the seat and gave David a huge hug and kiss.

As David came up for air, "I've missed you so much, but maybe we shouldn't be so demonstrative in front of your parents."

"Sorry, couldn't help it," Emma said. "I'm just so happy to see you. Park over there in front of the fourth garage door. If there's nothing valuable in the car, we'll just leave it there."

"Just my suitcase. I had to pack a dress suit and stuff for the lectures and talk. Pain in the ass to check through, not to mention the additional twenty-five bucks."

David grabbed his suitcase out of the trunk and into the house they went.

"Mom, you've met David."

"Hello, Mrs. Braza. Nice to see you again," David

said.

A brief moment of silence and no hugs of welcome passed quickly.

David opened his bag and brought out a bread mix. "My mom said I had to bring you something like a bottle of wine. But we all know that would have been a mistake. Emma says you're an amazing cook so I thought some genuine San Francisco sourdough bread mix might be different."

"Thank you. Very thoughtful," Clara said. She seemed pleasantly surprised and couldn't remember any of Emma's dates every bringing a gift, although none of them ever stayed in their house. "Oh, and please call me Clara."

"Sure, but I may forget."

"Joe will be down in a minute. Would you like something to drink?"

"A glass of water would be nice."

Minutes later, Joe Braza barreled into the room, hands in pockets.

"Dad, this is David Milton. David this is my father, Joe."

Sizing David up got Joe's attention. He had never seen a picture. David was almost four inches taller than Joe and in considerably better shape. Not what Joe expected. Joe, 5'10", maybe, had a moderate mid-age belly, and could easily stand to lose twenty pounds. David's blue eyes and light brown hair also didn't fit Joe's Semitic profile guess.

"Hello." *Joe said nothing more as he stood back two full paces from David. No nice to meet you, no call me Joe and Joe's hands stayed in his pockets.*

Oh well, David thought.

Emma, embarrassed at the cold welcome, said nothing.

Finally Clara broke the standstill, "Let's go out on the porch and sit for a little while. We have a little time to meet David and have a drink. Dinner is almost ready."

Clara served David a glass of water, Joe, a scotch on the rocks, and a poured glass of Pinot Gris for Emma and herself.

"David, Emma hasn't really told us a lot about you," Clara said. "You're a surgical resident. I know that means you're in training, but I couldn't tell you anymore."

"Surgical residency is usually a five or six year program which starts after four years of medical school. In July, I start my fifth year as a senior resident and will be done in June, two years from now. At that time I can start practicing General Surgery, unless I do a Fellowship, which is more specialized training. It's a bit more complicated than that, but that's the gist."

"How old are you?" Clara continued.

"I will be twenty-nine, next month. I was always young for my class. I was in a special accelerated undergraduate program at Cal Berkeley that allowed me to get into medical school at UC San Francisco a year early. I actually obtained my Bachelor's degree after the first year of medical school. After medical school, I decided that I'd had enough time in California, away from family, so I applied and was accepted into the surgical training program at the UW."

Joe finally entered the discussion, "Is it hard finding

a surgery job when you're done?"

"No, sir," David said, turning toward Joe.

Clara smiled at his attempt at respect.

"Actually there are twelve hundred unfilled surgical positions in the US now," David said. "I won't have any difficulty finding a job. In fact, the shortage of surgeons is profound enough that the US is letting in a good number of surgeons from out of the country. Most are well trained or pretty well trained, some not so good. Mostly from India, the Middle East, Canada and the UK. Also a good number of Americans are trained in Mexico or Italy and then make it back. I am thinking, however, of staying in academic medicine at a university."

As David finished, Alan Braza walked in.

"Hi everybody. I'm starved." Looking at David, "You must be Emma's new boyfriend. Darion or Darnell?"

David had stood and extended his hand but Alan had already turned toward Clara and made no attempt at shaking.

"It's David and you knew that," retorted an angry Emma.

"Whatever. Anyway, when we going to eat?"

Clara stood, exasperated at her son's totally inappropriate behavior. "We can eat now." She left for the dining room.

Alan and Joe moved to the corner of the porch for a moment as Alan whispered in his dad's ear. Joe nodded.

Emma had prepared David for the verbal slights, but the lack of social graces was particularly hurtful. David had quickly retracted his hand, but remained standing as they moved to the dining room.

Dinner was served by a lovely older Hispanic woman, Angelina, who had obviously been in the household for some time. The meal, mostly Mexican food, was delicious and filling. A dry white wine complimented the 'ensalada' and then a deep red Cabernet went well with the main course, carne asada with beans and rice.

Joe, being reasonably nice, so far, asked David, "Do you know anything about wine?"

"Actually nothing other than what Emma has taught me," David said. "We didn't drink much wine in our house growing up. Just maybe for the holidays. To me, initially, there were four types of wine. Red that tasted good, red that tasted bad, and white, same thing. Now I know that a deLorraine 07 Merlot goes incredibly well with hamburgers barbequed in this house."

Clara smiled and nodded, "A start."

David continued, "I may not have the palate to distinguish good and bad yet, but I am trainable. I've heard Emma use words like balanced, big, body, bold, bouquet, and buttery, just in the Bs. Then there is character, dry, earthy, fruity, full, mature, nutty, oaky, smooth, sweet, tannic, tart and woody. I can tell you what Emma tells me these mean, but I'm not sure I could distinguish them myself, yet. It's like a whole new language. Kind of like hepatic encephalopathy or Coccidioidomycosis."

"Hey," Joe said, "I know that, it's Valley Fever."

"Right, touché. Dr. Braza, I presume," David said.

Joe smiled. "Yep. We had a bunch of wetbacks from the San Joaquin Valley come up a couple of years ago and two of them had Coxi, Coxymosis or whatever. Sent their spic asses back pronto."

Emma glanced at David to see him grimacing at the derogatory slant.

After the maid cleared the dessert dished, Alan announced, “I'm beat and have had way too much to drink. I'm going to stay here tonight in my bedroom.

Emma glared at her mother, then back at Alan, knowing that Alan never stayed at home anymore. "We've already thrown David's stuff in that room."

"Well, it is my room you know," Alan said, calmly. “Let him stay in your room, that oughta' feel good."

"That'll be enough from you, Alan," Clara said. She realized that Alan had every intention of spoiling David's short stay. "Emma, you and I can move David's clothes down to the empty maid's room. It'll be fine."

"That's fine with me," David said. “I can give you a hand. I am exhausted from the travel, driving, good food and wine. What's the plan for tomorrow, if I might ask?"

"I'm going to show you the winery and the vineyards and introduce you to some of the people that have worked here since I can remember." Emma said, hoping for no other comments.

David stood, and looked to Clara, "Fabulous meal, Mrs. Braza, thank you, so much."

"It's Clara, and you're welcome. Do you have any breakfast likes or dislikes?"

"No, I eat almost anything."

"Bacon and eggs?" asked Clara.

"Fabulous," said David.

Alan, not wanting to miss a point, "You eat bacon?"

"Yep, do you?" asked David.

Alan, surprised by the response, said, "Uhhhh, why yes. I thought you people don't eat anything from a pig?"

David, showing great restraint, thought, *'you people', you're even a bigger asshole that Emma or Rafe warned me about.'*

"Some Jews don't," David said, "but most do. I eat anything." David then turned toward Emma and said, "Anyway, it's almost eleven, so let's get my stuff moved. Big day tomorrow."

David, Emma and Clara moved David's belongings in a matter of minutes. The second maid's room was actually quite nice with its own bathroom and double bed. David thanked Clara again for her hospitality and Clara again thanked him for helping Emma out.

David showered and changed into a T-shirt and boxers. He fell asleep in a matter of minutes.

Emma and Clara ascended the stairs together toward their bedrooms. Clara stopped Emma before the top step.

"Emma, he is nice and obviously intelligent. He is also much more handsome than I remember. I could like him. Dad, I don't know about. Alan is a piece of work right now. You obviously warned him that Alan would be a baby and I'm glad he didn't fall for it. I know it must have been difficult for him."

Emma smiled and gave her mom a hug, a kiss and a whispered, "Thanks."

Emma went to sleep by midnight, praying that her mother could hold the family in check.

Chapter 38

Dick Hawkins started positioning the DEA force at 10:30 p.m. on Friday night. Hawkins had William Baker take the best view site, while an officer from the Boise DEA office took the second view site. Both had excellent vision without glasses. Hawk and the four other agents parked behind a convenience store to the south of the Braza property. Two miles to the north the other five, led by Connors, sat in their cruisers. They all waited.

At 3:15 a.m., Baker radioed, "Movement eastern edge of the property, heading west toward the garage. Twenty to thirty feet at a time, then motionless." Baker assumed correctly that the intruder had come in on foot near the eastern service road. Hawk's group was closer to that entrance and dispatched the other group to guard and control all the other exits and entrances and to report any suspicious vehicles. Protocol called for full gear and fully armed with automatic weapons, night vision and two way communication.

Hawk's group arrived at the east service road, driving lights-off for the last half mile. Two hundred yards south of the service road they found a parked 2007 Honda Civic. Approaching slowly, the men found the Honda unoccupied. The driver side door had been left unlocked and car keys were located under the floor mat. The hood was popped and the battery disconnected. If the driver had a second set of keys, the first set meant little.

The second group reported no other vehicles present at, or near, any of the other service roads. Baker then radioed that the intruder had reached the Kia and opened the trunk. The second spotter came on to say that a second intruder was also on the eastern edge, fifty yards away and appeared heavily armed.

Hawk radioed the entire group, "Let both men finish their drop and we'll handle the take-down off property by their car."

Only Baker and the other observer remained in place watching the Kia and the Braza home for what was to be Act II of the plan - the arrival of the Walla Walla police to arrest Dr. Milton.

The intruder doing the drug drop closed the KIA trunk and walked slowly to his backup. Together they slowly headed east back toward the eastern service road entrance.

Twelve minutes later, two men exited near the east service gate and then sprinted to the Honda. They shut the door. Immediately, ten high intensity beams pointed at the car and the DEA agents approached with automatic weapons loaded and in position to fire.

Hawkins used a loudspeaker in English and Spanish warning them to open their windows and throw any weapons on the ground. They complied quickly. The cornered intruders were then instructed to open their doors slowly, exit the car and lie on the ground next to the car. The men complied without a struggle. Each intruder carried a loaded Glock semiautomatic pistol. A rifle was found in the trunk.

The two intruders, Alex Pesses and Dennis Vargas, had long rap sheets, but were penny-ante criminals. They were cuffed, placed in the back of one of the cars which returned to the waiting areas, five men to the north and five men, with the two cuffed intruders, to the south.

Harry Connors grilled the two intruders who seemed eager to cooperate. They said they were only doing a drop, and that they did not know what was in the bag, who the bag was meant for, nor did they know who had paid for the delivery. Everything was done through middle men. Realizing that cooperating now might make it easier for their lame excuse, they did have a list of car makes and license numbers that were not to be touched. The list contained the plates from the four Braza automobiles.

Chapter 39

At four thirty a.m., heavy knocking at the door and flashing police lights rousted the entire household, including David and the maid in the basement. The banging stopped when Joe opened the door. Clara, Emma and Alan stood behind Joe. At the door were eight Walla Walla deputy sheriffs led by John Specker, a senior detective of the Walla Walla County Sheriff's Department, and an old fishing buddy of Joe's. The entire contingent wore Kevlar vests and were armed with semi-automatic weapons.

"Gee Whiz, John. It's four in the morning, what the hell is going on?" asked Joe Braza.

"Hello, Joe. Hello, Clara," said Specker. "We received an anonymous tip earlier about a drug deal about to go down. Apparently there is a good sized amount of cocaine hidden in a rented Kia parked on your property. I have a search warrant signed by Judge Crogan. Sorry to do this, but we need to search the car and then your house, if need be. I'm going to have Officer Cruz stay in the house. Nobody leaves."

"There's got to be some kind of mistake. This isn't possible." Joe seemed sincere, and appeared both surprised and annoyed.

The young officer, Cesar Cruz, entered the front door. He shouldered his rifle and drew a service revolver.

Clara cried, "You can put that gun away young man."

Officer Cruz spoke up. "Sorry Mrs. Braza, protocol when drugs are involved. I will holster the weapon when Lieutenant Specker tells me to do so, not 'til then. Please everyone, have a seat where I can see you."

Joe shrank back into the living room and sat. He knew Alan had concocted something but a police raid was not what he thought might happen.

"Clara, can you get me a glass of water," Joe said. "I'm not feeling so well."

Alan sensing that his father might not be as thrilled as he was, offered quickly, "I'll get it for you."

Officer Cruz spoke up immediately. "No one leaves this room. Are there others in the house?"

Emma spoke up, "My boyfriend and the maid are in the basement."

The maid and then David, now wearing jeans and his T-shirt, appeared. "What's going on," David asked?

Emma grabbed David's arm. "David, the police are here. They said they think there is cocaine hidden in your rental car. Could that be true?"

David, surprised, said, "What are you talking about? No, no way."

Officer Cruz spoke forcefully. "Miss, please let go of him and have a seat. Sir, please sit down."

David spoke up again, "This is beyond absurd, or a mean joke. If there's anything in my car, I didn't put it there."

The officer, hand on his weapon, looked at David and shouted, "Sit your ass down now, buddy." He then looked at the maid, Angelina, and smiled politely. "Señora, por favor, siéntense."

No one spoke. Emma shook visibly. David sat, arms folded, still in a cloud as to what was happening. Joe seemed confused, as did Clara. Alan sat calmly, trying to hide a Cheshire cat grin.

Fifteen minutes went by and Joe Specker reappeared. "Whose car is the green Kia?"

"It's my rental, picked it up at the Spokane Airport around 4:00 p.m. yesterday from National Rental Car."

"Anybody been in it but you?"

"No, except for Emma who drove the last 100 yards up the driveway. I made a stop for a couple of Cokes before leaving the Spokane area. That's it."

"Your name please?"

"David Saul Milton, M.D."

"Well Mr. Milton, we found a bag weighing about two pounds in the wheel well of your vehicle. My educated guess is that it's uncut cocaine. We'll make sure what it is at the lab. I need to arrest you now. By protocol I need to handcuff you as well. Make it easy on yourself and don't fight it. You have the right to remain silent..."

David didn't hear the rest of his Miranda rights as Officer Cruz cuffed David behind his back.

"There has to be a mistake, this has to be a mistake," Emma screamed over and over.

Joe, acting disoriented, but finally realizing the seriousness of what was happening said, "David, don't say anything to anybody until you have a lawyer. I will call in the morning to get you one."

Clara and Alan said nothing although each had a different expression. Clara was simply dumbfounded. Alan was smirking. Alan now chirped in, "I know some guys who do criminal work. Yeah, don't say anything."

Cruz grabbed David by the arm and led him out the door and down the stairs. He guided David to a waiting police car using his baton, less than gently, to point the way. A tow truck had already started jacking up the back of the Kia to tow it away.

Joe Specker then announced to the room, "Clara, Joe, Alan and the rest of you please stay here at the house. I am going to have two officers search Mr. Milton's belongings and then bring them in."

"It's Dr. Milton. He did nothing wrong. This is a huge mistake," Emma shouted.

Specker, ignoring her comments, said, "Joe, can you show my officers where he was staying in the house? I am going back to Central to book Milton and then we may be back later today. I am so sorry for the intrusion but we've got over two pounds of what looks like cocaine."

Specker turned to leave, then turned to Joe and grinned, "Not looking real good for your guest, Joe." Specker closed the door as Cruz and another officer descended the stairs to search David's room and belongings.

The family sat in the living room. Emma crying, Clara and Joe stunned, and Alan sitting complacently with his arms folded, annoyed that his sleep was disturbed.

Chapter 40

During the entire time David sat cuffed in the back seat of the police cruiser, he kept repeating, "This is a terrible mistake."

Lieutenant Specker, sitting to David's left in the back of the police cruiser, was less than polite saying, "Shut up for the last time, buddy. So far Mr. Big Shot Seattle Hebe, it looks like all the evidence is against you."

"How did you know I was Jewish, Lieutenant?"

"None of your business, asshole, shut up."

David now understood the situation, unfortunately too clearly. Initially, he thought, or at least hoped, that someone had left the cocaine mistakenly or was using him or the rental car as a mule to transport the drug.

Could any human be so mean spirited to set him up on a cocaine possession?

David had heard all of the conversation with Joe, Alan and Clara except for a moment that Specker went back to say good-bye. With Emma present, Specker was not likely to be told that he was Jewish. David knew he had been set up, by Alan, Joe, or both.

David turned to the deputy sitting to his right, "Excuse me officer, what's your name?"

"Sergeant John Wilke."

"Well, Sergeant, you are my witness. Lieutenant Specker called me a 'Hebe', which is a derogatory way of saying that I am Jewish, which is true."

"Shut your mouth, asshole," said Specker.

David continued, "I never said, nor did anyone else say, during the arrest that I was Jewish. Which leads me to believe that the good Lieutenant knew who I was before ....."

Specker, listening to the accusation, hit David in the ribs with the end of his baton hard enough to hear a definite cracking sound like breaking a pencil. David screamed loudly. Specker followed the poke by saying, "I'd shut your fucking trap up completely if I were you. Wilke won't remember anything I tell him not to remember. Right Wilke?"

"Right, Lieutenant."

David, already bent over to the side, gasped for air and his breathing became shallow and rapid. David could not take a deep breath without intense pain in his left chest.

David knew that the baton had just fractured his ribs.

...

Specker and Wilke escorted David into the county jail. Another officer booked David and had him finger printed. David's breathing continued to be shallow and painful.

David was then taken to a small room to have mug shots.

"Please, do you have any Tylenol?" David asked the officer taking the photographs.

"Sorry, no, I have some ibuprofen, but I don't think I can give you anything. Against rules."

David, the surgeon, thought. *Ibuprofen wouldn't do. Inhibits platelets. Until I know I'm not bleeding, I need to stick to Tylenol.*

Pleading again to the photographer, he said, "I think I have a broken rib. Can I get a doctor to see me?"

"You'd have to ask the jailer, I think it's Lannie. I'm just the photographer."

"Will you tell him for me? They don't seem to be listening."

Flat toned, the photographer replied, "Sure, if I remember." He didn't.

Once placed in a holding cell, David asked the jailer, "What am I being charged with, I have the right to know? Also, I think I have a broken rib. I need to see a doctor." David was now spitting up small flecks of blood.

"Possession of an illegal drug with intent to distribute and resisting arrest. What, you a fuckin' doctor? How would you know you have anything? Just playing me, boy?" said the jailer, Lannie Waller, a grizzled 40 year veteran of the penal system.

"This is total bullshit. Don't I get to see a judge?" David could only talk in a low whisper-like voice. He had too much pain taking a breath deep enough to say more than a few words at a time or talk loudly.

"And I am a doctor and I think I have a broken rib...a fracture of a left rib can cause the rupture of the spleen or a lung contusion...and if I happen to bleed to death sitting in this cell,... the shit will hit the fan... particularly when you've been warned."

David stopped talking to concentrate on breathing.

"Like I give a shit. Court's open Monday afternoon for criminal hearings. You, or your lawyer, can enter a plea at that time. Until then you're mine. So shut the fuck up and sit down. There's a can in the back of the cell."

"Don't I get to make a phone call?"

"Yeah, you get one and Specker said you already made it."

"He's lying."

"You'd better watch who you call a liar, he's not a nice man," Waller smirked.

"I want an attorney."

"You had a chance when you made your call. You'll be assigned one from the PD office thirty minutes before you enter a plea. That's Monday at 1:30 p.m."

"I need to see a doctor, please.....I can't wait until Monday." David took a shallow breath. "I'm spitting up blood."

"Monday, that's just your plea. You ain't goin' nowhere soon. Not likely judge will give you bail. Too much drug and not being from around here. We've got you until they set a trial date. Doc don't come in til 10:00, 10:30 this morning. So shut the fuck up."

Specker walked back into the cell area and addressed Waller, "How's the asshole doing?"

Waller responded, "Making a shit load of complaints, detective. He said he didn't get to make a call. Says he's got a broken rib and needs to see doc."

Specker, uninterested as he leafed through a stack of papers, said, "I can't remember now. He may have made a call in the car. I'll get back to you on that. If he's got a broken a rib, it's his own fault for resisting. He can see the doc when he comes in. Don't call him early, costs the county hundred fifty bucks for nothing."

"Sure, Lieutenant," Waller said.

David sat in a heap, concentrating only on one

breath at a time.

I don't want to die.

In the cell with him were two clearly inebriated older men. They would be no help.

Chapter 41

At 6:00 a.m., Officer Cruz and his partner left the Braza house. Emma and Clara had fallen asleep on the couches in the living room. Without waking the two women, Joe and Alan snuck into the kitchen at 6:15 a.m.

"Alan, do you know what is going on here. Is this all your doing?" asked Joe.

"Dad, we agreed that you'd stay out of all this, remember," said Alan.

"Son, I didn't tell you to do *this*. I just didn't want him seeing Emma, but this is horrible. He could go to jail, lose his license. This is way overboard."

"I did nothing. Nothing at all." Alan said, realizing his dad still didn't really know anything for certain. Alan would keep it that way.

At the same time Alan thought to himself, '*Screw him. Emma was warned and warned again. If not by you, then by me. He got what he deserved.*'

Joe, still not sure said, "Alan, if you did something, you were wrong to go this far. Can you help undo it?"

"Forget about it, Dad. I didn't do shit. But even if I did, no way to fix it now. Not without putting me and maybe you and the business in jeopardy. Besides, if I could turn it around, I wouldn't. I don't want that weasel around here."

Alan and Joe turned to the door from the living room. There stood Emma, mouth agape. She had heard a good deal of the conversation.

A screaming Emma rushed Alan. She grabbed the only utensil on the kitchen counter, a large metal spatula.

"You fucking asshole," Emma screamed. "How dare you enter my life. How dare you decide who I can see or like. How dare you."

Joe tried to arm tackle Emma but her force carried her past a somewhat out of shape arm. She swung the spatula hitting Alan on the side of an arm raised to protect his face.

Both Joe and Alan were screaming, "Stop, Emma."

Joe grabbed Emma by the chest and pulled her up and away. She tried to kick Alan with her bare feet but he was already too far away and laughing.

Alan, jesting at his sister, said, "Shit, girl, if you're coming after me, use something like a knife not a spatula. Dumb ass bitch."

"Alan, shut up and get out of here. Now," Joe screamed.

"With pleasure." Alan left, but returned to his bedroom to get some sleep.

Clara entered the kitchen. "What's going on here?" she asked.

"Nothing Clara. Emma and Alan were fighting, now go back to sleep."

Emma, now in a heap on the floor next to the refrigerator, was red as a beefsteak tomato. "Alan did it, Alan did it, Mom," she cried. "He put those drugs in the car and called the police. He had no right to enter my life. I was happy. He had no right."

Clara looked to Joe, "Joe, is this true?"

"Mom, I heard them talking," Emma screamed. "Alan said that he did all this. I want to kill him. He can't ruin my life. It's not fair."

Joe responded immediately, "Clara, Emma, I don't know. I don't know if Alan is responsible, he may have just been spouting or gloating. He said he didn't do anything. I know nothing and I still don't know what happened."

Emma, crying again, said, "I've got to get to the jail and help David. Mom you've got to come with me."

"Clara, I don't want you leaving the house," Joe said. "You've not slept. Emma you too. Get some sleep and we'll work this out later in the morning. We'll need to find a lawyer for David. If he's not guilty, we'll sort this out."

Emma pleaded, "No, I won't sleep. Mom, please come with me."

"Joe, I need to be with Emma now," Clara said. "I'll rest later. I hope that Alan hasn't had a part in this. How terrible would that be?"

Emma and Clara quickly changed into jeans and shirts, sans makeup, grabbed two mugs of coffee, two untoasted popups and got into Clara's car and drove directly to the Walla Walla city jail.

At 7:00 a.m. the jailer, Lannie Waller, came back to David's cell and said, "Pretty girl out there, with her mom, says she knows you and she's local. Visiting hours ain't 'til 2:00, so I gotta send her away. She says she needs to see that you are alive. I told her you were breathing. But she ain't believing me. I'm gonna open the door for a second, so stand up at the cell corner so she can see you ain't dead, yet. That's all the time you're gonna get, got it?"

David moved to the corner of the cell and stood up on the bench so that his head was just under the top of the bars. He was guarding his left side but his bent appearance looked only as if he didn't want his head above the top of the cell. Standing hurt.

Emma appeared in the door scanning the room. "David, David," she yelled.

David knew the jailer would shut the solid 3" steel door as soon as she saw him.

He talked as loud as he could, "Call Rafe Gomez and get me a lawyer." The door slammed shut. With the distance, and the fact that he couldn't yell, he had no idea whether Emma had heard him. The door slammed with enough impact to shake the bars of the cell and Emma disappeared from view.

Emma saw David mouthing something with difficulty, but didn't hear a syllable. He was alive, that was all she knew. His look of utter despondency matched her feeling of total hopelessness.

"Shit, I knew I shouldn't have let the bitch in the door. Specker's gonna kill me", spit out Waller.

David slowly descended off the bench, felt light-headed and lay on the cold cement floor of the cell.

Emma bowed her head and put both hands on the impenetrable door for support. They were but twenty feet apart, but the chasm between them seemed intergalactic. Emma could only lament to the cold grey metal, "What have they done? What have they done? Please, David, forgive me."

Emma walked to the lobby and went to an unmanned information booth. On the counter lay a directory of numbers and rooms on a laminated piece of eight and one-half by eleven paper. Emma turned the sheet around and looked for Public Defender. Nothing. Next Emma looked for Prosecutor. Fourth Floor, Room 417, Extension 8444.

After parking Clara in the coffee shop across the street, Emma went up to the fourth floor. It was now 7:35 a.m. A plaque next to Room 417 read that the Prosecutor's office wasn't to open until 9:00 a.m. She could see through the window that people were already working. Emma banged on the door and kept banging until an armed sheriff appeared behind her.

"Miss, you can't be doing that," the sheriff said. "I suggest you leave the building and return after 9:00 a.m. when they open."

"I'm sorry. I just needed some information. My boyfriend just got arrested on a total bullshit charge. He was set up. I wanted to find him an attorney. I couldn't find a listing for the Public Defender's Office. Can you help me?"

"Yes and no," the sheriff said.

"What?" Emma asked.

"Yes, I can help you. No, you won't find one. Private attorneys do all the public defense work in this jurisdiction. We don't have enough bad guys in Walla Walla to support a full time PD office. Not like Seattle or Tacoma. If you cannot afford one, then a half an hour before your friend pleads he will be assigned a public defender."

"Do you have any recommendations?" Emma pleaded.

"I don't make recommendations, it's against policy. Now I'd like you to leave. Go home and come back."

Emma gathered Clara and headed back home. The Walla Walla Sheriff's officers had left. The house was quiet and Joe and Alan had gone back to sleep.

Chapter 42

Hawkins, Connor and Baker and the rest of the DEA force had returned to their positions after the arrest of the drug droppers. As before, the best view line belonged to William Baker. At 4:30 am, four squad cars from the Walla Walla Sheriff's Department entered the property, led by an older man in uniform. The approach to the house and the search of the car were strictly by the book, professional police work.

With lights from the house, patrol cars and flashlights, Baker had no problem filming and recording the entire scene except for conversation inside the house. Finally, a young man in cuffs was taken away in one car. The other two cars followed with a lone car left behind. Those officers departed sixty-five minutes later.

Hawkins had decided to hold off on presenting Pesses and Vargas until court convened at 1:30 p.m. Connors, who knew a number of the men in the Walla Walla Sheriff's office, called at 6:30 a.m. to ask about David Milton. Knowing the routine, he asked for the jailer.

Lannie Waller answered the phone.

"Waller here."

"Lannie, this is Harry Connors from the DEA. How ya doin?"

"Fine, Harry, what can I do for you?" asked Waller.

"You guys pick up a David Milton this morning on possession?"

"Yep."

"Plea at 1:30?" Connors asked.

"That's what Specker said."

Damn, Harry thought. *Specker is an asshole. Figured to be him.* "How's he doing? We may need to talk to him?"

"He's bitching like all of them. Claims he didn't do shit. He hasn't lawyered up yet that I know of. We'll get him a PD before the hearing. He's bitching that he has a broken rib, but I think it's just an act. They're all scum."

"Lannie, the guy is a surgeon, he might actually know."

Lieutenant Specker, who had walked into the jailer's cubbyhole, grabbed the phone from Lannie.

"Lieutenant Specker here, who am I talking to?"

"Lieutenant Specker, Harry Connors from the Spokane DEA."

"Connors, what displeasure hearing your voice," Specker said. "What can I not do for you?" Neither man liked the other.

Connors, trying to be nice, said, "We have an informant here in Spokane that says a couple pounds of cocaine was moved in the last few days for a sale in Walla Walla. Word has it you've got it. Right?"

"So, what if we do. We can handle it," said Specker.

"For drug deals this big, the DEA needs to be involved."

Specker, showing nothing but disdain for a fellow law officer, said, "Harry, go fuck yourself. We made the bust and we're taking all the credit. Not sharing this one, you guys did squat sitting with your thumbs up your ass."

"Glad you have no opinions, Specker, like always.

What time is he pleading? It's an open court and we need to be there. I assume 1:30, Monday, when Criminal opens?"

"At least you got that right. We're not releasing him to you without a fight. It's our case. How did you hear about this? In Spokane? That's funny because we heard the drug came from Portland."

"Sorry, can't give out my sources," Connors said.

"Well, nice to talk to you. Day late and a dollar short, as they say." Specker hung up thinking, *how did they hear about this in Spokane, this doesn't make any sense. I hope Alan isn't talking too much. He promised.*

Connors told Hawkins and Baker about the discussion, including the possibility that David Milton had a broken rib. Connors felt that Specker acted suspicious when he heard we had info from Spokane. Apparently, the deal came from Portland. He might smell a rat. Worse than that was David might actually be hurt. He had promised Rafe Gomez that nothing could happen.

Hawkins swore softly, "Shit. Shit Shit."

Hawkins certainly didn't want anyone trying to force a confession from Dr. Milton, possibly hurting him worse, if they hadn't already. Hawkins wanted the source of the cocaine. After all, finding the cocaine source was the whole purpose of the plan. But trying to wait to trap Alan Braza into calling the source seemed risky at this point. With consultation and agreement from Baker and Connors, the DEA officers decided they needed to pick up Alan Braza now, then bring all the information to the County Prosecutor by noon and get David Milton out of jail.

Chapter 43

At 8:45 a.m., as Emma was compiling a list of local criminal attorneys to call, three cars pulled up to the house. Out of the cars emerged, eleven men, heavily armed.

Emma went up to her parent's bedroom. Both were dead to the world.

"Mom, Dad, the police are back. I think you've got to get up again."

Joe jumped out of bed and looked out the window. "Not Walla Walla police or the sheriffs. Who are these guys?" He then noticed the large block letters of "DEA" on most of their gear.

"It's the Drug Enforcement Agency. They must be here to follow up or search the area again. Shit."

"Joe, should we get Alan up?"

"No, let him sleep. If they want him, they'll tell us."

The door knocking had already begun as the Brazas, already awake, descended the stairs.

These men, though armed, had their weapons holstered and were not wearing Kevlar.

"Mr. Braza, I am Richard Hawkins of the Drug Enforcement Agency, I am out of the Seattle office and this is Agent William Baker and Agent Harry Connors of the Spokane office. Is Alan Braza here in the house?"

"Yes, he's sleeping," said Joe.

"Would you mind getting him up, please."

"Clara, would you get Alan. I want to talk to these officers."

Clara went up the stairs quickly.

"So what's this about?" Joe asked.

Hawkins responded, "Actually, I am not at liberty to discuss anything at this point. We'll just wait for Alan Braza, if that's okay with you."

Emma, from behind her dad, started to speak "Sir..."

Joe turned quickly, held Emma by the shoulders.

"You are not to say anything to these officers about this morning," Joe said. "We don't know what is happening and we don't know what they want. So zip it. I mean it. Nobody says anything until we have an attorney present."

"Dad, I just want to ask if David is okay, nothing more, I promise."

"Okay, but that's all."

Emma asked politely, "Do you know anything about David Milton who was taken earlier this morning by the Walla Walla Sheriffs?"

"Yes, I understand that he was taken, miss," Hawkins responded, "But I can't discuss that either. Sorry. I'm sure he'll be okay. I would assume that he is still in the city jail." Hawkins had no intention of telling her about the possible broken rib.

"I was there earlier this morning but they wouldn't let me talk to him or see him, except for a second. He tried to say something but I couldn't understand him and they slammed the door."

"Sorry, I can't comment. I am sure he'll be okay."

Alan Braza descended the stairs, barefoot, half asleep.

Joe introduced Alan. "This is my son, Alan Braza. This is Mr. Hawkins of the Drug Enforcement Agency."

"Are you Alan Braza?"

"Yes I am."

"Mr. Braza, we're going to ask you to come with us now for questioning. You've not been charged with a crime but I am going to give you your Miranda rights. "You have the right..."

Joe Braza yelled at Hawkins, "You're not taking my son. He didn't do anything."

Hawkins, not liking anyone in his face, "Back off, Mr. Braza. He's not under arrest. We just need to ask him some questions. Take five steps back, now."

After finishing Mirandizing Alan, Hawkins continued, talking only to Alan, "We do not need to handcuff you, and we'd like you to come peacefully. I can get a warrant, if need be, but it'll be easier if you just come with us peacefully. You'll need to get dressed. We are going to an interrogation room at the city jail. If you, or your family, want to have an attorney present, that is your right."

Joe spoke emphatically and with deep anger. His face was contorted, neck veins bulging. "Alan, say nothing. I will get an attorney there as quickly as I can. Don't say anything to anyone."

"Dad, I understand. I didn't do anything," said Alan.

"Just keep your mouth shut," Joe said, loudly

Alan put his clothes on and returned.

Joe repeated forcefully, "Alan, say nothing."

Alan was escorted to an unmarked car, placed in the back seat and all of the cars then left.

Joe had tears in his eyes as Alan drove away in the police cruiser. He realized that Alan may have been involved in David's arrest and that he could be in serious trouble. He hoped not. He thought about how the DEA would have been suspicious of Alan. He could only think of one explanation. Joe was absolutely certain that Specker certainly wouldn't have called the DEA on Alan. He then lost all his composure, slammed the front door, spun around and confronted Emma.

"You ratted out your brother, didn't you?" Joe yelled, not asking a question, but accusing.

Emma, indignant, responded with a raised voice, "No, I didn't say anything to anyone. You were here."

Joe, his face almost a deep purplish shade, was screaming at Emma, "There would have been no reason to suspect Alan of anything unless you told someone."

Emma, now pleading, "I did not, I swear."

"You were just trying to protect your Jew boyfriend. I told you he would bring trouble and now look what has happened."

Emma screamed as loud as she could, "I told no one. Ask Mom, she was with me."

Joe screamed back with venom, "There was plenty of time for you to rat out your brother. Phone someone or tell someone down at the police station this morning. You told someone that Alan caused all this and now he's in trouble and we don't know if he had anything to do with it."

Emma, screaming back, losing her voice, "Dad, listen, I swear..."

"Emma, I'm through with you. You wouldn't listen to reason. I want you out of here. I've worked my whole life to make your life easy and you fucked me and fucked Alan. Everything you have belongs to my hard work, every piece of clothing, your car, your education, your trips, your phone, everything. All from me. I want you out of my life. I never want to see you again."

Clara tried to stop the two from killing each other and pried herself between them. "Stop this you two."

"I want her out of here, Clara," Joe said, pointing to the front door. "I don't care where she goes or what she does. I am sorry for her kidnapping, but she's changed. She's not my daughter. No child of mine would send their brother to the gallows, and for what, a Jew."

Emma, screaming again, "You're not fair. You never gave David a chance."

"I didn't want him here and you knew it. I want you out of here. Go live with your Jew, I don't care anymore."

Clara pleaded with Joe, "No, Joe, she can't leave. She's not strong enough for this."

"She was strong enough to not listen to us."

Emma, now with barely any voice, "I'll leave. I'll leave now. I'll just get my stuff and leave."

"Everything you have is mine. I want you out of here. I am done paying for you and your Jew friend."

Emma, crying, but speechless, stood back and pulled her cell phone out of her pocket and threw it against the closed front door as hard as she could. "Are you happy?" she rasped.

"Get out of here. And the car stays, everything stays."

Emma was dumbfounded. "I don't want anything of yours. I did nothing wrong. I said nothing to anyone about Alan, or you. I swear." Her voice was barely audible.

Emma took off her blouse and threw it at her father, who didn't flinch or move. Then she kicked off her shoes, and removed her jeans after taking out her wallet. She threw all her credit cards and cash and even the coins on the floor and hurled the wallet at her dad, now turned to stone.

"Happy now?" Emma said.

Clara was screaming, "Joe, stop this. Emma, don't leave."

mma started to head out the door and turned. "Dad, you make me sick. Mom, I love you, but I can't live with my father right now."

Emma, wearing only her bra and underwear, opened the door and walked down the porch stairs. She then stopped, turned around and walked back in the house and picked up her wallet. She quickly grabbed her driver's license and then threw the wallet back on the floor.

"The driver's license is mine. Fuck you." Emma turned, exited the house again, and walked down the stairs and away.

Joe stood motionless, felt nothing and everything. Clara feeling faint, started for the couch, but made it only a few steps and sat down on the floor in the foyer against a wall. She was too stunned to cry or speak as she watched her family unravel.

Joe went to the open front door. "Don't come back." He slammed the door hard enough that an entry wall sconce fell to the floor and shattered.

Emma walked fifty yards down the driveway before Julio, one if the groundskeepers Emma had known her whole life, stopped her. Emma could not speak. Baring his chest, Julio wrapped her in his sweaty work shirt and escorted her to a small house on the edge of the property where he lived with his wife, Chayo.

Upon entering the small house, Chayo became hysterical with fright, asking if something had happened at the house. Were there people hurt?

Emma speaking as slowly as she could with her voice almost completely gone, said, "No one is hurt, Chayo. No one is hurt. My father asked me to leave the family."

Chayo told her husband, "Get out of the house and leave us alone."

She gave Emma a T-shirt from their son's drawer and a set of old Nike warm-ups. Emma sat in the kitchen in shock, but at least covered.

Once covered, Emma told Chayo again, "My father asked me to leave the family. I will never come back, ever."

Chayo now worried that helping Emma might jeopardize Julio's job.

"We need get you away quick, Emma. What can we do?"

"Can I borrow your phone?" Emma asked.

Emma called Sophie in New Jersey.

"Hi Emma, how's it going?"

"Soph, I am in trouble, big trouble. I've lost my voice from yelling so I will talk slowly and softly, as long as I can talk at all. David was arrested and taken to jail. I think Alan had someone put cocaine in his car. Alan has been arrested too. My father blamed me for Alan's arrest and he threw me out of the house. I have no clothes or money. Sophie, what am I going to do?"

"Jesus, Emma, I've just started a summer job. I can't come back to Washington right now."

"Soph, I didn't expect you to. Can you wire me some money to get me by?"

"Sure, where?"

"There is a Western Union office in Walla Walla, I think it's called Money Shop or Check Store. It's on Wilbur Avenue. Send it there. Can you spare seven hundred fifty dollars? You know I will make it up as soon as I can."

"I'll send a thousand. I'll do it as soon as we hang up."

"Thanks. I will keep in touch someway. I won't have a phone but I'll have my UW email account."

"Where are you going to go?"

"Not sure. David can't help me and I can't help him. I'll just have to figure it out."

"Your dad really throw you out for good?"

"That's what he said."

"Wow. I didn't think it would go this badly. Shit. Keep in touch. Emma, we'll make it, you and me, someway. Okay?"

"Sophie, I've got to go now. I don't have the voice or strength to say anything."

"Emma, please, before you hang up, we'll get through this, you'll see. Good for you for standing up against your father. Be strong."

"Soph, I love you. I'll get in touch as soon as I land somewhere. I will try to be strong but I just don't know if I have it in me."

Emma asked for and received a five dollar loan from Chayo. Emma told her that the money would be repaid when she could.

Emma knew a public bus ran into Walla Wall about two miles from the Braza house. Five dollars would get her into the city. She borrowed an old pair of flip-flops, thanked Chayo for her kindness, and walked out the door. She walked out of the Braza world, the only world she have ever known.

Emma had only five dollars, no credit cards, and no voice. *I can't help David. He knows that our family caused his arrest and he will never have anything to do with any Braza, including me. I don't know what to do or where to turn.*

Emma arrived into downtown Walla Walla by noon and then walked to the Check Shop. She prayed that Sophie wouldn't let her down. Her driver's license was enough ID to get her the thousand dollars. She asked for change for one of the $100s. Before exiting, she noted telephone calling cards for sale and purchased Fifty dollars worth of calls within the US. *'More than enough for now,'* she thought. Emma then walked to the Greyhound station, about three-quarters of a mile away.

Chapter 44

The next few hours at the Walla Walla County Jail could only be described as a three-ring circus played in the key of B Flat Crazy.

After Hawkins and the DEA had collected, but not arrested, Braza and with the two intruders already in tow, they drove to the County Jail. The thought of putting Braza, if he confessed, the two intruders, and David Milton, in the same holding cell was close to comical. But the County Jail was the only facility available.

The two intruders, Pesses and Vargas, were booked into jail. Because Hawkins did not have the cocaine, he booked them for unlawful and unlicensed firearms and vehicular prowling. Flimsy charge, but enough to get them into jail.

Hawkins asked Connors to try to see how Dr. Milton was doing. Specker had given the jailer specific instructions not to let anyone talk to Milton.

Alan Braza was put in an interrogation room. A fancy three-piece suit lawyer sat beside Alan before any questions were asked. Specker was livid but neither he nor Hawkins said a word to each other.

Hawkins was pure pissed.

Specker was pissed and afraid. Afraid of what Braza might say.

Hawkins spoke to Braza for almost thirty minutes. On the advice of counsel he said close to nothing. He denied doing or knowing anything.

The attorney then spoke up. "Either arrest my client or let him go. You have no evidence. I'd like him released immediately or charged."

Hawkins had no options. He didn't have anything at this point to hold Braza. "You are free to go," Hawkins said to Alan and the lawyer. "You may not leave this jurisdiction until we've gotten some answers. Your attorney will tell you that fleeing is an admission of guilt, so stay put."

Alan Braza shook his attorney's hand and walked out of the jail. Alan made a call and Joe picked him up twenty minutes later.

It was now 10:45 a.m. Connors approached Hawkins. "We've got a problem. The doc just saw Milton. He's certain the doc's got some broken ribs and maybe bleeding into his chest or popped his spleen. They are taking him with armed guard to Walla Walla General. I couldn't talk to him but he's not going to make the 1:30 court appearance."

Upset beyond comprehension, Hawkins yelled every nasty word in his lengthy repertoire. He then took a deep breath and said, "I've got to get to the prosecutor now and lay out everything. You and Baker get to the ER and make sure Milton's okay. We'll deal with Braza and Specker later. We may have lost any chance to get the real bad guys. Shit, shit, shit."

Hawkins went up to the fourth floor and the prosecutor's office and showed his credentials to the front desk assistant. "Who was assigned Specker's drug case this morning?"

"Specker was here at 10:00 a.m. and went immediately to Alan Jones' office next door."

"Thanks."

Hawkins exited and went to the next office. The sign, in bold, read, **Alan Jones, District Attorney, Walla Walla County**.

Hawkins again showed his credentials to the secretary. "I need to see Mr. Jones."

"He's busy, officer."

Hawkins, almost yelling, "We can make this easy or make this hard. Lieutenant Specker badly misled Mr. Jones this morning. I need to speak to Mr. Jones now. I am not going to walk by you and bust in the door, but I will call the Attorney General in Olympia if I don't get a few minutes with him now. And I mean now."

Alan Jones, hearing the ruckus, poked his head out the door. "Everything okay here?"

Hawkins jumped at the opportunity. "Alan Hawkins, DEA. I need a minute of your time. You've been sold a bill of goods this morning. I need just a minute of your time."

"Okay, Mr. Hawkins, come into my office. Just a minute though. I'm really busy."

"Thanks." Hawkins knew that the explanation might take more than 30 minutes or an hour but once he started laying out evidence, tapes, and video he knew Jones would listen.

After listening to Hawkins and seeing the evidence, Jones needed no convincing.

Looking at his yellow legal pad and the notes, taken over the past half hour, Jones said, "I would have said thirty minutes ago, the case against Milton was rock solid, can't lose, slam dunk, easiest drug case ever. Wow, would I have been wrong."

"You got that right. Now what are we going to do?" said Hawkins.

"Well, we still don't know the supplier. You'll need to try to corner Braza, but if he's smart, there'll be no money trail. Not sure we'll have enough to even charge him with bad judgment. Specker must have gotten the tip from Braza or an intermediary, but Braza could just say he heard it from a guy he didn't know in a bar, yadda yadda. Specker did nothing wrong in arresting Milton, but Milton was also booked for resisting arrest and, in the scuffle, Specker poked him a bit too hard. He said, she said, and the other deputies are going to back up Specker."

"Specker's an asshole."

"Whatever," Jones said. "Best I can do at 1:30 is drop the drug charges against Milton and see if Specker will drop the resisting charge. I can say that if he doesn't, and the case goes further, Specker might get implicated. I'll present your evidence to him. He's somewhat of a mean sonofabitch, I admit, but I think he'll use good judgment and let this slide."

Hawkins was so despondent. "I have a court order to inspect Alan Braza's phone and bank records. You're right though. Likely, this whole case is going to fall apart."

Jones, understanding Hawkins's position, restated what he could offer. "I'll do what we can with Specker and the resisting charge. He won't be happy about losing the collar on the drug deal. He may have been set up as much as Milton."

"Thanks again. I've got to get to the hospital to see if Milton is okay. Does he need representation at the trial?"

"Only if Specker keeps the resisting charge, but I'll call you. Gimme your cell number."

Hawkins left and Jones barked to his secretary. "Get Lieutenant Specker back up here now. Do not take no for an answer. Tell him his case just turned to shit."

Specker was back up in five minutes from the jail. He was in Jones office for fifteen minutes. Yelling and screaming, Jones and Specker rattled a few windows.

Specker left, downtrodden and planned not going to the hearing. He'd give it to Sergeant Wilke. He'd make sure that Wilke supported him on Milton resisting, but he'll drop the charge if Milton promises not to charge him with assault.

What looked like an exciting day in court at 10 a.m. was, by 1:30 p.m., pretty tame. All charges against David Milton were dismissed. The two intruders, Pesses and Vargas, were booked on vehicular prowling and unlicensed firearms. Bail was set at five hundred dollars each and both were out on the street by 5:00 p.m. The case against Pesses and Vargas was weak other than the illegal weapons. The prowling was simply a misdemeanor. With their past records, they would likely get a thirty to sixty day sentence and then be back on the streets.

Chapter 45

David Milton was gasping for breath by the time the 'doc' for the county jail arrived at 10:15 am.

"I am Dr. Hofsepian. Mr. Waller tells me you are hurting."

David, using short breaths, spoke in half sentences. "I am a senior surgical resident at the UW...I was hit in the side...with a baton. I can't breathe....I am sure I have some broken...ribs. I may have a ...hemopneumothorax and...a ruptured spleen...I need to get...to a level I or level II trauma hospital...now. Please help me."

Alan Hofsepian was a simple family physician and used to short uncomplicated visits to the jail to supplement his salary at a local clinic. He did know when someone was sick, and David Milton was sick. Big time sick.

Hofsepian grabbed his stethoscope and a blood pressure cuff and quickly took David's vital signs. BP 90/60, Pulse 135 and weak. Respirations 40 - 50. David was sweaty, clammy and pale. His extremities were cold and his palm, when stretched, had no red in the creases suggesting profound anemia from blood loss. David had no breath sounds on his left side.

Hofsepian hurried out of the jail cell and ran at Lannie Waller yelling, "Lannie. Stop what you're doing. This guy Milton is deathly ill. He needs to get to the county ER now. He could die here in the jail. I mean now!"

Finally, someone had gotten Waller's attention. The Walla Walla county jail had a Hispanic druggie die in a cell two years earlier. The county lost fifty thousand dollars to his widow, countless hours of aggravation, and two incumbent supervisors had lost re-election as a result of the snafu. Waller, now motivated by an hysterical physician, moved quickly and called 911.

EMTs arrived in nine minutes and a deputy was assigned to Milton, who remained cuffed.

The EMTs radioed David's vital signs to Walla Walla General Hospital. Upon arrival, David was only semi-awake and the ER staff demanded the police take off the handcuffs and disappear.

IVs were started and the surgeon on call, Dr. Harold King stood ready. Dr. King was six years out of his residency and, fortunately for David, had done a trauma fellowship at Harbor General in Los Angeles. Hofsepian had called ahead to tell Dr. King about the transfer.

King rattled off a string of orders including IVs and 6 units of O negative blood on an emergency type and cross. He heard no breath sounds on David's left chest and guessed, at the least, that he had bled into his chest or a punctured lung, or both. Whether David had a ruptured spleen, King didn't know, yet. David needed a chest tube immediately.

One more quick order and a chest tube insertion kit dropped on the stand next to David's gurney. David, now alert enough, received a thirty second update and oral consent.

"Go for it," David, semi-alert, said.

Dr. King turned David left side up and anesthetized his lateral left chest wall with lidocaine above the bruise marks. A finger width incision down to the ninth rib was followed by a small incision into David's lung cavity.

"Ooow", David moaned.

Dr. King quickly inserted a large chest tube and secured it in place with sutures.

"Ooow, ooow", David moaned again.

The nurses, working quickly, hooked the tube up to chest suction. Five hundred ccs of blood drained immediately. A constant flow of air into the suction apparatus suggested that David had an air leak, that the lung had been punctured by the broken rib. The chest tube would keep the lung inflated and the lung cavity free of blood. David's blood oxygen saturation levels rose quickly to a more reasonable level at that point.

From the door to the treatment room, a technician yelled, "Hematocrit's 21%."

Dr. King, getting a quick glance at David's size and weight, told his crew, "Four to five unit bleed, so far. Keep those IVs running as fast as you can pump them in."

David's vital signs had now stabilized with two IVs running wide open, and the re-inflated lung.

A FAST ultrasound of David's abdomen at the bedside strongly suggested an intra-abdominal bleed. Given the location of the bruising and David's apparent blood loss, only a laceration of the spleen made sense.

David's first cogent comment followed, "I'm a senior surgical resident at the UW. I understand what is happening. Help me."

King responded, "David, quickly, you've almost certainly sustained a splenic laceration. With 4-5 units of blood loss already, you need to be explored now. I will try to salvage the spleen if I can, maybe use glue and sutures. I've had success with that more than a few times. If I don't feel comfortable, I will remove your spleen."

David was on the OR table within eighteen minutes. One unit of O negative blood was being given and another ready to follow.

Once anesthetized, Dr. King made an incision on David's abdomen. As soon as King entered the abdomen, he removed a thousand ccs of blood, mostly clotted. He quickly discovered active bleeding coming from the splenic area. King, moving quickly, but being mindful of the pancreas and stomach, mobilized the spleen and found a one inch splenic laceration just under a torn diaphragm. Dr. King closed the laceration with fibrin glue and sutures and all bleeding ceased. King re-explored the abdominal cavity and encountered no additional bleeding. Careful re-inspection of the splenic repair revealed no bleeding. King sutured the abdomen closed.

David lay in the recovery room for three hours and after a third unit of blood, his vital signs stabilized. David's blood work after three units revealed mild anemia, but adequate for a young adult. David would need no additional blood.

David, alert as the anesthetic began to wear off, gave his contact information to a nurse who called his father and the surgical office at the UW. The recovery nurse told David that all the charges against him were dropped and the deputy assigned to him had left. That information would not sink in for another day or two.

David, drugged to the max, then asked, "Is there a girl named Emma waiting for me?"

The recovery room nurse said, "No, I don't think anyone is here now, or has been here since you arrived."

Chapter 46

Emma could barely speak and her throat ached as if she had been gargling vinegar. She stopped at a super market and purchased a small roll of lemon Lifesavers to suck on, a toothbrush and a small tube of tooth paste. The first bus to Seattle would leave in sixty minutes, or to Spokane in thirty minutes. Emma decided on Seattle. More options. She bought a small ham and cheese sandwich and a Diet Coke. Big mistake. The Coke burned like fire on her raw throat. She poured out the Coke, upset about spending two dollars for nothing, and filled the screw top bottle with water from a fountain.

Emma sat and thought. She then went to payphone and, using her newly purchased calling card, made a call which lasted only a few minutes. Although Emma found it too painful to speak loudly or for too long, the call gave her hope. She had a hunch, followed it, and now, at least, she had a plan.

In the bus, Emma pulled her knees up to her chest and tried to rethink all the happenings in the past few hours, days, weeks and months.

My only true happiness and peace since the rape and assault had been the weeks with David before he left for San Francisco in February, and then when he returned in April. I hope he will be okay. I know he will have nothing to do with me, or my family, ever again.

The bus ride to the downtown Seattle bus station took five hours, with stops in Richland, Yakima and Ellensburg. She then took the commuter train to SeaTac airport arriving around 11:00 p.m. Her throat still felt like it had been sandpapered and, only a little voice would come out. She found a comfortable seat and stretched out. Surprisingly, even to Emma, she slept.

Awakened at 5:00 a.m. by the airport cleaning staff, Emma moved to another seat and awaited for the Alaska

Airlines desk to open at 5:30 a.m. She bought a one-way ticket for cash, using up five hundred fifty dollars of her remaining stash. The plane left at 11:20 a.m. She waited at the gate, lying in the corner. She asked the lady behind the counter to awaken her if she didn't hear the call.

"You okay," the agent asked?

Emma, voice still gone, said, "No, not really."

"I mean are you sick?"

Emma assumed that the agent wasn't going to allow a sick patient on the flight. Emma responded, "No, not sick, just hoarse from yelling." Emma then lied, "I'm fine."

Emma boarded the plane, which was only a third full, and moved just before takeoff to a rear row that was vacated. She put up the arm rests and lay down after the seat belt signs went off, keeping only the middle belt around her loosely. Emma fell asleep quickly.

At 1:45 p.m. the flight attendant nudged her to sit up and put on her seat belt. The plane made a rough and bumpy descent.

Well, this parallels my recent life.

Emma held on to both armrests and the plane touched down safely. She exited the plane by the back door gangway to a blast of intense, almost painful, heat. Her face burned after the air-conditioned confines of the Boeing 737.

Chapter 47

David's mother and father arrived at Walla Walla General at 10 p.m. and once they found David stable and had talked to Dr. King, left to get a hotel room. David's mother stayed the night in David's room and would be relieved by David's father at 4 a.m.

Clara Braza showed up at 11 a.m. the next morning. Luckily, neither Mike nor Laurie Milton was present in the room.

Clara, still unaware that the charges against David had been dropped, spoke quickly.

"I am so sorry about what happened. We are still not sure who did this or why."

She had some idea about Alan's involvement but would never say so. David turned away, looking out the window.

Continuing, Clara told David, "Emma and her father got into a huge fight and Emma's run away."

Clara now had David's full attention as he turned his head back to her.

"We don't know where she could have gone," Clara said. She had no money, no car, or credit cards. She just disappeared. Might you know where she went?"

"I have no idea," said David, still drugged. "You could check my apartment in Seattle, or call her friend Sophie. I hope she's okay."

"Anyway, I am sorry about all this," Clara said. "If you need something you can call me. Do not call my husband or the house. I will give you my number."

Before Clara could write anything down, David said, "I am unlikely to call any of you, Mrs. Braza, ever. You know why, and I know why, so let's not play nice."

"I am sorry again. I still do thank you for being nice to Emma when she needed it. I am so sorry." Clara meant it.

"Mrs. Braza, I am tired and want to sleep, if you don't mind."

Clara left, her eyes reddened. What had they done? What had Alan done? What had Joe done? This young man, who seemed quite nice, did not deserve what had befallen him.

Chapter 48

The subsequent investigation into Braza and Specker turned up nada, zilch, nothing. Braza had no money trail to follow and Hawkins assumed he kept enough cash at home to make the deal. His phone records were clean. Hawkins figured the seller used pay phones or personal contacts to arrange the drop. The list of license plates given to the intruders, Pesses and Varga, came from a man they'd never seen before, who gave them no name, just money, one thousand dollars, for the job and the list of makes and licenses of the Braza cars.

Specker admitted only that Braza gave him the tip that afternoon. When the tip was given, he did mention that his sister had a new boyfriend from Seattle, who was Jewish and would be staying at the house. Specker said that Braza said he overheard a conversation about the drug deal coming from Portland at a bar in Walla Walla a few days earlier. Braza had told Specker that he didn't know any of the people talking. He didn't even remember which of the three or four bars he frequented was the place that he heard the conversation. All the bars he mentioned said that Alan came in often.

The whole case fell into the toilet. The prosecutor's office said not enough evidence existed to get a grand jury to bite. The casualties included David Milton in the hospital, Emma Braza missing, Alan Braza off scot-free and Rafe Gomez angry enough that he wouldn't take Hawk's calls. The only upside mini-victory was that David Milton was alive, wasn't serving five years in prison or losing his license to practice medicine for a bogus possession and distribution. Hawkins last thought was, "My job sucks." He then forgot everything and went back to finding bad guys. He'd make up with Rafe Gomez later.

Chapter 49

It was the Sunday after Memorial Day, 2:10 p.m. At one hundred thirteen degrees, in the shade, plastic would melt on the dashboard in minutes. Esther Milton was waiting just inside the baggage area at the Palm Springs Airport. Emma, seeing Esther, started crying. But with no voice to shout out, Emma ran, ran to her only option.

Emma carried no luggage, no carry-ons, because she had nothing. But she did carry a hunch that this eighty-one year old would both understand her feelings and help her. Esther gave Emma a huge hug and led her to the car. Esther had left the car running with the air-conditioning on.

Emma wore the worn Nike sweat suit given to her a day earlier by Nadia, the wife of the groundskeeper. The threadbare suit was at least two sizes too big. Her uncombed hair, her dirty clothes and disheveled appearance highlighted the weariness in the slump of her shoulders. All expected, Esther thought, for someone lost. But her face carried a sadness that Esther had not seen often since the years after World War II.

"Let's not talk 'til we get back to my place," Esther said. "You can shower or take a bath and get into some clean clothes. Rachel has a full wardrobe of stuff that you can wear."

"Okay." Emma fell asleep in the car.

Once in Esther's garage, she awakened Emma and they entered her modern spacious desert house sitting just off the 10th tee of the Grove Course at Indian Ridge Country Club. They went into the largest of Esther's guest rooms. King bed, beautifully decorated, with a private full bath and shower. Esther had a small fully functional outside casita, but she thought, correctly,

Emma needed the security inside the house.

Emma lay on the bed, curled up, weeping softly. Esther ran her a bath, threw in some herbal essences, a new fragrant bar of oatmeal lemon soap, bath towels, wash cloths, and a fresh change of loose comfortable clothes. Some pajamas and a bathrobe and a pair of sandals -- all Rachel's.

Emma sat in the tub for thirty minutes and emerged clean, but not new.

She sat quietly on Esther's couch in the den near the kitchen and ate a small chicken Caesar salad from Trader Joe's and a Dr. Brown's cream soda. Esther said nothing, but watched. After finishing, she brought her plate and soda can back to the sink, rinsed the plate, put it into the dishwasher and put the can into the recycle bin that she found in the second cabinet door she opened. Even these niceties were not lost on Esther. She sat next to Esther, grabbed a lightweight tan Afghan that was draped over the back of the couch, balled it up and cuddled with it. She looked at Esther with despair and rasped, "I need to talk to someone."

"What am I, chopped liver, talk." Esther knew that the Yiddish funny line was lost on Emma, but Esther couldn't help it, it fit the moment. "Talk until you've said everything you need to say."

"I loved growing up in Walla Walla..." Emma continued uninterrupted and told of her wonderful life that nearly came to an end 21 months earlier.

"But the kidnapping and rape destroyed my entire world. My whole existence changed. Everyone that knew me changed, the way they looked at me and acted around me. Most that met me afterward, other than a few of my doctors and counselors, that found out about that terrible awful thing, made me feel like it was my fault or I deserved it. Sophie, instead of an equal friend, became a protector and mentor.

"For fourteen months I couldn't find a way out. I couldn't find myself, the old me. I couldn't escape. I was so tired of being afraid. Then I found David and for the first time there was a little light at the end of the tunnel. Then a bigger light when I came back from Mexico after Christmas and realized how much I missed him. At the end of those few weeks, before he left for San Francisco, I felt I might be through the tunnel into the warmth of daylight - even though it was January in Seattle. When David returned in April none of the luster had gone.

"But to be whole and complete, I needed, I wanted my family to accept me, the new Emma, and, therefore, accept David. I felt that I didn't have enough time or strength left to find someone else to help me find myself."

Emma stopped for a moment and then restarted, "No, that's not right, it's not that I didn't have the strength or time, I didn't want to find anyone else. I found David and I am so in love with him. I don't need to look any further. But I so wanted my mom and dad to be a part of my life, and to at least give David a chance."

Emma went on in detail over what she could remember about the last few days... "then, after I got the money from Sophie, I called you, hoping that you would understand my pain and know what to do."

Esther moved and sat next to Emma and hugged her for what seemed an eternity.

Emma had not brought up David's injuries, so Esther judged correctly that Emma was unaware of David's trauma and the emergent surgery. Esther made the call not to add anything to Emma's burdens at this point. Then she told Emma a few more of her concentration camp experiences. Experiences she had not told before, memories that could not go to sleep. Esther thought to herself that *misery must really like company.*

"Emma, our pains are so different," Esther said, "but they are still pains. I think you need some rest. Why don't you get some sleep. It's 7:00 p.m. and I'll try to find out how David is. When you wake up, we'll talk."

"I don't want anyone to know where I am yet, except my friend, Sophie," Emma said. "That includes David and your family. I am not sure my reasoning is sound, but I have to do some thinking. Is that okay with you?"

"Sure, although I don't agree with you, but I won't tell a soul until you tell me to."

Emma called Sophie's cell phone and left a message that she was in Palm Desert with David's grandmother and left Esther's Palm Desert number. "I'll call you tomorrow. No one, absolutely no one, is to know where I am. Please, no one."

Emma slept until 6:00 am. She arose, made some coffee and sat on the same couch with the same Afghan and waited.

Esther entered the den at 7:00 a.m. "I talked to David's parents last night," she said. "David was not prosecuted and all the charges have been dropped. It will not go on his record and it will be as if nothing happened. That's the very, very good news."

Emma smiled. "That's great news. But, but, how did that happen? Did someone confess? Is my brother arrested? I just don't understand. But, that is great news."

"Emma, I don't have any of those answers. All I know now is that David is not in trouble with the law." Esther waited for a few seconds to let what she had said sink in.

"The bad news, that you couldn't have known about, is that before the charges were dropped, he was injured by one of the police officers with a baton. He ended having some broken ribs and a ruptured spleen and lung."

Emma's eyes and mouth opened to their full extent and her hands came out of the Afghan to her mouth. "No. No. Is he okay?"

"He had surgery at Walla Walla General and received some blood, but is now resting comfortably and should be okay. He is still sick and not totally out of the woods, at least those are the words used by Laurie. But he's strong and they think he'll be okay."

"Has he asked about me?" asked Emma.

"Not that I know of, but I didn't ask. If I did, they might have suspected that you were here. But I am sure he's thinking of you. David's parents are in Walla Walla now. They'll bring him home when he's well. That's all I know and probably all we'll know for a little while.

"I am so scared. Do you know anything about my parents or brother?"

"No."

"Emma, I think it best if you stay here for a while and get your strength back. I don't think going home to Walla Walla makes sense."

"I don't think my parents want me and I don't want to go back there, ever."

"Ever is a long time," Esther said. "Maybe when this all plays out, your parents will see the miscalculations they've made. Do you have any other relatives or friends that might take you in?"

"Only Sophie in New York. That might be an option, but not right now. Does anyone know I'm here?"

"No, and our deal was that they won't find out from me."

"I need to set up a bogus email account and send a message to Sophie that I'm okay. I think my mom may have my UW password. I'll call Sophie later too. You'd really like Sophie. She's my rock."

Emma created a new address at gmail.com and emailed Sophie, "I am fine. Don't give anyone my new email address. I don't want to talk about anything yet. David will never forgive me." Sophie pummeled Emma with emails asking for information. Emma's only response was "He will never forgive me and I don't blame him. I am so sorry. I'll call you at 8:00 p.m., New Jersey time."

Emma looked at her UW emails. Nothing from David, but Emma thought it doubtful that he would have email access from a hospital bed in Walla Walla.

Chapter 50

Dr. King kept David in Walla Walla General for four days. David had a visit from a DEA officer, Harry Connors, who reiterated that all charges had been dropped. Connors, per Hawkins' instructions, did not tell David anything about the sting and DEAs role in the fiasco, nor did he tell him about Rafe Gomez's tip to the DEA.

Connors continued, "Also, Doc, all the charges for resisting arrest were dropped by the arresting officers."

"That's a joke, right?" asked David.

"No, not a joke, I wish it were. The Walla Walla sheriff, Lieutenant Specker, is not a good police officer or a nice man. Your injury was totally uncalled for. But pursuing assault charges against Specker would probably be a bust, especially here in Walla Walla. All Specker's deputies would support him."

David shook his head, then asked, what to him was the most important question, "Do you have any idea where Emma Braza could have gone?"

"Sorry, doc, dunno. I'll look into it." Connors had other work to do and he didn't look very hard.

Rafe Gomez showed up on the evening of day three. He felt responsible for David's injuries, but thought it best that David not hear that the sting had fallen apart and that he could have been forewarned.

"Why are you here? I had asked Emma to find you, but I didn't know if she heard me."

"She didn't call," Rafe said.

"She's missing. Do you know where she is?"

"No, I don't."

"Rafe, what happened to me? I was just coming for a visit."

"David, I don't know." Rafe hated lying to someone who had been so helpful to him and his family, but it served no purpose, at least now, to let David know the full extent of the total screw-up.

"Doc, I actually have to get back to Seattle tonight but I had to come and see you. I owed you that. Selma Rodriguez is here at the hospital, but I don't think you're going to make it to her house for dinner. She'd like a rain check, but she is going to have your mom and dad over for a real meal. I brought the van and I'm going to swap with your parents. They're going to take you back to Seattle tomorrow or the next day and you can lie down in the back."

Mike and Laurie returned for the rest of the day, except for dinner at Selma Rodriguez's house. The next day, David had his IVs removed and was discharged from Walla Walla General. His parents drove him directly to the UW ER where Delores Bryant met him. Armon Elliott, Chairman of the Department of Surgery, and one of the chief residents, Bill Phillips examined David. Elliott saw no reason to hospitalize David and discharged him to his parent's house to finish recuperation.

Elliott instructed David, in no uncertain terms, to rest and not to reappear at the hospital for at least a month. Elliott knew, as did David, that delayed bleeds from splenic injuries could occur in the first two weeks post repair. Once home, David spent much of the time searching for Emma. He emailed Emma's UW account every six hours pleading with her to respond, or at least say that she was okay. David received no responses from Emma and felt like he had fallen into a black hole.

David called or emailed Sophie every day or two to

see if she knew where Emma could be. Sophie told David she had wired Emma a thousand dollars, but then lied by telling David she hadn't heard a word since. She added to the prevarication saying that if she heard or received anything, she'd tell him.

Rafe Gomez came by every other day. He still didn't have the nerve and didn't feel it was time to explain what had happened. Or what didn't happen. He realized he might never have the nerve to tell David or anyone the full story and his part in it.

Chapter 51

Emma spent most of her time reading and thinking and reliving her past on Esther's couch. When not on the couch, she would sit in the shade and stare at the Little San Bernardino Mountains to the north or the San Jacinto Mountains to the west.

From Esther, Emma learned to play Spite and Malice, the Mexican Railroad game and the beginnings of Mah Jongg. Emma helped Esther start packing up for her return to Seattle for the summer.

Esther made her feel at home. Emma cooked and Esther chopped or Emma chopped and Esther cooked. They laughed a bit, cried a little more. Esther had funny stories to tell about David growing up.

Emma ended most of their long conversations with "He will never forgive me and I don't blame him."

Esther would always retort, "My dear, never is a long time and things change and people forgive. I know David and he will forgive you."

Emma talked to Sophie twice a day, often for an hour in the evening. She continued to make Sophie promise that she would tell no one her whereabouts.

"Emma, you are being unreasonable. You really need to call David," Sophie pleaded.

"I can't yet," Emma said. "I know that he will never forgive me."

"First, you don't know that. Second, you need him. I've talked to him every day or two. He misses you terribly and is scared because he doesn't know where you are. I hate lying to him. He has never said anything about being mad, only scared."

"I need time to think. My world is so mixed up right now. Try to bear with me."

Emma read all of David's messages to the UW mail account. All said the same. "Please write, call or text." But she didn't respond, she didn't know what to say. She thought, in her own mind, that he would never be able to get past the events in Walla Walla.

Despite her pledge of secrecy, Esther knew Emma needed to see David. In the end, nothing stops Esther, the Grand Manipulator, even promises.

From what she could glean from her children and her conversations with her grandson, David needed Emma every bit as much. Esther waited only for David to be strong enough.

David remained at his parent's house recuperating. Esther would call him every day from her cell phone, away from Emma. David told his grandmother that he couldn't stop worrying about Emma.

On day fourteen after the injury, Esther called David. By now, Esther knew that David's sadness revolved completely around Emma's disappearance. She always inquired how David was doing medically and what the doctors might be saying. David said he was now strong enough to return to work but Dr. Elliott remained adamant, and correct, that he not return until day twenty-eight, two weeks away. David remarked that he felt cold much of the time, most likely a result of his anemia.

Esther took a chance that the time had arrived to bring them together. Esther made the call pleading with David to come.

"David, it's one hundred five degrees and sunny here. I just sit in my house. I am going to send you a ticket to come down and spend your last week of recovery with me before going back to work. I will not take no for an answer. I am starting to pack up to go home and while I don't expect you to help, I could use the company."

"I don't know Gram. I don't really feel like travelling."

Esther, using her best grandmother logic started in on her grandson, "David, one, you've been complaining that you're freezing all the time. Two, it's hot as hell here. Three, I am asking nicely. Four, I am old. Five, I have never pleaded to you about anything. And six, and most importantly, I have things to tell you before I die. So come."

"Gram, are you sick?"

"No, David, I am just using manipulation to get you to see me."

"Okay, okay. I'll tell Mom and Dad. Then, I'll come."

"David, for God's sake, you're a surgeon now, you don't need to ask or tell anyone."

Using Esther's credit card, David booked the 11:24 a.m. flight for the next morning, to arrive in Palm Springs airport at 2:00 p.m.

Chapter 52

Esther had offered Emma two options earlier in the week.

"You can stay with me in Seattle, or you can stay here in the desert and close up the house yourself when you're ready to go, wherever you plan to go"

Neither option seemed good to Emma, but she opined, "I think I need to talk to Sophie about moving to New Jersey or New York. Sophie will be busy starting law school, but I am sure I could find a job."

Esther didn't think Emma was very convincing about heading east to even more unknowns.

To complicate Emma's confusion, she didn't know what to do about letting her mother know that she was safe. Clara had emailed Emma's UW account countless times and called Sophie repeatedly with queries about Emma's whereabouts. Sophie, the true friend, didn't provide any answers or solutions to the Brazas. To this point, Emma hadn't given her parents, even her mother, the satisfaction of knowing where she was or even that she was safe. But as Emma rethought the past two weeks, she believed that her mother didn't deserve not knowing.

After lunch, Esther announced that she had a hair appointment at 1:30 and would be back at 4:00.

"Oh, Esther. I am so conflicted on so many issues. I just don't know what to do. I probably need a haircut worse than you."

Esther said, "I don't think my hairdresser would work for you, but I'll ask her if she knows someone that can do youngsters. When I come back from the hairdresser, you and I are going to solve a bunch of your problems. I promise."

Emma's shoulder's sagged and she sighed, "I wish it were that simple. I just don't know."

Esther had no intention of getting her hair done. The temperature at the Palm Springs Airport was one hundred eleven degrees, but David found the desert heat almost comfortable.

Esther Milton waited out front.

Emma, wearing a loose T-shirt and a pair of short pajama bottoms, sat on her bed reading awaiting Esther's return. She heard the garage door opening and assumed that Esther had come back earlier than expected. No big deal, she'd yell hello and see if Esther needed help, in case she had done some shopping.

Before the house door from the garage opened, Emma thought she heard a different, but not strange, voice.

No, just me hearing things, she thought.

The door opened and the voice was there again, this time clear, crisp and glorious. She couldn't move. Was it an apparition, a ghost, God playing tricks?

"Gram, where do I put my stuff, casita or this bedroom?"

Emma jumped off the bed heading for the door when David turned the corner into the bedroom.

She bounced off David, fell back a step and then leaped back at him, grabbing around his neck. He dropped his suitcases and his arms encircled Emma.

"Emma!"

"David!"

"What is going on? Please tell me what is going on?"

"How did you know I was here?"

"I didn't."

"Why did you come?"

"Gram invited me for some R and R...Uh, I'm actually not supposed to be holding up this much weight."

"Oh, sorry." Emma went back to the floor. She hugged David as hard as she could. "Okay to hug you?"

"Sure." David turned to his grandmother standing in the hallway watching. "Gram, you've got a ton of explaining to do."

Esther could not wipe the smile off her face. "No matter how mad you two might be at me, watching the last twenty seconds made it all worth it. I am going to take a long, long bath. You two talk and then we'll go out to dinner."

"You didn't get your hair done?"

"Nope, had to pick up a grandson." Esther disappeared into the master bedroom and closed the door.

David and Emma sat on the edge of the bed in the guest room. Emma would not let go of his hand and sat next to him. Her T-shirt did little to hide her breasts. He had not forgotten how much he missed her.

"We have a lot of talking to do," David said. "I am so pissed at you."

Emma was crying again, this time more from joy, but touched with a bit of fear of what David might say or do next.

Emma started, in staccato, every thought she'd had over the past two weeks, "I never ever, ever thought you'd forgive me, I thought you were still in jail until two days later when your grandmother found out you weren't arrested but had been injured, why would you forgive me? I led you into a trap, you almost died, you might have never been able to practice medicine, you could have gone to jail, it was all my doing, I should have known."

David, always the calming seawall for Emma's tidal waves, said, "Emma, Emma, slow down. Slow down." He held her face in his hands. "I'm not angry about any of that. I know you didn't know and I don't blame you, even a bit. I swear."

"But David, it was my family that did this. My family. I am so ashamed."

"I am still not sure what exactly happened. I do know that your brother is a piece of work. Screw him. I'm angry because you disappeared and I couldn't find you. No, angry isn't the correct word, I was scared. You never can do that again. If I have to tag you with an implantable homing device, I never want you to disappear. It was so cruel. I was so sick and all I could think about was *were you safe*?"

Tears cascaded down Emma's cheeks.

"Your mom came to visit me the next day in the hospital," David said. "She was in and then she was out, but said you had run away. I told her to call Sophie and have someone check my apartment. Sophie couldn't help me either."

"I promise I'll never do that again," Emma said, wiping the tears with her T-shirt, "I just couldn't fathom you forgiving me."

She then told David the entire story, from her view, starting from the time he was taken away until she arrived in Palm Desert. “Grandma Esther has been amazing. I told her that I wasn't ready to see you until I knew you'd talk to me, to forgive me. I guess she knew."

David then chronicled his last two weeks. Heady stuff for both of them. David had learned that Alan would not be prosecuted for lack of evidence.

“Emma, the whole thing is still strange. I asked Rafe to look into it for me. But he called a few days later to say he couldn't get any additional clarifying information.

Emma, angrily responding, "I could testify that I heard him confess."

"To what end, Emma. It's your word against theirs. Your dad thinks you were the cause for Alan getting pulled in. And we both know that Alan isn’t going to admit to anything. Besides, sending Alan to jail isn't going to help mend fences."

"I never want to see my dad or Alan again. Oh, David. I am so sorry I got you into this mess. What was I thinking by bringing you home?"

They sat quietly for a few moments.

David said, "I've got to be back to work in twelve or thirteen days. Where are you going to go?"

"I don't know. I was thinking maybe of going to New York, get a job and live with Sophie."

"No way you're leaving me. No way. I've just beaten one rap. I wonder what the penalty is for strangling someone you're in love with?"

"Huh."

"Why don't you come and live with me. Remember the storage room? We'll get you a job and make you earn your keep."

Emma nodded yes.

David looked deeply into Emma's eyes. He couldn't live without her. He had been crazed not able to find her.

"Emma, I take it back. I can't have a girlfriend living in the building, it's against code."

"David, what are you talking about?"

"I want to marry you. I want you living with me as my wife, not girlfriend. I don't want to spend another day without you."

David kneeled by the bedside and put his head against Emma's belly, kissed it and then put his head up.

"Emma Braza, I love and need you, and will love and need you forever. I can only hope that you will love and need me as much as I love and need you. Emma, will you marry me?"

Emma thought for a second and considered being coy or playful and saying *how do you know I want to marry you. I may need to think awhile.* But she said, "Yes."

They both stood and embraced. "I love you so much," echoed back and forth.

"David, when will we get married?"

David thought, "Well, my parents, after my Walla Walla trip, are going to say, no, don't do it, not for a while. I am not even going to fathom a response from your family. Thrilled won't be on the list. Sophie will probably tell you absolutely no."

"Actually, Sophie said I should have already married

you. She said I'd never find anyone like you that loved me so much."

"A wise woman, a woman of distinction. Why didn't you tell me?"

"I wanted my family to accept you, first. I wanted that so bad. In my heart I know that my parents love me. What I mean is that I felt loved my whole life. I just wanted them to give you the same love, maybe not right away, but sometime."

"Do you need Sophie at our wedding?"

"She can't come back to the coast for a while. She has a new job and then starts law school."

Esther walked out of her bedroom. "Where do you two want to go for dinner?"

"Anywhere you want to take us. Gram, is the county seat and courthouse still in Indio?"

"Yes, of course, why?"

"You and Emma and I are going there tomorrow and then we're coming back here to pack up your house."

Esther asked, "What's at the courthouse, may I ask?"

"Emma and I are getting married and you're the witness."

Esther moved quickly to a chair and sat down. "Oh my God. I told Emma we'd solve her problems this afternoon, but I wasn't counting on this. You've got to tell your parents."

"They'll just tell us to wait. That I am being impetuous."

"You are being impetuous," Esther said. "Well, at least call them. You owe them that. They're going to kill me for this."

"Yeah. You're dead meat," David said.

David called his parents. Rather than being surprised, both had already said to each other that if David found Emma, he'd marry her.

When told that they wanted to get married the next day at the Indio County Seat, his mom said. "You know what, you're being impetuous. But, I'm not likely to dissuade you, so go for it, we'll throw a party for you two when you get back."

David's father agreed as well. They talked to Emma for a while and welcomed her to the family and told her that they'd all work together to try and patch things up with the Brazas, no matter how long it took. Emma started weeping again and thanked them profusely.

Twenty minutes later, on the way to the Fisherman's Market and Grill, David's cell rang with his mom's name on the screen.

"Mom?"

"No, you shit, it's me Rachel."

"Hi, what's up?"

"Mom told me you're getting married tomorrow."

"Yep."

"What time?"

"Dunno, whenever they open."

"No way, I'm coming down. I'm going to be there. You gotta wait for me," demanded Rachel

"Wow, sure," David said.

"I will find a flight into Southern California tonight somewhere."

"We'll be there, Rach, to pick you up."

David hung up and told Emma about their new maid of honor.

"I've got to call Sophie, now," Emma said.

Sophie screamed with delight. Emma and David promised that their first trip would be to the east coast to celebrate with Sophie and her family.

Sophie gave Emma one last piece of advice, "Emma, don't you think you need to let your mother know. I mean she might just come."

"I dunno. I've got to think about it."

"What's she going to say, no, don't get married. Remember, you're not asking, you're telling. Big diff."

Emma called her mom's cell using David's phone.

"Hello David, thank you for calling." Clara answered. "Have you heard from Emma? Do you know where she is?"

"Mom, it's me. I'm okay," said Emma.

"Emma, where are you? I've been looking for you for two weeks. Alan came home and wasn't guilty of anything. He doesn't know why they brought David in. Alan and Dad are still blaming you, but I told them you didn't do anything. When are you coming home? We'll talk to Dad and make this all work out."

"Mom, I am in Palm Desert."

"Palm Desert. That's crazy. Why are you there?"

asked Clara.

"Mom, it's not important why I'm here. I'm calling to let you know that David and I are getting married tomorrow."

"You are what!!" Clara exclaimed.

"I am getting married to Dr. David Milton of Seattle, Washington, tomorrow in Indio, California, at 3:00 p.m."

"Emma, please. Let's talk about this."

"Mom, I tried to talk and it almost cost David his life. And my brother is lucky he didn't end up in jail when the police came for him. They must have suspected or known something. I hadn't told anyone anything about Alan. I think that talking with Dad and you hasn't worked so well."

"Emma, please."

"Anyway, it's nice to hear your voice. 3:00 p.m., Indio Courthouse, tomorrow. David's parents aren't going to be here either. His sister will be my maid of honor. She's known about this for fifteen minutes and she's flying down from Seattle."

"Emma, please."

"Mom, 3:00 p.m., tomorrow, Indio. You've got David's cell if you need to reach me. We'll be back in Seattle in two days or three. When I get a new cell phone, I'll call you. Mom, I've got to go."

"Emma, please, don't hang up, don't do this."

"Mom, I love you. You've been an incredible loving and giving mom. Everything I am, or will be, is because of you. But you didn't protect me from Alan or Dad. I don't know if you could have, but you didn't try, and you knew they were wrong. You and Dad left me with no choices. Anyway, 3:00 p.m., Indio. Love you." Emma hung up and again the tears starting flowing.

Rachel arrived on the 11:00 a.m. flight into the Ontario Airport. Emma and Rachel sat in the back seat and jabbered the whole way back to Palm Desert, about ninety-five minutes. Rachel said she had packed a variety of clothes for both to wear.

Rachel commented. "I get to be a wedding planner. That is so cool."

David quipped to the back seat, "For sixty-eight bucks, two valid driver's licenses, two people who know you, a wedding is a simple as 1, 2, 3, I do."

Emma and Rachel wore Rachel's prom dresses, one from Rachel's junior year and one for the upcoming senior year gala. Emma was happy; T-shirts and jeans just wouldn't look right. Esther dressed to the nines and David had on a pair of slacks and a sports coat his dad had left in the desert.

The wedding at the courthouse went without a hitch. David had no time to buy a ring and spent one dollar for a temporary plastic ring from the Dollar Store. Esther surprised the newlyweds at the courthouse with her wedding ring as a gift, a two carat Marquise diamond on a simple elegant platinum setting.

"Why not, after all, first grandson to get married and I adore Emma," Esther said as David and Emma tried to talk her out of the gift.

The ring was a little loose, but no one cared. Afterward, the party of four went to Tommy Bahama's on El Paseo for dinner.

Rachel asked Emma, "So what name are you going to use?"

"I always thought that I'd use the name Emma

Braza," Emma said. But after all that's happened, I've decided to become Emma Milton."

Tommy Bahamas had a small band playing music. David and Emma danced, keeping in mind his injury. Unfortunately, the sidewalks roll up at 9:00 p.m. in the desert. The party ended at 9:01.

Esther suggested checking into the nearby Marriott for the night. Emma refused and their first night of wedding bliss was spent with David's grandmother and sister.

Chapter 53

David had twelve days left before returning to work. After getting the okay from Dr. Elliott at the UW, David suggested that he and Emma drive Esther's car back to Seattle rather than shipping it. Elliott demanded that David pull the car off the road every sixty to ninety minutes to walk around and stretch his legs to prevent blood clots. Emma would do the lion's share of the driving. David drove Esther to the airport and came back to pick up the new Mrs. Milton.

David had been gone almost an hour. It was now 11:00 a.m. The temperature was already one hundred six on its way to one hundred thirteen. They had planned to get on the road, heading west on I-10 into Los Angeles, as soon as David returned.

"Emma, I'm back."

“In here.” Emma was in the kitchen slicing apples and peeling tangerines for the car trip. "David, do you realize that this is the first time we've been alone in a house as a married couple? Come to think of it, in your apartment, people were always in the house, either above or below us, or both."

"Hey, you're right. Besides that, the neighbors to the north and south of Gram's house have already left for home. So...?"

Emma, not sure where David was going, said, "So?"

The smiling David said, "That means we’re totally alone and can make as much noise as we want."

"I was kind of thinking about that too. You're not going to bust your spleen open, are you?"

David smiled as he started on Emma's top button.

"David, I never believed that I could be this happy again. Sophie promised me that I would, but I knew she was just saying that to make me feel good."

David finished the buttons and slid off Emma's blouse.

"After a while," Emma continued, "I felt that I didn't deserve to be happy. That I was being punished for something."

David looked around and drew the kitchen and living room curtains. He then unsnapped Emma's bra and let it fall forward.

"Then after what happened at home, I felt for sure that I would never be happy, never be able to put my past in the past. I was just too damaged."

David pulled off his shirt and then slowly slid his open hands down her chest, circling her breasts and then back up to her face. "Emma, some might ask me, 'why you?', what could I possibly see in someone with your issues."

David kissed her lightly on the lips and continued downward, cupping her breasts, the nipples now taut. Stopping, he rose and looked Emma in the eyes, "If they are so insensitive to ask such a silly question, I will tell them 'I see everything you don't.'"

Emma and David didn't leave until 4:00 p.m., but two days later.

"Oh well", they laughed, the only person they scared was the Hispanic gardener who had come to fix a broken sprinkler the morning before leaving.

They drove until the early morning and stopped at a motel outside Modesto. They talked and laughed until David's incision hurt so much that he pleaded for Emma to stop talking for a while, at least until the pain subsided.

"Okay, okay, I'll shut up."

The next day, Emma sat in the passenger seat making various muffled animal sounds learned from twenty plus years in Walla Walla. David had to pull over and get out of the car so he could stop laughing. The next day they made it to Ashland, Oregon, in time to catch Romeo and Juliet at the Oregon Shakespeare Festival.

“Maybe not the best play. Romeo dies,” Emma said, afterward.

David, nodding, said, “Juliet didn’t do so good either.”

And the laughing started again.

They arrived in Seattle the next afternoon and went to Esther's condominium in Bellevue to drop off the car.

"So what took you so long?" Esther asked, not wishing an answer.

Emma and David did simultaneous shoulder shrugs. Rachel met them at Esther's with as much clothes as she could spare for her new sister-in-law. At least until she could manage some shopping. Emma promised to go with Rachel on Friday. Given David's limited budget, Emma and Rachel thought Ross Dress For Less and Marshalls made the most sense. They had dinner that night with David’s parents and Rachel.

"Thank you, so much,” Emma said. “I just wish my parents could or would be half as understanding as you three."

Laurie grimaced. "We're so sorry. Maybe things will work out down the line. My advice to the two of you is don't burn any bridges from your side. You did nothing wrong. Hold your head high and keep trying to reach out, without compromising."

Emma didn't need to nod that she understood.

When they got into the car to head back to the U district, Emma opened an wedding card from Laurie and Mike. Emma had been told not to open it until she got into the car, sure that it would be a sweet message, advice and a welcome. No message. A check for two thousand dollars with a Post-It note saying only "get some clothes."

At David's apartment's alley parking spot, they found two of the girls from the upper level in the back rummaging through the garbage looking for a missing locket. Both recognized Emma from her visits earlier in the year and both saw the armfuls of clothes that both were lugging.

"Hi, David. Hi...uh.." A wave to the forgotten name.

One of the girls, Casey Karson, the varsity sweep on the national champion eight women's crew, always had a wry comment. While pointing at Emma, she announced for the alley to hear, "Hey, Mr. or Dr. Landlord. My lease says I can't have guests more than three days at a time. From what you guys are carrying, I'd say, lots more than three days. Different rules for you?"

Casey, as tall as David and now likely, twice as strong, gave her best smile. David had lost fifteen pounds with the surgery and recovery. Her next comment would have been how he looked like shit and that he needed to come up for a meal.

David, smiling, countered quickly with his own made-up line of bull, "Clause 4, Section A, Paragraph III, Line 2 of your lease clearly states that a spouse can stay whenever and wherever she wants."

"No kidding, you guys get married. Hey, waz up, we weren't invited."

"No one was invited. Just eloped. Long story."

Kasey countered, "I don't believe you."

Emma held out her left hand. Esther's former and Emma's new wedding ring sparkled. Both girls whistled. "Not bad, not bad at all."

Kasey did a fake frown and said, "David, you promised you'd marry me."

"Oh, darn. Forgot. Maybe next time. My mistake."

All four laughed.

"Welcome to the Insane Asylum. Mrs. Milton, or are you going by your own name."

"No. Emma Milton sounds right, nice to see you guys again. Just Emma is fine."

"Congrats", again both in unison, but unison is what you'd expect from a NCAA championship crew.

On day twenty-eight post injury, Emma drove David to the UW Medical Center for work. As he had warned her on multiple occasions, his other wife was medicine. And this wife was as jealous as Snow White's stepmother. Surgical residencies are crazy and unpredictably busy. He would be home as soon and as often as he could be but he could never promise to be home at any certain time or to be available for any certain event.

Emma's only request to David that day was that when he had time he needed to call VISA to get Emma a credit card with her name on his account. He added that he'd break free and go with Emma to get a cell phone and get her signed up on his checking account. As it was, Emma had only David's computer to communicate with the outside. She immediately set up a Skype account and used David's credit card numbers to buy time. Her wallet had only her driver's license and a piece of paper mini-encrypted with David's social security number and his VISA account, expiration and security code.

Emma checked her email. Messages from Sophie, Rachel, a slew of sorority sisters and Francine Frost. None from her family. Apparently, Sophie had tipped off her sorority sisters about the wedding. Francine Frost, who in the end had been an ally, said that she'd like to see Emma anytime she was free. The sorority was empty for the summer and Francine was bored stiff. Sophie didn't have a Skype account on her cell phone, but did at home and they promised to video chat.

Emma took her check from Laurie Milton and the remaining one hundred thirty-seven dollars from Sophie's wire and drove David's car to University Village. She cashed the check at Wells Fargo and shopped for a couple of hours. In the end, Emma bought nothing. For the first time in her life, now that Joe and Clara Braza's unlimited credit wasn't available, Emma could no longer mindlessly buy what she wanted. She had never abused her parent's money but, then, she never gave it much thought.

As predicted, that night David was working in the hospital. The UW women's crew invited Emma up for dinner. They were fun and she knew that she would enjoy their camaraderie. She was thankful that the house, although segregated with different entrances, was always occupied at night. She told them as much as they needed to know.

As Emma was leaving to go downstairs, one of the girls told Emma that she wanted to talk to her alone. After dinner they went down to Emma and David's unit. The girl, Ava Richards, a junior from Spokane, told Emma that she knew about the kidnapping and so did Casey Karson. Casey and Ava had not told any of their other roommates, nor would they. Emma had not talked about it that evening. Ava told Emma that she was welcome to come up the stairs at any time, for any reason. She gave Emma a list of all their cell phone numbers and email addresses.

Emma thanked her with a big hug. "Thanks. David is away a lot. I think I'll be okay."

"We know, we hear the door opening and closing at 4:00 a.m. and then leaving at 6:00 a.m. all the time. Hope you can get used to it."

David called at 9:00 p.m. to say he would be stuck in the hospital that night and unlikely to come home until the next evening. Couldn't be helped. He promised to keep his phone on but gave Emma the number of Rafe Gomez, whom she may have remembered from their first encounter and the paging operator at the UW. At 11:00 p.m., Emma got into bed. She hadn't really been this alone in sixteen months. To make matters worse, the old house creaked. The girls upstairs, no matter how lightly they'd step, would move the old wooden floorboards. The darkness, the noise and the aloneness triggered memories. Emma didn't want to call David. He couldn't come home and her call would just make his evening more difficult. Emma called Ava, the girl from Unit #C.

"Emma, Hi, It's late, what's up?"

"Any chance you could come down here to #B for a second?" Emma asked.

"Sure, is there a problem?"

"I just need to tell you something, please. I will unlock the common door in the stairway, so you don't have to go outside. You just have to unlock it on your side and walk in. "

"Sure, I'll be there in a minute," Ava said.

Ava was through the common door into Unit #B. She had never seen the door opened before, even though she'd walked by it a thousand times.

"What's up, Emma? You okay?" Ava couldn't help notice Emma hands and lips shaking ever so slightly.

"David's at work. It's his first night back. And well, since my accident, I lived in the sorority with a roommate and then between home and then getting married, I've not really been alone."

"Emma, how can I help?"

Emma stuttering slowly, "Well, well, I didn't really know how I would be, and, and then I'd hear the floor creaking and..."

Emma was making absolutely no sense, none at all.

"Emma, are you scared to be alone?" Ava asked.

"Yes."

"Wow, Okay."

"I'm so sorry to bother you," Emma said.

Ava gave her a hug. "Hey, Plan A, I sleep down here. Plan B, you sleep upstairs with us. You pick."

"I don't want to weird out your roommates."

"Casey knows already. I am going to guess that the others would have found out in time. Tomorrow morning I'll have a talk with everyone."

"I can make up the guest bedroom next door," Emma said. "I'll keep the door open. That'll be perfect."

"Sure. Works for me. If you don't have a problem, then can we keep the common door unlocked permanently. I know we don't have anything worth stealing. The only thing you've got worth nabbing is David," Ava said, smiling.

Ava was back in five minutes with her pillow, cell phone and charger, and slept in the guest room. Ava kept her door open as did Emma. When Emma awoke, Ava had already gone and the bed was made. Emma would have to remember to tell Ava that she would clean up the room and not for her to bother.

Emma told David the next evening about her fears and Ava's sleepover.

"I'm sorry, I should have thought of that. Are the girls upstairs okay with all this?"

"They said it was fine with them," Emma said. "Ava talked to the group. Casey already knew but she explained it to the other four. They are all really nice. Anyway, one of them will stay in the guest room if you're not coming home. We'll keep the common door unlocked from now on. That okay?"

"Sure, perfect," said David.

The six girls and Emma became closer and closer as the year wore on. The six had re-rented until the following August. David would be gone, on average every third night. Most nights, when he was in the hospital, one of the girls would come downstairs to sleep. On some occasions, when one of the #C girls was gone, Emma would sleep upstairs. After 2 months of the shared units, Emma felt she could wean herself off the babysitters. Just having the common door unlocked would be enough security. Emma finally stopped the arrangement, but never re-locked the common door.

Chapter 54

The first weekend back from the desert as Mrs. Milton, Emma got the apartment up to snuff and then she and Rachel spent most of the two thousand dollars. Emma didn't realize how quickly two thousand dollars evaporates when you have nothing more. The closet and drawers seemed empty. David's schedule was not kind at the moment. David's injury and the subsequent absence of a month put a strain on all the other residents to cover. David owed coverage call to a number of people. They didn't really care that he was just married or injured. His problem.

"Congratulations David. You're on call for me on Tuesday and Thursday."

Emma needed to find a job. She and David had decided that she shouldn't reach out to her mother until she secured a job. She needed to show that she didn't need them to survive.

Emma did write a letter to her mother, giving all of her new contact information. She reiterated as strongly as she could that she had done nothing to implicate Alan. She had talked to no one at any time, before, during or after about David's arrest, his release, and Alan's questioning. She ended the note with...Love, Emma. Please call, write or email me. Emma made a copy of the handwritten letter on David's printer/copier. She would send a copy of the letter every Monday for the next three months. Clara did not write back.

Emma had always worked for her father in various helping positions at the winery. Seattle had no vineyards - it takes sun and someone forgot to turn on the lights in Western Washington. All the significant grape growing occurs east of the Cascade Mountains and Emma wasn't going to commute and wasn't going to leave Seattle or David.

Her college laptop sat in her bedroom in Walla

Walla. She would need to start rebuilding from scratch. She wrote out a resume, one page, concise. She used what little money she had left to buy a professional business suit for interviews.

She finally got a credit card, Emma B. Milton, and added a cell phone to David's account. She would need a laptop, but that was low on her list of priorities and way out of her current budget. She registered on the business contact website LinkedIN. She made a schedule of networking events held in King County. She made an appointment for an interview at the UW Business School job center and looked at web postings from the School of Business for job opportunities. She obtained some local trade dailies, and looked at Craigslist and Yelp. She made appointments and left resumés with headhunting firms that don't charge the client.

Mid-summer in Seattle, or any city, is not the greatest time to look for work. She was three to four months late, and many of the good jobs, of which there were few, had been filled. The workforce was also packed with students, many working for free to gain experience.

Emma had emailed Dr. Miller a couple of times and finally he responded. He had been on a scholastic junket to Russia teaching a course on Business Management. He would return to Seattle in a week but added that he was disappointed that Emma hadn't shown for the Business School Graduation ceremonies. Emma had been awarded her degree, Magna Cum Laude and was the only Magna graduate not to be present.

She emailed back, "I wanted to be there so badly. We have lots to discuss. I am happy to be alive right now. Whom do I call to make an appointment? Emma B. Milton."

"Mrs. Milton!! Wow. Mazel Tov," Miller responded. We do have things to discuss. Call Karen in the Business School Office and set up a meeting for next Thursday or Friday."

Emma Googled, 'Mazel Tov', and learned that it literally means "good luck or good fortune", but that it's used mostly for "congratulations."

Emma added the graduate honors to her resume. She decided to go on interviews for jobs that did not interest her, at least yet, for the experience. All the interviews went well and all the potential employers told her that she was overqualified.

She met with Dr. Miller who started the meeting reminding Emma how disappointed he was that she was not at the graduation. Emma then recounted the story of the trip to Walla Walla "in four part harmony", as Arlo Guthrie had explained in his 1967 hit song, *Alice's Restaurant.* Dr. Miller sat mouth agape as the story unfolded.

"Emma, I have had hundreds of students over the years, acting as advisor, mentor or proctor. I have never met anyone who has had your life experiences. Many bad, but so many, nonetheless. I will never again say how disappointed I was you not being here for the ceremony. I'm just glad you're in one piece. I don't have any job leads today as I just got back. But I hear of things all the time. I will find you if something comes across my desk. And Mazel Tov, Mrs. Milton, on the marriage."

Emma simply said, "Thank you."

After four solid weeks of looking Emma was frustrated. David had just started dealing with new residents and interns as well as running the service. A well-known fact in medicine is that one should never go to a teaching institution in July. The new residents don't know the facility, the computers or record systems, the help available, the nursing staff, etc, etc, ad infinitum. Emma was on her own. David wasn't kidding about the jealousy of his job. He did promise that, by the end of July, a lighter schedule and a little bit of normalcy would return.

Emma had still not heard from her family. As bad as the break up seemed, she could not fathom the total lack of communication. She asked Sophie to let her know if her parents reached out to her. "Just a line or something to see if I'm alive." But Sophie had not seen even a blip.

Emma, in desperation, called Francine Frost to see if she needed help with rush and the incoming pledges two months away. She said she might, depending how involved the other alumnae wanted to get. She didn't know if there was any money to pay her, probably not.

Chapter 55

Emma continued to search the web and the UW Business School postings for jobs. On a lark, Emma deleted the filter that required an MBA to qualify for an interview. Emma knew that she could not afford to return to school for an MBA, but she was curious about what might be available.

Within seconds of changing her bio, an opportunity arose.

A grant from a consortium of Italian wineries anxious to increase their exposure to the Pacific Northwest and British Columbia had been posted three weeks earlier. Apparently Italian wines underperformed severely in the northwest compared to other sectors of the US and Canada. The grant entailed studying the feasibility of implementing a promotional plan for Italian wines in the Northwest US and British Columbia with a funding of one and one-half million dollars over a two-year period. The salary for the six-month grant was thirty thousand dollars and the feasibility portion needed to be completed in ten weeks. The requirements included a minimum of an MBA and, at least, three years work experience in sales, marketing or public relations. A written grant proposal and an interview would be needed. The grant did not promise future employment, but didn't exclude it either.

The posting had been up for twenty-one days already, and the applications and proposals were due in five days on August twentieth. The posted schedule called for the first set of interviews on August twenty-seventh at 6:30 p.m. in the UW School of Business auditorium.

Emma emailed the link to Professor Miller and then called him.

"Emma, I am sorry, but you are not qualified because you don't have an MBA or the work experience.

But, I happen to believe that this job is uniquely perfect for you. All you can do is apply and try to get past their requirements."

The application energized Emma. She started to work on the project that evening. Dr. Miller helped Emma, as much as he could, writing the proposal. Emma knew some MBA grad students from her undergraduate classes that gave her some outlines of what employers expected in the application outline as well.

Her plans included pitching the wines heavily to Costco and the larger wine shops, a series of articles in local papers, as well as on-line marketing through Facebook, Twitter and other social media. Her senior project was about to come in handy.

She emailed Dr. Agotini in Italy and he gave some interesting history about the winery consortium that was sponsoring the grant. She called Ralph Potro and asked for some of his material. He said that he owed Emma big from the JDF talk and emailed her the slides she wanted. He did mention briefly that he had heard about her and her parents. He was sorry.

She spent the entire weekend developing a PowerPoint presentation as well as a complete proposal with budget for the ensuing two years.

When Emma turned in the application to the UW School of Business office she was told that eleven others had applied, all MBAs, looking for a new line of work. Most had graduated from the UW program, but the applicant list included two from University of Puget Sound, one from Stanford, and one from Harvard Business School. The business office clerk that accepted the application, seeing how young Emma appeared, asked if Emma had read the requirements and was she eligible to apply.

"I am totally appropriate for this grant."

"I didn't say appropriate, I said eligible. Fine, if they find you're missing something, they could ask you to leave."

"They won't, if they give me a chance," said Emma.

"I like your spunk, young lady, Good luck."

"I'd like to go last, if that's possible. That way if they disqualify me, no one has to wait. Possible?"

"Sure, I'll try. The interviews are a week from today and will be posted."

Emma wasn't sure that she would be able to even see the posting but she didn't want to draw attention to the fact that she didn't have an MBA. She called Dr. Miller who said he'd check for her.

Two days later she received an email from Dr. Miller. "August twenty-seventh, 9:45 p.m. The last interview."

Possessed with prepping, studying and practicing for the interview, Emma worked tirelessly. David said he'd come with her for luck. They both knew the real reason, although Emma had not had more than the occasional nightmare. David said Rafe Gomez would escort her if he became tied up in the hospital.

The evening of the interview, David signed out to the other chief resident. Emma and David left the apartment at 8:45 for the twenty minute walk to the business school. Dressed professionally in her one, and only, interview outfit, her hair in a tight bun and with little makeup, Emma felt prepared, but anxious. She could not hide that she was young, but she wanted to look as professional as possible. Emma tried to call Sophie on the walk, despite being three hours later on the East coast. Sophie had been warned that a call might be coming, but it went straight to her voicemail.

Emma left no message and put the phone back in her purse. She held David's hand as she said in a clear voice, on her own, "You gain strength, courage, and confidence by every experience in which you really stop to look fear in the face. You must do the thing which you think you cannot do."

"What was that about?" David asked.

"Oh, nothing. A quote from Eleanor Roosevelt that Sophie would make us say together when I had problems. It helped most every time. I'm okay to say it by myself now."

"Any other Emma-Sophie secrets I need to know, now that we're married?"

"Women need secrets to be mysterious. That makes you guys love us more."

"Well, I've got some secrets too."

"No, you don't, sorry Charlie. You're a big open book. But I love you in spite of yourself."

David smiled. He'd been outfoxed again.

Emma and David sat outside a small auxiliary meeting room off the auditorium. The building was eerily quiet. At 9:40, the interviewee before Emma exited. He saw Emma and David and assumed that David was being interviewed.

"Hey, good luck. This sounds like a sweet gig that could lead to big things. Where'd you get your MBA?"

David smiled, "HBS, 05, then London School of Business, 07."

"Wow. Good luck."

Emma elbowed David. "You are such a creep. Why'd you say that?"

"What was I going to say? It's not me, it's her. She hasn't gone to business school."

"The truth will set you free."

"That's only when the shoe fits."

A middle aged woman in a business outfit opened the door and said, "Emma Milton."

"Here, I'm here."

David squeezed Emma's hand as she disappeared through the door.

Four men, and the one lady who opened the door, sat around a large rectangular table. Already loaded and projected on a screen was Emma's PowerPoint program's first slide.

The man in the center suggested Emma sit, so that the slides were visible but close enough to the interviewers that a microphone wasn't needed.

The same man introduced himself as Vittorio Veliano. His accent suggested that English was not his first language. The other three men were introduced and nodded only. They looked American but Emma didn't presume anything. She knew the woman that had brought her in was not Italian.

"Signorina Milton. I see that you graduate from the University only a few months past. You don't have an MBA?"

"Signore Veliano. Sono sposato. Signora Milton, por favore."

"Ah, Mi dispiace. Signora Milton. Parla italiano lei?"

"Si, parlo italiano."

"Sei italiana?"

“No, Io sono americana.”

Mr. Veliano turned to the others on the panel and explained the tête à tête. That Mrs., not Miss, Milton was an American, but spoke Italian.

"Perhaps, Signora Milton, we will continue in English so the others might follow. Va bene?"

"Va bene. Okay," Emma said.

Veliano continued, “Again, Mrs. Milton, you don't have the qualifications for this job. You haven't an MBA and have not been in the work force for three years.”

Emma needed to be honest, but powerful, and she realized that this moment was her only chance.

"You are right, I don't have an MBA, nor have I been in the workplace for three years. But I am the best qualified for this grant. No one whom you have interviewed could possibly have my experience in the wine industry, both here and in Italy. I speak fluent Italian, French and Spanish. I am passable in German.

“There is no facet of the American wine industry, particularly the Northwest wine industry, which I am not versed in. I know a great deal about the Italian industry as well. I have visited twenty to thirty Italian vineyards in the past ten years, and I consider myself close friends with a number of prominent Italian vintners. I have been working with Washington State wines my whole life and know production, distillation, distribution and marketing. If it would please you, I would like to give my presentation before you dismiss me."

The panel looked at each other and nodded for Emma to proceed.

After her fifteen minute presentation, each panel member asked questions of Emma. Emma knew facts, figures, and had some experience with most of the queries. She admitted, quickly, ignorance for a few of the more esoteric questions about business projections. Some of the questions contained business verbiage that Mr. Veliano did not understand, so Emma translated and explained the question and her answer in English and Italian.

One of the other men spoke up.

"Mrs. Milton, I'm Ralph Reisner of Mitchell Reisner O'Hara. We're an advertising firm in Seattle and Vancouver, BC. How could someone so young possibly have adequate experience?"

"I grew up on a winery in eastern Washington. I will be the fourth generation in my family to be in the wine business, if you accept me. I will not let you down."

"Which winery?"

"deLorraine."

"Are you Joe Braza's daughter?" asked Reisner.

"Yes, yes I am."

"Well, that explains it. Impressive."

"Do you know my father?"

"Yes, I do."

"Mr.Reisner, I would be disingenuous if I said we're on good terms right now," Emma said.

"And why is that?"

"My dad wasn't very happy who I married. I am married to Dr. David Milton, who is a surgical resident here at the UW. If you call my father, I doubt that he'll be very supportive."

"Are you working now?"

"No. I can start on this project immediately and give it all my attention, one hundred ten percent."

Mr. Veliano jumped in, "Thank you, Señora Milton. I think we've heard enough and it's late."

"Molto grazie, Signore Veliano. E stato un piacere per me."

Veliano replied in English, "It was nice to meet you too. Good Luck."

Emma left the room, having no clue how they would deal with her.

Ralph Reisner called Emma early the next afternoon. After the niceties, he got to the point.

"Tell me more why your father is upset," Reisner asked. "Actually I made a few calls. He's disowned you, apparently."

"Yes, he has, but I'm working on that. He's mad because I married Dr. David Milton. David is Jewish. That's it."

"That's it."

"That's it, pretty much."

"Sorry about that. That's what I had heard too."

"Thank you for calling Mr. Reisner. I want to be in the wine business. It's in my blood. I would really work hard for you. When might you make your decision?"

"I expect you would work hard. We'll know sometime in the next ten days. A second round of interviews is slated for the top candidates."

"Thank you, Mr. Reisner. I hope to hear from you."

"Goodbye Emma."

Emma couldn't read the meaning of Mr. Reisner's call, so she remained hopeful. She could only wait now, and she hoped she had done well enough to get to the second interview.

Emma did not get a second interview.

No one did. Reisner called three days later.

"Mrs. Milton. Ralph Reisner again."

"Yes, Mr. Reisner."

"You've got the grant if you want it. You were right, no one was even close to your level of experience on the wine side. The business side is weak but we suspect that won't stop you. Besides, between you and me, you've got something to prove."

"Really. Oh, wow. Thanks, thanks so much. What happens next Mr. Reisner?"

"First, you can call me Ralph, since we'll be seeing a fair amount of each other. Can I call you Emma?"

"Absolutely."

"There will be a contract delivered by courier to you that will likely arrive tomorrow. Read it, sign it and send it back. The courier will return when you call them to pick it up. We'll have you down to our Seattle office next Monday, 9:30 a.m., Two Union Square, Suite 3750, thirty-seventh floor. Got that?"

"Every word, Mr. Reisner."

"It's Ralph."

"Ralph. See you next Monday."

"Goodbye Emma and congratulations. Your selection was not unanimous, so we're, so I'm, counting on you."

After Emma hung up the phone, she jumped on her bed, spread-eagled, pounded her feet into the mattress and screamed as loud as she could. "Yes, yes, yes."

Sixty seconds later Ava from Unit #C barged through the common door. She heard yells and wanted to make sure Emma was okay.

"Better than okay. Thanks." Emma would have to remember that the walls in the old houses sometimes have ears.

She called David and left a message. She called Sophie and left a message. She thought for a while, started and stopped a few times, then called her mother's cell phone. Clara answered.

Chapter 56

Clara did not recognize the name or number on the cell phone screen, 'E. Milton 206.746.5207.' "Hello, who is this?"

"Mom, it's me Emma."

"Oh...oh, well, hello. Are you okay?"

"Yes. Yes I am. I've missed you."

Clara cut to the chase. "Your dad has not forgiven you, Emma. Alan has convinced him that your husband set up this whole thing and it backfired on him. Alan is particularly mad at you for calling the cops on him without any evidence. He's convinced your father that David and, therefore, you are evil people."

"Mom, that is all so unfair and untrue. Why would David have himself arrested? That makes no sense. David and I have done nothing wrong. David almost lost his life. Are you aware of that?"

"Yes I am. But that doesn't change how your father and brother feel."

"Mom, you are my only hope. We did nothing. You never gave David a chance."

"Emma, I don't know what to believe. There's always a kernel of truth on both sides."

"Mom, please. Alan is not truthful at all. He tried to trap David. I heard him say so, and so did Dad.

"Alan denies it. Your dad believes him. Right now my hands are tied. Maybe later when memories aren't so fresh. Your father would be upset with me even knowing I am talking to you. He has said as much, that I should hang up if you should ever call. I can't deal with this now."

"Okay, Mom, but I want you to keep an open mind. One day, hopefully, you'll know what really happened. For now I am fine. I miss you. I even miss Dad too. By the way, I have a job."

Emma stopped and thought about telling her mother about her grant. Emma realized that if her mom told her dad, he could try to undermine everything.

"What kind of job?"

"Oh, just some grant to do some research I got through the business school. Mom, you have to believe me that I did nothing and neither did David. At least keep an open mind. I would love to see you, even if we have to do it secretly."

"Emma, I don't know. Not now. Maybe soon."

"Mom, I don't know if Dad scans your email, or if Alan does, but I am going to get a bogus email account that I will use only to write you. Reply if you want. I will get something that starts with Shannon and use Gmail.com. I will be selling kitchenware or something. Remember you can delete email from the inbox or sent mail and then go into the trash box and delete it again."

"I dunno, Emma."

"Bye, Mom. I love you. You were a fabulous mother and you've done nothing wrong, other than not protecting me."

Emma established an email account using ShannonPotts0101@Gmail.com. She sent her mom an email offering cookware from a company called PottsandPanz in Stowe, Vermont. Two days later her mom responded with "sorry. don't need cookware right now but if you have any great deals write me back."

Emma couldn't worry about her mother, or father.

She had a job. She made a list of everyone she had met over the years that might be able to give her advice. David would often say, good surgery comes from experience and experience comes from making mistakes. She didn't want to make mistakes that had been made before. She hoped that some of the contacts could at least tell her what would not work and why. She also needed one more business outfit for her Monday appointment. She couldn't wear the same clothes from the interview.

Monday morning came quickly and Emma arrived at Two Union Square, fifteen minutes early. She bought a decaf latte from the kiosk in the lobby, afraid that any caffeine would make her even more anxious. She went up to the thirty-seventh floor, five minutes early. As she entered the offices of Mitchell Reisner O'Hara, she whispered her Eleanor mantra for good luck.

She met with Ralph Reisner who then introduced her to two other ad executives, Marty Melior and Grace Gordon. Mr. Reisner explained to Emma that each of them had experience with the beverage industry, but none had worked with a foreign winery. Mitchell Reisner O'Hara had been chosen because they were not attached to any of the other large wineries in the Northwest.

Emma decided that for the first day she would listen, mostly, unless talk was absolutely necessary. These three knew tons more than she did, except about wine. Marty Melior's demeanor was flat, and Emma couldn't tell a thing about him or what he thought. Grace Gordon's visual sizing up of Emma, her new, and very young, cohort was not going well. If looks could kill, Grace Gordon's looks were death rays.

Listening worked for the first hour. Emma took notes. She had the impression that Reisner's two cohorts thought Emma might know nothing from the way she wrote and listened and said little.

Grace Gordon asked Emma about predictive

variables using jargon that only an MBA could answer. Emma admitted she didn't know the answers - yet.

Ms. Gordon grimaced at Ralph Reisner and looked daggers back at Emma.

"How old are you?"

Reisner interrupted, "Grace, you know that we can't ask that type of question."

Ms Gordon responded immediately, "Okay, fine. Then what's going on here? This 'girl' does not meet the criteria we set up for this job. So why is she here? Is this someone's girlfriend or cousin?"

Ralph countered, "Grace, let's take this outside the room."

They both exited into the hallway and shut the door. The walls were tinted glass but even the poorest lip reader could have made out "This is bullshit" from Ms. Gordon. Ralph held up his hands in the "stop" mode, shook his head, and said something that brought both back into the room.

Emma felt that she needed to defend herself if she was ever to gain the respect she needed for the job. Before either could speak, Emma stood and took control of the meeting.

"Ms. Gordon, Mr. Melior, you are both thinking that I am not qualified for this job and you are absolutely correct that I did not meet the criteria that were established. I understand your concerns. However, if you would think outside the box for a moment, the criteria were not robust enough to really find the right person. No experience with Italy, Italian wineries, wine production, distribution, transportation, and storage was required, or asked for. The same goes with the

Pacific Northwest wine business. I believe that if you had set your bar high enough, I would be the only one you would have interviewed. I've listened for an hour and now I'd like to educate you. Oh, and by the way, I am twenty-three."

And educate them she did. No notes, just twenty-three years of wine.

"Wine is not sugared water like a soft drink that can be made, packaged and sold in one continuous cycle. Wine is stored and aged. Some wines can come out quickly and some do better aging, particularly the heavier red wines. The vintner, if he, or she, knows their wine, will not release it until it is ready. Some years produce better reds and some better whites. Some years the wine crops are abundant, some not. Shipping from Italy and storage, once here, can be costly because of the refrigeration and temperature stabilization requirements. Labeling might be better done locally for a variety of reasons."

"Also, learning a little about the history of wine and wine from Italy might help generate an edge in promotion. Italy is the world's second largest wine producer after France. Greek settlers were growing wine in Italy first. The Romans started vineyards at least two hundred years before Christ was born.

"The Romans were more organized than any other winemakers, to that point, and pioneered mass production, barrel making and storage techniques.

"Italian wine is exported to almost every country in the world. Italians have the highest wine consumption per capita in the world at around seventy liters per capita. Italy's one million vineyards are spread through every region of the country, from the Alps to the tip of the Italian boot.

"Americans have pretty much learned most of the

wine types from the French and, to a lesser extent, the Germans. Italian wines share many of the same characteristics but are named differently. Italy does produce non-native and internationally better known Chardonnays, Gewürztraminers, and Rieslings in the whites but if this project is to succeed, Mitchell Reisner O'Hara will need to educate the North American wine lovers in wines that are pure Italian."

Emma then went through the characteristics, without looking back at her PowerPoint presentation, of Arneis, Catarratto, Fiano, Garganega, Malvasia Bianca, Moscato, Nuragus, Pigato, Pinot Grigio, Ribolla Gialla, Tocai Friulano, Trebbiano, Verdicchio, Vermentino, Passerina, Pecorino doc, Falerio, Carricante, Coda de Volpe, Cortese, Falanghina, Grechetto, Grillo, Inzolia, Picolit, Traminer, Verduzzo, and Vernaccia. She pointed out that only the Pinot Grigio, which in France is Pinot Gris, is a common American selection.

"In the reds, of course everyone knows Chiantis, which are actually in the category of Italian Sangioveses. These were Italy's claim to fame and come from Tuscany. Traditionally made, the wines are full of cherry, fruit, earth and cedar."

"In addition to Chianti, there is Rosso di Montalcino, Brunello di Montalcino, Rosso di Montepulciano, Montefalco Rosso, and others. The Sangiovese is also used in wines popularly called "Super-Tuscans," which are blends with Cabernet Sauvignon and Merlot."

"Other non-Chianti Sangiovese reds were Aglianico, Barbera, Corvina, Dolcetto, Malvasia Nera, Montepulciano, Nebbiolo, Negroamaro, Nero d'Avola, Primitivo, Sagrantino, Sangiovese, Rosso Piceno, and Rosso Piceno Superiore. Every one of these wines has a different characteristic.

In summary, our job is to make these household names like Bordeaux, Merlot, Cabernet and Pinot Noir. We need to make them romantically Roman. Once we do that, no one will want a wine from anywhere but Italy..."

Emma spoke for seventy minutes, non-stop and left the impression she could go on for seven hundred minutes if she were asked. Most of her eye contact was with Ms. Gordon, whom Emma figured to be her biggest hurdle. After Emma concluded her presentation, Reisner was grinning from ear to ear.

Grace Gordon stood and did a mock bow and exclaimed, "I am so sorry I misjudged you. Where did we find you? You act like you've been priming for this job for fifteen years. Incredible performance. Brava, Brava."

"Thank you," Emma said. "I've been priming for this my whole life. And Grace, I hope to learn as much from you as you learn from me."

"That's a deal. We're having five couples for dinner on Friday and I need wine."

"You let me know the menu and I'll get the wine."

Marty Melior just smiled. A smile that said, "*This is going to be big.*"

Reisner gave each a job, but most of the legwork and development was to be Emma's. They would meet every Monday at 9:30 a.m. for ninety minutes and more if needed. Reisner demanded that Emma use a special laptop that was specific for Mitchell Reisner O'Hara's firm. All the logins were protected and email and files were encrypted to guarantee that no other PR firm would get wind of the work product. The computer's hard drive would be divided electronically so that Emma could use it for private use as well. Reisner said that if she needed help transferring her own material to the new laptop, their IT department would help. Emma didn't let on that she had no computer.

"Sure, I'll bring mine in, if need be."

She was given a parking pass and a photo ID card. Emma was through at noon and exited Mitchell Reisner O'Hara with a new thirty-five hundred dollar MacBook Pro under one arm and David's briefcase under the other. She wasn't very good at whistling, but it didn't stop her from trying on the way back to her car.

Emma flourished under the tutelage of Ralph Reisner and Grace Gordon. Emma continued to get advice from Professor Miller, Dr. Agotini and lists of acquaintances in the wine business in America and Italy. Emma finished her final proposal two weeks early. Vittorio Veliano and two other Italian vintners returned to Seattle to review the final product. Test marketing and focus groups, along with retailers, thought the campaign would be brilliant. The Italian consul joined the group for a congratulatory meal. He remembered Emma from the JDF lecture and told the entourage how Emma had stepped into an impossible situation and made it her own.

Chapter 57

The launch started in the spring of the following year. Mitchell Reisner O'Hara offered Emma a position as an account executive with a starting salary of eighty-five thousand dollars yearly. The sale of Italian wines saw growth of over fifty percent the first year and another eighty-five percent the following year. By year three, the Italian investment of one and a half million dollars in Emma, Ralph Reisner and Mitchell Reisner O'Hara paid off with forty-five million dollars in profits to the Italian consortium. In addition, Mitchell Reisner O'Hara won three local and national awards for advertising. Two major beverage accounts switched to Mitchell Reisner O'Hara in year three, largely because of their success with the Italian wines. Three advertising agencies, one in Seattle and two in San Francisco, tried to lure Emma away. Emma would have never left Seattle, but Reisner wasn't taking any chances. Emma's salary was raised to one hundred thirty-five thousand dollars yearly, plus bonuses, for year three and, in year four, she was given another raise and was made a partner of Mitchell Reisner O'Hara. Emma completed her Executive MBA through the Foster School of Business at the UW, three years after graduation.

David Milton had finished his chief year on schedule and joined the faculty at the University of Washington as an Assistant Professor of Surgery. David was put in charge of residency training at the Harborview County Hospital and started to develop his own private practice at the UW specializing in laparoscopic abdominal oncologic surgery.

Emma continued to communicate with her mother using the Potts email but had not been back to Walla Walla or seen her parents since her excommunication from the Braza household by her father.

Emma's name and picture would show up in various

wine publications. Clara's only comments of support and, perhaps affection, came in a terse email stating how proud she was of Emma's achievements

Alan continued to blame Emma, and Joe continued to listen. Alan and Joe Braza's attempts to undermine Emma, when her position at Mitchell Reisner O'Hara became public knowledge, fell on deaf ears. She was already too popular and too valuable to be removed.

Emma was now twenty-seven years old, successful and powerful. David, thirty-three, was an up and coming academic star in the Department of Surgery. David and Emma moved out of the apartment on 16th when Emma made partner so that Mike and Laurie could rent it to students once again. They purchased their first house on 40th Ave East in the Madison Park area, a four bedroom split level rambler.

Esther Milton, in the absence of Sophie Picone, continued to serve as Emma's anchor. As Esther approached her eighty-fifth birthday and in seemingly good health, she died peacefully in her sleep of a stroke. Esther had been an active participant in a number of charities and had served as president of her synagogue, Temple de Hirsch Sinai, and the local chapters of the Jewish Federation and the American Jewish Committee. Close to six hundred people attended her funeral. Emma took Esther's death as hard as her natural children and spoke at the funeral of the incredible impact Esther had had in her life. She had been a role model for Emma in dealing with the tragedies that they kept hidden together. Emma would never forget her.

At Mitchell Reisner O'Hara, Emma now had two MBAs and four executive assistants working under her for the beverage and wine promotions. She sat in Ralph's office after the Italian account had been renewed for another three years, and they toasted with a glass of Chianti.

After the toast, Emma said, "I might not be drinking much wine for a while."

Ralph understood without asking any additional information.

Emma Milton officially announced her pregnancy four months later.

Emma and Sophie continued to talk, text or email each other on a daily basis. Meanwhile, Sophie had married Carl Hawthorne, a fellow classmate at Columbia Law School, and was practicing law in Morristown, NJ. Carl joined a large New York firm specializing in mergers and acquisition law.

The firm Sophie joined made her a partner when she brought her father's trucking business with her. She remained counsel for Picone Trucking but started to develop a trust, wills and estate planning practice.

Emma, David, Sophie and Carl would have at least one vacation together each year, alternating oceans, Hawaii, Bahamas, Cabo San Lucas and Turks and Caicos. Sophie and Carl had their first child, a girl, about the time Emma became pregnant. Sophie was thoughtful enough to have her baby on the day the doctors had predicted six months earlier. This afforded Emma the opportunity to be with her during labor and delivery, sharing responsibility with Sophie's mom and Carl. Sophie, with Carl's blessings, immediately named her Emma Picone Hawthorne, and Emma was appointed godmother. Sophie held off little Emma's baptism until Emma and David could return to New Jersey 6 weeks later.

Sophie promised Emma that, unless an act of God prevented it, she would be in Seattle for her delivery. Emma continued to work and had little trouble with morning sickness.

At twelve weeks, Emma had her first ultrasound. The gynecologist, Tracy Johannsen, an OB at Swedish Hospital, told Emma and David, “Both look great.”

"You mean the baby and me?"

Dr. Johannsen fully aware of her play on words, continued with a smile, "No. We didn't ultrasound you. I am talking about both babies."

"What, twins. You're kidding?" Emma and David said in unison.

"No, not kidding. Can't tell the sexes yet, but two there are."

Emma emailed Clara first, using the Gmail account, with the message "We have a pair of buns in our special oven. Expect delivery in 6 months. Are you interested in Bun Ovens?” She received no response.

The email to Sophie was followed in four minutes with a phone call. The laughing and screams of happiness lasted for half an hour.

Emma planned to work until the day the babies were born. She stopped going downtown to the office after thirty-six weeks.

Sophie's calls were now coming daily. "So, who's going to be there for the delivery, in case I'm late or you're early."

"David, of course. His parents don't feel comfortable and Rachel is away at University of Michigan. Soph, I haven't said this much to you, but I miss my mom. Particularly now."

"I bet you do. Sorry about that."

"Alan is running more of the business. I hear things and they've lost a number of key personnel because Alan doesn't know how to manage people. I also heard that my parents had to take out an equity loan on the winery after Alan lost money on a building project in Spokane. His third wife has apparently left him. These babies will be my parent's first grandchildren."

"Well, I'm sorry about your mom but I'm coming, so don't squeeze too hard. I've already got my ticket. My mother and mother-in-law will take care of little Emma. Can't wait to see you. Bet you're big as a horse."

"Neigh." Emma whinnied. Both laughed. "Talk to you tomorrow, Soph, okay? I do really miss my mom."

Sophie felt terrible that Clara, and Joe for that matter, were going to miss the birth of their first grandchildren. She thought about Emma's predicament for a good deal of time and discussed it with Carl. Sophie made the call.

"Mrs. Braza, this is Sophie Hawthorne, Sophie Picone Hawthorne, Emma's roommate from college."

“Hello, Sophie,” Clara said. “It's been a while. Nice to hear your voice. Are your parents okay?"

"Yes, thank you. Everyone is fine and they send their regards." White lies.

"What can I do for you Sophie?"

"First, this call is on my own. Not Emma, or anyone else put me up to it. Just me. I will get to the point. Are you alone?"

"Yes, Joe is working in the car shed."

"Well, here's the deal. I know you and Mr. Braza and Emma aren't speaking."

"Yes."

"It is possible that sometime in the future you and Joe and Emma will forgive each other, or reach an understanding or find out something you didn't know. It's possible."

Clara said, "I suppose it's possible. Joe and Alan are not likely to forgive Emma for calling in the police for a snippet of a conversation she claims she heard and that Alan denies saying and Joe denies hearing."

"Mrs. Braza, I've always been a straight shooter with you. Even when I had dyed hair and piercings and I know you remember those days."

"Yes I do."

"There will come a time when Emma will be forgiven. I know her and I know what she's capable of doing. The point is that your daughter is four weeks away from delivering your first grandchildren, twins. She came to my delivery and I am planning to come to hers. That said, she has said a couple of times that she wishes her mother could be there with her. Could you ever fathom not being with her for this event? If you do make up, and I know you will, you will kick yourself for not being there for her. She needs you, she wants you, and you should want it too."

"I don't know, Sophie. Joe would go ballistic. He blames Emma for ills that I know she has no part in. I know that Alan stokes the fires, despite my trying to reason with them."

"Mrs. Braza, Joe is not going to leave you if you show up for Emma's delivery. He may be mad for a while but he's not going to hurt you and he's certainly not going to leave you. Not after forty plus years. You've been an amazing wife and mother. Mr. Braza can go back to being angry after the delivery. You don't have to stay or even come back. But do you really want to miss this?"

"No, I don't want to miss it," Clara was crying. "And I miss Emma, but we can't forgive her for what she did. It was just too unthinkable. Joe and Alan warned her about being with David. She knew how they felt and yet she followed him."

Clara's comments struck Sophie deeply and profoundly saddened her. Clara hadn't listened to a word that Emma or Sophie had said or written over the past few years. Joe and Alan, with a constant and steady barrage of false information, had essentially brain-washed Emma's mother.

Clara continued as Sophie listened, "Sophie, let me think on it. I will have to discuss it with Joe. I can't sneak out. I can't act like Emma did, hiding her actions."

Realizing the conversation was going nowhere but to hell, Sophie stopped beating her head against the proverbial wall, "Okay. Okay. Mrs. Braza, give it some thought. Can I call you in a couple of days?"

"Sure, how about Tuesday at 10:00 a.m? I'm home alone then."

Sophie, surprised that Clara had even suggested she call back responded, "Okay, Tuesday at 10:00 it is."

Sophie was not optimistic, not even a little, but still there was a glimmer of hope. She called back Tuesday at 10:00 a.m.

"Hi, Mrs. Braza, it's Sophie. Have you thought about it?

"I would like to come. I really would. But I haven't the nerve to tell Joe about it. I can't sneak out of town. If I do and I'm caught it will only be worse. I really want to come. I will try to wait until Joe is calm and then ask. I think he knows she's pregnant but I'm not even sure of that. It's as if she doesn't exist."

"Clara, do you want me to call back or do you want to call me."

"Call back in a day or so. I'll try my best."

Two days passed.

"I discussed it with Joe and he went berserk," said Clara.

Clearly upset and sounding scared, Clara's revelation struck hard. Sophie had been with Emma scared and their voices sounded so alike.

"It was worse than I thought it would be. He called Alan, who came over and berated me as well. I can't take this. I am not used to this kind of punishment. I am so sorry, Sophie, I can't go."

"I am sorry Clara. I am so sorry. More for you than Emma. She's an amazing, strong, honest, intelligent and caring woman whom you raised and you're not getting any of the enjoyment out of her success. It's just too bad. I will let you know how things go. Okay?"

"Sophie, I've got to go, please."

Sophie did not tell Emma about their conversations. To what end?

Both Emma and Sophie knew that the delivery could be early with twins. But Sophie didn't have the luxury of taking off more than a week. A little luck was necessary. They talked and texted every eight hours. By week thirty-eight, Emma was having false contractions every few hours but nothing sustained. With six days to go to her due date, Emma had hard contractions for twenty minutes. She called Sophie, David, and Laurie Milton after ten minutes. Her bags had been packed for three weeks. Rachel, back from Ann Arbor, answered the phone at Laurie's house and said her mom was at the grocery store.

“Rachel, I think the babies are coming. I need a ride to the hospital.”

“I'll be there in fifteen minutes,” Rachel said.

Ten minutes later the contractions stopped. Rachel arrived, spent a little time with Emma and went home. Emma called Sophie back and told her about the false alarm.

"I can't stand this. You're going to have these babies in the next twenty-four hours. I am flying out this afternoon."

Sophie, the soothsayer, was correct. Emma went into labor at 10:35 p.m. that evening. Sophie arrived at SeaTac at 11:05 p.m. and took a cab directly to Swedish Hospital. She, David, and Laurie spent the next twelve hours with Emma until she was transported into the birthing room. Only David and Sophie came with her, one on each side, and watched her deliver two healthy baby girls. The first, five pounds eleven ounces and the second, a non-identical twin, five pounds eight ounces.

Sometime later that night when the hullaballoo had died down, Emma lay in bed looking and feeling a bit sullen. The babies had both tried breast-feeding with a little success but not much milk. The nurses were going to supplement them with some sugar water and try to let mother and babies sleep. David was sound asleep on the rollaway bed and everyone had gone home, save Sophie.

"A penny for your thoughts, Emma."

"Funny how things in life work out. I am so blessed right now. Two babies, yet unnamed. A wonderful husband, an incredible career, and the best friend anyone could ever have. Yet I am still missing something. I am missing my family. Anyway, I am so lucky, let's not dwell on the negative. Thank you, again, for being here."

"Wouldn't have missed it."

"We didn't want to jinx things by talking about names before they were born and healthy. David and I discussed this for a very short time because we both agreed. The first girl, in case there were two girls, is to be named Sophia Picone Milton. You have been so important to me that just the first name was not enough. Don't argue with me, even for a second. You know pregnancy, hormones, mood swings, yadda yadda. Just say thanks. Sophie you deserve even more. You will be Sophia's godmother and I expect you to be there in spirit for her. I will tell her the stories of her godmother and namesake over and over, so she knows how meaningful and important her name, your name, and you have been and will be to me."

Sophie was bawling by this point and gave Emma a huge hug. "Thank you."

David awoke and turned to Emma, who spoke, "I told Sophie the girl's name we chose."

"Cool." He fell back to sleep.

When the bawling stopped Sophie asked about the other girl's name.

"We are going to call her Esther Rene Milton after David's grandmother, Esther, and great aunt, Rene. We've talked about Grandma Esther before and how helpful she was to me in so many ways. Esther had a sister named Rene that gave her life so that Esther could live. Rene's story contains so much tragedy and she died young, but her story was so compelling and so much a part of Esther's that we felt the need to honor her."

Sophie nodded. "Emma, I will watch over and pray for Esther Rene Milton as much as I do for Sophia Picone Milton. I can't wait for our kids to be old enough to play with each other. My children will know about Aunt Emma and their Seattle cousins, I promise."

Emma went home the day after her delivery. A slew of close friends made cameo visits over the next few days. Rafe and Nadia Gomez called and asked if they could come.

"Of course," David said. "By the way, do you think you could drive Emma's friend, Sophie, to the airport?"

"No problema, amigo. We'll come in separate cars."

"I know you remember Sophie. She's the one you met outside the sorority that first night I scared Emma."

"How could I forget," said Rafe.

The next day, Rafe and Nadia came for a short visit very early in the morning. When introduced, Rafe reminded Sophie that they had met. She didn't remember until he explained that he was the UW officer that brought Emma back to the sorority after David had followed her into Anderson Hall."

"Wow, that was something. And look what it lead to," said Sophie.

They both nodded agreement.

Nadia, somewhat of a breast feeding guru, helped Emma with little Sophia and Esther. David helped load big Sophie's suitcase into Rafe's car and headed back to the hospital. Sophie and Rafe headed to the airport at 8:30 a.m. Sophie's plane would not leave for another three hours.

Chapter 58

On the drive to Sea-Tac Airport, Sophie was thinking about Emma and her family and said offhandedly to Rafe. "Too bad Emma's family couldn't be here. They are really missing out." Sophie had no idea what Rafe knew or didn't know.

Rafe had not really gotten into Emma's family life with David. "Why's that?" he asked.

"Oh, that's a bit of a story that you may or may not know. David went to visit Emma's family and someone had planted drugs in David's car. The police came and arrested David. It was all bogus and they threw out the charges but then, of course, David got his lung and spleen injured. Emma had overheard her dad and her brother, Alan, talking and her brother apparently admitted having something to do with it. But not very specific. Anyway the police came later and took her brother in for questioning. Emma's parents, or at least her dad, felt that Emma had told the police that her brother had confessed to being responsible. Her dad threw her out of the house and has never forgiven her and won't let her mother get near her either. Her brother is a piece of work and he apparently stokes the anger as much as he can. Emma has denied having anything to do with all this, but her father won't listen. Such a shame."

"Sophie, you're an attorney, right?"

"Yes, practicing in New Jersey."

"If I tell you something, is it considered attorney client privilege?"

"Only if I am your attorney"

"Well, counselor, I'd like you to be my attorney"

"Rafe, I'm expensive. Really, really expensive."

"I think you'll discount my fee when I tell you what I know."

Sophie laughed. "Your time as my client may be the shortest in history."

"I doubt it." Rafe began, “Here goes, so listen closely. I know a ton more than you, Emma or David, but have never told anyone. Rafe finished telling Sophie the saga, talking continuously for the forty minute drive to SeaTac Airport.”

Sophie was stunned, left speechless for a moment, and then said, "Why don't you just tell Emma and David what you told me?"

"Well, I don't know that David would ever forgive me for putting him in harm's way. He almost bought the farm. The DEA promised me that no one was going to get hurt and then the sheriff pokes him. What's Emma going to do with the information? She says, he says. Alan and Joe will deny all of this and we've only got hearsay, counselor," said Rafe, in his best *legalese*.

"Your cousin or his friend willing to step up?"

"No. Don't think so. My cousin might, but I don't even know who told him and he's not going to tell me. So it's hearsay again. There is no hard evidence."

"Well, here's a thought. There is likely not enough evidence to get to Emma's brother, you're right. But I don't care if Alan goes to jail, although I'd like it. I only want Emma's parents to hear this out. They can make their own decisions. If we could get Emma's folks into a room with all the players, you, your cousin, the DEA guys, the video tapes of the break-in, Specker's assertion that Alan had tipped him off, maybe they'll see what really happened. If nothing else, the DEA can tell Emma's parents that Alan was going to get picked up regardless and that Emma had nothing to do with it."

Rafe thought. "I don't know if we can get all these people together. Specker was apparently a friend of Joe Braza and he retired soon after this happened. After the DEA showed up, I suspect he knew he had been suckered into a setup and maybe afraid that David would pursue charges against him. Anyway he bailed out of the force, taking his thirty years and a pension."

"Rafe, couldn't hurt to try," Sophie said. "The DEA has to have some remorse about David's injury. Maybe you can ask, eh? Getting Specker personally to tell the Brazas that Alan had tipped them off would be fabulous, or that might be in the police records."

"Braza admitted that he'd heard it randomly at a bar in Walla Walla and told Specker."

As the two conspirators arrived at Sea-Tac airport Sophie added another thought. "Emma's mother's biggest fear is Joe throwing her out of the house too, just for befriending Emma. I do a lot of wills and estate work. I'll bet dollars to donuts that Emma's mother is the sole owner of the winery with clear title. Her parents must have left it to her, unless their attorney was a complete bozo. I'll need to see if I can get Emma's grandparent's will. Knowing that Joe can't really do anything to the winery without Clara may be a big stick to wag. At least maybe we can get him to listen. Here's my card. We'll need to talk some more. You're correct, by the way, I am going to do a deep discount on my services. Maybe some of Nadia's recipes as payment."

"Sophie, here's my card. If we pull this off, Nadia and I will come to New Jersey and cook for you."

They shook hands. Rafe took Sophie's suitcase out of the back of the car and they waved good-bye as she walked into the United Airlines terminal.

Rafe got back into his car and thought to himself

how he'd really love to square things for David and Emma and get the whole thing off his conscience. He still had the occasional nightmare about David croaking in Walla Walla. He mumbled a prayer to the dashboard Jesus as he drove off and added, "C'mon, Sophie, do your magic, and I'll work like hell on this end."

Chapter 59

"Hawk, this is Rafe Gomez."

"Hey Rafe, long time no talk."

"I'm still spitting nails about Walla Walla," Gomez said.

"So am I, fuck you, that's the business we're in," said Hawkins.

"But I'm willing to forgive if you can help me out."

"Depends on what you want me to do, Rafe. We go back a long way, but I don't owe you shit. You never returned my calls after I explained what happened. You know that I could not have predicted your buddy getting hurt. So can we put that behind us?"

"I'm sorry, Hawk. I do know how these things go. I was just so upset 'cuz I could have lost a good friend. I need to try and make this right."

"So what's on your mind?"

Rafe explained how Emma had been wrongly accused of ratting on her brother and the father wouldn't listen to her. He would try and get his cousin and, if lucky, the cousin's gang member to talk to the Brazas. Rafe wanted Hawk to bring himself and maybe one or two of Spokane agents to the same meeting. Rafe offered to pay for the transportation costs, which impressed Hawkins. Hawkins didn't realize the money was coming from Sophie. Rafe made clear to Hawkins that no one was concerned about nailing Emma's brother. They just needed to get Emma off the hook. Getting Joe Braza to come to a meeting would be difficult. The attorney friend of Emma was working on something to make him come. Hawk said he'd try but couldn't make any promises.

Sophie called a few days later. She had gotten copies of Clara Braza's parent's will that had been filed with Walla Walla County. Clara deLorraine Braza had been given full ownership of the winery and her brother, an attorney in Dallas, was to be paid half the appraised value of the winery over ten years at no interest. The note was paid in seven years giving Clara clear title to deLorraine Vineyards. If Clara were to die without a will, the winery would likely be divided equally amongst her legal children.

Sophie was concerned that a codicil may have been filed removing Emma from the will, but Clara would have had to sign a document of that sort, and it hadn't been mentioned. Sophie wondered how many things Clara might have signed over the years without reading or understanding the intent. The law firm that represented the deLorraine Winery was listed as the executor of the will. Joe Braza was not mentioned in the will. Clara owns the winery, free and clear. If there were a divorce between Clara and Joe, the increased assets of the winery would need to be divided equally but the winery would remain in Clara's hands. Sophie was hopeful, just hopeful, that this knowledge would spur Clara to force Joe to listen to whatever conference was set up.

Sophie and Rafe decided against contacting Sheriff Specker. They were afraid that he'd get to Joe Braza and render the plan useless.

Hawkins got back to Rafe and said that he'd bring the files and the videotapes and meet in Spokane with agents Harry Connors and William Baker, the two Spokane based agents. Rafe said he'd get back to him about timing.

Rafe's cousin, Rico Rodriguez was not at all happy. Rico certainly wasn't going to give anyone, including Rafe, the name of his gang member, not if Rico wanted to live very long. Rico didn't want the Brazas or the DEA to know who he was, in any way, shape or form. Rafe asked if Rico would allow himself to be interviewed in a remote location with a voice-changing device so he wouldn't be recognized. He said he'd think about it. Rafe called Selma Rodriguez who called her brother and told him that Rafe wouldn't screw him and that the family owed David Milton that much. Rico called Rafe back to say he'd do it but he'd walk if anything didn't feel right."

Sophie, knowing Joe Braza better than Rafe, said they needed one more piece. Someone that Joe Braza would trust, like a judge or politician. Sophie would try to get this information from Emma or Clara without letting on what she and Rafe were doing.

Sophie did some research and found out that judges were elected officials in Washington State and voters and companies could donate to their campaigns. Therefore, if Joe Braza or the deLorraine Winery had donated money to either a politician or judge their name would show up on filed election donation reports with the State of Washington.

Joe had donated five thousand dollars to two judges, Armon Hatfield and Elliot McAuliffe, both currently serving as Superior Court judges.

Sophie called Emma and after the usual mommy chitchat she threw Emma a curve ball.

"One of my partner's clients is trying to buy commercial real estate in Walla Walla County, and they've run into a snag. I don't know much about it. He's hired an attorney in Spokane to represent his client. They are scheduled for a hearing in two months and my partner is coming out to be second chair. They are assigned to a Judge Hatfield, but were told they might be transferred to a Judge McAuliffe because of scheduling difficulties. Because he knew I went to UW, he asked me if I knew either. I told him I didn't know any judges in Seattle, least enough three hundred miles away in Walla Walla. You know either?"

"Don't know Hatfield but McAuliffe is, or was, friends with my father. He used to work for the firm that deLorraine used as their legal counsel. He then ran for judge. I would think he's still a friend with my dad. He always seemed like a nice enough man."

They went back to mindless mommy chatter and said goodbye.

Sophie called Rafe and asked if any of the DEA guys knew McAuliffe. Turned out that Harry Connors did.

Everything was in place. Now they had to get Joe and Clara Braza to listen. Hawkins, Connors and Baker all agreed to go to Walla Walla, if and when the rest of the people could get there. Connors called McAuliffe and made an appointment to see him and drove out to Walla Walla the following week. He came with the official file from the DEA and presented all the evidence to the judge.

"Why me, Harry," McAuliffe asked. "I had nothing to do with this case in any way."

"We don't think Joe Braza will believe anything from people he doesn't know. He doesn't know any of us, but he does know you and donated to your campaign. We just want to see a wrong righted. The scope of this is to get Emma back in the family graces if possible. Not to incriminate anyone else, particularly their son."

The only hurdle left was to get Joe and Clara together, without Alan being present. Judge McAuliffe felt he could arrange the meeting but couldn't speak to whether Alan might show up. Connors told him that if they could start the meeting and Alan wasn't there, he would make sure no one else entered the property.

Rafe came out to Walla Walla and met with Rico. He brought voice changing equipment and set it up in his garage.

Rico heard the playback. "I like this, how much it cost?"

"Fifteen bucks off the web, try eBay or Amazon," said Rafe.

McAuliffe called back and told Connors that Alan Braza usually played cards Wednesday nights. He called Joe and told him that he'd like to meet with him and Clara.

"Why Clara? She's not involved in any of my business dealings."

"Joe, I have to talk to you about something that is extremely personal. I promise that no one is suspected of any wrongdoing and no one will be arrested or questioned after our meeting. I just need you to hear something that was presented to me. I need to do this to you two alone. You do not need a lawyer present but if you'd like one, that's fine. I guess we've been friends for a long time. You may just have to trust me on this one. I'd like to do it on Wednesday at 7:00 p.m. at your house. You can tell Clara that we're meeting. Should take about an hour or so"

"I don't know Elliott. This sounds fishy. What's it about?"

"I can't tell you," McAuliffe said.

The meeting was set up for Wednesday night. Joe called Clara to tell her what he knew. She cancelled out of a bridge game that had been set up at a friend's house.

At 7:00 p.m., McAuliffe pulled into the Braza driveway. Bill Harris, Joe Braza's personal attorney was already present. He, of course, knew Judge McAuliffe and after the usual pleasantries, Judge McAuliffe had everyone take a seat in the living room. The judge explained that a number of people would arrive in the next fifteen minutes. They needed to listen to the entire story that was to unfold, and they could ask questions if they wanted, but didn't need to. McAuliffe told the Brazas and Harris that what was to unfold was unusual and something he had never done before. He knew some of the people who were coming to talk and didn't know others.

The judge then reiterated his pledge, "I swear that no one will be arrested or charged with any crime, ever. This is an explanatory meeting, nothing more."

The explanation and pledge befuddled Joe and Clara and Harris. They knew not what to expect.

Rafe Gomez, Dick Hawkins, Harry Connors and William Baker arrived at 7:10. Everyone stood for the greetings.

Rafe introduced himself to the Brazas. "Hello Mr. and Mrs. Braza," and shook hands. "I am Rafael Gomez. I am currently the Chief of Security forces at the University of Washington. I grew up in Walla Walla and played football one year ahead of Alan. We weren't friends. Different sides of the tracks as they say. These three gentlemen are officers in the Drug Enforcement Agency. Mr. Hawkins is from Seattle and we served in the US Army and MPs together. Mr. William Baker and Mr. Harry Connors are from Spokane and I have not met them before this day. You, of course, know Judge McAuliffe, whom I also don't know, but who I gather knows Mr. Connors."

Joe Braza recognized the three DEA agents from the night that Alan was arrested and didn't like what was happening. "You are the guys that took Alan in, right?" Joe asked.

"Yes, sir, we are," said Hawkins.

"I don't like this. Shouldn't my son be here?"

McAuliffe spoke up, "Alan is not being questioned and will not be arrested or questioned as a result of this meeting, I promise, and so do the law enforcement people here."

Hawkins spoke up immediately, "That is absolutely correct, Mr. and Mrs. Braza. If you have questions for your son afterward, that is your prerogative. Again, we do not need to question him, nor will we in the future."

Joe turned to his attorney, "Bill, but I don't like this."

Judge McAuliffe spoke up, "Joe, Bill, I don't like it either. But you can listen and when they are done they will leave. You may ask questions if you wish. This is about the night David Milton was arrested."

Joe was not happy, but sat. Clara was confused. The Braza's attorney was even more confused. All took seats.

Rafe started, "Mr. and Mrs. Braza, I need to acknowledge first that I am friends with David Milton. Dr. Milton saved the life of my oldest son seven years ago. To that, I am, and will always be indebted to him. He has also taken care of my cousin, whose name is not important, who thought she had breast cancer. The brother of this cousin is a gang member here in the Walla Walla area. He is not, well, he's not a good person. But he called me because he knew that his sister thought the world of Dr. Milton. This cousin will have voice altering equipment so you won't know who he is. His English is just passable."

Rafe dialed a number on his cell phone and attached it to a speaker system.

"Hola."

"Hola. Without any names I would like you to tell me about the phone call you made to me 5 years ago."

In an electronically altered gravelly voice, Rico Rodriguez explained,

"I was meeting with my boys and one of us says he been approached by Alan Braza. Señor Braza, he want us to put fifteen thousand dollars worth of cocaine in a car of person he want for a fall. My friend no accept the job. When my sis tell me her doctor that helped her was coming to Walla Walla to visit the Brazas, I figure out who the man being set up be. Only since my sister been helped by this doctor, I try to help him. I call to Rafe to see if he could keep his amigo out of trouble."

"Thank you. We don't need you any further," and he hung up his cell phone. "I then called Dick Hawkins of the DEA, a friend, for help."

Joe Braza, now angry, interjected, "This is bullshit."

Clara responded, "Joe, calm down. Let them finish. We don't know where this is going yet and they've promised that Alan is not in trouble, right, Elliott."

Judge McAuliffe spoke up forcefully, "Exactly, Clara, Alan is not in trouble."

Hawk took over. "I told Officer Gomez specifically not to contact Dr. Milton and to stay out of Walla Walla. The DEA, and the DEA alone, would handle the rest. I did promise Officer Gomez that no one would be harmed. I was wrong, in the end, but we could not have predicted what happened. Anyway, I mobilized Mr. Connors and Mr. Baker here from Spokane. I had court orders from a judge in Seattle allowing phone taps on Alan Braza's home and cell phone. We never listened to any conversations at this house. We also got orders to inspect Alan Braza's bank accounts. Nothing was found on the phone records or at the bank."

Hawkins then went into detail about setting up for the drop and used his laptop to show footage of the break-in on the Kia, the planting of the drugs on his computer screen. He told of the arrest of the two intruders, Alex Pesses and Dennis Vargas, petty convicts with long rap sheets.

"They knew nothing of the source of the package they were inserting in Milton's car but they did have a list of car makes and licenses that they were not supposed to enter. Pesses and Vargas were arrested outside your property's east auxiliary road. They were not helpful and in the end served sixty days for illegal weapon charges and vehicular prowling."

Hawkins paused a moment to let his comments set in and then restarted, "Our plan at that time unraveled because of David Milton's injury, which turned out to be life threatening. What we were going to do then is now not important. We did feel we had enough to question your son but he said nothing and he had no bank or phone traces that would have implicated him. All we know for sure is the drug drop did occur, and it was cocaine. The prosecutor did not have enough to present a case to the grand jury. There was no money trail and the two intruders provided no additional information."

Hawkins paused again to let the information set in and then restarted, "The important points here are, one, we were always going to bring Alan Braza in for questioning. The timing of us doing that was pushed up by David Milton's injury and the need to get him out of jail and to the hospital. That likely saved his life. At no time did David Milton or Emma Braza know that this operation was in place, and to this day they still do not know. You two now know, Emma and David Milton do not. At no time, did Emma Braza speak to anyone in my office, the Sheriff's office, the Walla Walla PD, or the prosecutor's office about Alan Braza. We've presented all of this information to Judge McAuliffe only so that he might tell you that this is not something concocted by the DEA for any reason. Judge."

McAuliffe said, "Joe, Clara. I've seen these files. They are dated, official and are the truth."

Rafe stood up. "Mr. or Mrs. Braza, do you have any questions? If not, we will leave. If you want to call any of us later, I will leave a sheet with our numbers."

Joe spoke first. "This is bullshit. I have no questions."

Bill Harris spoke for the first time, "Alan Braza is not a suspect now?"

Hawkins answered, "Alan Braza is not going to be questioned. There is no hard evidence that he was involved. Only hearsay."

Clara looked saddened. "I have nothing to ask either. I am still not sure why you came."

Rafe answered, "We are doing this solely to clear your daughter's name. Nothing else. The DEA was doing this as a favor to me. She has been accused of informing the authorities that Alan was implicated in the purchase and planting of the drugs. That is not true. Alan Braza was going to be interrogated and possibly arrested as a result of the tip given to the DEA. In the end, no concrete evidence of his involvement, other than hearsay, could be found."

When Rafe finished, everyone sat motionless.

Rafe Gomez, sensing the failure of their mission, said sadly, "We will leave now. Thank you for your time. As we said before, nothing presented here will leave this room, unless you talk about it."

Without the Brazas offering thanks or saying good-bye the entire group departed. The DEA officers thanked

Judge McAuliffe as they entered their automobiles. McAuliffe was not looking particularly happy. He said a few words to Bill Harris, they shook hands, and both entered their cars and drove away. McAuliffe was certain that Braza would not be making a donation to his campaign in the future.

Rafe proceeded to drive back to Seattle and called Sophie from the car.

"So, how'd it go?" Sophie asked.

"We did everything we could. Joe Braza responded with 'bullshit.' Mrs. Braza said nothing. Your name never came up. I'm almost positive they don't know you had anything to do with this."

"Well, we tried."

"Yes we did," Rafe Gomez said. "But it ain't over 'til the fat lady sings. I guess we sit back and see what happens."

Chapter 60

"Joe, what was that about?" Clara was still confused.

"They were trying to blame Alan for everything."

"They said that no one would be arrested or questioned. I don't think they are going after Alan. Bill Harris is an old friend and he said that emphatically"

"Then why'd they come?"

"I think that they were here to... well, I'm not sure...but I think it was to let us know that our daughter had no part in any of this, none at all. Maybe we've been too hard."

"She still married that Jew."

"Joe, in the end, we forced her into it. No, you forced her into it. You don't know that they would have stayed together or married. They never said they were going to get married. They were just a young couple going out with each other. We gave her no options. You forced her out of our life."

"Clara, don't get into this with me. She didn't listen."

"No, that's not true. She listened and talked to us and told us what she was doing. We didn't listen. I've now missed the birth of our first grandchildren. I want to see Emma and see our grandchildren."

"I'm not sure yet. I'll have to think about it."

"I'm not asking you now. I'm telling you. Emma did nothing wrong and you overreacted. We gave her no options. She said from the beginning that she didn't know what was going on and we didn't believe her."

"You're not to talk to Emma. I have to think about this."

"We'll see."

"Not 'til I've said you can," Joe demanded again.

Clara started to tremble, "Joe, what's gotten into you? You've never been like this. You've changed. You're just being mean and stubborn now. You're not listening to me at all and you won't help me reason out this terrible mess. Maybe you, or we, need to see someone?"

"Clara, have I been mean to you, ever?"

"Well, no."

"Have I been mean to any of the people that work for me at the winery or work for us around the house?"

"No."

"Enough said. Our daughter was and is being manipulated by that Jew doctor. I've had it with her." Joe steamed out of the room, went to his study and slammed the door.

A few days passed and Joe and Clara did not speak of the meeting. In fact, they talked little, but Joe was a bit calmer.

At breakfast, three days later, Clara brought up her thoughts again, "Joe, I think we should reach out to Emma."

"Not yet. End of conversation." Joe stormed out of the house, without finishing his meal, and went to the winery.

Clara, talking to the front door, "Not the end of conversation to me."

Clara gave it some thought. She didn't know how they would even start to communicate. Clara decided that she'd call Sophie for advice.

"Sophie, this is Clara Braza."

"Hello Mrs. Braza."

"How are you and the baby and your parents? Kind of lost touch haven't we?"

"Uh, yes we have. Didn't have to Mrs. Braza. Didn't have to."

"I'm thinking that I'd like to see Emma or at least talk to her. I don't know what to do."

"What's holding you back?" Sophia asked.

"Joe doesn't want me to talk to her yet. No, stronger than that. He's threatened me if I do talk to her. I'm not sure why. I don't think she did anything to Alan, I mean with the authorities and all. We know some things now, I can't say what, that put Emma clear of all the blame. Still, Joe is emphatic that she's terrible and not to be trusted. I am actually worried that he's not processing information presented to him as sharply as he used to."

Sophie was not going to let on that she knew about the meeting.

"Mrs. Braza, Joe can't stop you. It's a free country, so they say. Just call Emma. Or if you like I'll call Emma and have her call you."

"I'm afraid of what Joe will do. I mean he does everything. I can't afford to get him angry."

Sophie thought this was as good a time as any to explain Clara's parent's will. "Mrs. Braza, I am an attorney and my specialty is trusts and wills and estate planning. The deLorraine Winery was started by your family two generations before you and when your grandfather died he left the winery to your father. When your father died, he left the winery to you. To you alone, and you have what is called 'clear title.' Not to Joe Braza, and not to your brother in Dallas, who received money for his share of the estate. The winery is yours alone to pass on. People will assets like this to their children. There are a host of reasons why this is done, but rest assured that Mr. Braza cannot take the winery away from you, unless you've signed it over to him."

"I've never done anything like that," Clara said. "I mean I don't think I've ever signed anything giving it away. I might have signed something that allowed Joe to take out loans against the winery, but that's it. How do you know what my parents did?"

"Because that's what I do," Sophie said. "You'll have to trust me on this. Your parents would not have left the winery to anyone outside the family. If Mr. Braza walks out on you, and I seriously doubt that he would, the house and the winery and the vineyards belong to Clara deLorraine Braza. It may be a little more complicated than that, but not too much. End of story. If you have any questions about what I've said, call your brother in Dallas."

After a bit more chit chat, Clara ended the call. She then called her brother in Dallas. Her brother, Jesse, confirmed what Sophie had been saying. The winery was in her name unless she had signed it away.

That night, Clara announced to Joe that she was going to call Emma.

"Not until I say you can."

"And what will you do, Joe Braza? You're just being stubborn and afraid to admit that you might have wronged our daughter."

"I'll do what I want. The money in this family has been made by me and you'll do as I say," Joe fumed.

Clara took a deep breath and collected herself. "Joe, you don't own me. You can't admit that you may have been wrong and so was Alan. Yes, you've made the winery successful, but who, actually, owns the winery? I mean, who is on the title of the house and winery and vineyards?"

"Who cares, I run them," Joe said, continuing to spew venom.

"Well, I care for one," Clara said. "Do you know the answer? If you don't, then I have a pretty good idea that the winery was left to me. I remember that we paid off Jesse after my parents died, he didn't want any part of it."

Joe said nothing more and stormed out of the house.

Clara decided a few things at that moment. *I am calling Emma tomorrow. I will start taking a little more interest in the winery. I need to get Joe to see Dr. Franklin. He just isn't acting normally.*

Joe had his first stroke with symptoms that evening. He came back to the house an hour after leaving. He had not gotten any farther than the garage. He told Clara that when he got into his car, his left hand and left side of his face went numb. The numbness lasted for ten minutes. Clara could see a little drooping of the left side of Joe's mouth and his speech was garbled. Joe also complained of terrible headache.

"Clara, I'm scared," Joe said.

Clara called Dr. Franklin immediately and told him what Joe had told her and how he looked. Without hesitation, Dr. Franklin told Clara to give him an adult aspirin and then drive Joe to the Walla Walla General ER.

"Joe will probably be okay, Clara," Dr. Franklin said. "I'll call ahead to make sure the ER knows that Joe is coming."

The emergency room physicians found nothing wrong with Joe's physical exam, laboratory tests and vital signs including a normal blood pressure, blood tests and EKG. The drooping at the side of his mouth, his garbled speech had completely resolved. A CT scan of the brain revealed no acute bleed or hemorrhage, but did suggest loss of brain tissue and old areas of infarction on the right side. Given the story, and with Dr. Franklin's consent, the doctors started Joe on a potent blood thinner to try to prevent additional strokes. Dr. Franklin referred Joe to the radiologists for more tests, which revealed an irregularity and narrowing of the right internal carotid artery, the big artery in the neck that goes to the brain. An MRI done the following day suggested damage to many parts of the right side of Joes brain, meaning that he may have been having small strokes for some time.

Dr. Franklin immediately referred Joe to a vascular surgeon in Spokane to have his artery repaired. In the meantime, Joe was to take it easy, reduce stress and not go to work. Alan assumed control of deLorraine.

Two days later as Clara and Joe readied to leave for Spokane, Clara called Emma with a cell phone from the garage. Sophie had told Emma that she had spoken to her mom about some estate issues and that a call from her mother could happen.

"Emma, this is mom," Clara said.

"Is everything okay? I'm so happy to hear from you."

"Well, Dad is going to Spokane tomorrow to see a surgeon. He had a little stroke but it all went away. I think they called it a TIA, or something like that. Dr. Franklin thinks he'll need his neck artery fixed. Apparently the surgery isn't too big a deal but if he doesn't have it, he could have a worse stroke."

"Do you want me to come to Spokane?"

"No, I think your showing up now will not calm Dad down, probably the opposite. But as soon as he's better, I am coming to Seattle to see you and the babies. That's a promise."

"Will you call me every day and right after surgery to let me know how things are going?"

"Sure. Sure, I will. We have lots of things to make up. How are the babies?

"They are fine, amazing, and a ton of work. Wanna help? Sophia is now almost 9 pounds and Esther is 8 and 3/4. Everyone says little Esther looks like me."

"Is Sophia named after Sophie Picone?" Clara asked.

"Yes. She named her daughter Emma. If she hadn't, I would have still named Sophie, Sophie."

"Who is Esther named after?"

"David's grandmother. I think I've mentioned her before to you, maybe not. She passed away recently. She was an amazing person and you would have enjoyed meeting her. She survived a concentration camp, Auschwitz. I miss her."

"Nice. Can you send me some pictures of the babies?"

"I have a bunch of pictures stored on a website. I will send the link. Just log in and feast your eyes. I'll set up both the ID and password for you as Clara and Clara. Mom, they are the most beautiful things in the world. Ever."

"I thought that about you. Still do. You'll understand when you're older. You will always be the most beautiful girl. Anyway I'll call every day when I have a moment. I hope everything goes well with your father."

"Who's running the winery while Dad is gone?

"Alan is."

"That okay?" Emma asked.

"Well some of the men don't work with him well. It's frustrating. I stay out of it."

"Maybe you shouldn't stay out of it."

"I'm planning to get a little involved. At least until Dad is better."

"Mom, a little involved won't do it. Alan could destroy deLorraine before Dad gets back to work. I mean it, Mom, get involved."

Clara listened and said nothing. Emma took this to mean that she understood. Emma continued, "Do you know the name of the surgeon Dad is seeing?"

"Yes, I have it here. Hold on. Dr. Kenneth Keyes, Vascular Surgeon. Do you know him?"

"No, but likely David does. Good luck, Mom. The kids are screaming to be fed and last I looked I have only two boobs. I feel like a moving feeding station right now, but I've lost weight, almost back to normal. I must be thinner below because my breasts must weigh a ton. Never had cleavage before but I don't think it will last."

"Emma, you are so funny. I miss you."

"Mom, I'm starting to leak. Gotta go. Can I call you?"

"No, not just yet, I'll call you."

Emma put down the phone, stunned. She wept softly while breast feeding. When done, she sent her mom the link to the online picture storage site and used her own email.

Bye Bye Ms. PottsandPanz.

She finished feeding and called Sophie to tell her about the unexpected phone call from her mother.

"Sophie, Alan is now running deLorraine. That's a huge mistake. I told my mother to get involved and I hope she's listening. Alan will just screw things up and Dad may not be able to put it back together when he's well."

When they were done talking, Sophie called Rafe, got his voice mail, and left a short message. "Bingo."

David called Kenneth Keyes. Keyes had been in the UW program and finished three years ahead of David. David told him not to mention that they had talked and gave him a bit of history. Keyes said he'd take good care of Joe Braza.

Emma emailed Clara that David knew Dr. Keyes and that he was an excellent surgeon and a good man.

Clara emailed back at 11:30. "Dad's asleep. Lot of that lately. You were right. The babies are the cutest ever. Can't wait to see them. You were pretty cute though. Esther looks so much like some of your baby pictures it's scary."

Chapter 61

Clara and Joe returned to Walla Walla seven days later. A portion of Joe's right carotid artery had been replaced with a vein graft. He did well, but was clearly feeling the impact of the surgery. Dr. Keyes opined that Joe might not be himself for a few weeks to months. Joe and Clara went to Dr. Franklin's office as soon as they returned to Walla Walla. Dr. Franklin would agree with Dr. Keyes.

Joe, voice unsteady, started in on Dr. Franklin almost immediately, "Doc, listen, I've really got to get back to work. The winery needs me badly. Alan is not ready to take over deLorraine, and if I'm not there, I'm afraid bad things will happen."

The doctor, prepared for Joe's pleadings, wouldn't budge an inch.

"Joe, going into the winery, or making any important decisions is just out of the question for now. You are not ready for that level of stress. We will take this week-by-week. I am not letting you leave this office until I hear you say to me and to Clara that you will not go back to the winery. If you won't do that, well, you can find another physician."

"Okay, okay," Joe said. "I'm not going back. But I can't promise how long I can keep this stupid-ass promise."

"I guess that depends on how quickly you want to have another, and possibly life threatening, stroke," Franklin said.

Clara jumped in, "That's it. I've heard enough. Joe, you are not going to work until Dr. Franklin lets you. End of discussion. Now get dressed so we can get home."

In the hallway, while Joe was dressing, Franklin addressed Clara about some of the issues that had been bothering her for a few months.

"The pre-surgery MRI suggested that Joe had moderate right sided brain damage which would affect the left side of Joe's body. I can't be sure, but I'd bet that some of Joe's personality changes and anger management issues might be explained by innumerable small strokes over time. The strokes did not cause his bigotry, but his ability to change, reason and understand might have been severely altered by the brain damage."

Dr. Franklin reiterated that Joe keep his stress levels to a minimum, and that going in to work, or even trying to run the winery from home, was out of the question for the near future.

At home, Joe took out his frustration on Clara, but she was unrelenting in not allowing him to return to work. She did calm the waters by saying that she would go into deLorraine herself, every day if need be, and report back to Joe.

Clara called Emma every afternoon while Joe was napping or out of the house working in the garage. Clara explained sadly that she couldn't really leave Joe just yet, and that Emma coming, with or without the babies, might not be a good thing just yet. Clara promised that she'd be in Seattle to see the grandchildren by the end of October, with or without Joe.

"Mom, what's going on at the winery."

"I'm going there tomorrow to check things out. I'll let you know."

Clara went to the deLorraine offices the next morning. She had told Alan that she was coming and wanted to learn a bit about the business. Alan acted dismissive of her interest in the winery, but, as usual for

Alan, he didn't care whether she came or not. When Clara did arrive, Alan was in his office, but not particularly happy or attentive. Alan's fourth divorce proceedings had glitches. Clara had known for years to stay out of his personal life. She and Joe had not gone to the third or fourth weddings, which had been held in Las Vegas. Alan left after forty-five minutes to see his lawyer.

The employees at deLorraine looked a bit down at the mouth. Clara had been coming to the winery, on and off, her whole life. She had never seen the place with so little life.

Not good, not good at all.

Clara walked into the office of Henry Watson, deLorraine's CFO and sat down. Watson had been at the winery for 30 years. Clara knew little about him other than seeing him, and his very tiny wife and very tiny children, at company events.

"Hi, Mrs. Braza. What can I do for you? How's Joe doing?"

"Thanks Henry, he's coming along slowly but we're hopeful for a full recovery."

"I certainly hope so. We need him here."

Clara stood up and closed the door. "Can anyone hear us?"

"No, not with the door closed," Watson said.

"Henry, Joe Braza is not going to be the old Joe. At least not for a while and maybe not forever," Clara said.

"I am so sorry to hear that Clara, we really need him."

"Henry, What's going on? I don't like the feel around here."

"Alan is just not a very good people person.

"And."

"Well some of the people are going to leave if Joe doesn't come back. We've already lost two key people in the distilling crew, Armando Ruiz and his cousin Hector Ruiz."

Clara interjected, "I remember Armando. Handsome."

Watson continued, "Armando was the senior sanitizer for the winery equipment and has been here for twenty-four years, his cousin, Hector, fourteen years. Alan berated Hector in front of the entire crew for being late. His wife had gone into labor that morning. Armando had Hector's work covered and then Hector showed up at 2:00 p.m. when Alan was making rounds. Alan wouldn't listen to his reason for being late and, when Armando tried to quiet Alan down, things got out of hand. Alan started in on Hispanics in general - lazy, stupid, whatever."

"That's terrible," Clara said.

"Anyway, Armando and Hector quit. Alan did not try to stop them. We will have to hire three new untested and unfamiliar people just to cover their jobs. We are going to have to cut production until the new people can get up to speed. We lost two of our senior foremen over the past year for much of the same reasons. Some of our suppliers are also fed up with Alan's treatment of the delivery people. Campenella's Supply has been bringing fertilizer here for two generations. Alan was inappropriate when a new driver of theirs backed into the loading dock. He did a little damage to his truck and none to the dock, but Alan read him the riot act and told him that he never wanted to see him driving on deLorraine property again. The driver was the husband of Campenella's niece. I would not be surprised if they ask us to find other vendors.

"Are there other fertilizer suppliers?"

"Nothing really until you get to Richland. We're going to have to pay for higher delivery charges."

"My goodness."

"Also, Mrs. Braza, Alan has taken out some loans against the winery. In all my years here, we had never carried debt other than the note owed to your brother when your father died. The bank was not happy about the second loan because Alan wouldn't explain what the money was to be used for. Since no collateral was mentioned in the documents, other than the winery, and with Alan's trips to Vegas, my first guess, and it's only a guess, is that he is accumulating gambling debts. Mr. Braza has Alan as a signer on the business's bank account."

"Joe knew about these loans?"

"Yes, but he seemed to shrug them off. Wasn't like Joe," Watson said.

"What's going to happen?" Clara asked.

"Getting to the bottom line, Mrs. Braza, Alan cannot run this winery. He doesn't have the skills or the interest or the love of wine like Mr. B does - or did. I want you to know that I will stay here as long as I can, no matter what. I hope you don't take this personally, but I think someone needs to know what I've just told you. Mr. Braza had such high hopes for Alan, that he'd mature. In fact, I would say Joe, for the past few years, was almost desperate that Alan would follow him in running deLorraine. But I don't see it, sorry to say."

Sweat poured down Watson's neck as he finished talking. He opened a bottle of water from his desk and drank half the bottle.

"Thank you, Henry, thank you for your honesty. This will stay between you and me," Clara said.

"You might talk to Sam Ayers, the vineyard manager. He's got some issues as well."

Clara's talk with Sam Ayers was an echo of the talk with Henry Watson. Alan did not have the skills to run the winery and could not get along with the employees.

Clara left the winery and drove to downtown Walla Walla. She entered the law offices of McLean, Harris and Ogden. She asked to see Bill Harris, counsel to the deLorraine winery. He was the son of Samuel Harris, the namesake of the firm and had taken over from his father twelve years earlier along with his brother, Albert.

Clara was in the office for three hours and made an appointment to return the next day.

She then visited the Bank of America office in Walla Walla and spoke at length with Henrik Swenson, Joe's private banker.

When Clara arrived home at 6:00 p.m., Joe was sleeping. She awakened him and he dressed and came into the kitchen while Clara was helping prepare dinner.

"What happened today at the winery?" Joe asked.

She told Joe none of the negative conversations or dealings that had occurred that day.

"The winery looks the same and everyone seems to be doing their jobs. I am planning to go back every day and see how many of the people I can meet."

Joe seemed pacified, perhaps too pacified, which shocked Clara. Clara pondered whether Joe's personality had changed more than she thought, or she was an extraordinary actress and liar. She knew, unfortunately, that she couldn't act or lie. Joe then begged off dinner and returned to bed. Clara called Dr. Franklin.

Dr. Franklin came out to the house the next day. He thought that Joe was suffering from postoperative depression. He called Dr. Keyes who agreed with his assessment. Joe was started on Zoloft, an anti-depressant. A local psychiatrist and a neurologist evaluated Joe and neither added anything to Dr. Franklin's diagnosis or treatment plan. All of Joe's physicians felt that he would not regain the energy levels necessary to run the winery in the short term and, because of the brain damage, possibly forever. When told about the continued anger at Emma, the psychiatrist and neurologist reiterated what Drs. Franklin and Keyes had said. Specifically, Joe's emotional reactions could have been partially a result of the brain damage suffered slowly over the past few years.

Clara called Emma every day to give an update on Joe's progress. Emma pushed hard to come home and see her father. Joe did not want to see Emma and would cry when asked. Clara stopped asking.

Clara made two more visits to the winery. Alan was not at work either day and no one knew where he might be. Clara needed help and guidance, and she wasn't going to get any assistance from Joe. Clara called Emma.

"Emma, deLorraine is in a bit of trouble. Alan has been taking out loans against the business and some of the workers have been needlessly fired."

"Mom, you've got to get involved as much as you can. Call me if you need some suggestions."

Clara met with the lawyers and bankers on two more occasions. She came home to an empty house after the last meeting. Joe was gone, as was his car. Clara immediately called deLorraine and asked to speak to Henry Watson.

"Henry, I assume Joe is there?"

"Uh, right. Mrs. Braza. And uh...uh." Watson said no more.

Clara, changing quickly to alpha mode, demanded, "Henry, tell me what's going on. I could be there in ten minutes if I have to, so there's no reason not to be honest with me."

"He's at his desk. He was crying earlier."

"What, why?" asked Clara.

"Joe came in, sat at his desk and seemed pretty normal for an hour or so. We were all surprised and excited. Then he went into accounting and apparently got confused looking at some simple shipping numbers. He then got angry, at no one in particular. I guess he realized that he didn't comprehend something basic that used to come easily to him before. The staff didn't know what to do, so they called me, and I put him in his office. I was going out to get him some coffee and a roll when Alan walked in."

"Uh, oh," Clara remarked.

"I told Joe and Alan I'd be back in a few minutes," Watson continued. "I didn't tell Alan about the confusion, not while Joe was there and listening. Anyway, when I returned, Joe was alone in the room, staring blankly at the wall and crying. Alan had left. I don't know what happened while they were together but his secretary, Mrs. Joyce, said that the door was open and neither raised they voices. "

Clara, wanting to know more, asked, "Did you tell

him any of the things we talked about regarding Alan?"

"Once he settled down he told me that the doctors were right about him coming back. He said, "Henry, I don't think I can run deLorraine anymore." Then he asked me whether I thought that Alan could run the business. I figured that it was as good as time as any to be honest with him and I told him, no, I didn't think Alan could manage deLorraine. He surprised me by saying that it was hard to hear that, but he agreed. He told me, perhaps, deLorraine should be sold. He did know of two wineries, one in California and Wenatchee Ridge Winery that had shown interest previously. I left, but Mrs. Joyce told me he then made a couple of calls, one to San Francisco. She was pretty sure that he was talking to some winery brokers about putting deLorraine on the market. After the calls, he left. I don't know where he was going."

"Thank you, Henry, for keeping me in the loop and being such a good friend of Joe's.

When Joe came home that evening, Clara had already figured out that getting mad would serve no purpose. Joe seemed ready to defend himself, but Clara merely asked, "Where did you go?"

"I went into work."

Still playing dumb, Clara said, "How'd that work out?"

"Not so good really. I am not able to run deLorraine anymore. When I told that to Alan, he merely shrugged his shoulders and suggested we sell the winery. That kills me, Clara. It's like a knife in the heart. Alan didn't seem to care. In fact, I felt he really wanted to be out of the business. After all I've done to set the table for him, he doesn't care at all, not a damn. So, he may be right, we may need to sell deLorraine."

Clara tried to act surprised but she had been hearing from the attorneys and bankers that selling deLorraine was likely the best exit strategy, although unfortunately, when done under duress, the sale price was likely to be significantly lower than deLorraine's true value.

"Who might be interested?" Clara asked.

"Mark Sullivan at Wenatchee Ridge had some private investors from Seattle that wanted to help him expand. I also know that Redstone in Salinas was looking to buy up here."

"Go slow, Joe. Big decision. Dr. Franklin was pretty adamant about lowering your stress levels. You do not need the stress of a long tough negotiation."

"Well, I called a winery broker in San Francisco and he told me that some feelers had been circulating for a few weeks about deLorraine, ever since my getting ill," Joe said. "The vultures were already circling. He thought we could be getting some requests to see deLorraine officially in the next week or two. He was pretty certain that any bids would be a fraction of deLorraine's worth. I so hate the thought that we might have to sell, and at a big discount. If we did, I feel like I betrayed your father, but I really don't see another option."

Clara sat motionless and quiet.

Joe looked so sad. "I don't really feel like dinner. I'm going to bed early."

The next morning, Clara called Emma and brought her up to date on the winery.

"Your father will never be able to run deLorraine again," Clara said. "The mini strokes have made his return impossible."

"Mom I've been thinking about this since your last call and I have talked to David," Emma said. "Give me half an hour, and then I want you to call someone that you know and will help. Here's the number."

Clara waited half an hour and then made a call to New Jersey to an attorney. "I need you badly. I need your help and advice."

"Mrs. Braza, what can I do?"

Chapter 62

By the end of September, harvesting and pressing of the grapes had been completed and the fermenting had begun. The fermenting period was a slow time for much of the staff and vacations were common. Clara had become a daily fixture around the winery. Clara's visits were more social than businesslike, but her presence seemed to raise some of the sagging spirits.

When asked why she had taken such an interest in the winery, Clara had the same answer for all. "I want to get the feel of the winery. It's been a long time and, for now, I will be Joe's eyes and ears."

All the employees, of course, asked about Joe and hoped he'd come back soon. They didn't ask just to be nice. They needed him and, since his surgery, Joe Braza had stepped back into the winery only once, and that visit had not gone well.

Alan, although technically running the winery, worked little to not at all. His divorce number four would be final at the end of September. Alan told Clara that he needed time off and that the staff could handle the work. He left for Maui with two friends and his golf clubs. He returned on October seventh.

Clara continued to meet regularly with Albert and Bill Harris, the attorneys for deLorraine.

Clara informed the entire staff that two large winery operations were coming to look at deLorraine, one from California and one from the Walla Walla area. The California group spent three days looking over the facilities while their accountants poured over the books. The eastern Washington group, the Wenatchee Crest Winery, came only for a day and a half. The Wenatchee Crest group was well aware of the deLorraine facility and the owners knew Joe Braza well.

Unfortunately for deLorraine, both potential suitors

knew Joe Braza's medical condition.

Clara asked Mr. Watson and Mr. Ayers to cancel all leaves for the third Monday in October and schedule a meeting of the entire staff of deLorraine at the Whitman Hotel in downtown Walla Walla. Clara also invited deLorraine's attorneys, bankers, teamsters, suppliers, and large shippers to the meeting.

Alan, back from Hawaii, spent very little time around the winery but, when seen, appeared to be in a very good mood.

Very few of the deLorraine employees understood the reason for the meeting called by Clara Braza. Most felt that Joe Braza would be officially stepping down as president of deLorraine. What would happen next was anybody's guess. Either, Joe would be replaced by Alan, or the winery's sale to the Wenatchee group or, worse, to the Californians. No other options seemed viable. Most of the employees hoped for a sale to a local company. To most, Alan taking over the reins of deLorraine was the most unpalatable. All realized that jobs would be lost regardless of options A, B, or C.

As the third Monday in October arrived, the casual observer would have seen little change at deLorraine. However, conversation amongst the employees during this period was focused on one point, and one point alone - "What's going to happen to deLorraine and our jobs?"

At the scheduled meeting, the presence of Armando Ruiz and his cousin, Hector Ruiz, and the management of Campanella's Supply, surprised the attending deLorraine employees. Both Ruizes had been fired by Alan two months earlier, and deLorraine had been forced to find a different supplier for fertilizer after Alan had torn into a Campenella driver. The Ruizes and Campenellas remained tight lipped about their presence, but clearly they must know something that others did not.

Alan sat in the front row and appeared in good spirits, really good spirits. At one point he was seen doing a Heisman Trophy stance. To a person, no one knew how to interpret Alan's good mood.

From the dais at the end of the room, Henry Watson opened the meeting and welcomed everyone. He then introduced Clara Braza to genuine applause. Clara had been a constant presence at the winery for more than a month, reacquainting herself with as many people as she could. Some even believed that option #4 was that Clara would try to run deLorraine.

Clara, looking radiant, spoke in a strong, clear voice, "Thank you, Henry, and thank all of you for coming. What I have to say is of monumental importance to me, and to you, and to this community."

"First, I want to thank all of you from the bottom of my heart for the kind words and notes hoping for Joe's recovery. Unfortunately, Joe will not be able to return in full capacity as president of deLorraine. We hope he will recover, but managing the entire business is, and will be, out of his scope."

A palpable mumbling of acceptance could be felt in the room.

"deLorraine has been a family held winery for three generations. Nothing would make me prouder than to have a fourth generation deLorraine continue the traditions. The importance of continuing these traditions would honor the century of work done by my ancestors. I feel strongly that these traditions should continue, if possible."

Clara made a definite pause at this point.

"But only if the new leadership has the potential to show the same dedication, capabilities and love of wine that my husband, father and grandfather showed over the past, many years."

With that comment, Alan Braza stood up and walked calmly, like a man with a purpose, through a door to the side of the large room. Most thought he would circle around to the back of the dais and make some kind of grand entrance. There was a mumbling in the room, just slightly audible.

Was Alan going to run the winery?

Clara continued, "Also, we have had multiple generations of employees in every facet of our business. Some third and fourth generation people are here, working with their parents and grandparents. The pride of being a deLorraine employee has not been lost on most of these hard and tireless workers, and we'd like to see that continue into the future.

“To that end, I would like to introduce the new management and CEO of deLorraine Winery to say a few words."

The door behind the dais opened and...

Chapter 63

3 weeks earlier

Clara Braza had called Sophie Picone Hawthorne. Emma had called Sophie thirty minutes earlier. Together a plan was hatched by the three women.

After Clara's call and request for help, Sophie hung up and made two quick calls. One to her husband and one to Emma Milton to confirm that her mother had reached out. Two days later, Emma Milton flew to Walla Walla. She brought David and her twin girls, Sophie and Esther, with her. Emma was joined by attorneys, Carl and Sophie Hawthorne and their daughter, Emma. The Hawthornes and Miltons stayed at the Whitman Hotel. Only Emma needed to stay out of sight.

The reunion at the hotel with Clara, Sophie Hawthorne's and Emma's families was tearful.

Clara walked into the George Suite at the Whitman unsure of herself. She had not seen her daughter in five years and had never met her two grandchildren.

Overcome emotionally in seconds by Emma, little Sophie, Esther, big Sophie and little Emma, Clara did not know which way to turn or hug next. Clara went from child to child to grandchild to grandchild, crying the entire way and saying over and over, “I'm so sorry.”

Clara knew Sophie and Esther's names and faces from the pictures she had been sent. She gathered the two and got down on her knees.

“I am your Grandma Clara. I know we haven't met, but I promise that I will make up for lost time. You two are so beautiful.” She ensnared both in a bear hug. “I will love you forever.”

The two girls, overcome by the attention, ran back to their mother's skirt as soon as the hug ended.

Clara finally stood and approached David, watching from the back of the room. "David," Clara said, "you have a beautiful family. I am so sorry for everything that has happened and only hope that you'll be able to forgive me someday. I am so sorry."

She gave David an unexpected hug that lasted long enough to say the sorry was meaningful.

Blame, recrimination and fault were never discussed that night, or ever in the future. Joe did not know of Emma's presence and was not invited. Sophie, Carl, Emma, and Clara met the next day at the offices of Bill and Albert Harris and a team of attorneys from their firm, McLean, Harris and Ogden. David went to visit Dr. Harold King, the surgeon at Walla Walla General who had operated on David's splenic injury.

As Emma's attorneys, Sophie and Carl presented Emma's non-negotiable demands to the deLorraine lawyers and Clara. Emma would assume complete control of the winery, and with the following provisos: First, Alan Braza would never step foot onto any deLorraine property again; and Secondly, Alan would be bought out of all deLorraine's holdings. Three current appraisals would be taken of the value of deLorraine and he would be paid 50% of the average appraised value over a 10 year period, at no interest. The payout was identical to Clara's brother's settlement when Emilio deLorraine died. Thirdly, Joe Braza would continue only as an advisor to deLorraine, with Emma having final say, in all matters.

Clara, who already knew what Emma's demands would be, met with her attorneys after the meeting. They urged her to accept. She did so without hesitation. The Miltons and Hawthornes then slipped out of town and went to Coeur d'Alene, Idaho, for a joint family vacation. They would return on the morning of the meeting.

Alan Braza, totally unaware of the meetings with Emma, was then called and invited down to McLean, Harris and Ogden. With Clara present, Bill and Albert Harris outlined the proposal already agreed to by Clara. Harris did point out to Alan that the winery was, and had always been, in Clara's name. Not surprising to either Harris, Alan was ecstatic at the deal offered him. Clara listened and said nothing as Alan left the law firm.

The law firm, in an attempt to get tentative bids on the worth of deLorraine, approached brokers to set up visits from interested groups. In the end, three wineries, two from California and one from eastern Washington, toured the facilities and submitted non-binding tentative bids. These bids were easily 50% below Emma's estimation of deLorraine's worth, but were expected because of deLorraine's tenuous status. These bids were used to calculate Alan's buyout.

Alan showed up at the company meeting and left before Emma's introduction as CEO. Alan would never be seen again by the deLorraine staff. He moved to Las Vegas four months later and never returned to Walla Walla. He continued to talk to his mother and father and they visited him in Las Vegas occasionally. Alan married for the fifth time three months after moving to Vegas. Alan's pre-nup agreement guaranteed that Number five will get little or nothing of his estate if the marriage ends.

The University of Washington Medical School had been looking for satellite facilities. The Department of Surgery was particularly interested in having rotations for their residents at facilities away from Seattle but within Washington State. Finding the right surgeons to head such satellites was a major sticking point. David Milton's suggestion that he run such a facility in Walla Walla came as a great surprise to the Department. But he was felt to be the perfect person to take on such a task. Walla Walla General accepted the University of Washington's joint agreement proposal quickly. David

Milton joined the surgical group at Walla Walla General and residents commenced rotating there within six months. Free housing for the residents and their families was provided in a nearby condominium complex. The rotation to Walla Walla quickly developed into one of the favorite and most productive rotations in the Department of Surgery system. One year after starting the program in Walla Wall, the Department of Surgery promoted David to Associate Professor.

Reintroducing Emma to her father was difficult. Joe remained angry and resentful, and felt betrayed by Clara and Alan. Joe's depression worsened. As a suicide prevention measure, Clara, on David Milton's suggestion and Dr. Franklin's support, removed all sedatives, sleeping pills and narcotics from the house as well as all the firearms. Clara continued to ask Joe to meet with Emma, which prompted only anger and resentment.

Strangely, Alan, before leaving Walla Walla, provided the most comfort to Joe by being honest – a trait that didn't come easily to him. Alan told his father, in a rare bit of reality, that he never liked the wine business and would have, without hesitation, sold deLorraine, if and when, he controlled the business. Joe and Clara told Alan about the visit by the DEA, Judge McAuliffe and Rafe Gomez. His response, "I'd rather not talk about it," was answer enough.

Despite pleadings from everyone that knew the family, Joe continued to refuse to see Emma. Clara, frustrated and having no clue what to do next, was given a tip by the housemaid, Angelina.

Clara returned home the next day with two granddaughters in tow, sans Emma. Esther and Sophie were told they were going to meet their 'secret grandpa.' Both girls brought books to be read.

Joe melted.

Afterward, he asked Clara if they were coming again. After two visits from his granddaughters, Joe, without prodding, asked to meet with Emma alone. Father and daughter met for two hours, and neither spoke of the meeting. Three days later, dinner at Joe and Clara's house, served by Angelina, with Emma, David and the children went as if no trouble had ever happened. Clara gave Angelina her Christmas bonus early.

Near the end of the meal, Joe asked Emma if she was using his old office.

Emma responded, matter of factly, "No, Dad, I've left it untouched. You are free to come back and help me anytime you want. I am using Alan's old office."

Joe said nothing and came back to deLorraine the next day. Ecstatic employees, happy to see him, greeted his return. Each and every employee told Joe, in their own way, that their prayers had been answered when Emma walked into the Whitman Hotel meeting.

Joe would make the occasional cameo at deLorraine, but never asked for, or assumed, any management role again. He was very helpful when Emma later decided to expand deLorraine by acquiring portions of wineries in Oregon and British Columbia.

Clara Braza again lost interest in the winery and spent most of her free time taking care of two, soon to be three, grandchildren.

Chapter 64

David Milton was seeing his usual slate of patients that afternoon. After two years in Walla Walla, David's practice was full. The Department of Surgery had been searching for another fulltime surgeon to join David.

His third patient of the morning was listed as a new patient, referred for repair of a left inguinal hernia. The top of the chart said "Mr. Erik Rawlins."

"Hello Mr. Rawlins, I'm Dr. Milton. I see from Dr. Hamilton's notes he thinks you have a hernia. Correct?"

"Yep, Doc."

David went through Erik Rawlins' history, past medical issues and did a complete physical examination.

"I understand that your wife is in the waiting room?"

"Yes, sir."

"I'd like you to get dressed and then both of you come into my office so we can talk about your hernia. I see you're a Lieutenant in the Walla Walla police department. How long have you been there?"

"Twenty-nine years."

"Lots of stories I bet."

Mr. Rawlins came into David's private office, joined by Rawlins' wife, Joanne. David rarely talked to patients about surgeries inside the exam room. David and the Rawlins would spend the next twenty-five minutes going over the hernia procedure, risks, benefits, and alternative therapies. Rawlins was given a consent form to review that listed all the topics they had just discussed.

Mrs. Rawlins paid attention to everything about the surgery. Erik Rawlins was looking around the room at diplomas, awards and family pictures.

"Doc, you're married to Emma Braza aren't you?" Erik Rawlins asked.

"Yes I am, but she goes by Emma Milton," David said.

"You know I was the one that took the call at WWPD when a random, retired Canadian police officer found her. It's an incredible story that has never been told that I know of. I never got back to that Canadian about his tip."

"Tell me. Hold a second." David punched a button and talked into his phone speaker. "Mildred, hold my calls for ten minutes. Thanks."

Turning to Rawlins, David said, "Go ahead, Detective Rawlins."

"Well, there was this retired Mountie heading down from Canada to Mexico or Arizona in his RV. He drives into a service station in Oregon where he sees these two bad guys who look like trouble in the bay next to him. The Mountie next sees the back of the car shaking like there's someone in the trunk......." Rawlins finished the story.

Chapter 65

1 month later, October, Vancouver BC

"Charlie, the phone's for you. It's Phil Gorman."

"Hey, Phil, for what do I owe the privilege?" asked Charlie Munro.

"Two things, first we've got a tee time at 1:00 p.m. if the god damn rain'll stop. Bill and Fred will be there."

"I know, I know, Phil. But honestly I can't wait to get south. This cold weather is killing my bones. What's number two?"

"Bill, Fred and I and our wives are going to the RCMP banquet next week. You're comin', eh."

"Shit, Phil," Charlie said, "I swore last year was it for us. I've told you that fifty times if I've told you once. They sit us way in the back and I can't hear or see a thing. No one remembers any of us. I feel lousy after I go. Like all those years meant diddly squat. You guys go, I ain't going."

"Lemme speak to Ruth."

"It ain't gonna make any difference. Ruth said she wouldn't go."

"I don't want to talk to you. Lemme speak to Ruth," Phil said.

Ruth picked up the receiver and greeted her friend, "Hi, Phil."

"Ruth, we're all going to the banquet. We've never missed one, ever. Us eight, while we're alive, promised that we'd go. Charlie Munro is coming if I have to come over, dress the son of a bitch, put him in cuffs and drag him. And I'm not kidding. We all go."

"Charlie, Phil says we're going, so we're going. If it doesn't work out this year I won't make you go again, promise."

Charlie Munro retook the phone but glared at his wife. "Ruth, why do you cave so quickly. These banquets are for the younger people still there. They don't care about us."

"Charlie, we're going. Look at it as a send off party for us heading south," Ruth said.

"Okay, okay, okay, Phil," Charlie grumbled. "Why can't I die in peace? Hell, that won't even work, they'll prop me up and drag me to these things after I'm dead and gone."

"Bye, Phil."

"Bye, and don't be late for the tee time."

Phil looked over his shoulder at Fred and Bill and the Superintendant of the RCMP for British Columbia and gave a thumbs up.

A few nights later, Charlie and Ruth and Phil and his wife, Mavis, drove down to the Bayshore Hotel. They parked their car on the street, three blocks away. Seventeen dollars for valet parking was too rich for them.

When they arrived at the reception area, Charlie, Ruth, Phil and Mavis found the other couples, Bill and Fred and their wives in the banquet registration area. The men put on sticky name labels and picked up seating cards. As before, they seemed to know fewer and fewer faces. The four old timers and their wives stood a bit apart, jabbering away. The Superintendant of the RCMP for British Columbia, E. Donald Richards, came by and personally welcomed them, by name, and said how much it meant to all that they come.

"Hey, Charlie, pretty nice of the 'Sup' to come by, eh?" Phil said.

"Yeah, that was nice," Charlie said. "First in a while. What table we at?"

"It's on your name label, We're all at table two."

"Probably started numbering from the back this year. Table one is in the kitchen," Charlie said emphatically, as if he meant it.

The dinner gong rang and the four retirees with wives came into the large dining hall. Table two was up front, just under the speaker's platform.

Visibly impressed with the seating, Charlie said, "Ruthie, Wow. Pretty nice. Did we pay extra for this?"

Phil couldn't hold back. "Charlie, shut up and enjoy the scenery, you're such an ornery piece of work."

"Thanks, Phil," as Charlie clenched his arms in front of his chest to assure that no good thoughts passed.

After the throngs were seated, Superintendent Richards came to the microphone. He did the perfunctory welcomes, and then he went off program.

"Tonight we have a couple of special guests who are going to tell a story and then make a presentation. Don't look at your program, it's not there."

Most of the attendees still checked their programs.

"First, I'd like to introduce a compatriot from Washington State, Lieutenant Erik Rawlins of the Walla Walla PD, a twenty-nine year veteran in law enforcement. Lieutenant Rawlins."

"Thank you, Superintendent Richards. Ten years

ago I was sitting at my desk on a Monday morning in Walla Walla. Absolutely nothing was happening. I picked up the phone a couple of times just to see if I had a dial tone."

Rawlins waited for the laughter to settle. Everyone in the room had been there.

"One of those days when you know nothing's going to happen. The day before, a shooting robbery occurred fifteen miles out of town that the County Sheriff's office had handled. Early in the morning, before I came on, someone called in that their teenage daughter didn't make it home. No one put them together."

Rawlins now had Charlie and Ruth Munro's attention.

"Anyway, finally a call came in. Our operator tells me she's got a Mountie on the phone in Oregon, and he needs to talk to me. A Mountie in Oregon, gimme a break, some kind of joke. Sounds like an Eskimo in Hawaii, but what the hell, I take the call.

"This guy was talking pure Canuck and at high speed. He tells me he's driving south in Oregon toward Mexico. He asks if I know about any bad guys on the run. At first, I thought he's crazy, then I know he's crazy. But, I tell him about the robbery and murder from the day before. We had no leads at that time.

"Then he asks out of the blue, is there a missing person too? Now he's got my interest because the missing teenager hadn't been made public yet. He swears that he's watching two really bad looking dudes on the run and there is something alive in the trunk of their car, kicking. The bad guys had already gotten back on the road but he's got descriptions, license plates, and car make. Damn if the license he gives me doesn't match the plate of the missing girl, who was driving a different make of car. Now I know my Mountie had hit the jackpot. I hung up and took it from there, but with a promise to call him back, which I never did. My bad.

"An hour later, two men are shot dead at a roadblock by the Oregon State Patrol and Salem PD Swat team. A young girl from Walla Walla, a junior at the University of Washington, locked in the trunk, was barely alive after a day of torture and abuse. She, by all accounts, would not have lived more than a few hours more. She was helicoptered to the University of Oregon, close to death. She was in the operating room forty-five minutes later to remove blood clots around her brain from head trauma. She barely clung to life for a few days before waking up. She lived, but it took a year of rehab, physical and psychological, to get her back on her feet. But recover she did, and she finished college. And then she flourished.

"But she never had the opportunity to say thank you to the RCMP and the man that saved her life. The man, sitting here in front of me with his lovely wife, Ruth, is Charlie Munro.

"Charlie, I would like to introduce you and the rest of the RCMP to Emma Braza Milton, the president and CEO of deLorraine Winery. She is here with her husband, Dr. David Milton, Associate Professor of Surgery at the University of Washington and head of surgery at the Walla Walla General Hospital and their three children, Sophie, Esther and Geoffrey."

Emma, holding a baby boy, with David and her two girls at her side, approached the microphone. Emma handed little Geoffrey to David and then faced the audience. When the applause stopped, the packed room was still and quiet.

"Thank you, Erik. Charlie Munro, you and I have never met. But we should have."

Emma started to tear and lose her voice. She

gathered herself for a moment and continued.

"Your police instincts honed over years on the RCMP saved my life. For that I can never repay you enough, nor can my husband and children ever thank you enough for your perseverance in seeing your hunch through. When the dinner starts, we hope that you and Ruth can join us at Table Six for a bit, and then return to your friends. Not as good seats as Table Two, but it was the best I could do. I think you have to know somebody."

The laughter was genuine.

"More importantly, in honor of your years of service to the RCMP, I am endowing The Charles Munro Permanent Trust fund with $2 million dollars to be used for education and scholarships for families of members of the British Columbia RCMP. In addition, deLorraine Winery will be providing the wine for the RCMP banquet every year as long as I am alive.

"I know that RCMP has rules about using only wine that comes from British Columbia at your functions. Not a bad rule, as the Okanagan wines are amongst the best wines in North America. But we, as you, live in a society of rules, and we must stick to the rules. It turns out that deLorraine owns interest in three wineries the Okanagan Valley, so meeting my wishes and your rules should not be difficult to follow.

"Also, I hear that you drive from BC down to Mexico every fall. I'd like to extend an invitation to you and your wife to stop in Walla Walla on your way up or down or both to visit our home and winery, forever. Again, thank you from the bottom of my heart. I think others have a little something to say too."

Emma removed the microphone from the podium stand and lowered it down to Sophie and Esther.

The young girls each put a hand over their eyes to

scan the audience.

"Which one is Mr. Charlie, Mommy?" Sophie asked, in a crisp loud voice,

"He's the man in the very front who's crying," Emma said.

Esther pointed and said, "There he is. See him, Soph?"

"I see him now. Why's he crying, Mommy?" Sophie asked.

"He's happy."

"I only cry when I'm sad. Mommy Is Charlie okay?"

"He's fine, Sophie, just fine."

In unison, the girls waved and said, "Thank you, Mr. Charlie for saving our mommy. We love you."

The entire auditorium stood for five minutes giving Charlie Munro the applause he deserved. Charlie cried like a baby and never missed another banquet.

Epilogue

Fifteen Years Later

One night, after dinner in the late fall, Emma Braza Milton took her son Geoffrey deLorraine Milton's hand and walked him into the vineyards where a new small shed had been attached to the back of a large storage garage.

"Mom, why do you always hold my hand so tightly?"

"Because I love you." Emma smiled. She still didn't like the dark, but her son's hand kept her safe.

The shed was locked. Emma had a key and they entered the shed and Emma turned on a small light. Pictures of Emma, her uncle Arnie, her grandfather and great-grandfather adorned the walls. Emma asked Geoffrey to sit and she picked up a small cutting of grapevine and asked Geoffrey what he thought of it. Geoffrey spun it in his fingers, looked closely, smelled it, and then looked back at his mother.

"These are the new Sauvignon Blanc vines from southwest sector that we planted two years ago."

"You're right. But I knew that you'd know," Emma smiled.

Emma then explained to Geoffrey the small scar on her right wrist given to her by her grandfather two years before he died. She explained that every picture on the wall represented a deLorraine that had exactly the same scar created by a deLorraine from the generation before. Each of the pictures represented someone who would dedicate their life to the deLorraine Vineyards. Geoffrey understood immediately the significance and sanctity of his mother's story and without hesitation unbuttoned his right sleeve and rolled it up.

James Gottesman M.D. is a Urological Oncologist who has been writing most of his adult life. He has authored more that a hundred scientific papers, medical book chapters, research grants, operative consent forms, and computer programs written in BASIC and HTML. *The Road Back Isn't Straight* was his first foray into fiction. Dr. Gottesman graduated from UC Berkeley and UC San Francisco Medical Center and did his Urology training at UCLA. He is a Clinical Professor of Urology at the University of Washington. He lives on Mercer Island, Washington, with his wife, Gloria, three sons, seven grandchildren and dog, Biscuit. He plays golf and has travelled much of the world.

Dr. Gottesman's books of fiction include *The Road Back Isn't Straight* (2013), *The Search of Grace* (2014), *Can't Forget* (2016), *Stab Wound* (2019), *An Enemy to Love* (2021), *In Flew Enza* (2022), *The Angel of North Africa* (2024) and *The Remarkable Rachel Romain.*

He lives on Mercer Island, Washington, with his wife Gloria and their dog, Biscuit, near their three sons and nine grandchildren.

www.ingramcontent.com/pod-product-compliance
Lightning Source LLC
Chambersburg PA
CBHW051544250626
47157CB00001B/172
9780615711249